Amazing Grace

A NOVEL

Hugo N. Gerstl

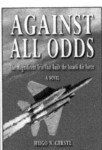
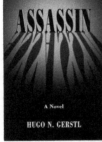
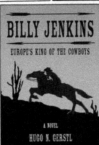
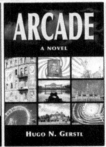

Amazing Grace

THE STORY OF GRACE O'MALLEY
THE NOTORIOUS PIRATE WOMAN

A NOVEL

Hugo N. Gerstl

PANGÆA
PUBLISHING GROUP

Amazing Grace
The Story of Grace O'Malley the Notorious Pirate Woman

Copyright © 2019 Hugo N. Gerstl
www.HugoGerstl.com

ISBN 978-1-950134-06-9
Pangæa Publishing Group
www.PangaeaPublishing.com

This book is a work of fiction. With the exception of certain anchors of fact, all the characters in this book are the author's creation. As in all novels, much of what occurs in this book originated in the author's imagination. Any similarities to persons living or dead or to events claimed to have occurred are purely coincidental.

Cover image:
Pirate steering wheel © Rceeh,
Pirate Boat,© Andreas Meyer,
Storm Credit line © Irina Efremova,
Ocean storm © Daniel Boiteau,
Dreamstime.com

Cover design and typesetting by
DesignPeaks@gmail.com

For information contact:

PANGÆA PUBLISHING GROUP
25579 Carmel Knolls Drive
Carmel, CA 93923
Telephone: 831-624-3508/831-649-0668
Fax: 831-649-8007
Email: info@pangaeapublishing.com

Dedication

This book is dedicated with love and affection to

The late, truly great **António Manso Pinheiro** (1942-2007)

Seldom has any human being displayed such an array of human qualities – a wise and gentle worldview, knowledge gained from a lifetime of sheer excellence,

And kindness unparalleled since Saint Francis of Assisi.

Yet, he wore his grace with such dignity
and lightness of spirit and generosity and nobility
That you would say he was an emperor who wore

a Crown of Feathers.

Alas, he went to his Maker too soon.
God willing, we will meet again
In a better place
And forever.

And

To Maria Correia
She must now live for two, and by her own life
Propel his eternal blessing,
As well as her own
5

Map of Ireland

"Grandma, can we talk for a while?"

"Of course, Maeve. It seems nowadays I have all the time in the world to talk, and no one wants to spend time talking with me. Your da's busy with his allies and your ma's probably busy arranging for your wedding. Six months, is it?"

"It is, and I'm frightened and unsure and..."

"Is it about losing your virginity?"

"*Grandma!*"

"Don't 'Grandma' me, young lady. Isn't that what frightens you most?"

She cast her eyes down. "Well... yes... but how could you know that?"

"You think your generation invented sex? Or, for that matter, love? You're how old, Maeve Dear? Seventeen?"

"Almost."

"And a virgin?"

"Of course!"

"You don't have to say it like it's some sort of badge of honor." I crinkled my face into a knowing smile. "If I may be blunt, little girl, that's one of the most pleasurable aspects of life. I think you're more worried that when you marry you'll be under someone else's control, that your life of freedom as you know it will be over."

My granddaughter looked quizzically at me. "Are you some kind of witch, Grandma, that you can see inside me?"

"Hardly, My Girl," I said, now openly chuckling. "It's just that I have been on this earth for seventy-two years and I've learned a bit about life, and what makes people think and act as they do." My thoughts wandered back, far back, in time, to a day when I was Maeve's age. I sighed involuntarily. "Girl, let me tell you, you may think you're at the end of your life, but you're not. You're only at the beginning."

"My da tells me you were a famous pirate. People called you the pirate queen of Connaught."

"Does he now?"

"Aye, and that the day he was born you were attacked by pirates and got up out of bed and shot them all dead, and that you met with Queen Elizabeth herself and, and..."

"You don't think he might be telling you tales?"

"My da doesn't lie!" she said defensively. Then, "Grandma, most people don't even remember anyone who died more than ten years ago. If they've done anything to remember, they end up as pages in a history book. No one even thinks that once that person lived and breathed – and did other things.

"When I was little, you told me stories about Ireland, about the Little People and the clans, and the wide open lands where you could walk for a whole day and never see another person. But one thing you never told me was the story of *you*. I know I'll have children some day. What will I tell them when they ask about my da and my grandmother and... and... the others that went before?" She was breathing rapidly, whether from fright or eagerness I didn't know. "It's six months before I marry, only six months before my own childhood is over. Please, Grandma, I'd feel so much happier if I could lose myself in someone else's life other than my own."

"Very well, Maeve, I don't know that anyone will ever remember me, but I can't see what harm it will do. Cuddle in next to me and I'll begin. 'Once upon a time there was a little girl named Grace...'"

Chapter 1

I was born Granuaile Ni-Mháille, which is the old Irish way of saying Grace O'Malley, on All Fools Day in fifteen hundred thirty, almost seventy-three years ago. My father, Owen Dubhdarra O'Malley, called the "Black Oak" because of his dark hair and his great strength, was a most important man, the chief of his clan.

When I was growing up he captained three galleys and traveled between the west coast of Ireland and the Spanish and French coasts. His boats seemed very small to be out on the great ocean, but they were seaworthy and satisfied our needs – large enough to travel the seas and small enough to hide in the tiniest bays and estuaries.

This was necessary since Men o' War, much larger ships, stalked the waters off western Ireland. You might ask why these ships would want to attack a small vessel like my father's. You want the truth? The ships that plied our waters engaged in lawful trade, but one never knew when one would be attacked by pirates who offered protection for a price. We feared not these pirates because... well, because not all of my da's trade remained entirely legal. Some called *us* pirates. We preferred to call ourselves guardians of Irish independence. We made sure our seas remained *our* seas, and that those who sailed our seas had proper respect for those who owned it.

My first adventure began in 1539, in my ninth summer…

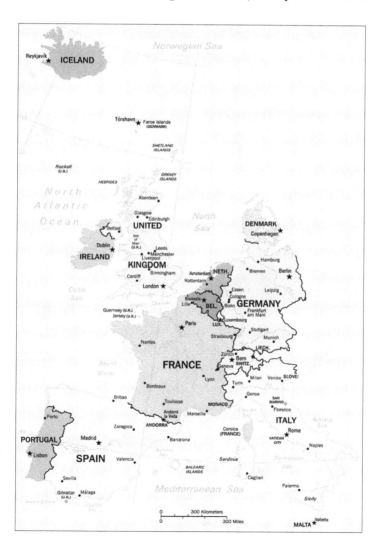

"I can't believe it!" I shouted. "You won't let me go sailing with my own father? If you want to stay at home on this little island, go right ahead and do it! It's so unfair! I'm an O'Malley, I am, and da told me the O'Malleys have sailed the seas for more than a hundred years!"

My father shrugged his shoulders and looked at my ma. I knew he wanted me to go, I knew how much he loved me. I was nine years old, quite small for my age – I'm told I could easily be mistaken for a six or seven-year-old – and he still bounced me on his knee every evening and sang sea chanteys to me. He'd be going away in a week and he'd be gone for... I don't know how long he'd be gone, but I'd probably be ten years old by the time he got back.

"But Grace," my da said kindly, "You're still a little girl..."

"I'm not a little girl, I'm nine years old!" I interrupted. "On my fourth birthday, you told me I was a *big* girl."

"And so you are," he said, lifting me up by my armpits and swinging me around lovingly. "I meant..."

"What your da meant," my mother said, "is that you're a *girl*. A very beautiful and very sweet girl, but girls don't go sailing, Grace." She sighed and continued, "Girls have different talents. Besides, look at your lovely, long yellow hair. If you went a'sea with your da, ye'd only catch that long hair in a hawser or some such, and it'd pull your pretty head right off your neck."

"I can tie my hair up in a braid," I replied stubbornly. "Then it won't get caught."

"Aye, but it *could* get caught, my little darlin'," da said in a way I knew closed off the conversation. "I'm not sayin' you'll *never* go a'sailin', my wee one. Just not yet."

"But, da," I protested. "You'll be gone for*ever*. I'll probably be old and married by the time you get back."

"I doubt it, Granuaile," he said. "Your ma is right. Ye wouldn't want to risk harming a single hair on your beautiful head."

My parents were really kinder than they needed to be. They didn't interrupt my tirade, not even once. But my da wasn't called Dubhdarra – the Black Oak – for nothing. He was a strong man, and his word was the law, and I knew enough not to contest it.

Without another word, I marched up the stairs to my bedroom and quietly closed the door. I was so angry I ripped all my clothes off the closet shelf and threw them all over my room. I thought it would make an impressive pile, but it looked pretty small, even to me. I climbed into my bed, face down, and started crying at the injustice of it all.

But I'm not a crier by nature. I soon sat up and thought seriously – at least as seriously as a nine-year-old can – about what my parents had said. "A *girl*" they had said, as if that were some kind of lesser being. "A girl with beautiful, long yellow hair, the kind of hair that could get tangled in all kinds of ship's machinery." The kind of machinery that could separate my head from my neck. As I thought about it more and more, the solution seemed so easy, so clear that I was amazed I hadn't thought of it before.

—⊪—

"Aieee!!!" My mother's scream of anguish when I came down the castle stairs the next morning seemed reward enough for what I had done last night. I hadn't looked in a mirror, so I couldn't tell how neat the job was, but I'd felt all around with my fingers that morning, and none of it had grown back.

"Owen! Owen, come quickly! Right now! This instant!" she cried. She breathed in and out so hard and fast I thought she might faint.

"What is it?" my da called back in a sleep-slurred voice. He'd obviously decided stay in bed late that morning.

"It's Grace!" my twelve-year-old brother Donal na-Piopa called. He could scarcely contain his giggle. "She's dressed like a boy. And she's... she's *bald* is what she is!" Big brothers can be so awful sometimes.

"Bald?" My da stomped into the dining room, where we'd all gathered around the huge oak table. "What foolishness is...? Why, bless my soul!" he said, doubling over with laughter. "'Tis true. The girl's bald as a stone. Grainne Mhaol – Grace the Bald."

"'Tain't funny!" my ma growled. "'Tain't funny a'tall, a'tall. Young lady, what's your explanation for this?"

"No explanation," I said calmly. I was amazed at their inability to see what I had seen so clearly. "You said I couldn't go sailing with da because I was a girl and because I had long, yellow hair that would catch in the ship's machinery and tear my head off my neck. Well, now ye've no worry at all, do ye? I've got less hair than Donal and less hair than da, so I surely won't catch my hair in any machinery. And, as you can plainly see, I'm not a girl anymore, at least not so's anyone can tell. So now I can go sailing to Spain with da."

"Saints alive!" my da remarked. "'Tis true what the girl says. Grainne Mhaol – Grace the Bald she is, and a funny looking, er, fellow at that. Now, do we reward such pluck with punishment or do we encourage such original thinking?"

My ma stood there abashed, not knowing what to say. Donal, bless him, sided with me, and said, "What harm could it do? Da'll be there and I'll be there, too, and how much can she eat?"

I glared at Donal, but in the end the Black Oak's great humor prevailed. "Very well, child," he finally said. "I see no good reason why you shouldn't go. Ye're nine and ye can read a bit. Ye may be a tiny mite for your age, but ye're strong. Ma, you can certainly manage the castle while I'm gone, and who knows? The child may learn something of value."

So it was that I began my first adventure outside the realm of western Ireland. I'd grown up in a solid three-story high stone fortress, Belclare, my father's ancestral castle, which abutted Clew Bay, an inlet of the huge ocean called the Atlantic. The thatch-roofed mud and stone cabins of my father's followers nestled around the outskirts of Belclare. The closest town of any size – if you wanted to call a hamlet of one hundred souls a town, was forty miles to the south. Much farther south and east was Galway, which was a real city – more than four hundred fifty people. For the first eight years of my life, we rarely ventured more than a day's journey in any direction.

During the summer months, our family sometimes joined my father's clan to live in a temporary summer dwelling, a *booley,* to graze our cattle herds in the uplands. I hated going to the booley, because unlike our castle, there was absolutely no privacy. The booley was one long room without any partition or separate rooms. There was a fireplace in the middle of the long room, an ever-burning log fire, even in the summer months. The booley had no chimney, only a vent hole for the smoke, and the building always smelled like smoke.

We ate well during the days and nights in the booley. Often, the clan would gather and we'd eat a whole beef or an entire sheep, which had been boiled and then roasted. The ladies laid on heaps of oatcakes. Beside each pile, there were always three vessels, one filled with whey-buttermilk, the second filled with sweet milk, and the third filled with ale.

My father, a tall, broad-shouldered, ruddy man, was tremendously strong. His hair fell to his shoulders and, as was the custom, it was cut in a *glib,* or fringe, across his forehead. He usually dressed in tight worsted trousers called *trews*, and a saffron-colored *léine*, a shirt with wide sleeves which fell loosely through the short sleeves of his tanned leather jerkin. He wore leather shoes and carried a *skeyne*, a knife, in his belt. His chieftain's cloak was fastened with a gold pin at the neck, and fell in folds to the ground.

My mother, Margaret, was my da's equal in every way. She was tall and slender and had a fair, clear-skinned complexion, save for the numerous freckles on her face. I got my bright yellow hair from her side of the family. She supervised the women's work – the spinning, weaving, and dyeing of our family's clothes, the churning of butter, the baking, the preparation of our household meals, and the upkeep of the castle. When my da was away on his sailing trips, ma was the glue that held the family together.

Unlike the landbound members of our clan, my da made the greatest amount of his living from fishing and trading. The O'Malleys spent much time building and repairing small, hide-covered coracles and curraghs. The majority of my da's time at home was spent supervising the maintenance of his three galleys.

Clare Island sat in the middle of Clew Bay. We visited the island quite often. While the eastern side was as quiet as a graveyard, the western coast always resounded with the

clash and crash of waves against the high cliffs. Often, my ma
would pack a lunch of cold roasted venison or lamb, turnips,
buttermilk, cabbage, and ale, and we would walk to land's end
where, according to my ma, monsters still lived. We'd ride over
to the island in a coracle barely large enough for the four of us.
Da and Donal would row together, propelling our small craft
smoothly over the glassine waters of the bay.

The adventure on which I was about to embark would
be different from those short journeys. I had seen my da's
galley many times before. While it was larger than any ship I'd
seen in Clew Bay, it seemed so *small* to go out on such a large,
treacherous ocean. Nevertheless, I had made such a tumult
about sailing to Spain with my father that I couldn't very well
back down now.

The night before we were to leave, my parents surprised
me with a set of clothes for the trip: two pair of boy's breeches,
three tunics, a heavy fleece overcoat, thick, warm stockings,
sturdy boots, and a felt bonnet of the kind worn by yeoman
sailors. I was overwhelmed. That night I hardly slept at all, so
excited was I at the prospect of the voyage.

My da had chosen a propitious month for the journey.
It was June, and the weather was as mild as it normally gets in
western Ireland, which is to say it was somewhat less gray, and
the sea, always wild, was at least more manageable than in the
fall and winter months. This was fortuitous, for the first day
on the water I suffered the onset of a most vicious illness. The
rocking of the galley was quite pleasant for the first hour of the
journey, and any fears I'd had about the danger of the journey
quickly subsided. I was having a wonderful time looking down
into the murky waters of the Atlantic, where large fish often
broke the surface. During that hour, I saw a most amazing

phenomenon: a school of small, narrow fish suddenly took to the air before my very eyes. They truly appeared to be flying. I'd never seen such a thing before then, but I have often seen flying fish since, and I've never yet lost my fascination for them. Da told me they flew to avoid being caught by larger fish, but their desperate efforts were not always successful.

Soon, the rocking effect of the water lulled me into a state where my eyes started getting heavy. Almost at the same time, I felt the beginnings of a churning in my stomach and a tightening in my lower neck, considerably less pleasurable than I'd felt only moments before. Soon, I felt nauseous, then extremely nauseous. Involuntarily, I leaned over the side of the galley and started heaving. But nothing came out. The harder I tried to vomit, the less happened. The world was spinning about. When I touched my hand to my forehead it felt wet and clammy.

"D – da," I barely managed to stammer. "H – help me. I think I'm dying." About that time, my eyes rolled up into my head and I started swaying. Now, dreading I'd fall over the deck even more than I dreaded embarrassing myself, I lowered myself to the ship's floor. The rolling feeling became more pronounced and made things even worse. I tried heaving again. This time, I was able to spew some of the contents in my stomach. In the past, when I'd been sick, as disgusting as it was, I'd felt better afterward. Not this time. As I wallowed about the deck in complete agony, truly hoping I would die, I heard voices, my da's and Donal na-Piopa's.

"Ah, poor little one," my da said. "'Tis the seasickness, it is."

"It affects everyone sooner or later," Donal said, not unkindly. "I remember when I suffered from it."

I felt someone very gently turn me onto my back and lift my head. Through a haze of dizziness, I felt, rather than saw, my da applying a cold, wet cloth to my forehead, the back of my neck, and my chest. That didn't help at all. I quickly doubled over again, my insides trying to spew themselves out. My da and my brother lifted me so that I could empty myself over the rail. I soon found this was only the beginning of my misery.

I don't know if it was worse when I lay down on my bed belowdecks, where it was warm and stifling, or when I was on deck and the cold wind chilled me so that I shivered uncontrollably, even when my brother had wrapped me in a heavy woolen sweater and greatcoat.

Although the last thing on my mind was eating anything, the ship's second in command forced me to swallow hardtack, old dried bread the consistency of a brick, and warm, watery broth. At first this made things even worse, but slowly – very, very slowly – the sickness started to abate. By morning of the third day, I felt very weak, but at least I was able to hold my food down.

I slept the entire afternoon, and when I awoke I felt almost normal. I shared the captain's quarters with my da and my older brother. The captain's cabin was the largest on the ship and was quite well-furnished. There were two two-level bunks, so four could sleep in the cabin, each bunk solidly attached to a wall by strong braces. Beyond the beds, there were two elevated chairs and a large table. My da kept large folios of charts on the table and on the adjacent, raised shelves, and these he consulted several times a day. Shortly after sunset, Donal and my da came into our quarters.

"Ah, I see you've recovered, m'darlin'," my father said.

"How can I ever tell ma?" I asked, embarrassed. "I've wanted nothing more all my life than to become a sailor and the first day out..."

"Ye're lucky it happened your first day out," he replied gently. "'Tis the seasickness and I've never known any sailor to escape it. Sometimes it happens early, sometimes it happens more than a year later, but sooner or later it happens to everyone who sets foot on a seagoing vessel. The lucky thing is that once you've experienced it, it hardly ever seems to come back. It's like a Baptism, it is. Well, Grace, ye've survived your first challenge as a sailor. I think from now on ye'll do quite well. I brought ye a little somethin' to help you speed your recovery."

He handed me a root of some kind, light tan colored, with a rubbery skin. "'Tis ginger," he said. "One of the best things I know for ending the seasickness once and for all." He cut a small piece of the root and handed it to me. The root tasted sort of sweet, sort of bitter, and spicy hot, but not unpleasant. "Chew on it a little at a time. It only takes a small amount to help," he said.

During the next few days, my father taught me how to read the charts on his captain's table and how to plot our course. At first, I could barely make out a few words on the chart, but I did get some idea of the route we were taking. Those maps were very detailed. Although they were large enough to spill over the sides of the table, each chart covered an area of no more than thirty nautical miles. They showed more islands than I ever knew existed. The bays and inlets were marked with numbers.

"Those numbers show the shallowest parts," my father told me. "We know the draft of this galley when it's fully loaded – how far down it goes into the water – and we make certain to avoid the shoals and the shallows. Many a good ship has run aground and thrashed its way to its death." I shuddered. "Don't worry, Granuaile," he continued. "These are very good charts – among the most important and valuable things I own – and I've been navigating these waters long enough to tell, even without the charts, when we're getting anywhere near danger."

From Clew Bay, we sailed southwest, past Slyne Head, the dreaded Cliffs of Moher, into the estuary of the River Shannon, where we stopped for fresh water and other provisions. I'd never been this far from home before, and I catalogued each new place in my mind. Every cape was called a "head," since it was a headland sticking out into the great ocean. Our next reprovisioning stop was Great Blasket Island, a gray, dour, windswept nothing of a place, which existed solely because of ships that stopped there. It was three miles off the mainland, but it was the only settlement of any kind we'd seen in four days. From there, I followed our direction south on the charts. Slea Head and Bolus Head and Sheep's Head. After the latter, we turned east into Bantry Bay, which was the demesne of a friendly king. We spent two days in Bantry town. The men ate and drank their fill at public houses along the wharf. I'm told they pursued other things as well, although I was not told what those things were. After we left Bantry Bay, we turned east, into the Celtic Sea.

"We've left the wild Atlantic," Donal told me. "From here it'll be much calmer, at least as far as Carnsore Point, when we'll cross St. George's Channel and Bristol Channel."

"Will we be in Spain, then?"

"Nay, child," my father said. "We've only made the smallest part of our journey."

"The smallest part? But da, we've been at sea for two whole weeks already."

"And we've got three more to go," he said. He went to the shelf adjacent to his table and pulled out another set of charts. The first covered a much greater area of land, and was not nearly as detailed as the others. He took my hand in his and pointed my finger at the large letters on the map. "Irelande," he said. "Englande, and France." He folded the chart over. The second page covered a similar area, the northwestern coast of France down as far as Cap Ferret. "'Cap' is the French word for 'Head.'"

During the following week, we followed the southern coast of England as far as Dover, which was a great city with more stone buildings than I'd ever seen before. Although the English Channel from Dover to Calais, on the French coast, was tumultuous, the seasickness I had suffered the first day out did not return.

Once off the coast of France, we remained close to shore, always keeping the land in sight. I learned that port and starboard referred to the right and left sides of our galley, and bow and stern meant the front and back, respectively. The farther south we sailed, the warmer the weather became. There were many days when I wore only the lightest of tunics over my breeches and allowed the warm sea breeze to pass over my bare arms.

Just north of Lisboa, which the locals pronounced "Leesh-bo-a," the wind slacked off and gave way to a sultry, uncomfortable heat. Two days before we got to Lisboa, there was very little wind at all, which meant that thirty men at a time took to the oars to propel our galley at some speed until the wind picked up once again.

When we reached Lisboa, a very grand and old and gracefully beautiful city, my da said we'd lay over here for three days to give the crew a chance to rest and relax, while he engaged in trading. "You and Donal and Paddy, he said," pointing to a roly-poly young sailor of about eighteen, "can spend the morning exploring Lisboa and I'll join you in the afternoon."

In answer to my questioning look, he said, "Ye'll be as safe with Donal na-Piopa and Paddy as with me. They're strong as bulls – and Paddy's almost as smart as one," he said, winking at me. "I reckon if anyone attempts to bother Donal na-Piopa's little, er, brother, he'll get a thrashing."

By that time, at least some of the hair I'd so smugly chopped off had grown back, so I didn't have to hide my head under a bonnet all the time. It was still no longer than a boy's, and since I'd not yet developed any womanly curves, no one aboard ship suspected I was anything other than the captain's younger son.

I enjoyed Lisboa immensely. The men there seemed much shorter than the Irishmen who manned our galley, swarthy, and quite handsome. I felt a wee bit of envy when I saw how stylish and beautiful the young women, some only a few years older than I, looked, and how the young men looked at *them.* There were hundreds, maybe thousands, of older women wearing long, sad, black outfits.

"They're widows, or their husbands have been away for months, sometimes for years," Donal said.

"Where do the men go?" I asked.

"Mostly to Africa and India. Lisboa's the capital of Portugal, a very powerful and wealthy country. I've heard that every man in the country is, or wants to be, a sailor. It's been that way for more than a hundred years and goes back to the days of Prince Henry the Navigator."

"A prince who was a sailor?"

"No," Donal na-Piopa replied. "Although he was called Prince Henry the Navigator by the English, he never actually sailed on any of the voyages he sponsored. Instead, he established a school for navigation, mapmaking, and shipbuilding. He wanted to find a route to the rich spice trade of the Indies, and to explore the west coast of Africa. The ships that sailed the Mediterranean were too slow and too heavy to make these voyages. Remember those beautiful, fast ships we saw when we sailed into the harbor?"

"Aye."

"Those are called caravels. They're lighter and much faster than our galley. They were designed at Prince Henry's school. Even after they were built, Prince Henry found it almost impossible to persuade his captains to sail beyond Cape Bojodor off the west coast of Africa. The captains told him that south of that point, the sun was so close to the Earth that a person's skin would burn black, the sea boiled, ships caught on fire, and monsters hid in the Green Sea of Darkness, waiting to smash the ships and eat the sailors.

"It took more than a dozen years before Henry convinced a captain to sail fifteen hundred miles down the African coast, but after that caravel came safely back home, Portuguese sailors realized they really could sail all the way to India, and come back as very rich men."

While my brother and Paddy seemed interested in discussing the commercial strength of the Portuguese sailors and the riches of India, I concentrated more on the sights of this large and beautiful city. Lisboa spread out along the right

bank of the very wide Tagus River, which debouched into the
ocean some miles to the west. Just north and east of where
we'd disembarked, there was a large and very dramatic hill.
I explored the streets and alleys of the Alfama and Mouraria
districts below the hill. I saw hundreds of shops and stalls
dealing in every kind of merchandise imaginable, silk from
the land of the Seres, spices from India and the new Ottoman
capital of Istanbul, flowers, and all kinds of food. The streets
were covered by square tiles. Some of the alleys were so narrow
there wasn't room for Donal na-Piopa, Paddy, and me to walk
three abreast. The more I saw the food stalls, the hungrier I
became, for the smells were exotic and enticing.

Donal and Paddy must have sensed my hunger, or
maybe their own, since the sun was now high in the sky and
the commerce in the streets seemed to abate.

"Aha, my worthies!" a welcome and familiar voice called
out.

"Da!" I exclaimed. "How did you ever find us?"

"It's no mystery," my father replied. "It's midday, and
most of the city's best, and cheapest, eateries are located in
Alfama. I took a chance that by following my nose I'd find you
sooner or later. Fortunately it was sooner," the Black Oak said.
"Of course, if you're not hungry..."

I glared at him and rolled my eyes. "I'm so hungry I
could eat a small sheep."

"Well, my darlin' – sons –" da said, keeping up the
pretense so that Paddy wouldn't become suspicious, "we're
going to try something different for lunch. Although they grow
plenty of sheep in the Portuguese hills north of here, I have a
feeling young Gra – Graham," he said, calling me by the closest
boy's name to my own, "might want to try something new."

My father herded us into a large, reputable-looking establishment, where he ordered lunch for all of us. The first thing I noticed was how wonderful the food smelled. When our meal came, I immediately appreciated how different – how deliciously different – it was from Irish fare or the food we'd been eating on board the ship for the past month. The pickled cabbage, salt beef, half-rotten turnips, and hardtack I was used to, gave way to rich and succulent fish stews, redolent with many fish and shellfish I'd never even seen, let alone eaten, before. Sardines and mackerel, octopus and squid, hake and cod, baked in a rich and savory tomato sauce, with onions, peppers, and beans. Bright yellow, saffron-flavored rice, washed down with purple-colored Port wine.

But the greatest treat was yet to come. At dessert, I had my first-ever orange. It was both sweet and slightly tart, and tasted nothing like the shriveled, sour limes my father had insisted we eat each day on our sea voyage. Da told me that oranges, lemons, and limes grew along the southern coasts of Portugal and Spain, and in the land of the Moors, on the continent of Africa. I cannot remember a better meal in my life. My father and brother teased me that if I didn't stop eating so much, I'd grow as round as a ball and so heavy our ship would be in danger of sinking from the extra weight.

As we left the restaurant, my da told us, "Until four hundred years ago, the Moors, who ruled southern Spain and all of Portugal, were the sovereigns of Lisboa. They built the harbors, shared in the Mediterranean Sea trade, and designed this fine city. Look at the hill above."

I did, and was stunned to see a huge, brooding castle.

"Castelo Sao Jorge," my father said. "The highest point in the city. The first fortress on that site was built seventeen hundred years ago – it's almost one hundred seventy times as old as you are," he continued, chuckling. "The castle you see today was built by the Moors. It's been a ruin since King Alfonso of Portugal captured it in 1147."

Despite my father referring to it as a ruin, I could still see several towers and look-outs. "Is there a way to get up there?" I asked, fascinated.

There was and we did. I'm certain I would have been agile enough to make the ascent, which was almost straight up, but my da preferred that we climb at a more relaxed pace, through a series of concentric streets that eventually brought us to the top of the hill. The view from the Castelo was amazing. I could see across the wide Tagus Estuary to the southern side and the districts of Barreiro, Montijo, and Almada. When I turned to my right and looked west, I could see all the way out to where the Atlantic began. Even better, a blessed breeze had arisen, and chased away the heat of the day. We remained atop Castle Hill for an hour. Meanwhile, Donal and Paddy had bade us farewell and started walking back down to whence we'd come. When we'd seen enough of Lisboa from the height of the castle, my da waved down a horse-drawn carriage.

"Why don't we simply walk back down?" I asked. "It's not that far."

"You're right, Granuaile, but we're not just going to the bottom of the hill. There's a very special place I want to show you."

The sun was midway between the zenith and the horizon when, two hours later, we reached the western edge of Lisboa, Belém, which the Portuguese people pronounced, "B'laine." I gasped as I beheld a huge tower of white and grey stone. "I saw that as we sailed in," I said.

"Belém Tower," my father replied. "It was built twenty-five years ago, during King Manuel's reign, as a fortress to guard the entrance to Lisboa's harbor. It was to be the last sight of their homeland the Portuguese sailors saw when they were about to embark, and the first thing they'd see when they returned home. But that's not the real reason I brought you out to Belém. Look yonder," he said, pointing inland to where a monstrously huge building stood about three hundred yards away. "The Jerónimos Monastery," my da said. "King Manuel's crown jewel."

As we wandered through the Moorish-style arches, we encountered walls and ceilings set with decorated, multicolored tiles, endlessly long halls, and magnificent rooms the like of which I had never seen before and have not seen since. We heard the gentle, soothing sounds of running water everywhere, which made the Monastery seem cool, even in the mid-afternoon heat. I saw architecture I could never have dreamed existed. The place was so magnificent that then and there my life changed its direction. I would never again be content to live the rest of my life on the boggy ground of west Ireland, not so long as I knew that the great sea almost right outside our castle door would lead to places and peoples, to foods and sights, to commerce and sounds as strange and as wondrous as I experienced that day.

Chapter 2

As we rounded Point Saint Vincent, which the Portuguese call Ponta da Sagras – they pronounce it "Sah-grahsh," I experienced another new phenomenon: bright, cloudless blue sky, an endless horizon, and a dazzling sunlight so intense it made my eyes hurt. It took less than a day after we entered the Gulf of Cádiz 'til we stopped to take on more provisions at Vila Real da Santo Antonio, the last settlement before we reached the Spanish frontier. Another day's swift journey and we reached Cádiz, which the Spaniards pronounce, "Ca-dith."

Cádiz stands on a peninsula jutting out into a bay, and is almost entirely surrounded by water, a large and thriving city, not quite as large as Lisboa, but very modern and wealthy. I was told this was because, like Lisboa, it was a major launching point for very long sea journeys. But unlike Lisboa, ships leaving Cádiz were not headed south to Africa and east to India, but rather to the far west, to the newly discovered lands of America. Like Lisboa, the oldest part of the city looked Moorish. Narrow cobblestoned streets opened onto small squares, and the golden cupola of the new cathedral loomed high above the whitewashed houses of the town.

We remained in Cádiz for two days. On the third day, my father took Donal and me to Jerez de la Frontera. "It's called 'de la Frontera' because three hundred years ago it stood on the frontier between Moorish and Christian lands. The English call this town 'Sherry,' because they had problems pronouncing Jerez in the Spanish manner," he said. "We're here to trade our wools and hides for wine, from which we'll make a great fortune."

"How so?" Donal na-Piopa asked.

"Some time ago, the English took a great liking to the sweet wine from this town. It's as cheap as water here, but as dear as gold in Brittania."

We spent the day in Jerez, and my father made certain I saw the Eleventh Century Moorish fortress, the Alcazaba. On the way there, we saw signs proclaiming there would be a show featuring dancing horses that day. Papa must have intuited that a girl and a horse are as natural together as sherry wine and a goblet, and it took very little of my begging and pleading to get him to take Donal and me to the afternoon performance. The horses really did dance, and I'd never seen anything like it. I began to think my father had had more than a hint of a plan in his mind when he allowed me to travel on this voyage with him.

We had left Ireland in June, and it was now mid-August. "Time to return home, so we can make it before the vicious winter weather sets in," my father said. "But there's one more place you must see before we embark. It's a day's journey from here and well worth your while."

We sailed south from Cádiz on August 18 and slept on board the galley. Next morning I awoke to a stunning sight: a single granite rock, nearly as high as a mountain, stood out in sharp relief. There was nothing of comparable size near it, and the land about it was flat as far as I could see.

"Jabal Tariq, the mountain of Tariq," my father said. "At least that's what it's called today. In ancient days, it was one of the Pillars of Hercules."

"*One* of...?" I started to ask. "But there's nothing else around. Did the other mountain sink into the sea?"

"No. Granuaile. You'll see when we climb to the top."

"Sort of like Castelo Sao Jorge?"

"Perhaps even more dramatic."

We made landfall on the leeward side of the promontory abutting the rock. There were several trails leading to the top of the monolith. At a signal from my father, we walked down the ship's gangplank and onto land. Although the rock seemed very high from the beach, it took us little more than an hour to ascend most of the way to the top. I'd gotten about three-quarters of the way up, when suddenly something very heavy pounced on my back and shoulders.

It happened too fast for me to be properly frightened. As I turned to see who – or what – my attacker was, there was a loud chattering and gibbering that seemed to emanate from my shoulders and was answered in kind from somewhere in the dry upper reaches of the rock. Then I saw my nemesis. It was no larger than a medium-sized dog, and it sat quite contentedly on my shoulder, scratching itself and sticking its tongue out.

"Barbary ape," my father said. "The only wild monkeys in all of Europe. They're greedy and very clever. You'd best keep anything of value in your pockets."

No sooner he said that, the macaque grabbed for my bonnet and happily placed it on his own head. Having got what he'd come for, he leapt off my head and prepared to scurry away, but not before I'd yanked my hat back. Frustrated, the monkey tried to grab it from me, but forewarned by my father, I held tightly to the felt bonnet. What could have been a furious tug-of-war ensued, but my da tossed half an orange to the monkey, who happily caught it on the fly, let go of the hat, now completely uninterested, and bounded away about thirty feet up the mountain. From his aerie, he glared at me to make sure I wasn't coming after *his* orange, popped the whole thing into his mouth, and sat munching contentedly.

I asked my da for another bit of orange, and when he gave it to me, I tossed it to the monkey as a peace offering. The animal caught the orange as quickly as he'd caught the first one, and jammed it into his mouth as well. Glancing once more in my direction, he nodded, as if to put an exclamation point to our encounter, and disappeared into the brush. Not long after that, we reached the top of the mountain. From there, I could see nothing but flat land, water, and haze, until my father turned me in a southerly direction.

On the far side of the water, I saw *another* rock, an exact replica of the one on which we were standing.

"There's your *other* rock," my father said. "In the ancient days, these two rocks truly marked the end of the world. From the Pillars east, sailors plied the Mediterranean Sea. No man ventured west of the Pillars. But there's an even greater division north to south. We're standing at the end of Europe. That other rock you see stands at the end of Africa. So now you've ventured from Ireland to the Straits. East of here lies Italy, then Greece, then the land of the Ottomans, and beyond that the Holy Land itself."

I was silent, taking in with wonder the vast significance of this point on the earth. We remained another hour on the rock before we made our way down. I saw one or two more apes, but none ventured close to us.

On the twentieth of August in the Year of Our Lord 1539, we embarked on our trip back to Ireland. We made numerous stops on the way, mostly to purchase trade goods to sell in England or Ireland. By the time we left Bordeaux, we were so laden with wine from Aquitania, I doubt if we could have fit another crate into – or onto – my da's galley.

The small vessel traveled slowly, for it sat low down in the water, at maximum draft. About that time, the lookout shouted, "Ship ahoy! Pirate vessel. All hands to deck."

"Damn!" my father swore. "Of all times for *us* to be attacked. Usually *we're* the attackers. Can you see any markings?" he shouted up to the lookout.

"It's a Portuguese caravel!" the man called back. "It's flying the English flag and it's traveling twice as fast as we are."

Our galley had one small cannon on each side of the ship, certainly not enough to take on a warship of any kind. However, we had fifty men and forty sidearms on board, so my da felt we could hold our own if our ship were not shot out from under us. While the invader was still a good half mile from us, my da came up to me and said quietly, "Granuaile, I won't be able to watch you during the coming hand fight. Get down below in the hold and hide there until we see how the battle is going. Don't be frightened, girl. We'll get through this and ye'll be all right."

Frightened? Me? I did not feel remotely frightened. I felt exhilarated and longed to be part of the battle, even though I knew I was probably only half the size of any of the sailors about to invade us. Da had told me to hide belowdecks in the hold. But I had a different idea where to hide.

The English pirate ship, which had no more cannon than we, resorted to grappling hooks to draw our vessel close enough to enable its invaders to board. From where I was hiding, I could see their numbers and ours were about equal. The hand-to-hand combat had been going on about five minutes. I kept my eye on my da and my brother, who were, between them, fighting four men. I knew the O'Malleys were excellent swordsmen, and in a fair fight, even with four of theirs to two of ours, I had no doubt we'd prevail.

Suddenly, out of the corner of my eye, I saw an English pirate sneaking up on my father, raising a dagger behind his back. With no thought for my own safety, I leapt from my hiding place, high up on the sail rigging, through the air and onto the pirate's back. I screamed at the top of my lungs, causing my father and brother to turn. What they saw was something no bigger than a Barbary ape, gouging the eyes of the attacker, kicking and choking him. The Englishman screamed in frustrated rage, clawing at his eyes, trying unsuccessfully to pull my hands away.

I kept screaming, but now the scream turned into an elated whoop. More English pirates stopped what they were doing and stood shocked at seeing a tiny harridan manhandling one of their own. When the English pirate finally managed to shake me off his back, my da charged the man who would have thrust a dagger into his throat, decapitated him, then turned and dispatched the other two attackers by smacking them in the head with the broad side of his sword. When one of them went down near me, I used all the strength and agility in my little legs to kick the invader's ribs until I heard a loud crack.

I felt the thrill of victory as the Englishmen retreated to their own vessel, but the battle was not yet over. Our men hurled lighted faggots onto the caravel's wooden deck, where the dry wood caught fire immediately. In less than half an hour, the ship that had so vigorously pursued us was yawing in its death throes. Its skiffs had been loosed, and its crew crowded into the small dinghies, leaving the caravel to die with not even one man left on board.

As night fell, there were loud hurrahs all over our galley, and much clapping me on my back and shoulders. But my greatest satisfaction came when I heard the crew congratulating my father and saying, "That young lad of yours, Graham? He's tougher than men twice his size, and when he grows large enough to be a mighty oak himself, ye'd better make sure he's your ally, not your enemy."

That night, and for the many left before we sailed back into Clew Bay, I knew for certain that my future lay at sea.

Chapter 3

Shortly after I turned fifteen, my da, with my approval, betrothed me to another man named Donal, this one named Donal O'Flaherty. They called him Donal of the Battles, because they said he was so wild and foul-tempered that he was always getting into arguments and fights with others. I'd met Donal a few times, and had never found him to be such a bad fellow. He was nineteen and the *tanaiste,* heir to Donal Crone, The O'Flaherty. The term *The* O'Flaherty meant Donal's father was the head of the O'Flaherty clan and the ruler of Iar Connacht and Connemara.

I rather looked forward to the marriage. I'd heard tell – and my ma had confirmed it – that the things that men and women do together when they're alone and in bed are quite pleasurable.

By that time, I'd become a regular crew member on my father's ships and, if I do say so myself, I was quite adept at the family business. I'd never doubted that I was as strong as any man, if not physically, then certainly intellectually, and shortly after the betrothal, I convinced my father the wedding should not be held at the bride's home, which was common in Ireland at that time, but rather at a place that I felt would be more appropriate, considering who I was. When I told my da where I wanted to be wed, he guffawed loudly, slapped both knees, and said, "Ye've got iron nerve, I'll say that f'r ye. Y'know…?"

"Yes, Papa, I know," I replied. "And I can't think of a more fittin' place. Ye've always called me your little princess, and in Ireland a girl's wedding is her coronation."

"You're serious, then?"

"Aye, and not only that, you can afford it."

"'T'wasn't the money I was thinkin' of, darlin'. It'll be early springtime. We can sail as far as Galway, but then we'd have to trek inland to avoid the fierce wind and waves that batter the coast. It may be a bit difficult for the great crowd of folk who'll be comin' in from Clew Bay and Connaught."

"How many do we have in our own party?"

"Two hundred. That's a lot of people to live off the land at that time of year. I think we'd best sail down and meet everyone at Galway."

"A shame," I replied. "I've always heard of the lovely wilderness area around Clifden and Kylemore, near where my new home will be, and I've always wanted to see the Twelve Bens," I said, referring to the dramatic mountains that surrounded the stunningly beautiful marsh and lake country. "Perhaps my brother and I could ride down and meet you at Galway?"

"It'd take you the better part of a fortnight," he replied. "You wouldn't risk harm from the populace, since it's O'Flaherty country, but I'm concerned that rogue highwaymen traverse that area at the beginning of spring, and they get pretty desperate when the pickings are lean."

"But, Da, would they attack two young travelers with nothing of substance to show?"

"Might. Y'never know."

I continued cajoling the Black Oak, harking back to my adventure when the English raiders had attacked my father's ship on that first voyage. "I've proved I can handle myself. Besides, 'tis easier for two to escape than many, should anything happen."

"Well... if Donal na-Piopa is willing to travel with you, and we know the exact route you're gonna' take..."

Thus it was that on the tenth day of March, 1546, Donal na-Piopa and I left Clew Bay, headed south. We each had a sturdy mount, and we brought along a pack mule, a jack, which was stronger and more energetic than either of the ponies. The day we departed Belclare castle, the breeze from the north was mild and pleasant. "A good sign," Donal na-Piopa told me. "We may even have sunshine today. Should we climb the Reek for luck?"

"Aye," I responded. "We'll be chasin' the spring as it comes north, so we may as well chase all the good fortune we can." Both of us were wearing heavy coats, boots, and head coverings. From a distance of twenty feet it was impossible to tell which was the girl and which the man. Soon we approached Croagh Patrick, The Reek.

Back when he was alive, the Sainted Patrick spent forty days and forty nights on the summit of the peak. 'Tis said it was from that summit that he chased all the snakes out of Ireland, and to this day there are none. It's been a place of pilgrimage for more than a thousand years. During summer, people climb to the top wearing no shoes, only their bare feet. However, it being very early spring and still cold, we let the horses and the mule do the work. It didn't take us more than a couple hours, since it was only twenty-five hundred feet high. Still, it was the highest part of western Ireland.

As many times as I'd been atop the mountain, when we got to the summit of Croagh Patrick, I still gasped at the view from the crest. It was so much higher than the surrounding bog land that I could see all the way to the horizon in every direction. The whole of Clew Bay lay at my feet. Clare Island was in the middle distance to the west. Looking south, I could see a series of high mountains in the distance, *Na Beanna Beola*, the Twelve Bens.

As we rode south, the animals ambled at a leisurely pace on a well-trod trail. Occasionally, each would nibble at a shrub or trailside bit of scrub, but since they'd been well fed before we'd departed, and it was early afternoon, they maintained a steady pace. I thought about my upcoming marriage. I wasn't frightened. It wasn't as if we were necessarily marrying for a lifetime. Under Brehon law, the ancient Celtic law, marriage in Ireland was more a contract than a love match. Donal O'Flaherty and I would be marrying for a year and a day. After that, either of us could decide to quit the marriage or continue it. There was no penalty either way.

As we continued riding south, heavy clouds obliterated the mountains in front of us, giving the landscape a dour, gray, hypnotic appearance. We heard thunder ahead and night was coming on. "There's a place up ahead where we can take shelter for the night," my brother said. "Since we'll be in O'Malley territory for the next couple of days, there'll be no shortage of available homes."

That night, we stayed in a single story stone house, which, while minuscule compared to the O'Malley castle, was large enough to accommodate us in separate rooms. There was

also a barn and fodder for our steeds. Dinner was simple but
ample. A huge pot of stew, consisting mostly of turnips and root
vegetables, with the occasional chunk of lamb, was hung over an
open fire throughout the year. The pot was replenished as need
dictated, with whatever comestibles came to hand, and both the
inhabitants and guests of the house dipped earthenware bowls
into the stew. Since it was winter's end, the meat was lean and
stringy, and there were plenty of onions, carrots, and beetroot.
The meal, while by no means sumptuous, was certainly filling
and warming.

Next morning, we were up early. After a breakfast of hard
bread and ale, we were off once again. The sky was completely
clouded over and a damp wind pressed in on us from the north.
We passed between gray, moody lakes and bogs, and hillocks
whose tops were obliterated – two or three of the Twelve Bens.
Sometimes, Donal na-Piopa would ride a few yards ahead, but
then he would slow down every few minutes to make sure I
was close by. During those times Donal was farthest ahead, I
continued musing on Brehon marriage.

Donal and I were marrying *Lanamnas comthinchuir*,
both partners of equal rank and property. Although the
marriage was arranged by our families, either of us could have
said no. Each partner would contribute movable goods to the
marriage, but each of us would retain our own land. There were
many degrees of marriage in Ireland. A 'soldier's marriage' was
a temporary situation that could last as little as a single night. I
giggled, thinking that might be quite exciting.

Just then, Donal came riding back. "Granuaile," he said
softly. "Three men have been riding parallel, on a trail above
us, where they think we can't see them. I haven't seen any
buildings in the area. I have a short sword and Da gave me

another, but we may be outnumbered. Do you think we should make a run for it?"

"No, they may have accomplices lying in wait. Let's just continue as we have and hope they'll keep their distance 'til we can find a safe place."

During the next hour, the three strangers remained separated from us by some three hundred yards. It was only when we entered a narrow defile that they made their move. They kicked their mounts into a trot, then a canter, until they'd passed us, then veered back to face us. When they were directly ahead of us, they turned their horses toward us and sat blocking our path.

"Ho, brothers!" Donal na-Piopa called out. "Greetings!"

The apparent leader of the group, tall, very thin, with a scrofulous salt-and-pepper beard, said nothing in response, but sat with his arms crossed, his right hand holding a short sword similar to ours, but rusted.

"I said, 'Ho, brothers!'" Donal repeated. "We mean you no harm. Please allow us to pass."

"I think not," the leader said in a surly undertone.

"Well, then," Donal na-Piopa continued. "If you won't let us pass, then we will pass without your leave."

"I think not," the leader said again.

"Outlaws are you then?" Donal said. "This is O'Malley land."

"*This*," the leader said, describing an arc with his left hand, "is *no* man's land unless you are prepared to defend it, O'Malley," he sneered.

During this exchange, I said nothing. I had unsheathed my own sword and rested it lightly on my pony's saddle, where the three antagonists could see it.

Donal and I and the three highwaymen remained at an impasse, glaring at each other for a short time, before the outlaws spurred their horses straight at us. In a blur of action, swords clashed and Donal was unseated from his mount. I let out an involuntary scream and I'm sure in that moment the attackers knew I was a female and vulnerable.

As Donal grabbed at his wounded arm, the attackers, unseated me and roughly tore at my tunic. They ripped at my lower garments. I shouted desperately while my tormentors rolled me over and over, toward some grass adjacent to the trail.

I was not about to submit to a brutal rape willingly. I lashed out at the men with my booted foot, catching one of them squarely under the chin. No matter my efforts, we were one badly injured young man and one woman against three large, powerful men.

I did not hear another person come up until he was, quite literally, upon us. As I looked up, there he was, taller and broader than any of the others. He was dressed head to toe in chain mail. "Cease forthwith!" the man called in a sharp, commanding voice. "You're dead if you don't!"

All movement stopped as though each person were frozen.

"Wh-, who?"

"Richard-an-Iarainn de Bourgo at your service," the man said.

"Iron Dick Burke?"

"Aye." In the same instant, he unsheathed a broadsword and smacked my three assailants so hard they fell, writhing, to the ground. "I believe you are Granuaile Ni-Mháille, an ally of our family?"

"That's so."

One would have had to be completely insensitive, if not totally dense, not to sense the electricity that passed between us.

"'Tis dangerous country to be travelin' in, even with a small army, during this time of year," Burke remarked. "Did not your father tell you that?"

"He did, but I've never before seen the Bens or Connemara."

"So you'd risk –?"

"Frankly, Richard Burke, I did not see that as a realistic threat. I'm not exactly dressed to go to a party, and I don't fancy myself the belle of Ireland."

At that, his eyes moved appreciatively from my face to my still half-exposed body. "Aye, there's a sweet country below and I could happily rest my weapon there."

"No man will travel this country until he has climbed all Twelve Bens in a single day," I responded.

"In that sweet country, I'll rest my weapon."

"No man will travel this country until he has leapt the River Shannon carrying twice his weight in gold, and struck down three groups of nine men with a single stroke, leaving the middle man of each nine unharmed," I rejoined, getting into the mood of this exciting game.

"In that sweet country I'll rest my weapon."

"No man will travel this country who hasn't gone sleepless from Halloween until Groundhog Day, when the ewes are milked at spring's beginning."

"Aye, and I would milk something else, too."

At that moment, Donal na-Piopa rolled over and moaned, punctuating our repartee. In an instant, Dick and I surrounded my brother and checked him over carefully.

"The puncture wound in his arm is superficial. He might have a broken collarbone as well," Burke said. Donal na-Piopa moaned louder. Burke retreated a hundred feet to where his own steed, a large, chestnut horse stood. He took a jar of some smelly unguent and a brace out of his saddlebag. He applied the salve to Donal's shoulder, then fastened the brace in such a way that it held his shoulder and arm in a secure splint.

We hefted Donal onto his mount. Then we heard other moans and turned toward the three attackers, who were in various stages of semiconsciousness. "What should we do with them?" I asked Richard-in-Iron.

"There's any number of things I could do," Richard responded. "Kill 'em for their discourtesy, which would at least make their waste of skin valuable as food for the worm and the carrion raptor. Turn 'em over to the shire-rief, which would be an expensive proposition because the county would have to feed them while they were waiting for the hangman. Or simply tie 'em up and leave 'em here to freeze and rot. What do you propose, Lady Grace?"

"Since they *almost* had their way with me, perhaps there's an alternative that would ensure they'd never try such a thing with any other woman. Geld 'em."

The three men were now quite awake and obviously terrified. They ignored one another, so intent was each in pleading his own merit. In the end, it made no difference. Burke did as I had suggested, and the attackers were left dazed and altered as the three of us took to the road once again.

It was now early afternoon. Neither the weather nor the landscape had gotten any kinder. The wind was sullen and cold. Donal na-Piopa was very much in pain, and my gentle words did little to ameliorate his discomfort.

"We'll be out of O'Malley country by tomorrow. I suggest we leave your brother at the nearest decent-looking house and prevail upon whatever man and his goodwife reside there to get your brother back to Clew Bay as soon as possible."

"But you said it would be unsafe for two to journey onward," I said, calmly. "How much more dangerous would it be for one?"

"What makes you think there'll be only one?" he said. "You're headed through Connemara to Galway if I'm not mistaken?"

"Aye."

"I'm headed to Athlone. What if I choose to accompany you?"

"You'd do that for me, Richard Burke?"

"Aye."

"Well, I can't promise you anything except my appreciation."

"Mayhap that'll be enough for now."

As Richard-an-Iarrain had predicted, we found a house within the next two miles. The owner was a loyal subject of Owen Dubhdarra O'Malley, who promised to assist the Black Oak's son in any way he could. The man's house was well and sturdily built. There was room for Donal na-Piopa and me in the main house, but not enough room to house Richard Burke as well.

"No matter," said Iron Dick. "I'm three-and-twenty and it won't be the first time I've slept with the horses and kine in the barn."

"Ah," I said playfully, continuing the teasing game we'd started earlier, "an older fellow you are then?"

"Mayhap, my girl," Dick rejoined, "but some say, 'the older the buck, the stiffer the horn.'"

After an evening meal that replicated the previous night's fare, I retired to my bedroom. Some time during the night, I awoke, got up, and silently left the room. I knew exactly what my destination was and what I intended to find there.

Next morning, disheveled and wonderfully exhausted, my hair askew and flecked with bits of straw, my eyes bright with the smoke from a distant fire, I staggered in stiffly, in exquisite pain. I collapsed on the pallet, mumbling inanities, and promptly fell asleep.

Some hours later I awoke, bathed, brushed out my hair, and came into the dining room. Iron Dick Burke was there. He looked quite haggard and spent himself. We sipped our warm ale and ate dark bread, rolls and butter, silently. From time to time, we looked meaningfully at one another.

Once we'd left the house and were back on the road, I kept shifting from side to side as I rode my horse.

"Grace?" he asked softly.

"It was wonderful," I said in a dreamy voice. "I always feared what it would be like. No more."

"But the pain?"

"'Tis nothing, Richard. It won't last. Ah, but the other..." I sighed contentedly.

"Soldier's marriage?"

"Mmm-hmm."

"But Donal O'Flaherty...?"

"He needn't know," I replied. "The only difference is he was going to marry a virgin princess. Now, he'll be marryin' a queen, or, at the very least, someone who'll know what to do once she gets into the marriage bed."

"Say you so?"

"That I do. Donal may be one with the 'troubles,' but he'll find his bride'll have none but the pleasure."

"What about me?"

"We'll see what happens now, won't we, Dick? A year-and-a-day need not be forever, but I'll keep an open mind – and, perhaps, when you're in the neighborhood, two friendly open thighs as well."

Chapter 4

The remainder of the journey to Galway went easily and without incident, save for the nightly fire that invariably erupted between Dick and me. From Clifden, we rode east at a leisurely pace through the southern escarpments of the Bens. I remember Kylemore Lake in the shadow of the Bens as one of the most beautiful places I'd yet seen. Southeast of Kylemore, the land flattened out, and we descended to Galway Bay. By the time we reached my father's galley, we looked as innocent as two babes. Only I was aware that our amorous couplings during the past several nights had been anything but innocent. Donal na-Piopa had returned to Clew Bay just before our parents' departure, and the Black Oak had learned from him how Iron Dick Burke had intervened and saved both his son and daughter from a dreadful fate.

"I'm beholden to you for squiring her here," my da remarked to Richard when they met. "You're from the Mayo Burkes then?"

"Yes," Richard responded. "A neighbor, matter of fact."

"After what ye've done for my kin, it would be unmannerly not to invite you to my Granuaile's wedding. Will ye be ridin' south with us?"

"Thank you, but no, Captain O'Malley. I'm on my way to Athlone and thence to Dublin on family business. During our journey here, Grace told me where she's getting married. I can't think of a more appropriate place for her to wed. How long has she been betrothed to the *tanaiste* O'Flaherty?"

"Nine months," Owen replied.

"Seems a good marriage." There was not a hint of emotion in his voice. "How come they didn't marry at Lughnasadh?" he continued, referring to the August Celtic festival, the time when most handfastings took place.

"Because she was only fifteen and she was a'sea with me at that time," my father replied.

"And because I didn't want to be a Teltown bride," I said. We all laughed. The largest Lughnasadh festival took place at Teltown, in County Meath. It's was a regular marriage market, where young men and women came to the festival for the purpose of finding a mate, but hardly ever knowing who their partner would be. A great number of them went through the Celtic handfasting ceremony. They would stay together for a year, then, often as not, they came back to Lughnasadh, parted company, and hitched up with a new husband or wife.

It took a week for our clan to gather the more than two hundred souls who'd make the trek south to Cashel, where I was to marry. During that time, Richard proudly boasted to me that his family, originally called de Bourgo, had come from Norman England and captured the territory from the local O'Flahertys in 1232. He had the good grace not to mention that he, Richard-an-Iarrain Burke, had also bested an O'Flaherty in being the first to capture my maidenhead.

"Galway became an outpost of the Irish frontier until a hundred fifty years ago, when the control of the city passed from our family to the fourteen merchant families – the tribes. Even today, Galway's called the City of the Tribes. Have you ever heard of America, Granuaile?" Richard asked as we walked through the modern streets of the town, marveling at the new stone buildings that seemed to be going up all over.

"I have. What about it?"

"An Italian fellow working for the Spanish, Cristobal Colón, stopped off in Galway for a few days before he set sail for the new world. He'd heard that the sainted Brendan had made an earlier voyage to the Americas, and he wanted to investigate whether that actually happened."

"Did Brendan actually make it to the New World?" I asked.

"Don't know," Iron Dick replied. "Will you miss me?"

"Don't know," I answered playfully, but a little sadly. "You certainly fulfill your promise, Iron Dick, but I'm betrothed to an O'Flaherty and I'd best act like it. It's been fun, hasn't it?"

"Aye, young Grace O'Malley, that it has. So ye'll be settling in as a goodwife, raising a gaggle of little ones?"

"I'll never settle in, so long as there's a sea to be sailed, new folks to be met..."

"Treasure to be plundered?" he said lightly.

"That, too. Ye've heard of our family business then?"

"The Black Oak is a legend in these parts. I imagine the acorn won't fall far from the Oak tree."

"Thank you, Kind Sir. Oh," I gasped, "what a wondrous church!"

"Collegiate Church of Saint Nicholas of Myra. Ireland's largest parish church. It's named after a Turkish fellow. Nicholas was the Bishop of Myra, on the south coast of the Ottoman lands. He secretly provided gifts of money to brides who otherwise would have gone without. Today, he's the patron saint of Christ's birthday Mass. Yonder is Lynch's Castle, home to the most powerful of the fourteen families."

By that time, it was nearing noon and we met my father for the usual fare of corned beef, cabbage, and Irish stew. "Pretty tame stuff after Portugal and Spain, eh, my girl?" Owen said.

"Yes, Da. You'd think with all the trading we do with those countries, we'd at least have learned some of their cooking secrets."

"That may be, Granuaile, but even though you've been sailing most of your life, most Irish would never think of leaving their land. They're comfortable with their lives and their food. I guess most Spanish folk feel the same way about their land. Of course, the Portagees, every other man-jack of them seems to be a sailor."

"And a sailor I'll always be."

"Wife or no?"

"Wife or no, Da."

"Well, Granuaile, Donal O'Flaherty'll have his share of troubles if he tries to control you."

From Galway, the O'Malley procession gathered at the east end of Galway Bay. There were two hundred eighteen of us, and a like number of horses, mules, and carriages. Since a goodly number of our retinue consisted of men of fighting age, we had little to fear from those whose lands we'd be crossing.

Just before we left Galway Bay, my da went over the route we'd take on the two week journey to Cashel with ma, Donal na-Piopa, who was recovering nicely, and me.

"We'll be leaving Connaught and entering Munster to-morrow morning. In two days, we'll reach Ennis, the largest settlement in County Clare. From there we'll cross the Shannon, the widest river in Ireland, into County Limerick. Brian Ború of blessed memory, who ruled there, kicked the Vikings out of Ireland five hundred years ago. To this day it's O'Brien country."

"What's the land like?" Donal na-Piopa asked.

"It's wonderful farmland. Same can be said for County Tipperary. It's less than a day's journey from Tiobrad Árann, the main town, to Cashel."

Because as the bride-elect, I was expected to be radiant and healthy for my wedding night, my father insisted I ride in a closed conveyance drawn by two horses, so I wouldn't catch a chill. Most of the time, my mother and I rode in the carriage together. Talk we did, and not much about the scenery,

Truth to tell, I was not heartbroken at leaving Richard Burke behind. My mother and I had always been close, and I could talk with her about anything. I'd already told her about Richard Burke, and she didn't seem at all surprised.

"Ma, won't... you know... cause problems when Donal finds out?"

"I very much doubt it," my mother replied. "Boys and girls have been doing what comes naturally from time out of mind. But just to make sure nothin's amiss, I've a wee trick up my sleeve." With that, she extracted a small bag of some smooth, transparent material from her bodice. "Made from a goat's intestines," she said. "On the night of the wedding, you pour a small amount of sheep's blood into the bag, and when you and he get into bed, you place it carefully under your bum. Then..."

"Ma!"

"Yes?" she asked, looking maidenly sweet and innocent.

"That's... that's fraud!"

"Granuaile, my darlin', have you never told a small lie to make someone feel better about himself?"

"Well... maybe a little one now and then. But what you propose to do is... well... different."

"How so?" she asked. "If it makes Donal feel like more of a man because he believes he was the first, what harm can it do?"

Later on that day, my father told me there'd be people from as far away as England, Spain, and even Germans from the Hanseatic League coming to the wedding, and that I might be called upon to talk about Irish customs with them. "Like how come so many people in Ireland are named O'-this or Mac-that."

"Oh, Da," I laughed. "How could they *not* know?"

"The Spanish would understand, because they've got '*de*' this and the Germans have '*von*' that, but the English can be a bit dense."

"But it's so easy. In Ireland the family is everything. Several families make up a *sept*, and several *septs* make up a *clan,* and several *clans* make up a *tribe.* All members of a tribe are descended from a common ancestor. If someone's name is *Mac*-something, such as *Mac*Malley, he was the son of Malley, and if he was named O'Malley, that means he was descended from the grandson of the Malleys. The head of each clan or sept is called '*The*' something-or-other, like you, Da. You're called *The* O'Malley."

"Aye, but I'll never be *The MacWilliam,* the head of all the tribes in Connaught."

"Who's The MacWilliam now, *da*?"

"Ulick Burke."

"As in...?"

"Richard-an-Iarrain's great uncle. Mayhap one day Dick could become The MacWilliam."

The next day, the landscape continued to flatten as we approached the River Fergus and the northern edge of Munster.

"O'Brien country?" I remarked to my father.

"And a perfect example of what we spoke about yesterday, Grace. Brian Ború united the whole of Ireland five hundred years ago. His son was called *Mac*Brian and his *son's* children were called O'Brian, which changed over the years to O'Brien. *The* O'Brien is to Munster what The MacWilliam is to Connaught."

Shortly before we arrived in Ennis, I pointed to a large fortress atop a rocky outcrop of land.

"*Dysert O'Dea*, one of the O'Brien castles," my da remarked.

I found Ennis to be a charming town, with narrow winding lanes and painted storefronts. We attended an early spring *fleadh*, a music festival, there. The number of musicians varied from soloists to as many as a dozen members of a band. Although I recognized violins – fiddles – there were many instruments I'd not heard before.

My favorites were the Celtic harp, which was quite small, and the *ullean pipes* – bagpipes. One of the musicians showed me how to play the instrument. I blew into a pipe at the top of a leather bag. This filled the bag full of air. I then continued blowing air into the bag, while she squeezed the bag with her left hand and arm. There were four other pipes attached to the bag. The first, and largest of the pipes, came out of the middle of the bag, and three smaller pipes, perforated with holes, came out of the lower part of the bag. When I squeezed the bag, a single-pitched, continuous low note came out of the largest pipe. Simultaneously, my fingers alternated along the holes in the three other pipes.

There were other instruments at the *fleadh* as well: flutes, tin whistles, and *bodhráns* – goatskin drums played with small sticks. I proved adept, not only at playing the bagpipes, but also at doing some spirited Irish dancing as well.

Chapter 5

Two days later, just north of Limerick, our entourage arrived at *Bun Raite*, Bunratty Castle, the huge and impressive seat of the O'Briens of Thomond. My father seemed awed, and well he might, since Bunratty was to the O'Malley Castle as the O'Malley Castle was to the stone house where we'd stayed the first night in Connemara. The Lord of the castle invited us to a banquet in my honor the following evening.

That night, my jaw continually dropped in amazement. The castle, a huge, well-fortified place, had been built a hundred years earlier by the McNamara family, but had passed shortly thereafter to the O'Briens. Even in those days, it was famous throughout Ireland for its magnificent banquets. The great hall could easily seat our entire retinue. The servings of food – whole roasted lambs and beeves, turnips, carrots, wild onions, spring greens, soups, stews, and after dinner sweetmeats, accompanied by mead – were beyond generous. The meal was followed by entertainments of every kind, and by bards telling wonderful and evocative stories.

I was particularly fascinated by tales about the Wee Folk – the Little People – the faeries and leprechauns of Irish legend.

These were not kindly little folk. Their smiles were said to have a cast of evil to them, and if they were not downright malignant and evil, they were certainly to be avoided, unless, of course, one could steal something from them and frustrate their nasty intent and their even nastier character. I heard so many tales of them that night, and, indeed, those same tales were replicated all over Ireland in the following years, that I couldn't remember them all. Of course, not all of the tales painted the wee folk as totally bad. Indeed, as I learned at a much later time... But that came much later.

Another tale I heard that night was the fable of the man and the lion. A man once invited the lion to be his guest and received the lion with warm and wondrous hospitality. The lion had the run of a magnificent palace, akin to Bunratty. There were paintings and sculptures everywhere, but what attracted the lion most were depictions of the noble lion and members of his tribe. There was, however, one remarkable feature common to all this artwork: no matter how they were represented, the man was always victorious and the lion was always overcome. When the lion had finished his tour of the mansion, his host asked him what he thought of the splendors of the place. The lion, ever a gracious guest, gave a reply that did full justice to the riches of the man and the wondrous skill of the artists, but he added, "Lions would have fared better, had lions been the artists."

Bunratty sat astride the Shannon Estuary, more like a huge lake than a river. Next day, however, when we reached Limerick and crossed the Thomond Bridge, I found that east of Limerick the river was simply another of many wide rivers that traversed the remarkably green and fertile land.

I became more anxious and subdued as we breasted the Slievanamuck Hills and Tipperary hove into view. It was the very end of March. My wedding would take place less than a week hence.

"Oh, Ma!" I wailed, just after we'd left Tipperary town. "Why did I ever let myself get talked into this? They say Donal has a foul temper and I've heard evil things about him. I've only met him three times and I'm expected to sleep with him within the week. How romantic is that?"

"A soldier's wedding it isn't," she said. "But you can always pretend..."

"Yes, there was that," I replied wistfully. "But that was only for a few days."

"This need only be for a year, Granuaile."

"But what if children come? There's got to be *some* loyalty. You and da have been married more than twenty years."

"Yes, dear, it seems to have worked out quite well. Did you know our marriage was arranged, too?"

"That doesn't surprise me."

"You know, Grace, if you truly wanted to get out of this, you could still do so."

"No, Ma. I'm committed for a year and a day, and I've heard every bride goes through what I'm going through. If he can do it, so can I."

We came into Cashel, a small market town, from the southwest. It was the last day of March, 1546, and that morning was sunny – the brightest day I'd seen since I'd left Clew Bay. Just after we crossed the River Suir, we rounded a bend and there it was: a huge green hill flanked by limestone outcroppings. Although the rock wasn't nearly as high as the Bens, it was even more dramatic, rising, as it did, from the surrounding flatland. The rock was ringed by a great stone wall and crowned by a huge cathedral, with Gothic towers. In the golden sunlight, the Rock was a stark, impregnable walled fortress-city.

"My God!" I breathed. "It's magnificent. All the stories I've heard..."

"Great place for a wedding, Girl," my father said. "If you're going to be a queen for a day or for your life, you couldn't get a better start than here."

When we reached the base of the hill, the procession stopped. I stepped out of the carriage with all the dignity I could muster. Waiting to help me out of the carriage was a man neither as tall nor as broad as Richard Burke, but attractive nonetheless. He had wide-set blue eyes and a neatly-cut red beard. His auburn hair fell to his shoulders. He was dressed in a tunic with a brocaded vest.

"Donal an-Chogaidh, Tánaiste O'Flaherty," I said formally, nodding slightly.

"Granuaile ni Mháille," the man said in an equally dignified manner. "Is it your free will to be bound to me for a year and a day?"

"I shall marry you, Donal O'Flaherty," I replied, "but no more be bound to you than you to me."

"That is acceptable to me," he said.

In this manner, Donal-of-the-Battles, heir apparent to the title "The O'Flaherty," formally asked for my hand, after which each of us retired to be with our retinue until three days hence at noon.

As I entered the Cathedral, the door was garlanded with evergreen branches. Donal wore black trousers, a white linen shirt, and a red waistcoat with green piping. He stood next to the priest as he awaited my passage down the aisle. In his left hand, he held a sheaf of wheat, in his right a dagger.

I heard a collective gasp as I appeared in the doorway and started my stately walk down the aisle. They say every bride is beautiful. I say with no false modesty, I was told later by several people that no bride ever seen looked as stunning as I did on the second day of April in the Year of Our Lord 1546, as I walked down the aisle of the Cathedral atop the Rock of Cashel. My blonde hair, now long and thick, was tightly braided, both behind and atop my head. I was dressed in a white gown, with a green sash, cut very low in front to reveal the tops of my breasts, a symbol that there would be plenty of milk when the babes came. My eyes were framed by dark kohl eye shadow. In my right hand, I carried a Bible. In my left hand, I bore soft woolen cloth, woven in the O'Malley colors and heraldic design, and a horseshoe.

As I reached my betrothed, the priest approached us. In the time-honored Celtic tradition, we faced one another. "Have you brought the gifts?" the priest intoned.

"Aye," Donal said. "Granuaile ni Mháille, I give you wheat to provide for our home."

"Donal O'Flaherty, I give you woven cloth to provide for our home."

"Granuaile ni Mháille, I give you a dagger for the defense of our home," he said, handing me the dagger.

"Donal O'Flaherty, I give you a Bible for the defense of our home," I said. "And I give you as well a horseshoe to hang over the door to our home, to bring luck and to keep the little people away.

Then, Donal reached out with his right hand and clasped my right hand. I, in turn, reached out with my left hand and grasped my bridegroom's left hand. Our wrists were crossed. The Priest took a skein of bright green ribbon from his vestments. He wound the ribbon around our wrists, over the top of one and under and around the other, thus creating the symbol of infinity. He tied the ribbon in a knot so that all could see. We had been joined in the ancient ritual of handfasting.

"Do you, Donal O'Flaherty take this woman to be your lawful wedded wife and promise to honor and cherish her for a year and a day, or mayhap more?"

"Aye."

"Do you, Granuaile ni Mháille take this man to be your lawful wedded husband and promise to honor and cherish him for a year and a day or mayhap more?"

"I do," I replied.

The priest uttered a short prayer and an admonition to us both to be faithful and loyal to one another, then pronounced us man and wife. The entire ceremony took less than half an hour.

As we turned to leave, we were confronted by a large, straw broom, which had been placed across the aisle, barring our exit. Still bound together, hand to hand, Donal looked at me and nodded. Side by side, we stepped over the broom together, eschewing the more traditional role of the man carrying the woman over the broom, so that all assembled would know this was a marriage of equals, neither subservient to the other.

The feast afterward was rife with toasts, dancing, drinking, and other activities that invariably take place between the young of opposite sexes, which might, in more straitlaced times have been looked upon as debauchery, but which, in the Ireland of that day, were well and eagerly accepted. The day had been warm and sunny, a good sign, and cocks and hens, symbols of courage and fertility, seemed to be everywhere underfoot during the festivities.

After our wedding night, during which I learned that men could be entirely different from one another in many ways, but that each could be, in his own way, deliciously exciting and consummately satisfying, Donal and I rode down to Dungarvan Harbor, from whence we would take passage to Portugal to begin our *Mi Na Meala*, our "Month of Honey." When we got to the galley, there was enough mead on board to last us through the month, as well as special goblets with which we would continually toast one another.

Chapter 6

I may have been sixteen, but I considered myself reasonably wise in the ways of the world. While my twenty-year-old husband had a reputation for being hotheaded and temperamental, he was clearly a man of intellect.

"We'll be walking on English soil in a few days' time, my love," he said. "The realm of King Henry, God be with him and keep him far from Ireland."

"He's on his sixth wife now."

"Aye. I hear she'll probably outlive him," Donal said, grinning. "They say his waist is fifty-four inches around, that he can hardly walk, and that he has to be carried everywhere by sedan chair."

"What a shame," I replied. "My father told me he was a vigorous man in his youth. My God, fifty-four inches around! That's more than twice my girth. He may have worn himself out by all that marrying. Would you be able to handle six wives, Donal?"

"It might be fun to try, but even Henry didn't have to deal with them all at once."

"Divorced, beheaded, died, divorced, beheaded," I said, counting the wives before Catherine Parr on the fingers of my left hand. "Henry's officially the king of England, but no one in Ireland gives a damn except those who've sworn allegiance to him through submit and regrant."

"That's rather an effective practice," Donal said. "Let's say The O'Boyle is the head of a tribe that commands large parts of Wexford. The English king, who wants to show his great power, lands a military force at Wexford. He prepares to wreak destruction on the town, but before he does, his emissary approaches The O'Boyle and demands that he swear fealty and loyalty to the English sovereign.

"'What's in it for me?' asks The O'Boyle.

"'There are two options,' says the diplomat. 'If you don't swear loyalty, our army will destroy Wexford and take it by force. You'll either escape or, if you don't, you'll be jailed and sent to England for a spell. Either way, you lose your land, your position, your cattle, and your subjects.'

"'And if I submit?'

"'Very simple. You make a public show of submitting to the King of England and swearing to be loyal to him. The king, in turn, grants you a Writ stating that The O'Boyle has sworn loyalty to England, and what better man exists to govern Wexford than The O'Boyle himself? The O'Boyle still rules exactly as he had in the past, except he is doing it in the name of King Henry and paying a percentage of his income for the privilege and the protection."

"Piracy at a higher level?" I said, jokingly.

"Protection at a higher level."

"How much of Ireland is under English rule?"

"Most of the south and east. Up in Connaught, no one has

yet submitted, and now the king is beset with his own problems, and I don't just mean the gout. His wife's a Protestant."

"That shouldn't be a problem," I said. "Henry broke with the Roman Church when the Pope refused to give him an annulment from Katherine of Aragon so he could marry Anne Boleyn."

"Yes, but Henry never considered he'd left the Catholic Church, only that *he* no longer felt obliged to swear loyalty to the Pope. His Church of England still practices exactly the same rites as the Roman Church. Catherine Parr's got other ideas. They say she's a follower of that fellow who died a couple of months back, Martin Luther. Of course, now that Luther's dead, the idea of a different kind of Christian religion may die with him."

Ten days after we'd begun the voyage, the ship's lookout spotted a ship gaining rapidly on us from the southwest. As he gazed through his telescope, he called down, "Pirate vessel! Black with three red stripes across the bow! Not flying any flag!"

"What arms do we have on board?" I asked the captain.

"One small cannon and fifteen small arms."

"Damn!" I swore. "I'd like to give the son-of-a-whore in command of that ship a lesson he'd not soon forget. How far are we from the nearest port, Captain?"

"Half a day out of Portsmouth."

I took a telescope from Donal. "The pirate ship's gaining on us. We haven't got a half day's distance – not even a half hour's distance." As if to underscore my words, the roar of two cannon erupted from the pirate ship. Their cannonballs struck water only a few hundred yards from the galley.

"How much more sail can we raise, Captain?" I demanded.

"We've got two masts. We can raise the mainsails and a jib on the bow, but it's risky if the wind comes up."

"If those bastards come much closer, it'll be much more risky. Raise all sails immediately!" I said. It was not a request, it was a command.

"Are you taking over as captain, My Lady?" the skipper, a subordinate to the O'Malley clan asked me.

"I am," I replied. "By your leave and under you, of course, Captain."

"Very well, Ma'am," he said. "All sails up!" he shouted, "Oarsmen, to your stations! Row at military ram speed!"

Before the crew on the pirate ship could react to what was happening, the galley pulled away sharply from the aggressor – half a mile, a mile. Soon, the pirate ship was a distant spot, dropping down below the horizon. Less than an hour later, a jubilant galley crew pulled into Sidmouth harbor. I was in a foul humor.

"Why the long face, Granuaile?" Donal asked solicitously.

"Because we had to run from those..."

"There's no shame in that. We outraced them to port."

"That is not the way an O'Malley has ever dealt with aggressors. I swear on my father's honor that I will never cowardly run away from battle again. Captain," I turned and faced him. "We will stay close to land until we reach Portsmouth. Then," I said, handing him a purse filled with gold coins, "you will purchase and install three of the stoutest cannon this vessel is capable of carrying and ten rounds of cannonballs for each gun. While you're at it, exchange that baby cannon we're carrying now for something more realistic.'"

"But Lady, you're on your honeymoon."

"Aye, and I will make certain that from here on, it will be a perfectly *safe* honeymoon. Is that understood?"

"Yes, Ma'am," the captain mumbled. As he wandered away from where I stood defiantly, I could hear him mutter, "Donal O'Flaherty may be Donal of the Battles, but if I were him, I'd not want to do battle with that hen."

Portsmouth was a huge, boisterous, and well-stocked city, whether one was looking for weapons, artillery, furs, or entertainments common to a sailor town. Donal and I met the captain on ship, shortly before sundown the following day, to see the fruits of his purchases. There were four relatively new, quite serviceable, medium-sized cannon. Since each sat on a two-wheeled conveyance, they were movable, and since each could be secured by heavy metal bracing, I found them acceptable for my needs. The captain had also secured forty balls and an ample supply of gunpowder.

"This pleasure boat is now a Man O'War, Lady," he said.

"Excellent," I replied. "If only..."

The following day, I left Donal long enough to go into town to pick up two purchases I'd made the day before. The first of the two items was a bright black-and-red silk shirt with matching waistcoat for my husband, who fancied himself a dandy. The second purchase was part of my own plans.

Two days out of Portsmouth, we were crossing the English Channel toward Cap de la Hague, when my wish came true.

"Unknown vessel several hundred leagues astern!" the lookout called. A few minutes later, he shouted, "Damned if it's not the same black pirate vessel with the red stripes that chased us into Sidmouth!"

I smiled to myself, but said nothing. The pirate ship closed the distance between us until it was less than a mile away. Our honeymoon vessel plowed on ahead, seemingly – deliberately – oblivious to its pursuer.

"We're close enough to Cherbourg that we can make port either there or at Alderney Island. Shall I trim sail and have the men row?" the captain asked.

"No, speed up! Let them think we're frightened and trying to outrun them. Better yet, let's head out to open sea. Make it look as though we're frightened and confused – the perfect victim."

"But, Ma'am..." I gave him a sharp look that silenced him. "Very well."

The captain gave orders and the galley sped up once again. The pirate ship turned course to its left, heading southwest. Its captain obviously knew that by coming up on the galley on the landward side, it would force us out to sea and would block any attempt for our ship to make a run back toward the land. The pirate vessel raised all its sails and closed to within a half mile of our smaller ship.

Meanwhile, our deckhands were moving the four cannon into place on the starboard side. The galley would have tilted hard left, but for the fact that several cannon balls were secured on its port side. The galley sat low in the water, now moving so slowly it seemed to be stuck in mud.

The pirate craft edged closer and closer – a quarter mile, an eighth of a mile, a hundred yards. The ships were now well beyond land, at the widest part of the English Channel, between Start Point off the English coast and Guernsey Island. Just as the pirate ship was drawing even with the galley, three things happened with such speed it seemed less than half a minute went by.

The first was that my huge flag, larger than those flown from the topmasts of many Men O'War, suddenly fluttered from the highest point of the galley's mainmast. The flag was bright green with a yellow circle in the middle. Inside the circle was a large red hen.

The moment the pennant reached its height, four almost simultaneous concussions, one immediately following the other, boomed with a crack louder than a thunderclap, as our galley's cannon fired at nearly point blank range. This was followed almost instantly by the explosive sound of heavy wood splintering and shattering. So accurately had the cannon fired, I couldn't even see four separate holes, but rather there was a single ragged gash, running from just behind the bow of the pirate vessel almost to the stern itself.

The third occurrence was that the pirate ship, which had absolutely no chance of healing from its mortal wound, started taking on water so quickly that in less than five minutes, faster than the pirate crew could react, the blazing inferno that had moments ago been primed to attack and plunder, listed on its side and its bow raised to nearly a perpendicular angle as the boat seemingly screamed in its death throes and started its inescapable slide into the slick, black ocean..

Amid desperate shouts and wails, the captain called out to me, "Shall we toss them rafts, Lady?"

"Why not?" I replied. "Mayhap they'd let us rot at the bottom of the sea, but I'll show 'em an O'Malley's made of better stuff!"

It took less than an hour for us to gather the crew of the erstwhile pirate ship aboard our galley. I was surprised to find the captain of that vessel was a young man, no more than five years my senior.

"Granuaile O'Malley, the daughter of the Black Oak?" he asked.

"Aye. You know of me?"

"I know of your father. It is my privilege to meet you. It is obvious you bested me as a sailor, and cost me a worthy vessel in the process." He appeared to be cordial and garrulous, and, surprisingly, I found myself charmed by the man. "I appreciate your saving me and my crew," he continued.

"Would you have done the same for me?"

"I don't know. I intended to plunder your ship, not shoot it out from under you."

"It didn't look like that to me when you chased us into Portsmouth."

"Ah, well. If I apologized to you for what I tried to do, you'd know it was false."

"I respect that. From whence come you?" I asked, noting his colorful outfit.

"España. I am Don Bosco," he said, holding out his hand. "As you have favored me with excellent seamanship and great compassion, perhaps I may some day be of service to you."

"One never can tell, Señor Bosco. Where would you have me drop you off? We've not enough provender on board to feed you and your crew for any length of time."

"Saving our lives is provision enough. The nearest landfall will be fine. We can make our way from there."

After we had deposited the pirate crew on land, my husband turned to me. "That was a noble and charitable act, Granuaile. I don't know if I would have been such a samaritan."

"Mayhap I made a mistake, mayhap not, but only time will tell. Well, My Dear, we've had a fine day's excitement, but it's our honeymoon and I'm looking forward to a different kind of excitement. I'm ready to start on a baby tonight if you are, Donal-of-the-Battles."

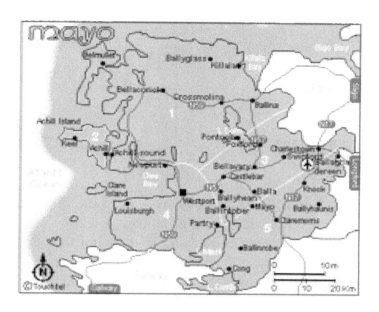

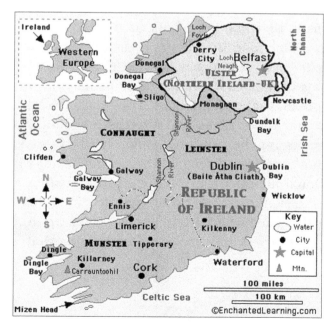

Chapter 7

And babies there were. Three during the first six years of our marriage, which meant, of course that the year-and-a-day got extended again and again, so that, political or not, it seemed we enjoyed a solid, stable match.

On return from our honeymoon, I was delighted to learn we would not be living at the O'Flaherty fortress at Ballinahinch, which was old, cramped, and drafty, but rather at Bunowen, a 'new' castle that had been built at the turn of the fifteenth century by Hugh Mór, Donal's great, great grand uncle. Within two months of settling down at Bunowen, Donal left to lead various small armies and collect taxes throughout his twenty-four town demesne in Connaught. This was fine with me.

At that time, I was five months pregnant, but due to my strenuous regimen of long walks, hard physical activity, and making other plans for my future endeavors, which I did not tell Donal about, I remained as lean and sinewy as ever, with just the slightest bulge at my midriff. Since Bunowen was very near the place where I had happily given up my virginity, I particularly loved the area of Connemara that encircled Bunowen.

The castle itself was a tower-house, with an attached enclosure to the north – the living quarters. It was quite spacious, but what attracted my sailor's eye immediately was its location, situated beside a very narrow and concealed sea-inlet, which merged with the Bunowen River, four miles southeast of Slyne Head. This narrow tidal inlet provided sea access to the castle, and a perfect place to hide the two or three galleys that would be essential to my plan. The castle was secure from attack from the sea, as one could only approach the O'Flaherty's home in a small boat or *curragh* from Bunowen bay.

My new home was separated from my father's territory by some of the wildest and most beautiful scenery in western Ireland. Bunowen was bounded on the northeast by the Twelve Bens. Far to the southeast, where I had often traveled on horseback, were the island strewn waters of Lough Corrib, that great inland lake-river that debouched into Galway Bay. All around the countryside, there were moors and rocks and the stony hills and cliffs of Connemara. Donal-an-Chogaidh's demesne contained twenty-four towns and numerous islands, including Imill, Omay, and Inis Lachan. Often on my walks, I saw deer, feral goats, wild pigs, and smaller game animals, and so many ospreys, egrets, and sea birds I couldn't even count them.

I was the dutiful wife, but spirited and independent, as my time grew closer. The surroundings were quite similar to my father's castle, but I often chafed and gritted my teeth during the numerous visits of the extensive O'Flaherty clan, who came to consult with my turbulent husband, the heir apparent to the clan leadership. I felt trapped by the burden of Bunowen's household duties. I longed for the excitement of life on the sea, but when my husband was not at Bunowen, I remained busy laying the groundwork for a far different life.

In May, 1547, I delivered my first child, whom I named Owen, after my father. I took to motherhood with the same total immersion as I did anything else I undertook. In place of my long walks, I now strolled more leisurely and more moderate distances, to a secluded glen or meadow, where I would patiently nurse baby Owen for what must have been an interminable time, but which seemed like only a few moments. I could stare at him for hours, as he balled his tiny fists, or followed the flight of a nearby bird, his eyes alight with the thrill of discovery.

I couldn't believe I could have given birth to such a perfect little boy. His eyes were as green as the shallow sea, he had his father's red hair, and his features were so beautiful, the curve of his legs, the plumpness of his arms. I have since learned over the passage of years that no matter how plain a child, when it's *your* child it's *always* the loveliest, the most beautiful, the smartest, and the most charming that God ever placed on earth.

Owen was my first and clearly my favorite. He was kind and compassionate to every living being, even from his earliest days. When he would suffer a bump, a bruise, the raging temper of his often irrational father, or the tenderness of my love, he would invariably treat each event with equanimity and boundless humor.

"He's much too nice for his own good," I confided in my mother. "I worry so for him, when he has to make his way in the cruel world of men and their wars. I only hope God will bless him with good fortune wherever he goes."

Two years almost to the day after Owen arrived at Bunowen, I gave birth to my only daughter, Margaret. One day, while I was nursing little Margaret and Donal was away on some exploit or other, four men came riding up to Bunowen Castle and asked to speak with me. The guard at the gate, thinking there must have been some mistake, responded that Master Donal was not in residence.

"It is not Master Donal with whom we wish to speak," the leader said courteously. "I am Edmund O'Flaherty, a kinsman, and I would like to speak with Lady Granuaile."

I heard the quiet urgency in the visitor's voice, put baby Margaret down, straightened my vestments, and went to the castle door. "Edmund O'Flaherty," I said, courteously. "Come in, come in."

He did, and introduced the three men with him, his sons. Edmund was a tall, dignified, and sturdy man of fifty, with graying beard and conservative bearing. "Your Ladyship, I hope we've not come at an inappropriate time?"

"No, I was just sitting here with Baby Margaret."

Edmund looked at his sons, who bowed their heads. "I'm afraid I have news that may be discomfiting," he said.

"Say it," I responded.

"It seems your husband Donal has been implicated in the murder of an ally of the O'Flahertys, a Burke."

I must have turned pale, for I felt my stomach churning. *Oh, God, could he have discovered my liaison with Richard an Iarrain?* I did not betray my emotions to the O'Flahertys, but said, quite calmly, "From whom did you hear this?"

"Roderick O'Flaherty, known to be a truthful and dependable man."

"I fear I'm losing my good manners, gentlemen. Mavis!" I called to my maidservant. "Tea and cakes for my O'Flaherty kinsmen, if you please."

"Yes'm," the servant said. She scooted out of sight and returned a few minutes later with tea, scones, and sweet cakes.

"Now, then, gentlemen," I said, when the four men were ensconced in chairs around the room's large fireplace, "What news?"

"Walter Fada Burke was murdered at Invernan Castle on Moycullen, down near Galway, when he and his father, David Burke, visited the castle.'

"David? The one who's married to Donal's sister Finola?"

"The very one. Walter was David's son, but not Finola's. Finola married David after his wife's death, and they had a child, Richard-an-Iarrain."

I felt my complexion redden, and I must have flushed noticeably, but I kept my voice quiet. "This Richard-an-Iarrain. What is his role in all of this?"

"None, Your Ladyship," said one of the O'Flaherty sons. "Richard is Finola's and David's son. David is next in line to become The MacWilliam, chief of the Mayo Burkes. Finola was concerned that when David died, The MacWilliamship would pass to Walter, her stepson. Clearly, she wanted The MacWilliamship for her own son, Richard."

"Eliminating Walter from the list of probable successors to The MacWilliamship increased the chances that Richard would become The MacWilliam when her husband was no longer around," Edmund said.

Iron Dick as The MacWilliam? Interesting. I wonder if...? Aloud, I said, "What would my husband gain from murdering Walter?"

"That's just it, Lady," Edmund continued. "While he's suspected of foul play, there's no proof it was him who did the deed. What's more, Donal has absolutely nothing to gain and everything to lose, since the Burkes and the O'Flahertys have been friends and allies for more than three hundred years."

"Is there to be a trial?"

"No, Ma'am," Edmund's youngest son, who'd been silent until now, said. "There's not enough evidence to bring him before a magistrate and there's been no public outcry or demand by the Burkes for retribution."

"No *public* outcry," I said. "But *privately*?"

"Ahem," Edmund cleared his throat and took a substantial gulp of hot tea before putting his mug down. "They say Finola promised Donal that when Richard became The MacWilliam, the Burkes and the O'Flahertys could, between them, control all trade into and out of Galway."

I stood up and paced the floor. I did not speak, but I nodded Edmund O'Flaherty to go on.

"Lady Grace," he continued quietly, "we've come to see you because the majority of the O'Flaherty clan has come to view Donal's increasingly irrational behavior as an embarrassment. As *tanaiste*, he stands to be the next leader of Iar-Connacht. We believe someone else should take the *real* control of the tribe's business."

"So you've come to me to enlist my aid in ousting my husband? You dare think I would betray my husband?"

"Ne, My Lady," Edmund continued in the same soft, unassuming tone. "He would remain the nominal head of the tribe."

"And the *real* power?"

"Lady Granuaile, we propose that *you* serve as that power."

"Me? *Me?*" I laughed heartily. "You're telling me the tribe would allow a *hen* to lead, when her husband, the rooster, is the nominal leader?"

"Precisely, Your Ladyship."

"You forget, gentlemen, I sleep with Donal O'Flaherty. How do you expect me to explain to him that our roles are suddenly reversed?"

"You don't need to explain, Lady Grace. Even as we speak, certain very senior and persuasive O'Flahertys are speaking with him. Although Donal is stubborn and can be quite vicious, something you no doubt know, he is by no means stupid. Frankly, M'Lady, I think Donal of the Battles considers himself too much of a high-risen gentleman to want to deal with the day-to-day dirtying of his hands."

"So he'd be free to continue doing what he's been doing all along?"

"Aye, collect taxes from the twenty-four towns in his demesne and play the role of the great Lord and beneficent Master of the realm."

"Interesting," I said, scratching my chin. "Would I be titled as well? I mean something other than 'the hen?'"

"Do you really need a title if the entire tribe knows where the real authority lies?"

"Mayhap, mayhap not. I'll need my own forces, of course."

"Aren't three ships and two hundred men enough?" Edmund asked.

Surprised, I put the back of my hand to my mouth and gasped. "How did...?"

"The O'Flahertys have sailors, too, Lady Granuaile," he said quietly. "We know you're still, and always will be, an O'Malley. You're a sea captain, regardless of your present role as wife and mother, and your ships are moored, for the time being, in Clew Bay, near your father's castle, am I not correct?"

"You have spies, Edmund O'Flaherty?"

He deflected the question. "Why do you think the O'Flahertys looked no farther than you, M'Lady?"

"No matter," I said, my mood lightening as I realized what he was proposing. "You'd have found out sooner or later, and frankly I'd rather have a ship full of O'Malley, McNally, O'Flaherty and Conroy clans than a ship full of gold."

"Well, said, Madame," Edmund said. "Does that mean you will assume the leadership and honor our request?" he continued, his eyes sparkling with hope.

"You'll supply me with O'Flaherty ships and forces who report directly to me?"

"Aye."

I excused myself for a few moments and went to my private quarters. When I returned, I bore two large flags in my hand. The first was the flag I'd had fashioned for myself in Portsmouth during my honeymoon. The second was the O'Malley Coat of Arms: a rearing stallion above a helmet and some bar-like objects. The middle of the Coat of Arms was a shield, in the very center of which was a large wild boar, with three bows and arrows pointed at it. At the base of the shield, there was a three-masted galley, and at the bottom, the words *Terra Marique Potens - Invincible on Land and Sea.*

"I want three each of these pennants to fly from the mainmasts of my three O'Malley ships. If I'm to command O'Flaherty vessels, I want smaller replicas of these flags, which I'll attach to the aft masts of those ships."

"It is said and it is done," Edmund O'Flaherty said happily, clasping my arm just as he would a man's arm.

When they left, I whooped with joy. My plan was starting to come to fruition. I had been in constant contact with my da, and he'd allotted me three of his older, spare galleys. On my own, I had slowly and quietly gathered a force of two hundred men, O'Malleys, Conroys, and McNallys. I had not planned on actually employing these forces for a year or so, because I wanted to wait until Owen was three and he could come with me. I would leave baby Margaret with my maidservants, at least during the early stages of my resumed career.

At that moment, Margaret began crying and I went over and picked up my baby girl. The commander of a fleet of ships, the real power of the O'Flahertys, the passionate wife and lover, and the silly girl-woman, instantly became the Madonna-mother. I carried baby Margaret gently into the nearby castle chapel and bowed my head in prayer as the tiny girl eagerly gave suck. In that moment, I was struck by what, to me, was a profound truth, and I have often thought about it since that day.

The revelation was this: From the moment of its birth, nature endows an infant with the instinctive ability to exploit its cry as the most potent and stirring vehicle of communication, complaint, and supplication. The baby senses the parent's absence as much as its presence; and, indeed, the demand for that presence to manifest itself is expressed forcefully and volubly by means of the baby's piercing and plaintive cry. That cry is essentially an act of *faith* – faith in the existence and proximity of 'the hidden parent' and in that parent's ability to supply all of the baby's needs. The baby may have had but one single experience of the parent's soothing presence, but forever afterward it has faith in that presence. It craves that presence and believes passionately that its well-being is intertwined with the parent.

The child that is taken away from its mother at birth will still cry out for that love and attention. It does not wait until its functions are sufficiently developed to appreciate the parent's relationship to it and responsibility for its well being.

It is the same with all of us who are God's children. Prayer is the ultimate and most developed form of that instinctive infant's cry. And because prayer is instinctive, we do not need to work at faith. If we have some serious misgivings whether God is "out there," then giving His presence the benefit of that doubt is certainly the safest bet. If, on the other hand, we are convinced that God is close to all who call upon Him, or even if we merely suspect that He is "out there," then the prayerful cry becomes natural and indispensable.

I uttered a small, silent prayer for the well-being of my children, and I prayed that I would be there for them whenever and wherever they might need me.

Chapter 8

1550 became 1551 and that year, in turn, became 1552, the year I gave birth to Murrough, my second son and third child. Of all the children I ever birthed, Murrough gave me the most trouble, even from the first.

At five years old, Owen was sturdy and kind to all. I had wanted Margaret to follow in my footsteps, and I was more than a little annoyed that she was so instinctively feminine. Even at the age of three, she was partial to lace and petticoats, soft stuffed animals and bisque dolls.

The world outside Bunowen castle was a world of great change, and not all of the upheavals portended for the good. King Henry had died five years before, in his last days, he had halfheartedly attempted to impose his "Submit and Regrant" practice on western Ireland. Although the Burkes submitted and were granted the strongest position of all, The MacWilliamship, my families, the O'Malleys and the O'Flahertys, resolutely refused to give in. Surprisingly, my people were left alone, and they continued to rule vast areas of Connaught, just as they had done for hundreds of years before the English yoke was cast upon the land.

After Henry's death, Edward VI, his son by Jane Seymour, ascended the English throne at the age of nine. However, Edward himself never actually ruled in his own right, and by 1552 it had become apparent to anyone of even moderate perception that poor Edward was doomed to a short life.

Although Donal and I were seeing less and less of one another as our paths diverged, we continued to hold banquets and festivals for our clans and our allies, and as I passed among our guests, I often overheard snippets of conversation and gossip from many of these revelers that gave me pause to think and piqued my own curiosity.

"Lucky for us, neither Edward nor his regents have bothered with Ireland. Some say the boy's got consumption and others say he's got some other strange disease. Either way, he'll likely be dead in a year or two, more's the pity. What then?" asked a garrulous older redbeard.

"Your guess is as good as mine," a tall young man of thirty responded. "I've heard that the Duke of Northumberland is plotting to have his daughter-in-law, Lady Jane Grey, take the throne when Edward passes."

They were joined by a short, exceedingly fat man, who said, "Parliament won't allow that. I say it will be Mary Tudor or Elizabeth."

"What is this world coming to?" the first man rejoined with a lighthearted but heavy handed attempt at humor. "Women rulers? Heaven help us!" I glared at him. "I'm sorry, Lady Granuaile. I didn't mean *you*, of course." I moved on to the next group.

"Mary'd be best for Ireland. She's Henry's daughter by his first wife, Catherine of Aragon, and she never left the Roman Church. Since Ireland's Catholic, she'd probably leave us alone to go our own way," a middle-aged woman of thirty said.

"Then there's her half-sister Elizabeth," her companion, a tall, balding man, replied. "Anne Boleyn's daughter is said to be the strongest of the three. I don't think things would bode well for Ireland with Elizabeth on the throne."

As I wandered through the crowd, I heard other, more wide-ranging comments.

"Have you read anything by that crazy Frenchman, Nostradamus?"

"God, no! What a fraud he is!"

"Why do you say that?"

"Anyone who dares to predict what will happen five hundred years from now has got to be crazy or a charlatan."

"Well, we say the same about the little people, don't we?"

And farther afield.

"They're persecuting the Jews in Bavaria."

"They're always 'persecuting the Jews' somewhere just about *everywhere*. I can't understand why those stubborn people don't simply convert, like the Spanish forced them to do. It would be such a simple world if only the Jews acted like Christians."

"Did it ever occur to you that it would be a simple world if *Christians* acted like Christians?"

When I say that our lives had diverged, I do not mean that Donal and I were any less stable than we'd been, although there was little of the early passion left between us, but rather that our *paths* had gone in different directions. Donal-an-Chodaigh O'Flaherty had always had a talent for offending people, and at twenty-six he was even less flexible than he'd been in his youth. As a result, in 1553 he was banned from trading at Galway, one of the largest centers in Ireland. He fumed with righteous indignation, but the banishment was not reversed, so he was forced to trade elsewhere.

By that time, my three O'Malley vessels and another three O'Flaherty galleys were regularly sailing to Scotland, Portugal, and Spain. From time to time, I would take young Owen, my favorite, with me, but for the most part, my maternal instincts were succored by the fact that I was "mother hen" to more than two hundred sailor-warriors. Thus, for the most part, I left my own children in the care of servants at Bunowen.

When I heard of my husband's banishment from Galway, I loyally sailed into Galway Bay in my fastest ships and intercepted merchants going to Galway. I would negotiate safe passage with these traders, and if they refused my demands, my forces would raid and plunder their ships. That was the first time I heard the name "the pirate queen," and I was not the least insulted by that sobriquet.

Mayhap, things would have turned out differently had I stayed home a bit longer. Owen and Margaret, who were now six and four, respectively, were well-mannered, kind children. Not so Murrough, who, even at two years, had his father's nasty disposition. Often, he would beat up on his sister and insult the women in the castle. But he adored Donal, trailed after him, and emulated him in any way he could.

It saddened me to see that when I was at home, little Murrough was invariably rude to me and seemed to take pleasure in frustrating my every overture. When I tried to strike him, he would simply run to his father and hold on to Donal's sturdy legs for protection. When I complained to my husband, he smugly said, "Boys will be boys. Ye wouldn't have him be like Margaret now, would ye? If he learns it's a big, rough world out there, he'll be better able to handle it."

"But Owen is different."

"Owen's a milksop, a mama's boy, and if you don't let him get some bumps or bruises, he'll be ill-prepared to deal with life."

That remark, and Donal's attitude, opened a yawning crack between us that had been just under the surface for months. I refused to even speak to my husband for two weeks. Murrough's attitude grated on me, while Owen's unconditional love drew me closer than ever to him. Although I fought against it, I felt a growing estrangement from my younger son. The mother's milk of human kindness was rapidly souring.

After his harsh words, a chasm now seemed to separate Donal and me. It was as if we had been living a lie, and now the bitterness was out in the open. In public, we continued to be cordial to one another, but while we still slept in the same room, I now contented myself with a separate cot in the antechamber.

One day, early in 1554, my ma came to visit. Three days earlier, I had heard disquieting news from my husband himself, and I spoke bitterly when my mother and I were alone.

"Donal has strayed from the marriage bed several times during the past year." My mother remained silent, keeping up with me stride for stride as we walked around a small lake. "You don't seem surprised."

"Should I be?"

"I suppose not," I said resignedly. "We've not slept together in months. It was probably inevitable, once I refused him."

"Weren't you frightened he'd beat you?"

"Not hardly," I said, with a caustic look. "Donal knew that if he took me on during the day, he'd best watch his backside when he was sleeping, lest he find a knife buried to the hilt just above his arse." I laughed with not even a hint of humor.

"Could it be that you were overwhelming him? Donal's not stupid and he's a proud man. Someone would have to be a total idiot not to see that the O'Flahertys look upon you, not he, as their leader."

"You're probably right, mama. Still, even though I don't want *him*, it's galling to know that he was the first to stray."

"Some men are like that." I looked questioningly at my mother. "Not your father, Granuaile. He's a good man, he is, and a rare one."

During the next few months, Donal was away more and more frequently and of substantially longer duration. Often, he took young Murrough with him. I didn't mind, and I was secretly pleased that neither Owen nor Margaret seemed to care either.

During the times that Donal was gone, which were more than half the year, I normally slept in the marriage bed, but neither a woman nor a man should ever be forced to abstain from very natural needs. Thus, two or three times a month, late at night, I must here admit that there were clandestine meetings...

As always, since I had no close female friends, I found my mother to be a wonderful and loyal confidante. "You know Richard-an-Iarrain's back in my life, mama."

"Is he the one who's been visiting at night?"

"Well..." I hesitated and actually blushed before going on. "There have been two others." My mother sat silently, making no judgment, urging me with her eyes to go on. "I don't know if all women are like me, but it sometimes takes more than one man to make a woman feel truly desirable."

"Tell me, Granuaile, before Donal strayed...?"

"There were none. Between the children and returning to the sea, even I would not have had the time or the energy."

I was now a robust twenty-four, a captain and a pirate, and while I still maintained a slender body, life on the open and windy sea had taken its toll. Despite my reliance on various emolients and unguents from as far away as France, Spain, and even China, my dry skin seemed to have aged me prematurely. Still, men seemed somehow drawn to me as to a magnet, and I returned their interest in kind.

"What if you were to get with child? What would folks say? What would Donal say?"

"Frankly, mama, I don't give a damn about what Donal would say. There are many ways a woman can avoid the burden of an unwanted child."

Still, I was not entirely happy with my life. I was beginning to realize that one person's life always seems so much better than another's. Everyone thinks his or her life is the worst, and they'd give anything to trade with the next person. Yes, there was plenty of excitement in my life, but there was hurt, too. While there were always men, and there was always *that*, I had never believed I could endure such pain as when my own child turned his back on me, or when I knew that other men were enjoying my body while my husband wanted nothing more to do with me.

Chapter 9

I had no awareness of when the man appeared next to me. I surmised he was my own age. He was two or three inches shorter than I, which would make him a little over five feet tall. His face was a shade too large, a bit too square for his body. He was dressed in workman's clothes of the kind common all over western Ireland. I had no idea of how long he'd been walking beside me.

"Is this a private lake, or can two lonely people walk with one another?"

I was too shocked to answer. His voice was gentle and his question was framed so simply. I said nothing for a few moments and kept walking. He made no move to rush me.

"How long have you been following me?"

"I haven't been following you."

"Walking alongside me, then."

"A while."

I shivered as a sudden gust of wind came off the lake. He took off the coat he was wearing and offered it to me. I nodded appreciatively and put it on. "How long is a while?"

"Three years."

"Three *years*? I don't believe you. I would have seen you."

"How many people have you *really* seen, Grace O'Malley? I don't mean those who pass through your life like so many shadows. Would you have picked me out in a crowd? Mayhap you never noticed me because you never *wanted* to see me."

"You're talking in riddles." In spite of myself, I smiled at him. The man was really quite attractive.

"My name's Ballyclinch," he said, as we turned inland, toward the hills. "That's my only name. I'm not married." He looked sheepishly at me. "I thought you'd best know that before you continued walking with a strange man."

Odd. This obviously intelligent man, who was not at all hard on the eyes, was more bashful than my daughter Margaret. For the first time that lonely day, I laughed. *Ballyclinch. Ballyclinch?* "Hello, Ballyclinch," I said. "I'm... well, it seems you already know who I am. Dare I ask how?"

"You may, but before you do, may I ask you some things that may answer your question?"

"Go ahead."

"Have you heard of the *little people*? Faeries?"

"Of course," I said, drawing away as a sudden cold chill enveloped me. But they're all old and evil and ugly, and..."

"Perhaps not all," he said, in that same gentle, soothing voice.

And thus it was that Ballyclinch and I began our first conversation.

During the next two months, he and I went on long walks every day I was in residence at Bunowen. I'd decided not to sail so much that summer. Donal saw no need to return home, and the children had been left in my mother's care up in Clew Bay. My dalliances had become boring. For the first time, I felt my life was not as centered as I wanted it to be. I needed to do some serious thinking to get my life in order.

I spent progressively longer parts of each day with Ballyclinch. During those balmy days, he would unashamedly regale me with faerie stories. My favorite story was about Liam Carney.

"Liam," he began, "the crippled son of a wealthy landowner, heard the clank, clank, clank of the leprechaun's hammer in the woods of Macroom town, in the southwest of Ireland. Following the sound, he approached the leprechaun. Knowing he had to capture him fast, Liam swooped him into his hand and glanced firmly at the wee man. The wise leprechaun tried every trick in the book to tear Liam's glance away, so he could escape. Finally, he gave in and began leading Liam to the treasure. Halfway there, the leprechaun told Liam that a beautiful princess was looking at him. Liam had been madly in love with her for years. Unfortunately, Liam was born with a physical disability so he was too self-conscious to profess his love for her. When the leprechaun mentioned her name, he was spellbound and whipped his head around to see the lovely maiden. However, she was nowhere to be found. He turned to curse the leprechaun in his grasp, only to find that the little man had vanished. Liam was out of luck.

"A couple days later, Liam heard the clank of the shoemaker's hammer again. This time, when he seized the leprechaun. Liam was livid. After giving the leprechaun a piece of his mind, the two of them began their journey to the treasure which the leprechaun promised existed. Further along the route, the leprechaun claimed he spotted the princess. Liam sneered and told the leprechaun he would not fall for that trick again. They kept walking. All of a sudden, he heard her voice. With that, he turned around, only to find no one. Once again, the leprechaun disappeared.

"Several days later, poor Liam was sorrowfully hobbling through the woods. Not only had he missed his chance with the leprechaun, but he never would be able to profess his love to the beautiful princess. Just as Liam's heart hit rock bottom, he saw the leprechaun in the bushes. He sneaked up, grabbed the little fellow, and demanded that he be shown the treasure. Knowing that Liam would pursue him until he got the gold, the leprechaun took him to the treasure. Here, Liam stuffed what gold he could into his pockets and took it back to his family's castle. On his last trip gathering the gold, he was so fatigued he fell asleep. During his nap the leprechaun cast a spell on him that cured his disability.

"As he was walking back from the treasure, he bumped into the princess. Speechless, he gazed at her. She returned his look of love. Not knowing he had turned into a charming prince, Liam was utterly surprised at the response he got from her. They spoke. She commented that he sounded familiar, but surely she had never laid eyes upon him before. Liam assured her she did, indeed, know him. It was Liam Carney himself. She had known how nice he was, but upon seeing him, she was absolutely swept away. They fell in love, got married and lived happily ever after. They ruled the village and Liam was known for his great generosity to the poor and disadvantaged."

"What a beautiful tale, Ballyclinch," I said. "Are you sure you are indeed a faerie? The tales I've heard about faeries cast them in such a poor light. Evil little old men, cobblers all of them, hoarding their gold."

"Like the Jews? Or the Gypsies?" I stared at him, waiting for him to go on. "I'm not joking, Grace," he continued. "The Jews and the *Rom*, that's what the Gypsies call themselves, have always been outcasts – thieves, cutthroats, penurious and greedy misers, killers, villains – should I go on?" His tone was edged with bitterness, but I was intrigued by what he had to say.

"Please do."

"The little people are no different. Society disdains them, mocks them. The reality is much different. We are five rungs below the lowest rung on society's ladder, simply because most people don't understand us – and they don't *want* to understand us."

"Like saying every Jew has a big, hooked nose, or they stick to money like glue?"

"Exactly. Or like saying every *Rom* is out to put a curse on the *Gadjo*, the non-gypsy, the foreigner."

I gazed directly at him. "*Are* the little people magical?"

"Yes, Grace, we are – in the sense that we see things from a different perspective – what we feel is a broader perspective – than those who share Ireland with us. Or in the sense that Jews believe they have a direct connection to God, or that *Rom* believe they have the ability to predict the future. But perhaps we shouldn't be talking like this."

"Why not?"

"Because my kind *does* have, as you would put it, 'eyes in the back of their heads.' They would feel I was betraying them by even speaking to you."

"So you – they'd – rather leave the prejudices as they are?"

"Yes, for their own safety and privacy. As long as you don't understand someone or something, you fear that person or that thing, and you stay as far away from that person or thing as possible. Like I noticed you recoiling from me the first time I told you what I was. Even if it means you say you've chased that person all the way across Ireland into the worst parts, the uninhabited rocks offshore. Even if that's a total lie, and the truth is that those same 'evil beings' chose on their own to move to these places, to get away from *you*."

"Me?"

"What the 'little people' would call 'your kind.'"

Without knowing it, we'd walked to the top of a small hill, from where we could see all the way to the Atlantic coast, some five miles away. Even though the hill wasn't high, as most hills aren't very high in Ireland, the view was astonishing: three of the Twelve Bens, an equal number of small lakes, windswept bogs and plains, and everywhere the emerald green color that pervaded the entire island.

I unpacked a lunch I'd made, cold lamb, sweet bread, cold turnips, and ale, and we sat companionably munching and quaffing for the next little while. "If your people are so set against your talking to someone of my kind, why do you do it?"

"Because it suits me," he said calmly. "And because..." He did not go on, nor did I push him that day.

I changed the subject. "Ballyclinch, you've referred to your people as the 'little people.' I won't insult you by comparing you to the size of those who live at Bunowen castle, and whom you've undoubtedly seen, but you don't seem that 'little' to me."

"Aye, and that's the problem," he said, sadly. "You see, among my own kind, I'm looked at as some kind of freak. I'm a good three hands higher than anyone in the settlement where I grew up. There's talk in the village I must have been a half breed, cursed by both sides. When I was a child, no one claimed me as their own. That's why I've got only one name."

"I never knew..." I said, choking up involuntarily.

"How could you know, Grace? You never even knew I existed until two months ago."

"So you've lived alone?"

"For the past eight years, since I was sixteen and ran away in misery rather than face the daily disdain of those in my village. It's not hard to live on your own. I can steal sheep or cattle as well as the next man. I'm sure that the 'larger people' blamed the loss of one or two lambs or beeves on the 'little people,' and that's just as well. I've amassed a comfortable little herd of my own, small enough that I can control it and guard it from thieves, more than enough to provide me with milk and food and hides for clothing and warmth."

"Where do you live?"

"In a cottage I've built with my own hands. Mayhap you'll see it some day, but I think it's time you were getting back to Bunowen and that I was going on my way."

I left Ballyclinch that day feeling he wanted to tell me more, but that it wasn't the time to do so.

Another three months went by. We talked about anything and everything. Ballyclinch was the first man who seemed to have filled the void in my life when Donal had abandoned his love for me. One afternoon, after we'd eaten the midday meal, Ballyclinch said to me, "Grace, you once asked where I lived. Would you like to see it?"

"I would, Ballyclinch."

"Very well, then, follow me."

We traversed the bog and before I knew it, we were on a narrow trail that led into the foothills of one of the Bens. We circled the mountain until we came to a remote place I'd never known existed, a series of hills that connected one mountain

with its neighbor. Here, the trail narrowed still more, and there
was not even a hint it had been traversed by any living thing.
Another half an hour, and I spotted a small but solid, stone
house at the top of one of those hills.

When we reached the peak of that hill, and the house
itself, the view was another of those heartstopping views I'd
seen all over Ireland. Green pastureland descended from the
edge of the house to a tiny, pearline lake. Just as we reached the
house, there was a cacophony of thunder and jagged streaks of
lighting. A moment later, it became almost as dark as twilight,
and rain started coming down in sheets.

"Quick, Grace, inside!" Ballyclinch commanded. I was
certainly not resistant to his request.

Once inside, I was amazed at how clean, well-kept and
comfortable the place was. I hadn't known what to expect. For
all my so-called talents in many spheres, I was not a particularly
good housekeeper, and Bunowen Castle was not, on most days,
the model of cleanliness. Donal cared not a whit what the place
looked like because, for the most part, he no longer stayed at
Bunowen.

The main room in Ballyclinch's house was a combination
living and dining area. Two deep leather chairs sat adjacent to
a fireplace that went from floor to ceiling. From three windows
on the far side of the room, we had a view of the fields and the
lake below, and another of the Bens in the distance. As I passed
through the house, I stepped into the bedroom. The view was
similar to what it had been in the living room, but even more
dramatic. There was a small fireplace in that room, and a large
bed which was covered with a goose down featherbed. Outside,
the thunder, the rain, and the howling wind increased, which
made being inside, and dry, and warm, feel even better.

Our first kiss was an accidental thing which we each seemed unconsciously to have planned. It was delicious and when it was over, we were both trembling. Ballyclinch held me tight, half-comfortingly, half something else entirely. His arms were strong, but he was very gentle.

"Is that how you treat all your visiting guests?" I finally asked, my voice husky.

"Only the beautiful ones." Ballyclinch tried to keep his tone light, but his voice came out a croak.

"Come on, my friend. Let's have some ale and continue talking before something happens that shouldn't." At that moment, I so wished he'd make what shouldn't happen *happen*.

Instead, he said, "Why shouldn't it happen, Grace?"

"I don't know, Ballyclinch. I'm married... But, since Donal... that hasn't stopped me. That is..." I found myself completely tongue-tied.

"Grace, when we talked some time ago, I wanted to tell you something, but I hesitated."

"I know."

He walked out to the porch, gathered two large logs, put them in the fireplace, and stirred the fire with a rod until the flame rose higher. For what seemed an endless time, we watched the red, yellow, and blue flames. They were hypnotic, and they kept either of us from saying anything. Finally it was Ballyclinch who broke the silence.

"I love you, Granuaile O'Malley. I've loved you for the last three years."

"Oh." *What a stupid, inane response!* My hands were wet and clammy.

"Did you hear me, Grace? I said I love you."

"Yes, I heard you, Ballyclinch." I felt tears come, happy tears, and I was powerless to stop them. "Oh, Ballyclinch, you've no idea how long I've waited to hear a man say that. I need so badly to be loved, and I need so badly to give my love. And since we met, I've felt the same. And now one of us has the courage to say it."

We kissed again, more tenderly, then much more passionately than the first time.

"I've never been with a woman. I've never even kissed or touched a woman in my life." Suddenly, his own eyes were bright with tears about to be shed. "No one –"

"Sssh," I whispered, putting my fingers to his lips. "Just hold me for a while, my darling."

He did, and it was warm and tender, but the fire in the fireplace was nothing compared to what was going through my body at that moment. He kissed me again, and as he did so, I reached over, gently took his hand and put it inside my blouse. He squeezed my breasts, gently at first, then with greater force, and both of us moaned.

And then...

I did not return to Bunowen that night, nor the day after, nor the day after that. When I finally arrived back, I limped slightly as I made it up the stairs to the bedroom and went straight to the mirror by my bed. As I appraised myself in the mirror, I looked nothing like I had looked when I'd last left Bunowen castle. My blouse was disheveled and looked like I had slept in it, which, indeed, I had. I looked flushed and consummately satisfied. When I tried to talk, my voice was hoarse and raw.

I had been told at various times through the years, by many men, that a woman is at her most beautiful after she has lain with a man, and has climaxed again and yet again. I flatter myself that I looked that way now.

For weeks afterward, Ballyclinch and I would meet almost every day. Going a day without making love was like going a day without eating or breathing. Once hooked, I had become addicted, not to the sexual part of our lovemaking, but to the intimacy, the closeness, the sharing of another soul with my own. Was I in love? That depends, I suppose, on how one defines love. Did I want to be with Ballyclinch – and did I feel that he wanted to be with me – every waking moment? Yes. Did I want to fall asleep in his arms, with him holding my breasts in his hands every night? Again, yes. Did I want to awaken each morning to find him snuggling against me, and feel his hardness as we turned to face one another and eagerly touch and thrill and tease each other, signaling the ultimate encounter where each one of us would be the winner? Certainly.

Actually, I felt very much like I had felt after my first night with Dick Burke. There were times when we never left the bed except to eat and do the natural things for two or three whole days at a time. It was everything I'd ever believed a woman could experience, and more.

I had no idea where the affair was going. I only knew I was blind to every man but Ballyclinch. The others seemed to realize my new-found feelings and accepted with equanimity that I no longer required their services, or needed or wanted them in my bed.

But things do not remain static in this life. I began to be haunted when I was not with Ballyclinch by worrisome thoughts. He told me he had run away from his village many years ago. Legend had it that the little people were not known to suffer a loss – any loss – happily. Ballyclinch might, as he had told me, be a half-breed, or he might not, but as long as he was out in the world of the larger folk, his own kind might fear disclosure of their secrets. I would have wagered that whether he knew it or not, they'd been watching him all these years. And if they had been watching him all that time, they'd know about us, and probably, for all I knew, had already seen us in our most intimate moments and postures.

I shuddered. Ballyclinch had told me on more than one occasion that the little people possessed a kind of magic. A conversation we'd had months ago now haunted me.

"Are the little people magical, Ballyclinch?"

"Yes, Grace, we are – in the sense that we see things from a different perspective, what we feel is a broader perspective, than those who share this island with us... But perhaps we shouldn't be talking like this."

"Why not?"

"Because my kind does have...'eyes in the back of their heads.' They would feel I was betraying them by even speaking to you."

"But surely, they'd see we were in love."

"Yes," Ballyclinch replied, "and just as surely they'd see it as an invitation to betrayal. I fear for you and I fear for me, Grace," he said, holding me tightly to him. "And what I foresee does not augur well."

"We could run," I said stubbornly.

"To where, Grace? To a different land? I told you the little people have a broader perspective, that they see dimensions of space *and time* as one."

Involuntarily, I started crying bitter tears. They wouldn't take Ballyclinch from me, they couldn't take Ballyclinch from me, I wouldn't *let* them. But if what Ballyclinch said was true, and my rational self fought with my heart and convinced me it *was* true, we were trapped, with no escape route open. Ballyclinch held me gently until my sobbing subsided.

"On the other hand," he finally said, "You are the queen of the Irish seas, and if the little people want to engage my love, then they choose to engage me as well."

I pretended to be comforted, but I was not. That night, I stayed awake a long time after Ballyclinch had descended into a peaceful sleep. I'd always felt I was as strong-spirited as any human being alive, but I was not one of the little people, and while my powers were superior to other human beings, I knew there were powers beyond my comprehension. And that was the reason I found myself trembling uncontrollably and unable to sleep for most of the night.

Chapter 10

"Lady Granuaile, are you all right?" Edmund O'Flaherty asked gently. As always, he was a gracious model of propriety coupled with warmth.

"Of course, Sir Edmund. Why do you ask?" He had asked me to come to his castle, eighty miles from Bunowen.

Now, O'Flaherty closed the door to his private room and bade me sit. "Port?"

"Please."

He poured me a goblet of purple wine and then one for himself. "May I be frank, My Lady?"

"Have we not always been such?" I had genuinely liked him from the very first.

"Very well. We are deeply grateful for what you've done – what you are doing for clan O'Flaherty. We are, for the time being, at peace and we are enjoying prosperous times. But we've also become aware, ummm, become aware..." he hesitated.

"You said we'd be frank, Sir Edmund."

"I did." He seemed embarrassed to go on.

"Does this have to do with Donal?"

He rose from his chair, stirred the fire in the adjacent fireplace, returned and sat next to me again.

"Your silence is answer enough, Sir Edmund. If you're trying to ask me if things are all right between Donal and me, I tell you, as my friend they are not. You must be aware, then..."

"Yes," he said simply. He put his right fist over his mouth and coughed uncomfortably.

I sat with my hands folded over one another in my lap. Some silences are oppressive and some are comfortable. The silence between us was somewhere in between these two extremes. It was Edmund O'Flaherty who spoke first. "Do you plan to leave him?"

I was stunned by his statement. Although there were many things on my mind, I had never given any thought to divorcing Donal-an-Chogaidh O'Flaherty. Could he have been thinking of divorcing *me*?

Sir Edmund, who must have been anticipating my own thoughts, said, "I am asking you, Lady Granuaile, because any such decision would be yours to make, not Donal's. True, he remains the *tanaiste*, the heir apparent to The O'Flaherty, but the clan has let it be known in no uncertain terms that he would lose that position immediately should there be a divorce."

I breathed a sigh of relief. From the way Edmund was speaking, I surmised that, regardless of his personal feelings toward me, Donal was astute enough to know the continuance of his position was irrevocably linked to my success, and in the complex manner of internecine relations between the clans of Connaught, Sir Edmund was letting me know the last thing the *clan* wanted was to lose me as its *de facto* leader.

I nodded demurely at Edmund O'Flaherty, quietly acknowledging I understood what he was implying.

"My Dear," he continued. "You must feel great personal hurt. I look upon you as a treasured daughter. I simply wanted you to know that if you were to have... other interests... the clan would turn a blind eye."

"Thank you, Sir Edmund," I replied. I said nothing more, neither admitting nor denying anything.

"The castle's gardens are beautiful at this time of year," he said. "Shall we walk outside awhile?"

"Changing locales, changing subjects?" I asked, smiling for the first time that day.

We emerged into sunlight which, while not blindingly bright, was clement for a summer afternoon in this part of Ireland. As we walked along paths bordered by boxwood and blooming roses, I asked, "Sir Edmund, what news on England's latest efforts at submit and regrant?"

"Mary Tudor's trying to turn back the clock in her own country and she hasn't had time for Ireland, not that Connaught would ever submit."

"Elizabeth's been released from house arrest at Woodstock Palace."

"Philip's doing, not Mary's, and now her king-husband's gone back to Spain for an indefinite time."

I nodded and we continued walking. My mind wandered. "Sir Edmund, what do you know of the Little People?"

"Now that is certainly an abrupt change in the conversation. Why do you ask?"

I stooped down and picked a few stems of clover, savoring their sweet, clean aroma. "My da once mentioned that you, perhaps more than anyone else in these parts, know truth from myth."

"Ahh," he said, smiling. I could surmise his secret pride that I had spoken thus. "Well... I wouldn't say I'm *the* expert by any means, but I have made it a point to learn what I could about them. Any reason for your interest, Lady Granuaile?"

"Mayhap, mayhap not," I said, hoping my tone appeared lighter than it seemed to me.

"There're lots of fables about them. Little old men, greedy shoemakers, and such." He looked more serious. "You're not looking for those kinds of stories?"

"No, Sir Edmund."

"Truth is, Granuaile, they're called the Little *People*, not simply Little *Men,* and if they're to perpetuate their kind, they must mate, so there must be women as well."

"Do you believe they really exist?"

"Aye," he said quietly. "Although not in the way we imagine them." Something in O'Flaherty's tone led me to believe he knew more than he was letting on.

"If these people *were* to exist, and I'm not saying I believe they do..."

He looked at me archly, his eyebrows raised. "I think perhaps we should continue this discussion in a more private place," he said.

How long have you been following me? Three years. I don't believe you. I would have seen you. Mayhap you never wanted to see me. Our kind have eyes in the back of their heads. They could be anyplace and you might never know it.

Once ensconced in his study, Edmund O'Flaherty continued, "You've seen them, then?"

"I never said that."

"A few moments ago, you said, 'If these people *were* to exist...' I didn't allow you to finish the question."

"Where would they live?"

In response, he chuckled mirthlessly. "Oh, My Dear, western Ireland is so sparsely inhabited, they could live almost anywhere. If discovered, they could pick up and be gone in a whisper."

"But wouldn't they want some permanence, just like the rest of us?"

He raised his eyebrows again. "Did you say *permanence*, Lady Granuaile? You, who live to be on the high seas?"

"Like most other people, then."

He walked over to a desk and returned holding a large map of Ireland. "How many islands lie off the western coast?"

"Hundreds. Thousands."

"Does that answer your question?"

"Yes and no."

"Is there a reason for your interest, Lady?" When I didn't answer, he said, "The O'Flahertys used to own Inishbofin before the O'Malleys seized it a hundred years ago."

"Inishbofin? The island of the white cow. Are you saying...?"

"No, Lady Granuaile. Far too inhabited for the likes of the Little People."

"You're talking in riddles, Sir Edmund. There must be all of four families on the whole of Inishbofin."

"Aye, four families too many as far as the Little People are concerned. But continue south," he said, his finger describing an arc from Inishbofin to the western edge of Slyne Head. "You've sailed this route many times?"

"I have."

"And you're familiar with all the coastal islands?"

"Perhaps not all of them."

"Suppose some islands existed much farther west than shown on this map, out where the ocean is wild and forbidding. Would you not admit they *could* exist?"

So they'd never need to come to Ireland itself. And they'd be left alone except in legend. "Sir Edmund, you mentioned that the Little People perpetuate their kind. Would it be possible for one of them to mate with a normal-sized person?"

"I can't see why not," he responded. "Except for their lesser height and stories about their magical ways, they've always been portrayed as having human characteristics."

"Like a horse and a donkey producing a mule?"

"I hadn't thought of it that way. Is there something you'd like to tell me, Granuaile?"

"No... yes... I don't know."

O'Flaherty sat quietly. He placed his hands together, steepled his fingers, and created a cup in which he rested his chin.

They say when two people share a secret, it remains a secret only until it is disclosed to another person. Once told, it takes wing and spreads quicker than legend. I knew this, but I also knew that it is human nature to *want* to disclose certain things, particularly when they have to do with love. Thus it was that Sir Edmund O'Flaherty was the first – and the only – human being with whom I shared the knowledge of my affair with Ballyclinch. I never even told my mother, and to this day I remember Edmund O'Flaherty with gratitude, for he never betrayed that secret.

"You told another person about us?" Ballyclinch asked, not so much angry as fearful.

"I did."

"Then we may as well say goodbye, Darling Grace. He'll no doubt want to see for himself and then the others of my kind..."

"I think not," I replied. "He gave me his word."

"The word of a man."

"Aren't you showing your own prejudice?" I said sharply. "You who told me about how the Little People were vilified?"

"They're not to be trusted."

"And I am?"

"You're different, Grace."

"How?"

For the first time since we'd come together, we felt a stab of uncomfortable tension. Neither of us broke the silence, even when we walked down the hill to the edge of his land and I continued walking alone to Bunowen.

We never know when the last time will be.

Donal returned to Bunowen Castle two days later. He was so courteous and so solicitous that when he sought to come to the marriage bed that night I did not refuse him. I saw nothing wrong with this. Despite what had happened on both sides, we shared a history and three children together. Perhaps... But then my thoughts went back to Ballyclinch. I felt genuinely torn between the two of them.

The rapprochement between Donal and me continued during the entire week he stayed at Bunowen. Ballyclinch only fleetingly entered my thoughts. The leaves of August began to brown, and I longed not so much for either man as I longed to sail to Spain, perhaps for the last time that year.

After Donal left, I felt it was time for a serious talk with Ballyclinch. Neither of us knew or could tell where our affair was headed, but the time for us both to deal with the taut strings that tied us sexually and emotionally together had arrived. Besides, matters had been left uncomfortably unresolved when last we'd parted.

On an uncharacteristically sullen day in September, 1555, I trekked through the bogs and valleys to the hidden hills where Ballyclinch lived. The wind picked up when I started to ascend to his cottage. Strange, there seemed to be no cattle about, and an eerie silence hung like a heavy fog. I knew Ballyclinch had an unobstructed view of the pathway to his home, and I found it disquieting that he'd not come bounding down the trail to meet me as had been his custom. Surely he couldn't still be angry with me. Could he have somehow found out that Donal had been home for a week? *Our kind has eyes in the back of our heads.* I shuddered.

No sound greeted me as I approached the house. Even stranger, no response came when I knocked on Ballyclinch's door and called out his name. Frantic, I pushed the door. To my surprise, it opened easily.

"Ballyclinch," I called, softly, then louder. No response! Even more unnerving, only cold ashes lined the fireplace, and the normally spotless cottage had an air of abandonment and desuetude. I felt a prickliness in my skin as I approached the bedroom door, the place where we'd shared our bodies and our passion.

"Ballycl –" I started to call out again, then froze in my tracks and stared in sheer horror. Ballyclinch lay in his bed, his face remarkably handsome and at peace. From the neck up it appeared he was sleeping. But his body had been slit from neck to belly, then across his chest cavity, in the shape of a jagged cross. What slime there had been had either been cleaned away or it had congealed and dried. Just to the left of his head, someone had placed a bunch of dried clover and, on top of that, a small medallion.

No one heard my scream. No one saw me vomit until my insides and my throat felt as jagged as the knife wounds that had killed my beloved.

I remained in this place for two days. During that time, I somehow managed to gather my wits together long enough to bury Ballyclinch in a bower of clover overlooking the lough on his property. As if driven by gods or demons, I cleansed the cottage. I didn't eat during that time, and I felt weak with hunger and an unconquerable emptiness. With my last strength, I dragged three large logs inside, placed them in the fireplace, and lit a fire. I watched as the tinder caught, then the logs caught and a large fire roared. Ballyclinch would have liked that. With not a backward glance, I left the cottage and returned, dry-eyed, to Bunowen.

"Sir Edmund...?"

"I know. Quiet, child." He held me in his arms. I felt as comforted as when my da, the Black Oak, had held me when I was a little girl. I had no one else to whom I could turn.

"Why?"

"There is no why. There is only `who.'"

"Donal?" I asked in shock.

"No, My Dear. Donal never knew and you never gave him reason to know,"

"Who, then?"

"This is going to be very hard for me to say, and almost impossibly hard for you to hear. From the medallion you brought me, I can only conclude it was Ballyclinch's father."

"His father? But how could that be? He told me no one ever claimed him as son."

"One can never know whether or not it was his blood father. Let's just say it was the father of his village."

"How could you possibly know, Sir Edmund?"

"They say they have eyes in the back of their heads," he said. "They claim they possess powers beyond any human reckoning. For the most part, that may be so. But there are a few of us, very few, who take time to look, to listen, and to learn their ways."

Even in my misery, I thought it best not to question Edmund O'Flaherty. There are some things best left unknown.

Weeks went by. Although I was consumed with the tasks of caring for my own children and with the necessity to publicly appear to be conducting family and clan business, I seethed with slow-burning anger and hatred. What made it even harder was that I could not mention anything to anyone, and so I suffered alone.

One evening, just before sunset, a stranger came to Bunowen bearing a message from Edmund O'Flaherty. When I opened the envelope, it contained only a few words. "Go softly to Ballyclinch and finish the work."

Not even my great and frustrated anger and rage prepared me for what I saw. What remained of a smallish stranger hung from a large meat hook beside Ballyclinch's fireplace. Around his neck hung the medallion I had seen when last I'd been inside this cottage. The unknown man was still alive. Barely.

He had no power to implore me with the bloody stumps of arms he had left. His one eye fixed me with a stare that begged me to kill him. He couldn't speak. His tongue had been cut out. Nor could he hear. There were other things. Perhaps it was an undeserved kindness that I plunged my dagger into his heart right then. But I couldn't allow even so loathesome a creature to suffer any longer.

Immediately thereafter, I gathered all the wood that remained in a large pile just outside the house. I moved all of the wood into the cottage itself. Because the autumn rains had not yet come, the wood and tinder were dry and leapt into flame almost immediately after I lit them.

This time, when I left what had been, in happier times, a nest for Ballyclinch and me, I looked back for a long time, until I was satisfied that all but the stone exterior was no more than a charred shell.

Sir Edmund O'Flaherty never mentioned anything to me again, nor I to him. I was greatly saddened when that great and good man died of a mysterious accident the following year. And I still wonder...

Chapter 11

On November 17, 1558, Queen Mary of England died at the age of forty-two. During her reign, Mary's weak health had led her to suffer two false pregnancies, so she left no one to succeed her. Although she had enjoyed tremendous popular support and sympathy during the earliest part of her reign, she lost almost all of it after marrying Philip of Spain. The marriage treaty between them had clearly specified that England was not to be drawn into any Spanish wars, but this guarantee proved meaningless. Philip spent most of his time governing his Spanish and European territories, and little of it with his wife in England.

For her persecution of Protestants, the queen had earned the appellation "Bloody Mary." Indeed, during her five-year reign, two hundred eighty-three individuals had been burned at the stake, twice as many as had suffered the same fate during the previous century-and-a-half of English history, and even more than had suffered a similar fate during the Spanish Inquisition.

Mary's half sister, twenty-five year-old Elizabeth, three years younger than I, assumed control of the British throne immediately on Mary's death. She was crowned queen of England two months later, on January 15, 1559. There was no Archbishop of Canterbury at the time. Since the senior Catholic bishops refused to participate in her coronation because they considered Elizabeth to be illegitimate and because she was a Protestant, the relatively unknown Owen Ogelthorpe, Bishop of Carlisle, crowned her. Elizabeth's coronation was the last one during which the Latin service was used.

Shortly after ascending the throne, Queen Elizabeth started to undo all of what her Roman Catholic half-sister had done during her five-year reign. She required the use of the Protestant Book of Common Prayer in church services. Concurrently, she ended Mary's Communion with the Catholic Church and assumed the title *Supreme Governor of the Church of England*. Under Elizabeth's direction, Parliament passed the Act of Supremacy, which required public officials to take an oath acknowledging the Sovereign's control over the Church or face severe punishment. Many bishops were unwilling to conform to Elizabeth's religious policy. Those bishops were removed from their positions and replaced by appointees who would agree with the Queen's decision.

For the first time since her father Henry's death, Elizabeth saw to it that England turned its eye toward her other realm, Ireland. The western part of our island, and the fiercely independent province of Connaught in particular, were not pleased.

Alas, between my youngest son, Murrough and me, there was no peace. At seven, he was a terror, often beating up his two-years-older sister and disdaining my attempts to mediate between them.

Donal and I had settled into our separate lives. The hurt of our mutual betrayals had cooled, and we had achieved a peaceful *modus vivendi* – so much so that every three months or so, sometimes more often, we joined forces in the bedroom, although the lovemaking lacked fierce passion.

Owen, now eleven, was quite the gentleman. As he had matured, my brother had taken my firstborn under his wing on those occasions when I sailed. Margaret stayed with my mother at those times and Murrough happily spent his time with his da.

I now commanded four O'Malley vessels and four O'Flaherty ships. Since Donal was still banned from trading at Galway because of his reputedly violent temper and the troubles he'd allegedly caused, we raided and pillaged those ships bound for or coming out of that city. It mattered not whether those vessels were English, Irish, or Spanish. If they wanted to deal with the largest market in that part of Ireland, and that market thought it could prohibit me and mine from trading there, Galway and its tribes could face the consequences.

Three times a year, usually during the more clement months, I traveled outside the Irish realm, usually to Scotland, Spain, or my beloved Portugal, where we sold the produce of Connaught and Connemara – hides, wool, sweaters, and building stone – in more lucrative and less prohibitive markets than Galway. When we returned from those exotic places – my countrymen found them exotic, but I was very much at home there – we brought back wines, spices, glass, iron, rich silks, and fine fabrics. We found a ready and highly profitable outlet for our goods among the Gaelic and Anglo-Irish lords of Connaught, who preferred to purchase from me at cheaper rates, rather than pay the high import tolls at Galway.

This so irritated the good citizens of Galway that they requested help from their English overlords. Their earnest request availed them not at all.

No less profitable, albeit of much shorter duration, were the trading trips we made to Munster, Ulster, Scotland, and England itself, and for the most part I left the running of those missions to subordinate captains.

My da, Owen Dubhdarra O'Malley, was now fifty-seven, and while he was still a man of great personal force and unimagined strength – at least to me – he seemed content to abide within his barony, Umhall Uachtarach, the Upper Owel, which the English called Murrisk.

"Aye, My Granuaile, I'm now of an age when I leave the excitement of the seas to young folk like you."

"But da, ye're still a young man ye'rself," I protested.

"That may be, but I'm happy to accept the hundred milk cows, hundred hogs, hundred casks of beer, two small ships, five horses, five swords, and five changes of clothing I receive as tribute from the O'Malley clan each year, without risking my own hide any longer."

"Quite a retirement, Da."

"That it is, my dear, but that's been the way of the O'Malleys for eight generations, and I'm not one to argue with tradition." My father seemed unhappy, as though the world might be passing him by.

"Don't you sometimes miss the excitement of it all?"

"I thought I would, but after you've made more than a hundred journeys, you sometimes get to wondering whether one day your luck will run out. There've been some times when the sea's been high and I've run into storms where I wondered if that was the one that was going to take my ship and my life with it."

"But Da, you've always been cautious."

"So have hundreds of others whose boats are now hiding

places for the fishes and other sea creatures. Not to mention those of our kind."

"Pirates?"

"And others. It seems nowadays every third vessel's looking for a way to make a profit off the labors of others."

"You make it sound as though there's something immoral about what we do."

"I didn't mean that at all, Granuaile. But it's gotten so we have to protect *ourselves* from pirate ships, and who knows where that will lead? Sooner or later, I fear every merchant ship will be accompanied by a Man O' War, and then the only ships pirates will have left to prey upon will be their own."

We were seated in my da's favorite room, his study, high up in Belclare Fortress-Castle, overlooking Clew Bay and Clare Island to the west. As my father and I drank warm ale and ate from a plate of oatcakes my mother had made, it seemed Belclare was so much smaller and older-looking than it had been when I was small. Still, my parents had taken steps to beautify the fortress. For one thing, engineers had devised an ingenious method of heating water at various levels of the castle, then piping that water under the stone floors so that the rooms were warm and cozy, even without a smoky fireplace. For another, winches and pulleys had been so arranged that food, drink, and even furniture could be hauled from the bottom to the top of Belclare without the need of traversing the hundreds of steps from the ground to the rooftop.

I wondered if I would feel as my father did when – if – I reached his age. I felt a stab of my own mortality as I realized that many men in my own crews were younger than I, and I was not yet thirty.

Still, I had immense respect for my father. In his time, he'd sailed from Clew Bay, which was large, and his fleet was open to attack by English Men O'War, even when in his home port.

By contrast, my demesne at Bunowen was small, narrow, and well-hidden. True, the English could, if they were so inclined, easily blockade the tiny inlet leading to the castle, but they faced numerous risks in so doing. First, Bunowen was situated so the large British ships could not navigate the inlet. Any attempt to lay siege to the castle itself was doomed, since we grew all the food we needed and we were well-supplied by friendly clans in Connaught. It also seemed rather trivial, if not downright silly, to waste the resources of a large Man O'War by blocking a minute inlet.

Most dangerous, however, was that as *de facto* leader of the O'Flahertys and with immediate access to the O'Malleys, it was within my power to call upon both those clans to send galleys of their own to surround the English blockader, and either starve that large ship into submission or blast it out of the water. Indeed, over the years we'd seized cannon and supplies from such vessels on enough occasions that by the spring of 1560 they did not pose a credible threat to my operations.

During my time with my parents, I relaxed more than I had in many years. All three children were with me, and, surprisingly, even Murrough seemed more civil and decent to me while he was in the company of his grandfather.

My stay at Belclare was interrupted early in April, a month after I had arrived. There had been disquieting rumors concerning my husband. Donal had attacked the neighboring territory of the Joyce clan on Lough Corrib, the largest lake in western Ireland, the month before, and while the results of his latest battle were inconclusive, a messenger from the O'Flaherty clan reported that the Joyces were furious that Donal had seized one of their major castles on the lough and claimed it for his own.

Less than a week after my thirtieth birthday, a rider came upon Belclare so rapidly that his mount was frothing at the mouth. "Lady Grace!" he exclaimed, his own face red from the exertion. "Your husband, Donal-an-Chogaidh has been killed!"

"How?" I demanded. I was surprised at my calmness in the face of this calamitous news. Although I cannot say there was great passion, or even love, left between us, we had become companionable of late.

"He was killed by Joyces, who trapped him while he was hunting in the mountains. 'Tis said that they were lying in wait for him after he'd successfully defended *Caislean-an-Cullagh*, the castle they claimed he'd stolen from them!"

"The Castle of the Cock?"

"Aye, Lady. The O'Flahertys called it that because your husband showed the courage of a cock while defending that castle."

"What happens now?"

"The Joyces have been celebrating his death for the last two days, while those inside the castle are said to be trembling. They're crowing that with Donal-an-Chogaidh gone, the castle and the land around it will be theirs for the taking."

"Is there no general among the O'Flahertys with spirit to avenge my husband's death?"

"No one has come forward. After all, the castle does lie in what has traditionally been Joyce country."

"How long before the Joyces attack?"

"Tis said it will take them ten days to marshal all their troops and storm the stronghold."

"Hmmm. Ten days, you say?"

"Aye."

"How long have you been riding?"

"Two days, My Lady."

"And the O'Flaherty forces? If they were inclined to raise an army, how long would it take to get to the castle?"

"Two days, mayhap three, My Lady."

"Very well," I said. "But I fear I forget my O'Malley manners. You are..."

"Damon O'Flaherty, Lady Granuaile."

"Come in, Damon O'Flaherty. Let us at the very least prepare you a decent meal and a good bed on which to lay your head this night."

That evening, after Damon O'Flaherty had retired, my father, my mother, and I held a miniature O'Malley war council.

"Why would you want to avenge Donal? The O'Flahertys are a friendly clan, but they are not O'Malleys, and the Joyces have been neither friend nor foe," my mother said. She, more than my father, knew of the real relationship between my late husband and myself.

"And you're a sailor born, my dear daughter. Is there some demon inside you that insists you fight battles on land as well as on the sea?" This from my father.

"You're both right," I replied. "If I'd be doing this, I'd do it not for the memory of Donal, who was difficult at the best of times, but in honor of a gentleman who did me a great favor once, Edmund O'Flaherty."

"Aye, he was a very good man, indeed," my father replied. "The most honorable and trustworthy of the entire O'Flaherty clan. But a land battle?"

In response, I pointed to the O'Malley coat of arms, which hung proudly in the front hall. "Invincible on land and sea," I said. "Do you still have any questions, da?"

Chapter 12

"We must move quickly," I announced to my two hundred O'Malley, McNally, and Conroy forces. "We'll have to circle southwest to remain in O'Malley land until we join up with the O'Flahertys. Then we'll approach the Cock's Castle from the west. We've no worry of anyone attacking us from the south, since what's not O'Flaherty country is Burke land."

"There is a small problem you may not have considered," my father said. "The Joyces control all the land between Loch Mask and Loch Corrib. While your kinsmen at Ballinahinch Castle report they have seen the fire signals from the cock's castle indicating it's still in O'Flaherty hands, the Joyces have encircled it on the three land approaches. You'd have to break through a well-entrenched army just to get to the castle."

"An approach from Loch Corrib?"

"Possible," my father said, "but I doubt you could reach the castle quickly enough."

"What then?"

"You need a large, friendly force to divert the Joyces' attention so you can reach the castle. The O'Malleys can marshal enough of a force from Murrisk, but it would be better if you had a second diversion."

"Hmm." I said, then mumbled under my breath, "friendly thighs may entice friendly forces."

"What?" my father asked.

"Oh, nothing. I was just thinking aloud," I replied. "You've just given me an idea where I can find a large friendly force. Carraigahawley, Rockfleet Castle."

"Burke country," my father said, admiringly. "Richard-an-Iarrain's castle. The Burkes are the largest and most powerful clan in all Connaught. D'you think he'd remember you after all these years?"

"Mayhap," I said, smiling.

My own two hundred men functioned so well together that I completely trusted my cadre of twenty-five lieutenants to lead them where I asked, without question or demur. Within the hour, they'd left Murrisk Castle at the southeast corner of Clew Bay, headed toward their rendezvous with the O'Flahertys at Ballinahinch. Meanwhile, I engaged a small boat to whisk me to the northeast corner of Clew Bay and Carraigahawley in two hours.

I spent a lovely night there, in what could be called animated conversation with Iron Dick Burke. The following morning, Richard signaled every Burke stronghold within twenty miles, and before noon, the Burkes had raised an army of four hundred men, many more than the diversionary force I'd hoped for.

Riding side by side at the head of the Burke aggregation, Richard and I reached Loch Mask by nightfall. From there, we could see the signal fires from *Caislean-an-Cullagh*, the cock's castle. The message was grim. The Joyce clan had mounted a naval blockade as well as the land siege, and now the castle was surrounded on all sides. It was clear from the signals that neither the O'Flahertys in the castle nor the Joyces surrounding it had any idea that forces were, at that very moment, approaching from the south and the west, let alone that the largest force of all was descending from the north.

"What say, M'Lady?" Richard asked. "By noon tomorrow, we'll be in Joyce country, and with luck they may still be unaware we're at their back."

"Richard-an-Iarrain," I responded sharply. "Grace O'Malley has never relied on anyone to bring her good fortune. How well do your kinsmen know the land between here and Lough Corrib?"

"Like the natives they are," he replied.

"Very well, then. I should like to address your clansmen."

"Can I stop you?" he asked, grinning.

"Not really."

Shortly afterward, Richard had gathered his forces in a semicircle around me. "My lions," I said. "If I live a hundred years, I'll never be able to properly thank you for coming to my aid." I specifically neglected to say "to the O'Flahertys' aid," because I knew there had not always been the best of blood between the Burkes and their neighbors to the southwest. "May the road rise up to meet each of you and bless you with sunshine, beautiful women, and many sons." A collective cheer went up.

I continued, "I hear tell a Burke can sleep a mere four hours a night and be fully ready to capture a castle or a woman!" There was raucous laughter and "Hear! Hear!"

"Very well, my hearties," I said. "Ye'll now have your chance to prove it. A quick meal, a short rest, and we'll be on our way to Lough Corrib." I held up a large purse of gold coins, which I ceremoniously handed to Richard-an-Iarrain Burke. "My friend Iron Dick will hold this sack as a symbol of my good faith. If you can make it to Lough Corrib before the sun breaks over the eastern horizon tomorrow morning, I will hand Richard Burke a second like bag of gold. Richard, I will trust you to distribute the bounty in shares to each of these fine young men."

Now the shouts were overwhelming, and uniformly positive, and there were calls of, "Why wait? Let's start now!" But I knew the importance of their being rested when they started, for the true test would occur when we reached Lough Corrib. I prevailed upon them to save their eagerness and marshal their strength for the coming battle.

We started out an hour before midnight. Richard counseled the men that they must travel with no more sound that a hunter would make when approaching a frightened animal. It took us little more than four hours to reach the outlying ranks of Joyce forces.

So silent were the Burkes as they surrounded the Joyces that I could have sworn there were only four men rather than four hundred. So cocksure of their position were the Joyce attackers, that they'd not even posted sentries on their northern flank. Only their carelessness rivaled their audacity. At a signal from me, the Burkes, screaming and shouting like banshees from hell, cut and hacked their way through the Joyce camp. I never stopped to count how many were killed or maimed during that ferocious assault. Our victory was so swift and sure that the Burkes completely encircled the land around *Caislean-an-Cullagh* before the sun rose that morning.

But while I was now installed in the castle, the victory was far from complete. By the time the sun reached its zenith, the Joyces had redoubled their forces and brought in friendly clans from the east. My McNally, O'Malley, and Conroy soldiers had not yet arrived. Meanwhile, the Joyces had rallied their allies. *Carean-an-Ullagh* had been a Joyce stronghold. They hated the churlish Donal-an-Chogaidh, who'd initiated the land grab of the castle, and believed he was nothing more than an upstart thief.

All that day and into the night, the battle for the castle continued, inconclusive and deadly. I stood on the ramparts watching the battle going on all around me, when the Joyce forces breached the castle gates. Hearing the sound, I reacted by shouting to my own allies, exhorting them to save the castle from the invaders. A moment later, I found myself barely conscious on the floor of the rampart. As I put my hand to my cheek, I smelled a sweetish smell and felt a slick wetness. Believing I was perspiring from the excitement, I looked at my hand and found it covered in blood.

I couldn't stanch the flow of blood from my face. The lights from the castle fires rapidly dimmed. I sensed myself being gently moved down a staircase. Surprisingly, I felt no pain. I tried to speak, but my jaw did not working properly and I couldn't find voice to express my thoughts.

"She's taken a fire arrow in her cheek." I heard a number of worried voices around me.

"Will she survive?" An anxious voice, a woman's as best I could make out.

"Don't know," another voice replied. "Looks like it took off most of her cheek. Thank God it didn't pierce her eye. Whether she'll ever talk again, I can't say."

"Where's my cheek?" I managed to stammer.

"Still up on the rampart, M'Lady," a man's voice said.

"Get the damned thing, get a medicus here if we have one, and sew it back on."

"But Lady..."

"And get me whiskey and plenty of it. I don't want to be conscious when it goes back on." Everything went blue, then black, then nothing.

When next I returned to consciousness, I felt such great pain that I screamed in sheer agony. It felt as if a hundred devils were clawing at the skin around my cheek. Mercifully, someone gently opened my mouth and poured a goodly slug of whiskey down my throat and I lost consciousness once again.

It took four days before I could communicate on a rational basis with anyone. By that time, the pain, though vicious, was tolerable. The medicus, a swarthy young man, approached me and said, "M'lady, thank God you're out of danger."

"My face?" My voice sounded strange to me, mushy.

"Ah, you can speak. That concerned us."

"My face?" I repeated in what I hoped was a firm voice.

"I cannot predict what it will look like in the future. It will be months before the swelling goes down. M'lady, I am not a trained physician. I believe there will be a large scar between your cheek and your eye and down along your jaw. I don't know what this will do to your speech, but God willing..."

I sank back on the pillows beneath my head. At this moment, I did not have time to consider this worrisome news. "How goes the battle?"

"It goes on, Lady Grace, but when you were so viciously injured, those in the castle took heart. A day later, the O'Flahertys arrived, and a few hours after that, they were joined by the McNallys, O'Malleys, and Conroys. They were beyond furious when they'd heard what had happened to you."

"Then I'm not too late to take part?"

"M'lady, you're in no condition to..."

"Don't you *dare* tell me what I am or am not in condition to do! Take me to the tower rampart immediately."

"But M'lady?"

"Do you hear me? I said *immediately* – this very minute!"

"Yes, My Lady."

I had very little strength. I could not stand on my own, and I could not project my voice. One of the young pages who had helped carry me up to the tower rampart devised an ingenious contraption in which I could lie back, nearly seated, with most of the weight off my legs, but it would appear from a distance as though I were standing. That same young man rolled a piece of hide in the shape of a cone, then cut the smaller edge so I could hold it against my mouth. This would allow me to project my voice by many degrees as it amplified any sound.

At my command, four drummers stood, two on each side of me, and beat a loud tattoo so their attention focused up to where I sat-stood. When the Burke and O'Flaherty troops saw me, a loud roar ensued. That roar spread to where the McNallys, Conroys, and O'Malleys were positioned, and the roar doubled in volume. At the moment the roar crescendoed to its peak, two huge flags fluttered from the masts atop the tower: my many-years-old personal pennant with the hen in the circle, and the O'Malley coat of arms.

"Granuaile! Granuaile! Granuaile!" resounded from the ground surrounding the cock's castle. I raised my right arm in salute to my armies and praised their valor in a very few well-chosen words. Somehow, I managed to remain strapped into the standing-sitting contraption for half an hour, and in that time the fervor of our troops renewed. The young man who'd helped me, seeing my near collapse, made haste to withdraw me from the sight of the troops, which was just as well, for they had more important things to do than cheer.

By the following morning, when I painfully awoke, a herald rushed to the castle keep with the news that the enemy had been vanquished. By sunrise, they had dispersed to the north and to the south, to the lands of the Joyces and their allies.

Covering my face with a mask, I asked the herald, "Is there more to report?"

"Aye, Lady Grace. Richard-an-Iarrain asked me to convey to you that the castle is no longer called *Caislean-an-Cullagh*."

"What say you? But that cannot be. We have successfully defended this castle."

"That is so, My Lady, but such courage have you shown in this battle that ever since your banner rose over this place, the troops have started calling is *Caislean-an-Circa*."

"The *hen's* castle?"

"Aye, Madame. Donal-an-Chogaidh is dead. He fought with the courage of a cock, but he died nonetheless. You fought with the courage of a hen, and you survived to prevail. Henceforth, this castle is named the Hen's Castle to your everlasting honor."

Alas, glory is a fleeting thing. I have learned several times that the moment you have won a battle, you are celebrated in story, song, and even legend, but the appreciation in your own time and among your own allies for what you have done declines daily.

I had saved an O'Flaherty castle from recapture by what most probably were its true owners. I had done this as the leader of the O'Flaherty clan, even though my late husband had borne the title The O'Flaherty. Within a fortnight of Donal's death, those around me advised that while I had certainly done a far better job than Donal-an-Chogaidh could ever have done, the O'Flahertys would not let the title The O'Flaherty pass to a woman. By that time, Owen was nearly grown and Murrough, who had never been partial to me, elected to move in with O'Flaherty clansmen.

More disappointing news continued. Under Brehon law, as the surviving widow of The O'Flaherty, one-third of my late husband's possessions belonged to me. Unfortunately, Donal had very little left in the way of movable personal property, although he had castles at Bunowen and Ballinahinch. He did not really own the Castle at Lough Corrib, since he had died before it had been won. With Edmund O'Flaherty dead and his sons embroiled in their own ambitions, I could not count on any support from them.

It took me eight months of hard negotiating, and I must say that the Burkes and the O'Malleys exercised great pressure on the recalcitrant O'Flahertys, before we came to settlement. The O'Flahertys would quitclaim the Hen's Castle to me, provided I agreed to waive claim to any O'Flaherty property, whether in Donal's name or otherwise. By this time, Owen sat warmly in the O'Malley camp, so little settled on him, while Murrough had so ingratiated himself to the O'Flahertys that he received three times his older brother's bounty. My daughter Margaret, as a woman, received nothing, it being assumed that when she married, her husband would bring sufficient estate to properly care for her needs.

I was pleased to have a castle of my own. I had already established myself independently from the O'Flahertys, securing my own livelihood through maintenance by land and sea "protecting" ships entering Galway Bay and Clew Bay. But as the year 1562 began, my personal life was deeply troubled.

Chapter 13

Although I commanded power and respect, I was not yet thirty-two years old and already a widow. I did not want to give up my womanly needs, but as I looked in the mirror, I could not help but see that my sadly disfigured face had not healed properly. My appearance terrified me. I looked like a gargoyle on some Gothic church. Worse, as grotesque as I appeared, I kept returning to look at myself in my bedroom mirror.

As months passed, an inner darkness clouded me. I had not returned to my beloved sea since the battle for Hen's Castle. My negotiations over my late husband's estate had taken place by means of posted letters. Although my erstwhile lover and present friend Richard-an-Iarrain Burke constantly assisted me, I had never, in all the months since the battle, allowed him to look at my face.

I felt like a grisly monster, certain that any man who looked at me would want to get as far away as possible, and as quickly as he could. As February became March and March became April, I secluded myself more and more in the Hen's Castle, where no one could see me. I socialized not at all, not even with my closest family. I spent most of my waking hours either crying bitter tears, looking in my dreaded friend-enemy, the mirror, or drinking myself into oblivion to stifle the pain that simply refused to go away.

By the middle of April, the mirror revealed a still more horrid sight: I had gained an incredible amount of girth. I had always been so proud of my lithe body and my ability to engage in any strenuous physical activity. Now, I could not make it up even one flight of stairs without stopping to catch my breath. Yet I remained powerless to stop gorging on food and consuming large quantities of whiskey.

During that period, I thought quite seriously of ending my misery by leaping off the tower rampart, the very place where I'd achieved my greatest glory. What glory? What use had my life been? I had succeeded in a man's world. I had commanded ships and I had commanded men. So what? If it hadn't have been me, another human being would have filled that role, perhaps better than me. I had had a marriage that was neither success nor failure, three children, one of whom refused even to talk to me. I wondered how many people had died because of me.

The second week in May started with an insistent pounding on the door of the castle. I heard the sound of a strong, manly voice and immediately shriveled up inside. *Oh, God, no! How can I turn him away?*

Before I had a chance even to call down to my castle staff, I heard my father's stolid steps as he climbed to the third story, where I sat in a small, dark room. He turned into the room as if he'd known exactly where I'd be, then sat down in the only other chair in the room. He'd not seen me for six months or more, and if he was shocked at what he saw, he didn't show it.

He sat silently, his broad hands in his lap. Before many minutes had gone by, I started weeping more copiously than I had in weeks. The deep sobs racked my cumbersome body and tore at my soul. I had no idea how long I cried, nor did I recall when he got up, walked over, and cradled me in those huge, masterful arms that had held me as a child.

"Oh, Da, Da," I wailed.

He started singing to me, a song he'd sung when I was three years old, or even younger. He kept singing and I kept crying, and time lost all meaning. Eventually, my sobbing slowed and my breathing became easier.

"Granuaile, my Granuaile, isn't it time you stopped blaming yourself for what happened?"

"That's... that's easy for you to say, Papa. You're... you're still the handsomest man in all Ireland, and I'm... I'm..."

"You're still my same beautiful little girl, Granuaile. Do you think I'm so shallow that all I see is the outside? You haven't changed a'tall," he said. "Except maybe to become yet more courageous."

"Courage? Courage, you say? If I were even remotely courageous, would I have let myself come to this?"

"Courage comes in many different forms, Grace. You did not hesitate to assert your rights against the entire O'Flaherty clan. 'Tis only when you had won yet another battle that you went inside yourself and found some poison you didn't even know about."

"You've no idea how often I wanted to die, simply to end this all."

"It took courage not to do that."

"I suppose," I heard myself say, the first hopeful words I'd said since I could remember.

"Do you think you might have yet more courage?"

"Meaning what?"

"Granuaile, 'tis dreadful when a beautiful girl ceases being beautiful in her own eyes, and that's what happened. What if I were to tell you there's hope that you'll be beautiful, even in your own eyes, once again?"

"It's cold in here, papa. I've been so cold all these months, but I've never wanted to light a fire. I wanted to stay out of the light, where no one could see..."

"Ah, Granuaile," he said, walking over to a small fireplace and tossing two logs as though there were small sticks, into the pit. He lit the fire, and soon it roared and I felt warm. For the first time in a long time I didn't care if he – or anyone – saw me.

"I want you to come to Portugal with me, Grainne," he said, reverting to a nickname he'd not called me for years and years. "I know that's one of your favorite places on earth."

"But..."

"No one need see you, if that's what you're worried about. I'll make sure you go to my cabin the night before we leave, when there's no one on board. It's late spring and I've no worry about the weather. You need not leave the cabin for the entire journey."

"Why do you want me to go?"

"There's someone I want you to meet."

"In my present condition? Isn't that the greatest cruelty you could visit on me?"

"I think not, my dear. Do you trust your old father?"

"Always and forever, papa."

"Then trust me now."

Sixty-year-old Doctor António Manso Pinheiro had thinning gray hair, clear brown eyes, and hands much softer and smoother than mine. While he dressed casually, his nails were neatly pared and a pleasant fragrance danced about him. When we had arrived at Doctor Pinheiro's clinic on the western outskirts of Lisboa, he had ushered us into his private chambers within a very few minutes. The doctor appeared quite courteous, but an infinite sense of calm confidence and gentleness emanated from the man. Not once during our lengthy interview did he patronize or talk down to me.

"Do you prefer I call you Madame O'Flaherty or Captain O'Malley?"

I smiled – or at least my face moved in as much of a smile as I could muster. "No one has called me 'Captain' since..."

"Since the incident where you showed such heroism at the Hen's Castle?"

"You know...? But how could you?"

"I make it a point to learn everything I can about someone who has honored me by asking for what small assistance I can give. I don't know what your experience with physicians has been, but I feel that unless I know the *whole* person, I might callously consider someone as a mere 'patient.' Now, I can keep speaking to you in the abstract, or you can tell me whether you'd prefer to be called Madame O'Flaherty or Captain O'Malley."

"Granuaile or Grace would be fine," I said, flushing with pleasure.

"Then you must call me António."

"But you're a *doctor*!" I exclaimed.

"Does that make me any more or less of a human being than you?"

"No."

"Well, then, it's Grace and António. We can call the old fellow 'Captain' if he wants," the doctor said, winking at my father.

"Doctor Pinheiro, I'd be careful if I were you," my father said, more relaxed than I'd seen him since the day he'd come to the Hen's Castle to fetch me. "I would say we're of an age, you and I. Perhaps you may *look* younger, but I'll wager..."

Doctor Pinheiro excused himself for a moment and returned bearing a tray with three glasses of the marvelous Port wine and some oranges and pastries I'd remembered enjoying as a child when I'd visited Lisboa for the first time. "I thought it would be more conducive to our little chat if we fortified ourselves."

Talk then turned serious. "Doctor Pinheiro, do you believe you could help my daughter?"

"Yes, I do, Captain," the doctor replied. Turning to me, he said, "Grace, from what I've learned of you, I believe you'd respect plain talk instead of airy pretension. Thus, we should be completely honest with one another."

"I would prefer that, António."

"Good," he said. "Let me start by saying whoever tried to deal with your wound did you a terrible, and I'm sure unintended, disservice." The man's voice was beautifully soothing, well-modulated and as gentle as the man himself. "But I've seen far worse. Look up, please," he said. I did, and he placed a piece of string, marked off in segments, to my cheek. So soft was his touch it felt like a feather. "Good," he said, moving the string to my other cheek.

"Shall I look up?"

"Please."

He took more measurements from my left cheek to my left jaw, and from my right cheek to my right jaw. Then, he measured from my left earlobe to my nose, then from my right earlobe to my nose. When he had finished, he carefully drew some lines and wrote some figures on a piece of paper on his desk.

"Doctor...António...?" I started to ask. "You said you'd seen worse?"

"Indeed, my dear. But I fear I've forgotten my manners. Here I am asking you to put your trust in me and I've not even told you about myself. Sometimes, but not often, when some patients know the type of medicine I practice, they believe I'm in league with the devil, and they can't wait to leave, never to return." He winked and I felt this good, good man would never do anything to hurt me or let me down.

"Because of the type of medicine you practice?" my father asked.

"One could say that, Captain O'Malley. I studied primary medicine at the University in Lisboa, but I didn't feel that medicine as practiced in Western Europe had the flexibility I thought it needed. I'd heard stories of other theories of practice. Since my parents were well-established, I was able to travel to Morocco, Egypt, and even further afield, to Persia and India, where I found there were indeed different methods."

"As advanced as in England and France?" I asked.

"Much more advanced. It was then I decided my life's calling was surgery. I spent two years in Egypt, a year in Persia, and two years in Varanasi, India, at the Sushruta Institute."

"The Sushruta Institute?" my father asked.

"Yes. The school, a teaching hospital named after Sushruta, whom many call the father of surgery. Sushruta lived and practiced more than two thousand years ago. He wrote a book, the *Sushruta Samhita*, in which he described over one hundred twenty surgical instruments and three hundred surgical procedures. He classified human surgery into eight categories. Can you imagine, he was doing the kind of surgery I'm doing today six centuries before Christ?"

"You're convinced all your training was worth it, António?"

"I am, Grace. During my medical training, I was not only allowed to observe, but fortune allowed me to apprentice to master surgeons. Their practice focused on serious burns and other types of surgery. I must have participated in over a thousand surgeries during those five years. During my free time, I also became a student of the human condition."

Doctor Pinheiro extracted a leather-bound book from his bookcase. *"The Guide for the Perplexed,"* he said. "Written by a Jew named Moses Maimonides, who was born in Córdoba, Spain, but who moved on to Egypt. He was what I've always longed to be – a physician and surgeon, a philosopher, and, most of all, a man possessed of love for his fellow men."

He signaled us to sit in two comfortable chairs adjacent to a low table, covered by several large charts. "Now Grace, you probably wonder why I measured your face, but you were so helpful and courteous that you kept silent." He pointed at a diagram of a human face on the table, where lines and numbers corresponded to measurements he had made. "This shows what we have come to know as a 'normal' face."

I noticed that the measurements were close, but not exactly the same in the distances between eye and jaw, and the like.

"In a few cases, the face is perfectly symmetrical, but in most instances, there are slight differences. That's what makes for a more interesting, often more attractive appearance. The most obvious example I can think of is a woman's breasts."

I blushed, embarrassed that he would talk about such a thing so openly, but he continued in the same direct manner. "I say this entirely as a clinical observation, and I use this because it's something every adult who has ever been married can well appreciate. In eight out of every ten women I've observed in thirty-five years of practice, a woman's left breast is measurably larger, sometimes significantly larger, than the right breast."

"I can appreciate that, I said," this time without embarrassment. "But what does this have to do with me?"

In reply, Doctor Pinheiro walked over to his desk and brought back the paper on which he'd written down the measurements. "These are the observations I've made on your face." He went over the writings with his right index finger. "You've probably looked in a mirror several times since you were wounded – don't feel ashamed, everyone so afflicted does that – and observed that your face seems to droop."

I looked down at the floor.

"The reason it looks that way is that your facial muscles have lost tone on one side and contracted on the other, which has pulled your face more out of symmetry than it should be."

"And the puffiness and jagged scarring?"

"Most likely caused because when the skin from your cheek was reattached, neither it nor your face had been properly prepared. My guess is that the dirty skin putrefied at the time it was sewn back on. Once it was in place, the skin continuing to rot. You and I are both blessed that you came here as quickly as you did."

"Would it have gotten worse with time?"

"Definitely," Doctor Pinheiro said, "and more painful as well."

"What do you propose to do, Doctor?" my father asked.

The surgeon put the first large page on the floor and pointed to the next page. This page showed a number of serrated lines and arrows.

"The first thing we will do is locate a part of your body where there is healthy excess skin. You have gained weight during the months since the incident?" It was not said judgmentally, but matter-of-factly.

"Yes."

"No need to be embarrassed, Grace," he said. "Such things are not unusual when one perceives of oneself as ugly. Don't look surprised, I told you I was a student of the *whole* person. This is a natural reaction. In your case, it is a good thing."

"Why do you say that?"

"The human skin can stretch. As you gain weight, the skin expands to adjust to the larger size. We will cut from an area where there has been expansion, so that..."

"You'll what?" I said. I felt myself starting to breathe rapidly and shallowly.

"Cut from an area where there has been expansion. That way, when you return to your normal weight, the skin won't hang in folds where it had expanded."

My father put his large hand over mine and patted it comfortingly. My own hands felt cold and clammy as Doctor Pinheiro continued.

"I'll try to make this as brief and direct as I can," he said. "What I am going to do will be very painful, but that pain will be masked by mandrake root and morpheus poppy, so you will be unconscious when we do this. In a few moments, I will look over your entire body – you may cover your most private parts,

of course. I will select the best area of excess skin to match
your other cheek. My assistant and I will slice thin layers of
that skin, cleanse it carefully, and keep it moist while I remove
the diseased skin and the scars on your face. We will cleanse
the area of your face where we have cut, removing every bit of
dirt and infection we can find. Then I will carefully shape the
healthy segment I have cut from the other part of your body, so
that it matches what should be the normal symmetry of your
face. During this entire procedure, you will not be conscious of
what is going on. Are you all right?"

"A bit shaky, Doctor."

"António."

"António, then."

"Again, My Dear, your reaction is typical. Since you've
already shown you're more courageous than most, I'm telling
you all this now, so you'll have ample opportunity to deal with
your fear before the operation. More port?"

"I think I will have some, yes."

At that moment, we heard a loud thump. I turned in
the direction of the sound and saw that the Black Oak had
fainted and fallen off the chair. Doctor Pinheiro quickly rose
and administered smelling salts to my father. "As I said, you're
more courageous than most..."

For the first time in nearly a year, I found myself
laughing heartily, not at my father's unfortunate reaction, but
at António's quick and incisive humor. As the doctor called
for an assistant to help lift my father, he poured me another
draught of port. Once my father had been safely, if groggily,
moved to another room, the surgeon continued.

"When your face and the new skin patch are properly
prepared, we will fit one to the other and carefully stitch them

in place with very fine thread, creating enough of a flap that your body will accommodate to the expansion and contraction while the healing is taking place. For the next months, I will carefully observe you and make any adjustments I feel are necessary. During that time, I will place you in the care of Maria Correia, my most trusted associate, who is as close to me as a daughter. It will be her responsibility to feed you and exercise you properly, as well as to help you reclaim your emotional health."

"Will I look...?"

"The same as you did before? That, my dear, is in God's hands."

Chapter 14

My father said his goodbyes in late September and left for Ireland the day before I'd gone into the operating room. We both knew if he didn't leave soon, the winter winds that whipped the Atlantic would keep him in Portugal until the following spring. He promised to keep in touch with me and ensured that I had more than sufficient money for my needs. He'd paid Doctor Manso Pinheiro before he departed and left a substantial account with which to pay any other expenses.

"Papa," I'd said. "Do you really think Doctor António will be able to help me?"

"I do, Granuaile darling," he replied. "Between the doctor and the great, good God, one has to trust *someone*."

"I'll miss you, Da," I said.

"And I you, my sweet child. But come early spring..." he didn't finish the sentence, and I didn't press him.

Time lost all meaning during the next several days. Although I'm told I was in great pain and screamed and begged for death as a release, I truly have no recollection of those events. Doctor António, or to be more precise his angel of mercy, Maria Correia, told me later that she'd sat at my bedside for hours at a time, and that whenever I awoke and stirred even slightly, she administered a new dose of mandrake root or morpheus, sometimes both, and followed that by dabbing port wine on my lips to keep them moist.

Human curiosity, particularly a woman's curiosity at what she looks like, is one of life's strongest motivating forces, and I grew anxious to see what God – more particularly what Doctor António Manso Pinheiro – had wrought.

I had been fully conscious for the first time since I'd gone into Doctor Pinheiro's operating theater when a new fear assailed me. I could not see a thing. The world was dark, even though my eyes were open. Had António's work rendered me blind as well as unsightly? My nervousness led to panic and I tried to talk. What came out of my mouth was only a muffled moan.

"Do you want more medication, Lady Grace?" The voice was as gentle as António's, but feminine. I shook my head as violently as I could. "This is the first time you've been fully awake in many days," the voice continued. "You can't see and you can't speak, and you are undoubtedly very frightened. Please don't be." I felt a hand softly, comfortingly squeezing mine. "Don't worry, you are not blind and you will be able to speak in the future. Your entire head, but for your nose, is swathed in bandages, to keep you from becoming infected and to keep your face moist until the new skin and the old make friends and start to heal together."

Just those very few words, spoken as gently as they were, cooled my fears and I relaxed.

"The more you can accept what is happening to you, the faster you will travel on the road to recovery. Every day, we will change the bandages and apply fresh creams and ointments to aid in the process. As Doctor António observes the healing process, the bandages will become progressively lighter, and he will begin a regimen of massage and exercise to strengthen your face muscles."

I drifted into slumber. The angel's words faded but she still held my hand in hers.

Another period of time went by. One day, I awoke to find I could see, and even speak a little. The first thing I saw was the woman with the soothing voice.

"Good morning, Lady Grace," she said in the same tone she had used each day. "I promised you you would see again, and now you can." She smiled.

As I carefully observed the woman, Maria Correia, that first morning, I tried to sear what she looked like into my memory, in the event I lost my newly-recovered sight once again: two or three inches taller than me, and more powerfully built than her voice had sounded. Her dark, short hair had a few flecks of gray. I gauged her age at about thirty-five, not much older than me. While she did not exude remarkable physical beauty, she appeared by no means unattractive, with eyes, which, like António's, were brown and very large – and consummately gentle – eyes that looked as welcoming as a mother's eyes when first she sees her newborn baby. As soft and caring as she had been, her roughened hands had obviously seen hard work.

"If Doctor António calls me by my first name, there's no reason you cannot do the same. Please just call me Grace, or Granuaile, if you will."

"Oh," she said, putting the back of her hand to her mouth. "I will do so, but only if you call me Maria." She continued, "You can see because we've taken the bandages off your eyes and you can speak because we've removed the covering from around your lips. You're still bandaged up, though."

"What do I look like?"

"Truthfully I can't say. I don't know what you looked like before. Your face is still quite swollen, but Doctor António told me he's very pleased."

"Can I see myself?"

"If you mean would I stop you from looking, the answer is no. But all you'd see is two eyes and a mouth."

"When can I...?"

"When Doctor António says so, and not before. He's very strict in that way. There's still quite a distance to travel before he'll allow that to happen and there are no mirrors in this place."

Another week went by. Now my face was covered by only a thin layer of linen. The next regimen of my healing process began when Maria approached me one morning and said, "How would you like a short holiday away from the clinic?"

"More than anything," I replied earnestly.

"Good. It's time to start moving you out of here and back to the outside world. I've just added an attic onto my home, so that when my sons return every other month from the university they'll have a place to stay. They're away now, and I've had no guests since my husband passed away a year ago. You can stay with me if you'd like."

"But my face...?"

"We'll cover it with a scarf and you'll look like everyone else in the street. In case you were unaware – oh, I forgot, how could you be aware, it's been almost three months since you've been with us? It's November, and even in southern Portugal the air can be cold. Don't worry, I've got plenty of bandages and dressings at home."

"Doctor António taught me exercises for my face," I said.

"Yes, and now we'll start on other exercises as well. You've actually lost quite a bit of weight while you've been here. Now it's time to firm up your body. But we'll talk about that over the next few days."

The "next few days" turned out to be three weeks. Maria, my constant companion, and I walked several miles each day. In her simple, clean home, the attic was the newest part of the house. Maria refused to coddle me. She gently, but firmly, let it be known that if I wanted a helping hand, I would find it at the end of my arm, and that I could climb the stairs to the attic as well as she could.

I could find no mirrors in Maria's home and when we were out and about, I was so bundled up I could not have seen my face even if I had found a mirror. At the beginning of the third week, Maria took me back to the clinic, where António inspected my face and pronounced that the last of the bandages could come off, and while I should be careful to continue wearing the scarf when I went out, I could now go about indoors without any facial coverings.

"May I see myself, Doctor?" I asked.

"No, my dear. Not for at least another week."

That week might have been the slowest in my life, but for the fact that Maria took me on an excursion to Sintra, a village nestled in the mountains between Lisboa and the sea. Maria arranged for a private carriage to take us to that magical town, which lies less than twenty miles from Lisboa itself, but is a world apart.

Lisboa had turned blustery and cold, and the countryside to the west of the city displayed stark, bleak hills. Scarcely five hours after we left Lisboa, we came into a dense glade of green forest, verdant even this late in the year. Immediately beyond the glade, I saw high stony peaks, not unlike Ireland.

"The Serra da Sintra," Maria explained. "Those mountains separate the Portuguese plain to the north and the estuary of the *Rio Tejo* to the south. When we get to the top, we'll see *Cabo da Roca*, the westernmost point in Europe."

"When we get to the top," I repeated. "I don't see any roads up the mountain."

"There aren't any, Grace," Maria said cheerfully. "But it's a long, lovely walk."

"A long, lovely walk"

"Yes, but we won't make the ascent until morning."

We located our night's accommodations, a simple and unpretentious inn, close to the center of town. Since it was still early afternoon, Maria suggested we walk about the town. A slight, warm breeze blew off the mountains. I could well have wandered through the warren of narrow streets and markets without a scarf covering my face. However, I still had no idea what I looked like, and the idea of removing the scarf in public frightened me. My mind's eye recalled the grotesque-looking person of several months ago, and I had still not been allowed to view myself after the surgery. Maria said nothing, but in deference to me, she, too, wore a scarf over her face, although most people walking in the streets did not.

As we passed over a bridge which traversed a verdant canyon, I saw two huge, cone-shaped towers on the other side of the declivity.

"The monks' kitchen," Maria said. "The best known landmarks in the entire town. Built about a hundred years ago, they serve a very useful purpose. They're the vents from the royal kitchen. They go from very wide at the bottom to very narrow at the top so they can keep in heat during the winter, yet provide fresh air during the summer months."

"Those buildings beyond the chimneys – the National Palace?"

"Yes. There are two buildings because of the two strong personalities who had them built, King Joao, who built the closest building a little more than a hundred years ago, and the great King Manuel, who built the larger building half a century later."

"The same King Manuel who built Belém Tower and the San Jerónimos Monastery?"

"The same."

"Does the king live there all year 'round?"

"Oh, no. He's expected to be seen everywhere in Portugal. But the palace doesn't stay empty, even when he's not here. Just about any time of year, you can see poets and other writers strolling through the gardens or outside in the courtyards."

As we came closer to the palace, I saw hundreds, perhaps thousands, of beautiful ceramic tiles adorning the walls and even the walkways of the palace. It was not the first time I'd seen *Mudejar azulejos* tiles. Indeed, from time to time, we had carried such tiles aboard my family's ships and sold them for a dear price in western Ireland. Since we'd not applied for nor received a royal invitation, we could not go into the palace itself, but it was impressive, even from the outside.

After a sumptuous dinner of fish stew, saffron rice, and rich pastries, washed down with the ever-present port wine, we retired early and I slept as peacefully as any time I can remember.

Next morning, I awoke to see mists rising from the town into the surrounding mountains. I felt rested and ready to attack what Maria had told me would be a long, lovely walk. We ate a fortifying breakfast of dark rolls, rich butter, and wine-flavored jam, then began our ascent, which was not an easy one. I found, however, that the weeks of ever longer walks had firmed my muscles and I was able to climb without running out of breath.

As we climbed ever higher, the sun broke through the mists, and the day was clear and beautiful. A few hours after we started, I looked down and gasped at the sheer loveliness of the walled town below. It was as beautiful as any work of art I'd seen before or since. Several minutes later, we came to a half-ruined, but still magnificent castle. Its perimeter walls appeared to be dug into the two mountain peaks surrounding it.

"*Castelo de Mouros*, the Moorish Castle," Maria, my ever-knowledgeable guide said. "The Moors built it at least seven hundred years ago, when they owned most of what is now Portugal. King Alfonso conquered it in 1147, but not without a fight."

"Even in its present state, I can see it must have been larger and more elaborate than any of the castles where I've lived."

Maria smiled. "Ah, Grace, I would not know such things, since I've never traveled farther than southern Portugal. I'll take your word for it, though."

After we ate a picnic lunch the inn had prepared, we spent the next hour gazing at the town below and rummaging around the ruins of the castle. Maria told me we'd only need to climb for a short while to get to the summit, which looked to me to be about as high as Croagh Patrick, twenty-five hundred feet above the surrounding terrain. When we reached the crest, the view was as breathtaking as that from Saint Patrick's mountain, but it was far different from Ireland. For one thing, there was bright sunlight, something exceedingly rare in my country. For another, the green forests on the eastern side of the mountains, gave way to scrubland and then to flat, dry plain to the south and west, all the way to where the *Rio Tejo* joined the Atlantic Ocean in the distance. Instead of the wild, rocky, and always restless clashing of ocean against stark rock so common to the Irish coast, this land sloped gently down until it met an ocean that seemed as quiet as a lake. This was a sunny land of shorter shadows.

We descended from the Serra da Sintra. Twilight had fallen by the time we arrived back in Sintra's town square, exhausted and fulfilled from the day's adventure. Once again, I slept the sleep of the blessed. Next day, we wandered through the streets of town again, then took a much gentler hike through nearby woodland, and soon another day had passed.

On the fourth day, we returned to Maria's house. When I asked Maria to tell me honestly how I looked, she gave a noncommittal shrug and said, "I think it's best you ask yourself that question, three days from now."

During the following days, I found myself becoming more and more anxious. My appetite had disappeared, and I found little to do. During the time I had been staying with Maria Correia, I found that she, like Doctor António, had a copy of Moses Maimonides' *Guide for the Perplexed* in a prominent place in her bookcase. I recalled Doctor Pinheiro's laudatory words. With nothing better to pass my time, I hefted the large, heavy book out of its place and started reading it.

After several hours, I found myself entranced by the questions raised by this long-ago doctor and philosopher: Did the universe have a beginning? Will it ever end? What is the nature of evil? Does the complexity of organic life imply some kind of rational design? The first part of the book dealt with the nature of God and concluded that God could not be described in human terms. More important to me was Maimonides' admonition, so similar to my own thoughts, that to be a successful human being, man or woman, one must consider all theories put forth by anyone, and not simply adopt one and disdain others.

Then I reached a passage dealing with medicine. "The Law permits as medicine everything that has been verified by experiment." This reflected exactly what Doctor Pinheiro had told me was his philosophy, and I found myself comforted and much calmer as I awaited the day of reckoning.

Finally, the day came when Doctor Pinheiro had promised I could look at myself. That morning, I was so nervous that I awoke before cockcrow. I was unable to eat breakfast and my stomach felt alternately tied up in knots and loose with diarrhea. When I came downstairs, Maria greeted me with a smile and handed me an extraordinarily seductive red peasant skirt, white blouse, and green sash, which she said I should wear.

"Are you crazy?" I asked. I had seen slender young girls wearing these outfits during the summer, beguiling every man who crossed their paths. "I am a thirty-two-year-old mother, with a son who's nearly a man full grown. I saw what I looked like when I left *Caislean-an-Circa* several months ago. Are you trying to mock my pain?"

Immediately, I felt guilt for what I had said. Maria Correia had become the closest thing to a woman friend I'd ever had.

She'd shown me nothing but kindness, even in the hardest times, and here I was repaying that kindness by snappishness and ingratitude. "I'm sorry, Maria, truly I am," I said. "Forgive me for such a selfish and self-centered outburst."

Maria shrugged and simply said, "You might want to try the outfit on and see if it fits."

I returned to my room. Simply to please my friend's generosity, I disrobed and put on the shirt and blouse. I was surprised – shocked is a better word – to find that the clothes fit me perfectly. When I returned, Maria held out a warm felt coat, and once again I wrapped the scarf around my face.

Since I had traveled between Maria's home and Doctor Pinheiro's clinic several times during the past three weeks, I knew it would take less than an hour to get to the clinic. I am not exaggerating when I state this was quite probably the longest hour of my entire life.

When we arrived, António had not yet come to his clinic, which was unusual because I'd always known him to be so punctual. As minutes went by, I became concerned, then worried. Near the front desk, I saw something I'd not noticed before, a spring-wound clock that actually counted minutes and hours.

As I was staring at the clock, a very familiar voice said, "Ah, yes, My Dear, my latest little acquisition. Peter Henlein, an inventor in Nuremberg, Bavaria devised this gem about thirty-five years ago. What a shame. As marvelous an invention as it is, I am still late. No worry, though. Follow me if you will into my examining room, so I can see if everything looks the way it should. A nice outfit you're wearing, by the way. My granddaughter, who's fourteen, started wearing them earlier this year, and I haven't quite gotten used to the fact that I'm *grand*father to a beautiful young woman."

Maria followed us into the examining room, where Doctor Pinheiro used a measuring string of the same type he'd used months ago, and wrote notes down on a similar pad. From time to time, he would grunt noncommittally, but other than that he made no comment.

When my anxiety had risen to a point where I was about to lose control, António remarked, "Did you have any questions, My Dear?"

"Yes," I blurted out. "Was the operation a success? When will I get to see what I look like?"

In response, António cupped his jaw between the thumb and index finger of his left hand, and his eyebrows knitted in a slight frown, as though he were deep in thought. "Ah, yes, I knew there was something I had forgotten. This is the day I promised you'd be able to see God's handiwork. Very well, why don't you go into the adjoining room and draw your own conclusions?"

With trembling steps, I walked into the room which was lit with olive oil lamps. The first thing I noticed was a clear, silver floor-to-ceiling mirror, the largest I'd ever seen. Almost concurrently, I saw a reflection in the mirror. It was my reflection, but it *wasn't* my reflection. My face was mine, but it was somehow more youthful, firmer, and decidedly lovelier than I had ever remembered it being. As I stepped back, I noticed there were two other mirrors, one on each side wall of the room.

I looked first in one mirror, then the other, to see if perhaps the first mirror had been lying to me. The images I saw were identical. There was no question that I had never looked so enticing, so seductive. The slender woman in the mirrors smiled at me when I smiled, touched my cheek when

I touched my cheek, and was unable, even as I was unable, to find anything other than the slightest, almost invisible, line on her – *my* – face.

I kept turning from one mirror to another, back and forth again, for what must have been a very long time. Then, uncharacteristically, I burst into tears of joy, tears of thankfulness. What had been pent up inside me now came spilling out. Finally, Maria and Doctor Pinheiro entered the room quietly and unobtrusively. "Well?" António asked.

In my confusion and delight, in the realization that I had been handed my life and my youth back, I blurted out what was probably the stupidest and most insensitive remark I could have made at that moment. "Doctor António, you were right."

"How so?"

"My left breast really is larger than the other one."

"That may be so," he said, "but I've brought you a small gift that may help balance things out." He took a large volume from Maria and handed it to me – *The Guide for the Perplexed*.

I was so overwhelmed at that moment I didn't know what to say. Opening the cover, I saw an inscription that had been meticulously and carefully written:

"Maimonides said,

'The love of God is acquired when a person examines the world and feels overwhelmed by its grandeur and beauty.'

Now you, Grace, are part of that beauty,

And what greater proof is there that God exists

and that He is good?

With love, António and Maria"

And the tears began anew.

Chapter 15

I spent a part of the winter in Portugal. I enjoyed the university town of Coimbra, almost in the center of the country. The university, which had moved to Coimbra Castle from Lisboa twenty-five years before, perched high atop the city, seemed far different from other schools because it consisted of not one, but several colleges, not all of them run by religious orders. From Coimbra, I went to the valley of the Douro River, a great and beautiful wine-growing area in the north, where I spent many days reading, relaxing, and taking long walks through the hills above that lovely river.

My father came to fetch me in the early spring of 1563, just ahead of my thirty-third birthday. As a birthday gift – and, as he said, in celebration of my return to life – he surprised me with one of the most precious gifts I'd ever received, a well-used but serviceable caravel, that wonderful type of sailing vessel that originated in the school of Prince Henry the Navigator a hundred years ago. This ship, much smaller than the large and cumbersome galleys, ideally suited both my needs and my desires.

Seventy years earlier, the discovery of the new world by Cristobal Colon had proved the value of this new type of ship. The *Nina,* a caravel, had clearly been the best of his three ships. The *Nina* sailed so much faster than his flagship, the older and larger *Santa Maria*, that she constantly had to wait for the rest of the expedition. Although the *Santa Maria* had been wrecked, the *Nina* returned safely to Spain, through the worst storm in living memory, and crossed the Atlantic several times more. Her design had drawn on lessons learned from Arab dhows, which in turn had been inspired by contacts with the land of the Seres over the preceding several centuries.

I couldn't wait to sail back to Ireland in my caravel, which I immediately renamed the *Sea Ghost.* The sleek ship had two masts and lateen-rigged sails, a round, broad hull, and a high bow and stern, but it was not nearly as bulky as my other ships. The lateen sails fascinated me. They swiveled around the masts, ensuring not only that the caravel traveled faster than galleys, but also that it could make headway even in the presence of headwinds. Moreover, the use of the rudder at the stern post greatly increased its handling qualities.

My father had most considerately brought a large crew with him, so he spared fifteen men to accompany me back to Ireland. Although the *Sea Ghost* could easily have outpaced his galley, I hung back so it would not look like the daughter was challenging her father.

Just off Marazion, a three-masted pirate galley gave chase to my father's ship. Although neither he nor I worried about this, since we were within an hour of Newquay, it gave the *Sea Ghost* an opportunity to show her superiority in pursuit and encounter. So quickly did my caravel cover the distance between the invader and my da's galley that I slipped between the two ships before the intruder could fire on its prey. Our four cannon quickly sent a message to the alien that it would be far safer to move as quickly as it could into other waters.

"Ahoy! Have you bested me yet again?" came a call from the pirate ship.

"Indeed, Don Bosco," I shouted back. "That'll teach you to attack your betters!"

He bowed sweepingly. "Godspeed, Grace O'Malley. Imagine what we could do were we to work together!"

We arrived safely back in Clew Bay by the first of June, 1563, and surveyed not only my surroundings, but my family's position as well. The Black Oak still held the castles of Belclare and Clare Island. My brother Donal na-Piopa, had established himself at Cathair-na-Mart. It distressed me that the English had further encroached on Connaught. The O'Flahertys and even the Burkes had submitted to the Crown, but the O'Malleys still maintained their independence, since our clan had remained neutral during the Burke rebellion earlier that year.

With my father's protection, Clare Island soon became my stronghold, and from there, using the *Sea Ghost* as my most frequently-favored vessel, I freely engaged in maintenance by sea. Word filtered to me that my activities off the coast of western Ireland disturbed the English Earl of Sussex, Thomas Radclyffe.

Fortunately, Radclyffe had his own problems, which kept him from dealing with me. He had just returned to Armagh to renew his unsuccessful war with Shane O'Neill in Ulster. He had failed, both in open warfare and by attempting to procure The O'Neill's assassination. Thus, left relatively undisturbed, I continued to involve myself in the affairs of Connaught province.

Clare Island and Clew Bay afforded a natural protection for my ships, and the inaccessible nature of the area acted as a deterrent to would-be intruders or pursuers. My castle on Clare Island, very near my parents, perfectly suited my needs. I had an all-encompassing view of the wide expanse of water surrounding the island, while the castle itself could not be noticed by passing shipping from any great distance. A gray old tower, perched on a cliff, it hid a wide, lofty cavern, a perfect retreat for the *Sea Ghost* and its attendant galleys, beneath it. A slippery stairway led up one-hundred-twenty steps to the lowest level of my castle.

With Clare Island in my hands, I could monitor everything that went on within the bay. I watched ships en route north to Ulster and Scotland, or south to Munster and Spain. My crew either provided these vessels with pilot services, or we plundered them, whichever we considered appropriate at the time. As to those ships we boarded, we were reasonable in our demands – a good parasite never demands too much from its host – and we were careful not to shed blood, if possible, in order to avoid concerted government action against my operations.

Between the plundering of lucrative cargo, the levying of tolls in return for a safe passage through my demesne, and the provision of pilot service for foreign vessels on their way north, the success of my maritime activities more than satisfied the needs of our community and guaranteed my men's loyalty to me as their chief.

As 1563 gave way to 1564, I was reasonably content, and but for my continuing heartbreak over my complete estrangement from my son Murrough, now twelve, who had switched his allegiance to the English-vassal part of the O'Flaherty clan, my family remained close to me. Owen, although formally an O'Flaherty and now near seventeen and fully grown, searched for a suitable wife, as my Margaret, fifteen and ripe for handfasting, searched for an appropriate husband. My parents, now in their mid-sixties and still healthy, constituted a force to be reckoned with in all of Connaught.

Still, there was something missing. I had been without a man for nearly two years, and although my life was far from empty, I have found that it is a natural need not merely to copulate – although I cannot deny that such activity was not consummately pleasurable – but also to have someone with whom you can share your most intimate feelings, someone who can provide a sanctuary from the toils of the day and the disappointments of life. In short, someone to love and who is willing to return that love. And I'd not had such a love since Ballyclinch.

Such thoughts beset me on the first day of February in that year, when my followers and I had decided to make a pilgrimage to the holy well of Saint Brigid, located in a quiet corner at the northwest edge of Clare Island.

Brigid had never been dominated by any man. Although 'tis said she was more than passing beautiful, she refused to marry the suitor her father had chosen for her. She further vexed her father by being overly generous to the poor with his milk, butter, and flour. Finally, she gave away his jewel-encrusted sword to a leper. At this point he became quite comfortable with her decision never to marry and to take the veil. With seven other young women robed in white, she took her vows before Saint Mel of Armagh, the abbot and bishop of Longford. Alas, Saint Mel, a doddering old fellow and nearsighted as well, mistakenly consecrated Brigid a *bishop*.

When she sought land for her community, she asked the King of Leinster only for as much as her cloak would cover. The cloak miraculously spread over the whole of the Curragh.

At nineteen, in the year 470, Brigid founded a monastery at Cill-Dara, the church of the oak. Nuns and monks lived under the same roof. During her seventy-four years, she traveled by chariot throughout Ireland, converting Gaels to Christianity. It was said that she cured lepers, that she gave speech to the dumb, that she turned water into ale, and that she turned stone into salt. According to legend, twenty virgins tended a perpetual fire in Brigid's monastery, but she is best remembered because of her supposed visit to a dying pagan chieftain. While she prayed, she plaited rushes into a cross. The chieftain heard her account of the cross as a Christian symbol, and was converted and baptized before he died. It was still customary in my day to make pilgrimages and to plait Saint Brigid's Crosses, in the hope that they would protect the household in the year ahead.

Although I was never obedient to tradition simply for the purpose of being obedient, I saw no harm in accompanying my friends on pilgrimage, if for no other reason than to honor their beliefs. The stormy, dour day became even more uncomfortable, with a biting wind from the southeast, as we approached Saint Brigid's well.

I heard, or perhaps I imagined, a faint sound coming from the direction of Achill Island, some ten miles north. As I looked toward the sound, I saw what seemed to be a ship foundering off the coast. Accustomed to being vigilant in my demesne, I always kept a telescope near to hand. The law of the sea held that if a ship went down, its contents were the property of whoever salvaged them first.

A ship risked the storms so common in the late winter only if it could be assured of great rewards. Although the weather looked very threatening in the vicinity of Achill Island, my ships would be the first to make it over to that large island. And if, perchance, the ship had not sunk or run aground, it might still be ripe for assistance, mayhap even plunder.

I concluded my homage to Saint Brigid as quickly as courtesy allowed. Within half an hour, I had hurried back to my castle, rustled up a small crew, and set sail for Achill in the *Sea Ghost,* with one of my lieutenants trailing me in a galley. We sailed into the very teeth of a vicious gale. It took the better part of an hour for me to negotiate around the south coast of Achill Island. As we reached the southwest corner of the island, I beheld a large galley breaking up on the rocks.

Obviously, we were here first and we controlled the area around the rocks, which would guarantee us primary rights of salvage, but the law of the sea also provided we must search for, save, and assist any survivors before we plundered. The survivors were only five, and by using a longboat, we managed to get them aboard the *Sea Ghost* in a fairly short time.

The gale did not let up, but we entered a very small bay, which was protected from the force of the storm, and which was near enough to land that I called out to the oarsmen that I would go on shore and search for anyone else I might find. During the next hour, I slowly walked along every crevice, crevasse, and declivity of that bay, looking for signs of human life. I found ten bodies, all men, and all dead. There was nothing more I could do for them.

When I had reached the far end of the cove, I stood at the edge of a tiny peninsula. To my left, the waters of the bay were relatively calm. To my right, the sea pounded furiously against the rocks, the spume often rising higher than my castle on Clare Island. I heard faraway shouts from the men in the longboat, urging me to get off that peninsula and return to the safety of where they were berthed. I turned to go back. At that moment, I heard a soft moaning sound coming from the direction of the ocean-facing rocks.

I looked back toward to where the strange sound was emanating and saw there was a minute shelf of flat rock less than three feet above the surf. I beheld what looked like a dark-gray being – fish, whale, monster, I knew not what. I edged closer to the ledge very carefully and the moan became weaker. It would be another five feet before I reached a point where I could see what animal was making the unutterably forlorn sound.

Unaware of the precariousness of my footing, I slipped and fell, and started rolling toward the rocky end of the peninsula. Although my knees and arms were scraped and bleeding, I somehow managed to make purchase, just before I came to the end of the rocky outcroppings. From this point, it would be easier to see what beast or being was most probably dying on the ledge below.

I looked over the edge of the rock, toward the shelf, and in that moment, I felt weak, nauseous, and utterly helpless. I could not speak a word, so shocked and dizzy was I from what I saw. It couldn't possibly be, not in a million, million years. With the last of my strength, I raised my head again and forced myself to peer over the rock. I knew either that I was seeing an apparition or that I had gone utterly crazy. Nothing in the world could possibly have prepared me for this, but as I raised my head and looked down a third time, I was utterly convinced this was not a figment of my imagination.

I was looking into a face that was gray and barely alive. It was Ballyclinch.

Chapter 16

Despite the whirlwind of feelings coursing through me, I somehow made my way back to where the coracle's crew was waiting. I told them I had found one survivor alive, but only Christ knew for how long, and that we must make haste to help him. I did not mention to anyone that I knew the identity of the survivor as well as I knew my own heart.

The three crewmen, all larger and stronger than I, lifted the survivor from his ledge-trap and gently brought him around the cove to where the longboat was anchored. I said not a word on the trip back to the *Sea Ghost*, but merely stared at the semiconscious man. For the first several minutes, while we were still in the bay, my heart pounded so hard that I feared, much as I knew how senseless this sounded, even to me, that my three crewmen could certainly hear it beating.

As I slowly calmed down, I realized this was not Ballyclinch. After all, the last time I saw him... I willed myself not to think of that heart-shattering time. Although he was lying prone in the bottom of the coracle, I saw that unlike Ballyclinch, he was a good half-foot taller than me, and where my Ballyclinch's hair had been dark, this man's hair was sand-colored. While his face bore a striking resemblance to Ballyclinch, he was younger than me, whereas Ballyclinch had been older. This man looked no more than twenty-eight.

By the time we reached the *Sea Ghost*, the storm had passed. The caravel's winch lifted the longboat with ease, and crewmen, at my direction, carefully carried the injured man to my cabin and laid him out on my bunk. By nightfall, the stranger was ensconced in a bedroom in my castle.

Over the next several days, I spoon-fed the man warm broth, which I had cooked myself. I baked fresh bread and made sure it was thickly spread with newly-churned sweet butter from our creamery. I changed his linen and buzzed about him like an overprotective mother. Ballyclinch had been taken from me once. I would not let 'him' be taken from me again.

I was almost giddy with happiness when he first opened his eyes, a pale blue in contrast to Ballyclinch's rich, dark brown color, and mumbled his first words. He spoke in a dialect I couldn't understand. When he saw that I could not fathom a word, he switched effortlessly to Gaelic. I recognized his accent was Scottish.

"Have I died and gone to heaven, Lady?" he asked.

I felt a flush creep from my chest to the top of my head. "Nay. You are in the west of Ireland – on Clare Island."

"South of Achill, then?"

"Aye."

"I remember a sudden horrid storm as we rounded Achill Head. The last thing I remember is screaming and prayers."

I thought it best not to mention that his ship had foundered and broken up on the rocks southeast of Achill Head and there had been only five survivors, all of whom had been taken to Kildawnet Castle at the southeastern end of Achill Island.

"I'm called Hugh de Lacy," he said. He was not my Ballyclinch. My Ballyclinch was really, truly dead and buried, as I knew deep in my heart that he had been. But this man, who could easily have been a taller, younger version of my lost love, was now quite alive.

"From whence hail you?"

"Glasgow."

"You're no friend of the English, then?"

"Not hardly."

"I'm Granuaile – Grace O'Malley."

"The female pirate?"

"You've heard of me?"

"Aye, it's said you control all of Clew Bay and its surroundings. But no one told me you were so attractive."

"Oh?" I changed the subject very quickly. "Would you like me to stoke the fire, Mister de Lacy?"

"That would be kind of you." The activity gave me something to take my mind off the fact that my legs felt disconnected from my body and my forehead felt as though it was perspiring profusely. "More tea?"

"No, thank you. Are you married, Grace?"

"Widowed. You?"

"Not married and never have been. My brother and I live in Glasgow when I'm not a'sea."

"A girl in every port?"

"No."

There was a distinct buzzing in my head. I'd not felt this aroused since that first night with Richard-an-Iarrain Burke, eighteen years ago. "How old are you, Hugh deLacy?"

"Twenty-six."

"I've cooked up some fine Irish stew for you, if you'd like."

"Aye, that I would, Grace O'Malley. I believe I'll be needing all my strength in the next days."

I was thrilled, not only by the words, but by the promise in Hugh deLacy's eyes when he said those words, and I imagined what it would be like when... and we both knew that there was no question of "if", but rather a question of "when."

The next few days raced by. I found myself dressing in the Portuguese skirt, sash, and low-cut blouse that Maria had purchased for me in Portugal, and I made certain to bathe daily, something I wasn't used to doing on the high seas. I even touched the area between my legs and dabbed my own scent behind my ears and between my breasts. 'Tis said that a woman's very personal scent is the most sexually enticing to a man.

During the next days, Hugh deLacy's eyes followed my every move, particularly when I bent over to feed him. One afternoon, I made sure my castle was empty but for Hugh and me. As I reached over to serve him a cup of ale, my breasts brushed against his hand. That was all the encouragement he needed, and certainly all the encouragement *I* needed. He pulled me over to him. Our first kiss was everything I thought it would be, and more. A moment later, he moved his hand to my breasts. I couldn't shed my blouse fast enough. The last two years evaporated in the maelstrom of our passion.

The first time did not take long, and when it was over, we were both trembling from head to foot. It was as if Ballyclinch and Iron Dick Burke had merged into one, Ballyclinch's tenderness and Richard's thrusting strength, and it was more satisfying than either of them singly. We could not have slept for more than an hour when I awoke, reached down, and within moments we came together again. It was just as wonderful the second time, and the third. We collapsed in each other's arms, and by the time the sun came up the next morning, we had made love twice more, each one better than the last. For the next several days, our passion continued unabated.

"It seems you certainly got your strength sufficiently back, Hugh deLacy," I teased.

"Aye, Grace O'Malley. And you are so much woman, you would entice a stone to turn hot or a sponge to become hard," he said, grinning.

"So what do we do with the rest of out lives?"

"I cannot think that far ahead, but I know one thing: there'll never be another woman like you in my life."

"Ah," I said, with just a touch of melancholy. "But when you are at your very peak, thirty-five or so, I'll be well into my forties, and you'd probably want to trade me for two twenty-year-olds."

"I very much doubt that, Grace."

"Stay with me, then."

"Aye, with pleasure – with *more* than pleasure, actually," he said. "But I would like to ride to Kildawnet to see how my companions are doing."

"Returning to Scotland?"

"Nay, my love, you've no worry about that. It'll simply give us both some time to realize how unbelievably perfect we are together, and make us more anxious than ever to continue where we left off."

"You're sure you'll be safe on Achill Island?"

"I'll stay as far inland as possible."

I reached into a nearby closet and brought out a beautiful bow and a quiver of arrows. "Bring me a deer when you return. I'll make us venison stew, and then..."

Words were a burden, and for the next several minutes we did not let them burden us.

Next morning, a brisk mid-March day, the sea between Clare Island and Achill was almost as calm as a lake. I gathered a crew of four. Hugh deLacy and I boarded a coracle for the fifteen minute ride to landfall at Achill. As we parted, we were singularly proper toward one another. I told him I'd return and meet him at Kildawnet two days hence, and we both promised each other a taste of the heavenly delights we would share when he came home.

During those two days, my mind was in turmoil. What if he really decided to go back to Scotland? What if he wanted to go a'sea? As I well knew, the ocean could be a never-ending siren song, which called to mariners throughout their lives. It did not concern me that he might fall for another woman. I was certain he'd never find another woman as attuned to him as I.

On the morning of the third day, I hungered for Hugh deLacy's strong arms and his body more than for food. As the sky lightened, I navigated the passage between the two islands. By the time the sun burst through the clouds, I'd piloted my coracle to Kildawnet Castle. I waited impatiently for the time Hugh had promised he'd be at the dock. An hour passed, two, and still no sign of my lover. After another half hour, I climbed onto the dock and impatiently approached the castle gate.

"Who comes?" This from the sentry.

"Granuaile ni-Mhaille. I'm looking for Hugh deLacy."

"He went out hunting in the hills yesterday morning. He has not yet returned."

"But he promised..." For the first time, I felt panic rising within me.

"He was to have returned yesterday afternoon, M'Lady."

"Did he leave word with anyone?"

"He did not. If he would have, I'd have been the first to know."

While we were talking, a man on horseback thundered up to the castle keep. Both man and beast were breathing rapidly.

"G-Guard!" he stammered. "I must speak with the rest of the survivors immediately!"

"What news?"

"It's Hugh deLacy. The McMahons, who claimed he was poaching on their land, seized him in a neutral glade last evening. They murdered him without trial."

My agonized scream must have been heard as far away as Clare Island. Then, mercifully, I fainted.

Chapter 17

The Little People had taken my Ballyclinch from me, and there had been nothing I could do about it. Edmund O'Flaherty had given me vengeance of a sort, through what trickery I never found. But the McMahons were not Little People. They were human beings, neither stronger nor smarter than I, and they could be killed the way human beings had killed one another from time immemorial: create a large enough hole in their bodies and they would expire. The McMahons had brutally murdered my Hugh, without cause and without shame, and now a lesson must be taught.

For the better part of a week, I was consumed by unbridled fury. But I knew from my own experience that one fights at the greatest risk when one is so aflame that all danger and reason is ignored. After the first week, I concluded that killing one McMahon or a dozen, or even a hundred, would do nothing more than prove I was as brutal as they. No, the McMahons would have to suffer in a more meaningful way.

The next large body of water north of Clew Bay, abutted by Achill Island on the south and Erris Head to the north, was Blacksod Bay, and at that Bay's eastern extremity, where it joined the Irish mainland, was the spiritual and functional headquarters of the McMahon Clan – Doona Castle. It would benefit me not at all to annihilate McMahon men, women, and children. It would be spiteful, vengeful, and beneath my station to do so. The McMahons must be humiliated.

My crew and I took shelter that night at Kildawnet Castle, a huge, square, dour, and consummately bleak monolith where I'd learned of Hugh's untimely death. I had learned early on that one's survival often depends on not underestimating an enemy – any enemy. While the O'Malleys controlled Kildawnet, the McMahons commanded the entire land area surrounding the castle.

Our assault on the McMahon stronghold at Doona called for a bold strategy. On the face of it, there was no way we could surprise the McMahon naval forces from the sea. Doona Castle commanded an unparalleled view of both Blacksod and Bellacagher Bays. The route from the sea was disadvantageous. The only other water route was via the narrow strait from Kildawnet north into Bellacagher. That would be equally unavailing, since it would take only two McMahon ships to blockade the neck where the strait joined the Bay.

The lay of the terrain ruled out an assault on Doona from the water. Our allies, the Burkes, and our own O'Malleys maintained a huge presence south and east of McMahon country, but the Nephin Mountains effectively guarded Doona against a land attack. An immediate attack on Doona appeared out of the question. I would have to ponder the matter more carefully.

During the next weeks, I positioned several O'Malleys at strategic points around Doona Castle – close enough that they could seek out any weak links in the defense perimeters of the fortress, yet far enough distant, in various hills, valleys, and crevasses, that they could not easily be seen. I had selected my spies carefully. They had to blend in with the landscape, so even had they been seen, none would be memorable. All my men wore gray tunics and buckskin jerkins, with no jewelry or adornments of any kind, so they were indistinguishable from any local peasants. To complete the charade, some would masquerade as shepherds, others as ploughmen, still others as cattle drovers.

Their reports painted a fairly complete picture of Doona's layout and its security measures. "We've heard nothing but talk of an O'Malley raid," one of my men said. "They're saying there's no telling when ye'll attack, but they've no doubt you'll do so before winter."

Another said, "Some of the McMahons are talking about suing for peace, but the vast majority feel that would be humiliating, since that would amount to sanctioning a poacher on their land."

"Oh, so?" I said, arching my eyebrows. "What are their defenses like?"

One of the younger and brighter of my forces, a man who'd served with distinction aboard one of my galleys, sat on a flat plot of ground, which he scraped clean with a stick. Then he started to draw figures in the earth. First, he placed a large "X" to denote Doona castle. Instead of a moat surrounding the fortress, there was a sturdy, gray eight-foot high stone wall that encircled the keep. There were two breaks in the wall. The perimeter of the wall ranged from one hundred to three hundred feet from the castle, depending on the distance from Blacksod Bay to the west.

The field inside the wall was devoid of trees, which would enable the inhabitants of the fortress to have a clear, unobstructed view in every direction. The fields leading to the wall were divided by wooden fences, which bisected the land surrounding Doona into two equal half-circle segments.

The McMahons, like most of us in Western Ireland, measured wealth by the number of sheep or cattle controlled by the clan. Cattle stealing had been a way of life in Ireland since time out of mind. Indeed, the great epic of our land was *The Cattle Raid of Cooley*. Queen Maeve and Coohoolain were as real to us as neighbors just over the hill. Cattle or sheep raids in broad daylight were not nearly as common as night raids. Thus, the McMahons, the O'Malleys, the Burkes, and virtually every clan in Connaught, functioned in much the same way: a few shepherds or drovers remained with their charges during the day. Some of these were slackards and most were downright lazy, since the job was the most boring one imaginable, and since there were always two or three dogs that did the *real* work of keeping the sheep in line.

Shortly before sunset, the dogs, shepherds, and drovers would round up the sheep and beeves and herd them through the gates in the wall. The cattle would pass through one gate, and the sheep through the other. Since cattle and sheep are not boon companions, each felt more at ease on opposing sides of the wooden fences. The shepherds and drovers would count the number of their charges each night, to ensure that none had been stolen. By that time of the day, the sun was just about to set, the shepherds or drovers were weary, though God knows why, from their supposedly exhausting work in the fields, and the cattle and sheep, eager to get to their nighttime pastures, bunched up at the gates.

"With all that confusion," the earth-artist said, "the herders usually sit as far back from the gates as they can, to avoid the smell and the noise. They let the dogs do the work, and they figure they can both count and nip some whiskey at the same time."

"How do they count the animals?" I asked.

"They estimate," the man replied. "It's comical to watch them. They'll sit together drinking. Every so often, one of them will look up and say to the others, 'I'd say there were twenty just went through the gate,' and another would respond, 'Seems right to me.'"

"It's a wonder they don't lose half their livestock," I said, archly. "What happens afterward?"

"There's a second, outer perimeter wall," another man, a graybeard, said. "There are huts and cottages between the first and second wall. That's where most of the Doona McMahons live. The McMahons have more than a hundred troops between the walls to protect the castle. Anyone approaching has to navigate through two sets of stone walls. Given the setup, it's almost impossible to breach both sets of walls."

"Almost..." I mused, smiling. "How many head of sheep and cattle do the McMahons keep at Doona?"

"I'd say two hundred of each, plus another sixty lambs and a like number of calves."

"How many McMahons live in the castle itself?"

"No more than twenty-four, M'lady." This from a graybeard.

"What are you thinking, Granuaile?" one of my most trusted senior lieutenants asked. "I've seen that half-smile before."

"Oh, nothing, nothing," I replied. "By the way, have you ever heard of a sailor named Odysseus?"

"Can't say I have. Is he from around these parts?"

"No, neither these parts nor these times."

When I confided my plan to Richard an Iarrain, who had become one of my closest friends as well as my sometime lover, he whistled appreciatively. "You'd have made one hell of a general!" he exclaimed.

"I've got two perfect little girls for the deception. I need forty soldiers."

"I'll find them from the Burkes and the Conroys. "All of 'em, would have to be well-hidden during the day. When will you put them in place?"

"No more than an hour before the roundup."

"Anything else you'll need, Grace?"

"Yes, half a dozen kegs of whiskey to make sure our McMahon friends are happy and well-nourished when they've completed their day's work."

"Clever girl," he said, squeezing my arm. "Anything else you need?"

"Burke land is far enough away from McMahon country," I said. "I'd need a fortnight to train my forces and I'd like to do it here."

"Your wish is my command," he said, bowing gracefully. "Ye'll spend the night, then?" he asked, grinning.

"Aye. No reason my soldiers should have all the fun."

Within a week, my loving friend proved to be as good as his word. He'd gathered forty men, all relatively small and able to blend into the landscape. None weighed more than eight-and-a-half stone. All were thin, wiry, and fit. The oldest of them was in his early twenties.

The little girls were no more than nine years old, small for their ages, but very bright. They reminded me of myself when I'd first gone to sea. It took almost no time at all to teach them what we wanted them to do. Richard an Iarrain selected two large wethers – castrated male sheep. "Much more docile than rams and, unlike ewes, they're not constantly eyeing the rams. They'll be perfect for our needs. The shearing season was long gone, and the sheep were well into their thick winter growth. After we'd chosen the wethers, we shaved their bellies and fashioned the shavings into woolen patches, which we tied to the children's backs and sides.

Next, we bound the girls, stomachs up, to the underbellies of the sheep by means of stout leather straps. Each girl wore a belt, which housed a scabbarded short sword on one side, and each carried a small cutting knife, to slit the leather straps when the time came. The sheep's' long fleece hung well below their bellies, making it impossible to see them, even had they not been wearing the woolen patches on their backs and sides. If anyone, shepherd or drover, were to place their hands below the sheep, they would feel nothing but greasy wool.

For the next few days, we practiced tying the girls to the sheep for lengthening periods of time. By the fourth day each was so used to the other they could easily accept the closeness of one to the other for two hours – much more than the time we'd need.

Next, we taught the sheep and the girls to travel a short distance, then longer distances, bound to one another. Then, we let the sheep run with the flock, so they would get used to being among their own kind while bearing their new "growths."

"They look very natural, and they don't seem to notice the extra weight they're carrying," Dick remarked on the fourteenth day. "How are you going to infiltrate them into the McMahon herds?"

"Two days hence, five or six Burkes, who're not at war with the McMahons, will drive forty sheep south, heading for *booley*. They'll ask permission of the McMahon shepherds to cross the land. In the process the sheep will become mixed up, dumb animals that they are, and when the Burkes leave McMahon land, they'll have the same number of sheep, but *different* sheep than when they started. Our wethers, carrying their 'baggage,' will be right at home among the McMahon herds, and when they're driven home to Doona at night..."

Two hours before sunset, five Burke men approached the shepherd. "We're beholden to you for allowing us to travel over McMahon land, my friend," one of the Burkes said. "I promise we won't tarry long and we'll make sure they won't graze your land any more than necessary."

"'Tis not a problem, 'tis an honor. Ye'll put in a good word with The MacWilliam?"

"Aye, we'll certainly do that, but my boys have somethin' more fittin' than a good word," the Burke man said. He reached into a cart and pulled out three small kegs.

"A bit of whiskey, is it?" The shepherd's eyes brightened in anticipation.

"Aye, Burke's best," he said, handing one keg to his McMahon counterpart and placing the two remaining gifts at the other man's feet.

"Go in peace, and the Saints bless Ye," the McMahon shepherd replied.

Just before sunset, the Burkes traversed the last narrow strip of McMahon land. Before they crossed onto their own land, they made sure to present another highly appreciative McMahon shepherd with three more kegs of whiskey.

Come sunset, the shepherds met at one gate, the drovers at the other, as the dogs herded their charges into the inner fields around Doona Castle. The McMahon shepherds, garrulous in anticipation of a lubricious early evening, counted the flock in a desultory manner. Unknown to the Burke shepherds, unknown to our O'Malley soldiers situated a few miles south, and unknown to any but Richard an Iarrain Burke, there were not forty soldiers but forty-*one* invaders, one of them a woman, who had managed during the day to slowly infiltrate themselves between the outer and inner perimeter walls, and who were now ensconced in narrow trenches at the foot of the closest wall to the castle. Thus it was that I was able to hear the shepherds as our wethers passed close to them.

"Generous people, those Burkes."

"Aye, ye can well afford to be when ye're the rulers of Connaught."

"May not be for long. They say the Burkes have submitted to the English."

"Nahhh, 'twould never happen."

"Has happened," said high-pitched voice, obviously belonging to a young man. "My da said he saw Shane MacOliverus, The MacWilliam himself, speaking with Sir Henry Sidney, the newly-arrived English lord deputy of Ireland, and they seemed quite friendly."

I stiffened involuntarily for an instant, then relaxed. There'd be time to speak with Iron Dick about this later. Surely his clan wouldn't... But I had other things to think of at that moment. As the flock entered more confined quarters, their noisy bawling and bahh-ing made it impossible for me to hear anything else the shepherds were saying.

After the sheep passed through the gate and found themselves in the far more spacious inner field, they relaxed. When the last of them had entered the field, I heard the gate clank shut, with the solid sound of heavy metal banging against stone. A moment later, I heard bars sliding into place. As night fell, it was apparent that no one was going to get into or out of the inner perimeter walls until the morning. The castle was as secure as the McMahons wanted it to be.

They hadn't reckoned on us.

When half an hour had passed, it was completely dark, but for the light radiating from Doona Castle and from the smoky fires of the huts and hovels, the cottages and public houses outside the walls. The noise emanating from the latter covered any sounds we would have made, but the little girls had been trained to be silent. We would assemble just outside the castle as soon as we could safely do so without being seen or heard.

So it was planned, and so it happened. All of us were aware it would not be long before our wethers would lie down and rummage around on the ground, so we had to make sure not too much time passed before we extracted ourselves. At the same time, the girls could not escape from the wethers too quickly, for these were not small animals, and the drop, even from a height of only two or three feet, could injure them were they to fall back-first onto rocks. Shortly, the girls cut themselves loose and, as quietly as we had taught them, they tiptoed to the closest gate, where the two soldiers, who had been charged to help them open it, were waiting. More silently than any of them, I scurried behind them to the gate. Even in the dark, I could see my men's eyes grow wide when they saw I was there. They'd been told only that they'd meet the leader at the castle gate, and would be given further instructions at that time.

Although they were surprised, I slowly moved my right hand, palm down, so they'd know to be silent. I spoke to them in a low voice, knowing that a whisper would carry much farther than if I kept my tone conversational. "Those inside the castle know that absolutely no one except their own could get inside the inner wall. Thus, if we bang on the door, they'll believe it's one of their men. We needn't make a loud noise. One of the servants or a keeper of the keys is bound to be close to the entry."

When the door was opened, we overcame the man who opened it, and we quickly dispatched the two dozen inhabitants of the castle and sent them to their Maker.

Next morning, the McMahon forces awoke to a bizarre and unexpected sight. My hen flag and the O'Malley pennant fluttered from the top of the castle tower. The two gates to the inner courtyard remained sealed. When the McMahon soldiers tried to enter, they heard a loud tattoo from outside the *second* wall as a huge force of O'Malleys, McNallys, Conroys, and Burkes erupted into the area between the first and second walls. So surprised were the McMahons that they did not resist when Richard an Iarrain called out to them to throw down their arms and evacuate the area. 'Twas thus that I avenged the murder of Hugh deLacy. 'Twas also thus that I attained another castle of my own, as well as yet another name, for thenceforth the McMahons referred to me as "The Dark Lady of Doona."

My demesne now ranged from all but the northeastern side of Clew Bay in the south to Blacksod Bay in the north, and it was staunchly, fiercely Irish. If the English thought they would easily conquer the west of Ireland, they had not reckoned they'd have to deal with me.

Chapter 18

By the beginning of 1566, when I was not yet thirty-six years old, the only territory around Clew Bay *not* held by the O'Malleys was the northeastern corner. That fact had not gone unnoticed by me, and I realized that if I were to consolidate my power base, I'd need a more inland fortress and safe harbor, Carraigahawley – Rockfleet Castle – at that time owned by none other than Richard-an-Iarrain, Iron Dick Burke.

Dick had been my first lover. We'd always been the closest of friends, and from time to time, we'd continued to share our bodies as well, for two decades, more than half my life. There was no question we were more than compatible with one another in every way. Each of us had scaled not one but several pinnacles in our lives, and I realized that when all was said and done, perhaps he'd been the true dominant love of my life, more steady and certainly-longer lasting than either Ballyclinch or Hugh deLacy. Plus, unlike the others, he was still alive, and, at the moment, he was a widower and available.

I was still widowed and there was no one else of interest on my horizon. As January became February, I thought more and more about the advantages of such an alliance – a marriage

– with Dick Burke. Richard was prominent and powerful, chief of the Burkes of Carra and Burrishoole. With good fortune, he might one day become the *tanaiste*, the heir apparent, to the title "The MacWilliam Iochtar," head chieftain of all the Burkes of Connaught, which meant the ruler of the largest and strongest clan in the entire province. The MacWilliamship was, at that time, held by Shane MacOliverus.

I was every bit Richard's equal, for I had amassed my own reputation as the pirate queen of western Ireland. Both of us were successful and independent. Unlike my marriage to Donal-an-Chodaigh, a marriage to Richard would be far less antagonistic and far less competitive. Richard was as secure in his position as I was in mine. We did not have to prove anything to one another, nor did we have to compete for the attention and adoration of our minions. I was no longer a flighty young girl. This time it would be different.

As I planned my campaign, I discovered this would not be the first O'Malley – Burke marriage. In the fifteenth century one of my ancestors, also named Grace, had married one Thomas Burke. I'd even seen a silver gilt chalice that had been given by Thomas and Grace to the Burrishoole Abbey in 1494.

One evening, late in February, I visited Richard-an-Iarrain at Rockfleet Castle. I have since seen numerous palaces with grandiose and embellished towers, turrets, and crenellated walls. Rockfleet would never compete with any of these. It was squat, stark, dour, and plain, built to withstand the largest force that could be mustered in these parts. The tower castle was built entirely of brick and rock, a bleak, square structure with narrow peepholes rather than windows. It sat on a rocky outcrop, far above the surrounding valley, overlooking – commanding –

Clew Bay. The roof was steeply pitched and there was a tall chimney protruding from the top rampart. Unlike Doona, there were no perimeter walls, no pastureland, and no moat surrounding the castle. It was, from the outside, as stern and forbidding a structure as existed anywhere in Connaught.

From my many visits to Carraigahawley in the past, I knew that the harsh exterior masked a comfortable, if boldly masculine, interior. There were four floors in the building, each ten feet high from floor to ceiling. Its furniture was heavy rather than graceful, but, like the castle itself, conveyed a feeling of robust strength. One could find candles and oil-lit lamps everywhere, and servants ensured that the place was both clean and well-lit day and night.

"Ah, Granuaile," Richard greeted me warmly, folding me in his strong arms. "To what do I owe this latest visit? D'you need men for an army, a guard as you ply the seas?"

"Oh, come on, Dick," I said saucily. "I don't come a'visitin' only when I need your help. On second thought, it seems the last few years have been that way, doesn't it?"

He patted my rump companionably. "And I thought you made those trips to Rockfleet just because you wanted my body."

"Aye, that, too," I shot back. "Of course, I've never heard you complainin' much, Iron Dick."

"You give as well as you receive, and I must say, Grace, you're much more of a woman than ye were when first we met."

"Two decades, Dick. Are you going to stand there pawing me in the entry hall, or are you going to invite me in?"

Dinner was Spartan, but filling, dark bread, thick stew, mutton, carrots, onions, and turnips. "Dick, every time I've visited, I've eaten this, or something similar."

"That's pretty much what I eat every day and night."

"The bachelor's life?"

"Aye. The cook certainly isn't very imaginative."

"Seems like you need a good woman, my friend."

Later that evening, after we'd done what we did so well over the years, and which left both of us sated, spent, and immensely satisfied, I sat up, well aware that his eyes were glued to my breasts. "That was lovely, wasn't it?"

"Wonderful."

"Ever thought of making it permanent?"

"What do you mean?"

"Settling down. You're forty-three and a widower, Dick. At that age, many men have had their fill of wenches and such. You never remarried?"

"Haven't found the right woman."

"How d'you know that? Every man's capable of finding the right woman."

"Mayhap, but it's a woman's way to tie a man in knots, make him a prisoner of the home, and nag when he leaves. Once a cow has roped her bull, that's all the sex he'll see for awhile."

I reached over and gently rubbed the hair on his chest. "Doesn't have to be that way if the woman's 'her own man,' so to speak."

"What are you getting at?"

"Well, take you and me. Supposing – and I'm just saying 'supposing' – you and I were to tie the knot. You wouldn't expect me to be a homebody and I wouldn't expect you to stay at home and coddle me every night. Besides, have you ever wondered what kind of a baby we'd produce?"

Richard reacted differently than I thought he would. No loud protests – and no romantic protestations of love either.

More of a thoughtful silence, as if he were analyzing and considering the advantages and disadvantages of such a match. After a while, he said, "You'd expect me to be completely faithful to our marriage bed?"

I laughed. "For the most part. At least for as long as we were married."

"That's what I like about you, Grace. None of this 'promise me you'll love me now and forever' stuff."

"Dick, we're not children anymore, even though you were my first man. I'm a widow, you know about Ballyclinch and Hugh deLacy. There've been others."

"I'm not even going to ask if I'm the best," he chuckled.

"If it'll make you feel like more of a man, you're pretty damned high on the ladder."

"If it'll make *you* feel better, you *are* at the very top of the ladder."

"As long as I'm beneath you," I teased. "Well?"

"I can't say it isn't an inviting thought. Politically it would be good for both of us, and I can't deny we're well-matched in every other way I can think of."

Chapter 19

Richard and I married at Rockfleet Castle in March of 1566, two weeks shy of my thirty-sixth birthday. It was a small wedding party, since neither of us was in the first blush of youth.

For the first month after our wedding, I took stock of my new home at Rockfleet. It may not have been spectacular – truth to tell, it was not even attractive – from the outside. Once inside, a spiral stone staircase wound past the lower levels to the main living area on the fourth floor. The ground floor was earthen. The second and third floors were made of timber, and a concave stone ceiling separated the third and fourth levels. The fourth level had a flagstone floor, which made it completely separate from the first three levels.

The main room on the fourth floor was a large living room, twenty feet long by twenty wide, and ten feet from floor to ceiling. Its focal point was a large, arched fireplace on the west wall. There were two *hobs* – stone seats – on either side of the fireplace. To the right of the fireplace, a small, oblong slit window allowed the light from the west to penetrate and light up the near corner of the chamber. To the left of the fireplace, an arched doorway led to the main stairway. There were additional slit windows on each wall. Within a fortnight after we'd married, I prevailed upon Dick to have masons construct a loophole in the south wall of our bedchamber.

"Why would you want such a thing, Granuaile," my strong but complacent husband asked.

"Security," I said, and offered no further explanation.

When he saw the use to which I put the loophole, he guffawed loudly. "Seems to me you love the *Sea Ghost* more than you love me."

"Mayhap, mayhap not," I teased. "Granted, you keep me much warmer in the kip than the caravel, but it's brought me great good fortune and I want to make sure it continues to do so."

I thought my contrivance was quite clever. The *Sea Ghost's* hawser, that cable used in mooring the vessel, was run and attached to our bedpost each night as a precaution, lest someone make the foolhardy mistake of trying to relieve me of the caravel. This device served the double duty of enabling my men to communicate an alarm directly to my quarters in case of a surprise attack.

From our living quarters, a further flight of stairs led to the ramparts above. On the east wall of the fourth floor, we'd installed an arched doorway, which led to a sheer fifty foot drop to the rocks below. This, too, had more than one purpose. If an attacker somehow made it to the fourth floor, Richard and I could either escape through the drop-off to a secret balcony, or, more likely, we could help an invader out the door and to his death or, at the very least, serious injury, on the sharp rocks below. During my tenure at Rockfleet, we never had such an attack, but we certainly did engage the doorway for a more practical purpose. We used it as a loading bay, through which we hoisted heavy and bulky goods from ground level by means of multiple pulleys.

The south side of the castle was built for our own comfort and cleanliness. It housed a tiny alcove, which contained a stone privy with a direct outlet to the tide of Clew Bay – a simple but ingenious feat of plumbing.

The view from the west window and from the ramparts was magnificent. Even more to my liking, no vessel could enter the inlet off Clew Bay without my observing it from the safety of my new home. For this reason, more than any other, I enjoyed Carraigahawley far better than my former residence on Clare Island.

This was a time when England was more and more incursing into Connaught, and even more into Mayo. While Rockfleet Castle was protected by its hidden inlet, much as my former home at Bunowen had been protected from the sea by *its* hidden inlet, Clare Island, where I'd harbored my ships for the past two years, was exposed. I had often feared my ships would be at the mercy of the English should Sir Henry Sidney, England's Lord Deputy, send a war fleet large enough to savage my small fleet of four galleys and a caravel.

In June, 1566, Richard left Rockfleet for the first time since our marriage, on some Burke business or other. I actually looked forward to a brief respite from my husband, for while I dearly loved Dick, being with him every day for more than two months had exhausted me. Unlike Donal-an-Chodaigh, who'd been a tentative lover at first, and boringly uncaring afterward, Iron Dick Burke's passion was rekindled every night he and I came together, which meant almost every night, except when I had my *menstruus*.

Dick was gone until the beginning of July. By that time, even before I'd missed my monthly curse, I was quite sure I was with child, Perhaps it was because of the nesting urge that I made many changes to Rockfleet during the month Richard-an-Iarrain was gone, softening what had been the masculinity of the place before I'd become mistress of the castle. I covered the stone walls and floors with sheepskins, tapestries, and huge, colorful carpets, many of them from the Ottoman Empire. I kept a peat fire burning in every fireplace where we lived, so that the fire suffused every place on that floor.

I quickly filled previously unused corners with my own implements, as well as with exotic spices, spoils, and the treasures of my trade. I brought in crockery, cookware, and such, from Clare Island. Within two weeks after Richard had departed, I installed my own furniture, which I'd shipped over from Clare Island.

"Quite the homebody, are you?" Richard asked, his eyes alight.

"Just makin' things more comfortable while my husband was away."

"Aye, that has a nice ring to it."

"What, you being away?"

"No, you goose," he said, swatting at my bottom.

"Careful, darlin'. You may hurt someone else..."

With a whoop, Richard picked me up bodily and swung me around. Later, after we'd celebrated his homecoming in a more meaningful way, Richard put his arms around me and gently stroked my breasts. "Why didn't you tell me sooner?"

"Seems to me I could have, had you been anywhere nearby. Who knows where ye've been gallivanting around to this past month, or whom ye've been gallivanting around with?"

"Shameless woman," he said, but softly and happily, as his fingertips gently traced circles around my nipples. "Ye're not worried I'd stray, are ye?"

"Dick, if the first month of our marriage was any harbinger of things to come, it might have given me a chance to get my strength back if you did have some ladies on the side," I said, fondling him in his most personal place. "I imagine had we been married from the first, I'd have had a dozen babies by now and been completely worn out. What kind of business were you on?"

"More troubles over the English submit and regrant policy. I fear it's become more submit and less regrant nowadays."

"And the Burkes? How do they stand on the question?"

Richard rose from the bed, stoked the fire in the fireplace, and wrapped himself in a thick Turkish robe, a gift I'd had ready for him when he returned. "Like all the other clans in Connaught. Half of 'em are fiercely independent and the other half seem to know it's only a matter of time before the English take over anyway. God knows they've got the money, the army, and the ships. I think God also knows *they* believe they've got God on their side."

"How do *you* feel, Richard?"

"Cautious."

"Because you want The MacWilliamship?" I meant no malice by the remark, but I saw my husband's face and neck flush red. "That's not a secret, Richard-an-Iarrain. They say you're favored to be the *tanaiste*, and Shane MacOliverus won't last forever."

"How do *you* stand, Granuaile ni-Mhaille-Burke?"

"Careful I suppose, just like you. We have to live on this island, and as a sailor I, if anyone, should know that before I start a voyage, it's best to find out which way the winds are blowin'."

And the winds did blow, and they were fair trade winds, and by September I was a'sea again. On my first voyage beyond Clew Bay, I felt a bit queasy, but it was not seasickness. It was the same morning sickness I'd endured three times before, and I closed my mind to it. 'Twould be unseemly for the pirate queen of Connaught to be hampered by a natural condition that would pass in a month or so.

Trade was so brisk that summer that my fleet had no time to prey upon other vessels. Nor did any ships attack us, for the *Sea Ghost* and her sisters had amassed a reputation of invincibility. In view of my conversations with my husband, and my own knowledge that England was making a very public show of trying to consolidate its power on the lands and seas of western Ireland, I carefully avoided engaging any ships that flew Queen Elizabeth's flag.

By the time I returned home in early October, I was gratified to see that my husband had arranged a surprise for me. As the *Sea Ghost* pulled into the inlet adjacent to my castle, I saw that Rockfleet now flew two flags from its ramparts, the Burke colors and my own flag. In my absence, Richard had commissioned a bright new Hen's flag, the largest I'd ever seen. He was wonderfully solicitous and we were companionable in every way.

The best thing about our relationship was that from the time we married, neither of us had hampered the other with unreasonable demands. It was this trust, and our own history, that led us to the most serious talk we'd ever had, and it happened one night when I was four-and-a-half months pregnant.

"Granuaile," he began. "What do you think of our marriage so far?"

"I've never been happier, never felt more secure. I love you, Richard."

"And I you, my Grace. More than anyone and more than anything. That means I must do everything in my power to ensure that you remain happy and free."

"You're talking in riddles, Dick," I said, feeling a sudden dryness in my mouth.

"What if you were to dismiss and divorce me the day before our year's marriage is ended?"

"Are you crazy?" I felt hot tears come to my eyes. "Is there someone else?"

"No, my Grace, and I give you my word on my life there never will be."

"Then why would you even bring up such foolishness? I'll have none of it."

"Hush, woman!" he said, more sharply than I'd heard him speak before. "Have I ever, in the more than twenty years you've known me, done anything – anything at all – to hurt you or betray your trust?"

"N... no," I stammered, still heartsick at what I was hearing.

"Trust me then, Granuaile. No matter what is *publicly* said, you and I will continue as man and wife 'til the day the first of us dies."

"Go ahead," I said. I had now been sufficiently mollified that I could listen with an open mind.

"You saw the Hen flag flying from the ramparts?"

"I did, and you could not have given me a finer present – other than yourself, of course."

"The English are well aware of your feelings against them, Grace. They know you'd sooner die than submit. Lord Deputy Sidney as much as told me the English have been watching your activities very carefully."

"You've spoken with Henry Sidney?"

"I have. Don't get me wrong, both you and he know that I feel uncertain about what will happen in the future, but that shouldn't stop me from dealing with the man."

"Go on."

"Rockfleet commands Clew Bay, yet it's much less exposed than any fortress in County Mayo. It's a safe harbor for you and for your ships. I'll not insult you by pretending that part – I hope only a small part – of your plan in marrying me was motivated by your desire to gain control of Carraigahawley."

"I've never kept that a secret from you, Dick, and, yes, it was only a very small part of why I wanted to marry you. But where is this leading?"

He rose from the stone seat adjacent to the large fireplace, stirred the fire, added some more peat, and brought two mugs of honeyed mead, one for each of us, back to where I sat. "Suppose I were to absent myself from Rockfleet for a fortnight, just before our one year anniversary. Suppose during that time, you were to bring in your military forces. And suppose when I returned you were to call out from the ramparts, 'Richard-an-Iarrain, I dismiss you and this castle is now mine!'" He grinned.

"But that would be unfair to you. Where would you go?"

"I've thought about that, darling. If I were to have a castle closer to the center of Burke land, farther south, say, near Lough Corrib..."

"*Caislean-an-Circa*, the Hen's Castle," I said, my mind now very much attuned to the game. "So *publicly* I would be ousting you from Rockfleet and making it my own, while privately I'd deed the Hen's Castle over to you, thus putting you in a position to keep a close eye on The MacWilliamship."

"Not to mention keeping a much closer watch on which way the winds are blowing, my dear."

"But our relationship...?"

"Not one bit different that it's been up to now. I pledged you my troth and if you'd like I'll find an officiant who will privately marry us for a lifetime and a day, with a signed and sealed commitment to you that on my death you and our child will inherit every stick and stone of my property. We'll be with each other as much, mayhap even more, than we've been before, and we'll have two places to be with each other, not just one. If need be, we'll be together when I sally forth to battle, and we'll be together on the *Sea Ghost*, but one thing I can, and will, promise you. We *will* be together. Now, My Darling Grace," he said, as he stood up, vigorously ripped my blouse off, held me against him, and pressed his bare chest into mine, "shall we seal the bargain?"

On the last day of February, 1567, Iron Dick Burke returned home to find his wife standing atop the ramparts. "Sir," I shouted down to him. "I no longer consider our marriage binding. Henceforth, Rockfleet Castle is mine. You are dismissed!" At that moment, two hundred men emerged from the castle and set up a human barrier. "My forces have gathered your belongings, and they will escort you off what is now my property! Begone, sir, and good day to you!"

Looking suitably dejected and downcast, Richard-an-Iarrain allowed himself to be led off the land around Rockfleet Castle without demur. I discharged my forces to return from whence they'd come and spoke only a few quiet words to the captain of my troops.

"You've told him when to return?"

"Aye, My Lady, one hour after sunset."

I was now at the end of my eighth month of pregnancy – truly 'great with child.' I waddled uncomfortably back into the living quarters. That night, when Richard returned, we lay in our marriage bed, gently holding one another, but doing nothing more, for that was all the loving we needed that night. And we laughed at the deception we had wrought.

Chapter 20

I'll never know what possessed me to clamber aboard the *Sea Ghost* a week later. Perhaps it was the lure of the sea, perhaps it was that I'd not been on the *Sea Ghost* – my greatest love but for Iron Dick Burke – since December's winds had blasted Clew Bay and the ocean beyond, and perhaps it was that with warm spring air finally cutting through winter's chill, I simply felt the need to go a'sailing, even if for a short while, one more time before the baby was born.

I'd promised Richard it would be only a short journey, no farther than the mouth of the Shannon River, and I'd be back in less than a fortnight. Richard cocked his head uncertainly. "Does it matter what I say, Granuaile? Has anyone ever been able to stop you when you got it in your head to do something?" He chuckled, held me close – well, as close as my greatly expanded girth would allow – and kissed me gently just before I boarded my flagship. "Be safe," he said. "Remember to come back quickly. The queen should give birth to the princeling in her own castle."

Richard had also convinced me that while I was the undisputed captain of the fleet, I should, for this one voyage

198

only, allow myself to be cosseted and treated as a passenger of honor. He'd made certain that the captain who was piloting the *Sea Ghost* had brought in a capacious and marvelously comfortable bed, which he'd installed in my captain's cabin, and that there would be a sentry at the door ensuring my every comfort. For the first time in my memory, courtesy of my husband, a midwife was aboard ship for the voyage.

The weather was clement as we began our short voyage. That was a good thing, because I'd planned to sail far west, giving wide berth to Galway Bay, an English stronghold. Just beyond the Aran Islands, our three ships turned east, to hug the coast off Clare County. I'd felt so happy to be at sea once again, that I spent the better part of each day on the deck, surveying my empire.

We were less than a week out, just north of the Shannon Estuary, when the pains began. I felt some discomfort, but it was nothing I couldn't handle. By that evening, the pains had increased substantially, both in measure and in duration. They were now coming every few minutes.

I stifled my need to cry out as best I could, but now the contractions were coming very rapidly indeed. "Crewman!" I called out, in what I hoped was as calm a manner as I could muster. "Get the midwife! Quickly!"

The young man returned less than a minute later, looking miserable. "Captain, My Lady," he said. "The midwife's never been on a ship before. She's in her quarters, retching up her insides and moaning. 'Tis the seasickness, and there's no way she can attend you."

I must have sworn, but there was nothing I could do. I'd have to find a way to give birth myself. "Get the captain, then." When the captain came down to the cabin, I said, "We have a problem. There is no midwife and my time has come much sooner than I expected. Is there anyone aboard ship who could at least cut the cord when the baby comes?"

"Ship's cook," he said uncertainly.

"Get him down here, then! Quickly! Aiieee!" I screamed with the pain of the sharpest contraction yet. Of all the foul luck! In spite of the pain, there was nothing worse that could happen. Or so I thought.

At that moment I felt the greatest contraction. I pressed down as hard as I could. I heard voices, but I must have gone in and out of consciousness. I have no recollection of how much time went by, but when I came to full consciousness again, I found myself holding a ruddy-faced baby boy, who was lustily bawling. I pressed the baby to my breast, where the little fellow began quickly and vigorously giving suck, heedless of what was going on around him. After my newborn son finished nursing, I fell into an exhausted sleep.

Some hours later, I heard and felt a tremendous crashing sound, and the *Sea Ghost* shuddered. "Captain!" I shouted. "What in blazes was that? I thought you'd steered us clear of the storm."

The captain was down to my cabin in an instant. "I did, My Lady. It's not the storm. We've just been attacked by a Moroccan pirate ship!"

"Signal our other ships to attack!"

"They've been blown back toward land. I'll do what I can to carry the fight to the enemy.

An hour after that, the captain was at my side. "How goes the battle?" I demanded.

"Poorly, My Lady, very poorly. We may lose the ship."

"*Are you out of your bloody mind?*" I exploded. "I gave birth less than twelve hours ago, and you're now telling me this could be our grave? These are Africans, for God's sake, bloody

Mohammedans who have no business in our waters to begin with! And you're saying they want to tangle with *me*?"

The captain looked downcast. "If only you could..." he finally mumbled.

"*WHAT*? Are you completely crazy? What is it you don't understand about the fact that I gave birth to a baby less than a day ago? What kind of foolishness is this?" I was livid with rage, both with the obvious incompetence of this idiot and with the threat that *my* flagship, *my Sea Ghost* could possibly be lost.

Meanwhile, the baby refused to let go my breast. I lifted him off me as gently as I could and placed him in the captain's arms. "God damn you to hell!" I swore viciously, but quietly enough so that only he could hear me. "May you be seven times worse this day twelve months from now, since you cannot do without me for even one whole day!"

Blessedly, I felt no pain, only supreme anger, as I threw on a loose-fitting garment, grabbed a loaded musket from the gun rack in my cabin, and staggered up the stairwell onto the deck. I was completely oblivious to what must have been the shocked stares of my men. The Moroccan vessel was within a hundred feet of the *Sea Ghost,* closing fast, and preparing to ram us, when I took aim at the leader of the pirate gang.

"You want a fight? Very well, arseholes, you've got a fight. Take this from unconsecrated hands you pigshit pirates! You dare mess with the queen in her waters? Here is your reward!"

With that, I emptied the loaded gun at him. The pirate leader spun about from the force of the blow and dropped sharply to the deck, dead and, so far as I could make out, mostly decapitated.

"All right," I shouted at my troops. "Anyone not doing exactly as I say – *exactly* as I say and *right now* – will get the same treatment as that pirate scum!"

The battle took less than half an hour. The invading pirates were demoralized by the loss of their captain, while my own men were heartened by the half-crazed harridan who'd made such an unexpected appearance. I was greatly pleased that I, myself, fired the first cannon shot that tore into the enemy vessel's mainmast. Now the roles of the ships were reversed. The *Sea Ghost*, which had sustained some damage to its aft mast, gave chase to the enemy vessel and once we'd reached that sorrowful ship and secured it with our grappling hooks, our men were quick to board it.

In the vicious hand-to-hand fighting that followed, we dispatched all thirty remaining pirate hands, while losing eight of our own. At the end of the day, we bound the enemy pirate ship to the *Sea Ghost* and hauled it into port in the Shannon estuary, where I added a new vessel to my fleet, albeit one that would need substantial repairs before it would again become seaworthy.

I returned to my cabin, took back my newly-born son, and lay back exhausted on my bunk. The baby, completely uninterested in what had gone on outside and uncaring about his mother's discomfort or her heroism, started his own squalling, and refused to be quiet until he had once again grabbed firmly onto my breast. Within a short time thereafter, we both fell into a blessed sleep.

Thus was born my fourth child and third son, Theobald, whom I named Tibbott-na-Long – *Toby of the Ships*.

Chapter 21

As time went on, only the outside of me grew older – my body and its presentation to the temporal world. Inwardly, I attained to a certain age, and stayed there throughout my whole remaining life. That perpetual inner age of different individuals may vary I suppose, but in general I suspect it gets fixed at early maturity, when the mind has reached adult awareness and acuity, but has not yet been calloused by habit and disillusion; when the body is newly full-grown and feeling the fires of life, but not yet any of life's ashes. The calendar and my mirror and the solicitude of my juniors might have told me I was getting older, and I could see for myself that the world and all about me had aged, but secretly I knew I was still a young woman of nineteen.

They say that if one looks back through the tunnel of years, there are a few times that stand out. My initiation into womanhood by Iron Dick had been one of those times. 1570 was another.

In that year, I was at the peak of my power and wealth. I commanded an unbelievable fleet of twenty ships – galleys and caravels – an unheard-of crew of nearly a thousand sailors, and a standing army of five hundred soldiers. I owned castles from

Doona in the north to Belcare in the south, and from Clare Island in the west to Rockfleet at the northeast corner of Clew Bay. My herds of cattle and flocks of sheep were almost beyond counting.

Shortly after my fortieth birthday, my daughter Margaret married a different Richard Burke – a nephew once removed from my own Iron Dick – and a more wonderful husband I could not have imagined. Indeed, I often joked with Maeve that had she not wed young Richard – who was nicknamed "the Devil's Hook" – I'd have adopted *him* and disowned *her*. He was to prove a stalwart friend and ally throughout his life and mine.

My Owen, now twenty-three, remained as close to me as ever, and he, too, was happily married to yet another Burke, Catherine, the daughter of Edmund Burke of Castlebar. My only disappointment remained my estrangement from Murrough, my second son, and although I often wept in the privacy of my own chambers at my loss of him, I realized that while you could give birth to someone, things simply did not work out the way you wanted them to. In Murrough's case, I had to admit I did not feel a mother's love for him. I didn't even *like* him, and I am sure the favor was returned. Among other things, Murrough was quick to embrace the English invaders. He was among the first to turn his back on his heritage and his people, and to proclaim the sovereignty of England and the primacy of the Protestant religion.

As for my own Richard-an-Iarrain, we'd dropped the pretense of being divorced two years before, and although we seemed to lead separate lives, our separations were matters of business necessity and our own political needs. During the times we were together, our loving friendship was such that it seemed we'd never been apart.

Baby Toby was aptly named. From the very first, he traveled with me, and happily, aboard the *Sea Ghost*. By 1570, when he was three, he'd been to more countries than my husband, more countries than almost any man or woman living in Ireland.

The next few years were happy and contented ones for me. Many times while on board ship, I spent countless hours gambling at dice or cards. Although I never won or lost any great sums, I learned the rules and strategies of the various games which served me well when we went ashore. We ranged the seas from Ireland to England, France, Portugal, and Spain. Sailors, generally of the lower class, oarsmen and seamen and such, usually gathered at public houses in every port, while most captains and officers preferred to dine with the merchants and the moneyed class of the cities.

I took care not to dress in my finest raiment, nor did I dress provocatively, although I am vain enough to say here that I could still have done so. Indeed, since my hair was now cut quite short and I generally wore loose trousers and nondescript sailor blouses, I could easily have passed for a man of early middle age. I was nearly as tall as many of the men in the public houses, and I kept my voice low-pitched. Mostly, I listened rather than spoke, and it was in these places that I learned from the loose-lipped seamen what ships were in port, what cargo they were carrying, and whence they were headed.

In this way, my fleet was easily able to attack and relieve several fat, unsuspecting vessels of their bounty. The captains of these ships never knew or suspected how my crews had learned so precisely where these ships would be and when they would be at their most vulnerable. From time to time, I would come across my old friend and erstwhile enemy, Don Bosco, and we would regale ourselves with tales of life on the open sea. Bosco, like I, didn't hesitate to frequent the seamen's pubs.

Each of the large galleys under my command was armed with more than sufficient cannon for our needs, and were capable of carrying sixty or seventy men, plus twenty or thirty oarsmen to work every boat. When the winds were favorable, which was quite often, I experienced the exhilaration of full sails driving our ships. At that time, there were plenty of oak woods at Murrisk – O'Malley country – which supplied material in great abundance. While, at any given time, I'd have hundreds of men at sea, I also had scores of talented shipwrights to make certain my vessels were kept in the most serviceable and seaworthy condition.

My castle at Carraigahawley had the best harbor in Clew Bay – safe, deep, and well-sheltered. Few dared enter the waters of Clew Bay because of the dangerous reefs and currents. The very remoteness of the land deterred intruders and pursuers alike.

With such a fleet at my disposal, well-manned, well-equipped, and surfeited from the spoils of the sea, my aggregation of fine men was more than able to hold its own against all comers, even the much larger English vessels that dared not follow us into the creeks and island channels of the bay. My fleet of swift ships could sail into shallow waters or endure the rough waters of the Atlantic. Often, we waylaid merchant ships bound for Galway, the city that had closed its ports to all O'Malley vessels. Once on board, I negotiated with the captains of those ships, levying tolls and providing pilots for safe passage. If my offer was refused, my men would simply loot our host's cargo and pluck the best of it for ourselves.

If I had a single fault, it was that my seamen and I were not very scrupulous in selecting our enemies. We lifted and carried off whatever came in handy on sea or shore, and we didn't care whether our prey was Celt or Saxon, Englishman, Scotsman, or Moor. This want of discretion was eventually to lead to my undoing, but that was some years in the future.

Despite my successes at sea, by 1574 it became obvious to me, as well as to the O'Malleys and our allies, the O'Flahertys and Burkes, that the English lion was grabbing more and more of western Ireland in its claws. Slowly at first, then with increasing alacrity, the list of those patriots who submitted to Queen Elizabeth's yoke increased from a trickle to a mighty deluge. Still, I refused to acknowledge the sovereignty of any but myself.

In July, 1569, Lord Deputy Sir Henry Sidney appointed Sir Edward Fitton as the first English governor of Connaught. As President of the Council of Connaught, Fitton effectively occupied the position of Lord Deputy when Sidney was absent from the province. I had heard tales that Fitton was a quarrelsome man, not given to compromise of any kind. When this proved to be true in the southern Connaught, I redoubled my efforts to assert my independence.

Not five years later, in February, 1574, I received word from my O'Flaherty and Burke spies that Fitton was preparing a war fleet to attack and lay siege to Rockfleet Castle. His fleet, under Captain Martin, would leave Galway on March 8. The first week in March, I counseled with my husband, that strong and wise warrior. "They're going to attack by land and by sea and Captain Martin will lead the sea forces. Do you know anything about him, Dick?"

"He's not a bad man, Granuaile. He's a plodder, no great lover of Edward Fitton, but he'll do what he's told."

"Initiative?"

"Not much, so I hear. Not known for his aggressiveness, but he's quite stubborn."

"Do you think he'd be a match for my ships?"

"On an individual basis, no, but he's supposedly mustering twenty-five ships. Those extra five could make the difference between victory and submission."

"What advice can you give me?" I asked. Even though it was early March, the wind was cold and biting on our hill overlooking Clew Bay, and both of us wore heavy woolen coats as we walked over our property.

"Leave no more than five of your smaller vessels at Rockfleet. Keep at least fifteen ships in Blacksod Bay. They should carry no extra weight and all cargo should be stowed at the castle, in case you need to bargain for time. Once your ships arrive at Blacksod Bay, I'll be waiting at Doona Castle with extra cannon and ammunition. When your ships leave from the north, they'll be floating Men o' War."

I mulled his idea over for a few moments. After a while, I said, "If I have spies, there's no question that Fitton has spies as well. He doubtless knows about Doona. I wouldn't be surprised if he has reserve forces between Erris Head and Blacksod Bay, lying in wait for our ships to come north. As soon as his forces spot us, they could trap us in Blacksod Bay and probably blast us out of the water before we made it to Doona."

Richard scratched his beard, which I noticed was now salted with light gray. "What about Kildawnet?" he asked, referring to the castle on the southeastern edge of Achill Island. "You could safely negotiate the strait between Clew and Blacksod Bays."

"Not good. All the English would need would be a single ship at each end of the channel and they'd effectively cork the bottle." Of a sudden, the answer came clear to me. "Bunowen."

"The castle where you lived with Donal of the Battles?"

"It has its own safe harbor hidden from view," I continued. "It's so far south of Clew Bay that Martin's fleet would be headed straight around Slyne Head and wouldn't give it a thought. Let's go inside," I said, shivering. "I'd think better if I could thaw out in front of a roaring fire than if my mind froze out here."

Once inside, my plan became solidified. "Can you bring some of your cannon south instead of north?"

"Certainly. It's all Burke, O'Malley, and O'Flaherty country."

"Good. I'll send six ships north to Blacksod, one at a time. Ten ships headed south will make it look like we're on a trading mission to the Continent. The southbound ships will turn east just south of Slyne Head and reprovision at Bunowen. If Martin's ships are coming north and they see my ships going south, they'll think we've left Rockfleet defenseless."

Six days out of Galway, on March 14, 1574, Captain Martin's expeditionary force sailed into Clew Bay and "trapped" me in my castle at Carraigahawley. Once at the foot of the hill, his sea forces laid siege to the castle from the water, and his contingent of two hundred soldiers set up a siege line running north from Castleaffy, five miles south of my castle.

For the first few days, no guns were fired except five or ten desultory shots from the ramparts of Rockfleet. These did not stop the English from reconnoitering the area, scouting for any defenses we might mount from the land side. Our forces must have appeared meager compared to Martin's troops – less than fifty lightly-armed guards, who spent more time inside the castle than outside.

The English ships promptly ringed the four small vessels we'd left adjacent to Rockfleet. On the third day of the siege, a signalman from one of Martin's invaders demanded we surrender the ships to the enemy forces. We did not respond, since we'd abandoned the ships and no men were on board. Nevertheless, it took the pigheaded English fully a day to realize this. When they finally boarded those vessels, they were frustrated when they found that the ships were not only devoid of men, they were devoid of *anything* – no provisions, no guns, not even sailing instruments.

Nine days after the siege had started, on March 23, 1574, an army of five hundred Burkes, more than twice the size of the English land contingent, flowed onto the grounds of Rockfleet from the northeast. Stunned, the English land forces retreated south and regrouped a mile east of Murrisk Castle. The following morning, the enemy was even more flabbergasted when another two hundred O'Malley forces emerged from Murrisk Castle. The English troops surrendered without a fight, leaving the inhabitants of Carraigahawley free to move landward at will.

Still, no one moved out of Rockfleet Castle. As night fell on the 24th, the English sailors slept on board their ships, secure in the knowledge that they still commanded Clew Bay and that they had acquired four ships in the bargain, each of which was now occupied by Englishmen and their allied Galway tribesmen.

As dawn gave way to morning on the 25th, the Englishmen were nervous, but not overly concerned when half a dozen O'Malley ships entered Clew Bay from the north and proceeded to head directly toward Rockfleet. Martin sent half of his armada to confront these six vessels, all of which flew the Hen flag. The English had drawn within half a mile of our easterly-bound vessels when ten more large ships entered Clew Bay from the south. These, too, flew the much-feared Grace O'Malley pennants.

The odds in the middle of Clew Bay were now sixteen to twelve, and while both sides' ships prepared to engage one another, the boom of eight large cannon fired from Rockfleet Castle quickly neutralized four of the English ships still laying siege. The English still held a numerical advantage but the invaders were now hemmed in, and they were in unknown, inhospitable waters, whereas we were on our own land. At that moment, the Burke soldiers started firing from land, and the English skeleton crews aboard our four smaller vessels were quickly overrun by Dick Burke's army. Now the odds were just about even, save that our four vessels were still unarmed.

It was then that a very strange and unexpected thing occurred. Three of the English vessels, including Captain Martin's flagship, broke off the engagement and headed west to the open sea. I could never figure out why they would have done such a thing, since even I believed that the enemy forces might eventually have beaten us by sheer attrition. At that moment, I remembered my husband's admonition that Martin was a cautious sort. He'd already lost four ships, by no means a horrendous number and by no means a crippling blow, but he realized he'd have to report those losses to Edward Fitton, who would not be pleased. Martin apparently determined that the most prudent course of action would be to cut his losses to a minimum, particularly since he'd realized that the land siege had been broken.

This was the ideal moment to make my first public appearance in many days. Accompanied by a phalanx of Burke troops, I boarded the recaptured *Sea Ghost*, and once I had satisfied myself that the English had done no harm to it, my men installed four cannon on my flagship. The *Sea Ghost* was faster than any of the English ships, and no sooner had my regular crew boarded the caravel, then I gave chase to the largest and slowest of the departing English galleys.

To my great satisfaction, the *Sea Ghost* caught that enemy vessel just as it was leaving Clew Bay for the open ocean. The battle lasted not very long and, because of our knowledge of the rocks and shoals in that part of the sea, the conclusion was assured. However, at the last moment, I relented and contented myself with demolishing the aft mast of that ship.

Knowing that the *Sea Ghost* could outpace any of the enemy vessels, I bore down on Captain Martin's flagship. When I was within a mile of that hapless vessel, I raised the white flag denoting truce, not surrender. Martin's flagship raised a white flag as well, indicating its willingness to parley. As the *Sea Ghost* drew abreast of Captain Martin's ship, I signaled my intent to come aboard. My request was granted, and I was shown down to the captain's cabin, which was spacious and finely outfitted, but no more so than my own flag vessel.

Our talk was brief and, given the events of the past several days, cordial. Martin was a man of my own age and height, stocky and barrel-chested. His hair was thin and he made no attempt to disguise the gray in it. His brow was furrowed, whether in worry or anxiety I could not tell.

"Lady Grania," he opened, bowing slightly and using one of the English versions of my name. "I salute you for outmaneuvering my fleet. But why did you give chase, then raise the white flag?"

"Captain," I rejoined in the same respectful tone, "you were indeed a worthy adversary. May I ask why you abandoned the battle when you might have won?"

"Because you had one advantage I hadn't considered, even though we were evenly matched. You had almost unlimited reserves on land because you are a Burke as well as an O'Malley. I assume that sooner or later the land forces would have signaled every O'Malley and O'Flaherty ship within a hundred miles to come to your aid. Between the two of us, I don't share Fitton's disdain for the Irish, but I had to obey my orders. I've done so, for whatever good it did. My disgrace is that I've lost four ships."

"Possibly five."

He blanched. "Is that why you've chased me down?"

"No, Captain Martin. You've proved yourself a gentleman as well as an officer. I came to tell you I could have destroyed your large galley, which is at this moment lying dead in the water at the southwestern edge of Clew Bay, surrounded by three of my own fleet. I did not destroy the boat, and if you'd like I'll be happy to escort you back so you can retrieve your ship and your men. I imagine you'll be able to figure out how to bring that ship back to Galway."

At that he bowed. "You are gracious, Madame. No wonder they call you the queen of western Ireland. Whatever befalls both of us, Lady Grania, I wish you well."

"And you as well, Captain."

Thus it was that Captain Martin returned to Galway, his tail partially – but not completely – between his legs, as they say. Two hundred of his land forces would be marched back to Galway in disgrace, and four English vessels would now be added to my own fleet. Given the English penchant for counting every penny, they were perhaps more embarrassed by the cost of this unsuccessful attempted siege than they were at the loss of English lives, which was minimal, certainly no more than five. As for our contingent, we'd suffered no losses, not so much as a single man.

And at the end of the day, I maintained my undisputed independence. For now.

Chapter 22

In 1576 there were momentous changes in Ireland. Sir Henry Sidney, the Lord Deputy, visited Galway in March and ordered the submission of the Connaught chieftains and lords. Shane MacOliverus, The MacWilliam Iochtar, was at first unwilling to come to Galway, but the Lord Deputy ultimately convinced him to come. Once there, he and Sidney came to agreement, wherein The MacWilliam agreed to hold his lands in the name of the Queen. In exchange for MacOliverus paying two hundred fifty marks sterling and feeding and equipping two hundred soldiers, horsemen, and footman for two months each year – not a particularly burdensome sacrifice – The MacWilliam would be able to go on exactly the way he had before. There was another benefit. MacOliverus was knighted, and Sir Shane MacOliverus, as he would henceforth be known, received sufficient remuneration from the Crown each year to equal what he would pay out on behalf of the new overlords.

Nevertheless, on its face this was a complete submission. The MacWilliam agreed to eschew Gaelic laws and customs and obey the laws of England. In a strange and unfriendly city such as Galway, it was the safest and most sensible way out at the time. Surrounded by the might of English administration and power, it was not the place for MacOliverus to reveal any misgivings he might have had about the terms of his submission. However, Dick advised me that Shane MacOliverus and Henry Sidney were very much men of the world, who knew that once safely back in his own territory, The MacWilliam would give the articles of submission a very wide interpretation.

The O'Malley, not my late father, but the current O'Malley, Melaghlin, submitted as well. These two events caused me to realize that as independent as I continued to be in my own realm, that of the sea, the beginning of the end of the ancient Irish order in the Kingdom of the Umhalls had arrived.

Although my husband, Richard-an-Iarrain, had been elected *tanaiste* – he was first in line to become successor to The MacWilliam Iochtar when Shane MacOliverus passed, the submission of The MacWilliam to the Crown meant it was less certain that Dick, who'd proudly maintained his independence from England, would succeed to The MacWilliamship. Consequently, I felt it was vital to my own political aspirations that I at least meet with the Lord Deputy – "beard the lion in his own den," as they say – so that each of us could take the measure of the other.

I arrived in Galway on April 4. By order of the Lord Deputy, the *Sea Ghost*, which had been denied entry into Galway for many years, was allowed to dock at that city's municipal wharf. I was surprised to find an escort awaiting my arrival, even more astonished when I was treated with deference normally accorded the highest ranking dignitary as I was transported to the Lord Deputy's palace.

When I entered the grand hallway, I was greeted by Sir Henry's son, Sir Phillip Sidney, a man of middle height, dignified, and quite handsome, with long dark hair. He wore tight white breeches, and a red waistcoat with gold piping. He reminded me strikingly of my son Owen. I felt an immediate warmth for this young man.

"Madame Burke-O'Malley," he said, bowing low. When he raised his head, he was smiling warmly. "I must say your reputation has more than preceded you. It is my distinct privilege to meet such a courageous woman."

I blushed at Sir Phillip's sincere charm, and responded, "I daresay, Sir Phillip, you remind me of my eldest and beloved son, Owen."

"So we are both immensely pleased to be in each other's company?"

"That we are. You are the eldest, I believe, of seven children?"

"Aye." His Gaelic was flawless. "You've studied up on our family, then?"

"I have, Sir Phillip. Your father's only a year older than I, and he's amassed not only great power, but a reputation for astute diplomacy as well. Will I have the pleasure of meeting him on this trip?"

"You will, Madame Grace," a new voice said. While Phillip and I had been talking, an older version of the son had entered the room, dressed similarly in breeches and waistcoat. Sir Henry wore a lightly powdered wig, the symbol of his authority.

"Sir Henry," I responded, curtseying.

"Shall we adjourn to more private quarters?" the Lord Deputy inquired. "I see you've been somewhat entranced by my son and he by you. Would you mind if he joined us?"

"Of course not," I replied.

Sir Henry led us down a narrow passageway that depended off the entrance hallway. That hall, in turn, led to several doors on either side. The Lord Deputy pushed open the second one to the left, and bade us follow. This room was far less formal than the more grandiloquent portico through which we had entered. It was, I estimated, twenty feet wide by thirty feet long, half again as large as the great room in Rockfleet Castle. The walls were paneled with wood, and a large bookcase was filled with volumes, the vast majority of which were in Latin. The large windows looking out onto the courtyard were framed by heavy, brocaded curtains. The room was furnished with comfortable sofas, chairs, and settees.

"I'm told you're partial to Port," Sir Henry said. "May I offer you some?"

"Thank you, yes," I answered. He poured from a large flask, then filled his own and his son's glasses.

"To friendship," he toasted, "even though in the past we have had our differences." I could see where the son had acquired his charm.

"To friendship," I responded.

"Would you prefer I call you Madame Burke, Grace, Granuaile, what?" Sir Henry asked.

"Whichever suits you, Sir Henry." I noticed that despite what each of us must have been led to believe about the other, the interview was starting off cordially.

"William Martin told me you were most gracious in victory. I thank you for not retaliating against Galway. Mister Fitton was not, I fear, noted for his diplomatic skills."

"Captain Martin was, himself, gracious enough to leave me with four new ships, although my shipwrights had to work long and hard to make them seaworthy again."

At that, we both laughed.

"Tell me, Grace, what made you decide to come here? I won't pretend I'm not aware of your fierce desire for Irish independence."

"Independent I am, Sir Henry, but you needn't worry that I'm another Shane O'Neill."

"Ah, you know about the troubles, then."

"I do." We sat in companionable silence for a few moments. "You've avoided the direct confrontation by elevating Calvagh O'Donnell, O'Neill's rival."

"I prefer not to have to resort to nastiness if I don't have to. If I may ask again, why did you come to Galway?" He stood up and walked over to the window, then looked back at me.

"To work out an accommodation, Sir Henry."

"I notice you did not use the word 'submission.' What kind of accommodation did you have in mind?"

"May we talk candidly, Sir Henry, with the understanding that this part of our conversation will go no farther than the three of us?"

The father looked to the son, who nodded acquiescence. "All right," he said.

"If I were to 'submit' at your invitation, I would be seen as having sold out to the English interests and I might be hated by certain O'Malley and Burke factions, even though both The MacWilliam and The O'Malley have submitted. My lack of submission wouldn't mean much of anything to you, since, as a woman, I have nothing to submit except a fleet of ships and a few castles. I am not a chieftain of any clan."

"Mayhap not," Phillip interjected, "but you're reputed to be the queen of western Ireland and the queen of the seas, and I was not trying to falsely flatter you when I said you are a most notable Irish woman."

"Thank you, Sir Phillip. I appreciate your courtesy. Gentlemen, my proposal is really quite simple. If I were to submit, it would be one thing. On the other hand, if I were to *voluntarily* provide my ally and sister, the Queen, with three galleys and two hundred fighting men, without any talk of submission or hierarchy, each of us, England and my own realm, would profit mightily."

Sir Henry sat on a chair opposite me, leaned his head on his chest, and closed his eyes. "When is a submission not a submission?" he asked rhetorically. Opening his eyes, he smiled with genuine warmth. "What's in it for you?"

"Several benefits," I said. "I remain free to roam the seas..."

"As long as you don't molest Galway," the Lord Deputy interjected.

"Aye, done." I said. "Equally important, my husband is the *tanaiste* to The MacWilliamship."

"Richard-an-Iarrain," Sir Phillip said.

"Yes, and I wouldn't want to see him supplanted because our family was viewed as noncompliant. It's become clear to me that as the power and influence of the English crown has encroached more and more on the affairs of my country, the Queen's representatives – particularly your Lordship – wield more power and influence than even the highest ranking Gaelic chieftain."

Sir Henry nodded but said nothing. I continued, "I have seen mightier leaders than me take their *bonnacht* from Elizabeth and survive. What I propose is simply a recognition of the present political reality."

"And that is expedient to you?" Sir Henry intoned.

"Expedient to both of us, Sir Henry. My *alliance* with the English instead of my *submission* connotes a marriage of equals. I need good relations with England. England needs to have me nominally subordinate. Even though we both know in private that my alliance, submission, call it what you will in

Galway, does not necessarily mean any change in my activities in Clew Bay, the Irish public will see only that one of their own respects and recognizes English authority."

"Very clever, Madame Grace," Sir Phillip said. "Both sides come out the winner and both sides proceed with business as usual."

Sir Henry nodded sagely. "In the few brief moments we've spent together, we've achieved what would otherwise have taken many months – painful months, I might add. Earlier, I toasted friendship, not knowing whither it would take us. Now," he said, raising his glass again, "I propose a toast to you, equal queen – and that's in private, of course – and to your long life and every success."

"And I to you, boys," I responded, eschewing any hint of formality. "Even though I shouldn't call you a 'boy' Sir Henry, as you are one year my senior."

Shortly thereafter, Sir Henry excused himself, leaving me with Sir Phillip. Very shortly, we became "Phillip" and "Grace," and during the next few days, Sir Henry's son proved a most companionable escort, as he showed me about Galway. The city had greatly expanded in the thirty years since Iron Dick and my father had squired me about that town. Church steeples competed with new university buildings, and the port had expanded to meet the needs of the day. Galway was very much a capital city now, and it was to western Ireland as Dublin was to eastern Ireland.

On my last day in Galway, Sir Henry gave me the rare privilege of a request that I conduct him and his entourage on a boat trip around the bay, as he wished to view the city's harbor and its defenses from the sea. I cheerfully complied with the request, but, business being business, I demanded one shilling in payment for this service. He stared fixedly at me for a moment, then burst out laughing as he handed me the shilling. "You are indeed the *pirate* queen," he said.

Over the years, I had pretty much learned to control my temper. However, there was one instance that took place a few months later when I was engaged in a trading trip that had taken me to the west coast of England and thence to Dublin. At the northern end of Dublin Bay there is a bulbous peninsula, Howth, on which sits a great and noble castle, far larger and more refined than any in western Ireland.

To understand what led to my anger, one must know that we Irish are the most hospitable of people, and the western Irish are the most courteous of all. It was expected that if someone from a friendly clan, or even a neutral clan, appeared at a castle, day or night, the owner of that castle was expected to show the utmost warmth to such a guest. This displays nothing more than good breeding and good manners.

On my return from England that propitious day in the summer of 1576, I landed one of my larger galleys at Howth. From there, I proceeded directly to the home of the lord of the manor in search of hospitality, as was the time-honored Gaelic custom. The gates of Howth Castle were locked, which was not surprising, it being the dinner hour. But what shocked, angered, and deeply offended me was that I was refused admission to the castle and rudely turned back because, I was told, the lord was at dinner and would not be disturbed.

I was livid at this callous disregard for the basic principles of Gaelic hospitality and I stormed from the castle in a rage, my eyes fixed on the road which led back to my ship. Just as I was leaving the grounds, I heard two voices within several feet of me. I looked up and saw a lad of perhaps seven, and a young woman who appeared to be his caretaker.

"Nana," the boy said, "we'd best be getting back to the castle right now. My da will be angry if he finds I'm not at dinner."

"You're right, young Edward. We wouldn't want to keep the lord of Howth waiting,"

They turned to go back to the castle and in that instant I brandished my short sword and seized the child, who acted as though this were simply another game. "He's mine for a while," I told the maid. "You may go in alone and tell your lord that if he wants to see the lad again, he can deal with Granuaile ni-Mháille of Connaught."

Terrified, the young woman turned and ran toward the castle, while I led the boy by the hand to my galley. The boy had never before sailed on a galley, and he was thrilled at this new adventure as we plied the waters of the Irish Sea and eventually sailed up the west coast of Ireland and into Clew Bay. My son Toby, who'd accompanied me on the journey, was three years older than young Edward Howth, and they quickly became boon companions, making the time pass even more quickly.

Upon my return to Rockfleet, I found an emissary from the lord of Howth, who had ridden headlong across Ireland by land, waiting at my castle gate. Being myself obedient to Gaelic custom, I invited him in. He breathed a sigh of relief when he found that the Howth heir was safe, and, indeed, quite happy with his new playmate.

"Lady Granuaile, my lord offers his most profound apologies to you and his regrets at the infamous way in which he treated you. He begs the safe return of his son, and is willing to pay any price for that."

"You may tell your lord that if he wants to plead for his son, he can come here himself and do so," I responded coldly.

Within a fortnight, the lord of Howth presented himself at Rockfleet. He echoed the sentiments of his courtier, prostrated himself, and vowed he would pay any price I asked. When the boy came running into the room where we were seated and saw his father, both parent and child shed happy tears at seeing the other, and I must say I was moved by this display of filial affection.

"I don't want your money or any of your property," I said.

"But my child...?"

I shooed the younger Howth out the door. "I don't need your child either. I have four of my own, thank you. What I need is your courtesy and respect."

"Aye, and that you shall have henceforth and forevermore."

"Brave words, Lord Howth. Words that will disappear on a gust of air no sooner than the moment you have your son back. I want something more tangible than that."

"Anything," Lord Howth said. "Say what you want and I will grant it to you."

"Very well, Lord Howth," I said, going over to a nearby desk and extracting two pieces of parchment and a quill pen, which my father had given me many years ago. The quill was one of my most treasured possessions. In the time-honored tradition, it was made from the outer left wing of a live goose, and it had been taken in the spring, twenty-five years ago. The left wing was favored because the feathers curved outward and away when used by a right-handed writer. "I want you to handwrite my conditions in duplicate, and I want one man from your entourage and one from mine to witness the writing. Each of us will keep a copy in our possession."

The lord of Howth looked at me strangely, not knowing what this obviously insane woman confronting him would demand. When the four of us, Howth, the two witnesses, and myself were assembled, I said, "Here are the conditions. In return for your son, you must commit in writing that the gates of Howth Castle will never again be closed against anyone who requests hospitality – *and* that an extra plate will always be laid at your table – always, as long as there is a Howth Castle, even if that be forever – as a reminder to you and to those generations that follow you, of your commitment."

The lord, relieved at the simplicity of this request, readily agreed, hand wrote, and signed the twin documents, after which he was allowed to leave Rockfleet with his son. Toby and Edward promised to remain lifelong friends and, surprisingly, they have remained friends, albeit at some distance. And I am told that to this day there is an extra plate set at Castle Howth for every meal.

Chapter 23

If 1576 was one of my brightest times, the following year was dark indeed. By then, I'd been sailing the high seas for more than thirty years. I was aware that youth is impetuous and in my younger days I'd often taken risks that, as I grew older and more experienced, seemed to me to be irresponsible, even stupid.

I've heard that God looks out for the very young and for drunks. At forty-seven, I was neither. I fancied myself the queen of Connaught and certainly the ruler of the seas of western Ireland. How could I possibly have been fooled by one of the oldest tricks known to sea captains the world over? And yet that is exactly what happened.

In the spring of 1577, I was returning from a brief, successful trading voyage to Waterford, one of my favorite towns, since it had steadfastly remained independent. As my three ships sailed leisurely west and up the coast from Kenmare to Castlemaine and from Tralee Bay to the Mouth of the Shannon, there wasn't a public house where we stopped that was not abuzz with the rumor that a huge galleon, laden with gold bullion, was at that very moment two hundred miles southwest of Kerry Head, and that pirate vessels were settling around that ship like flies on a piece of honeyed bread. Thus far, the galleon had avoided problems because it was surrounded by four heavily-armed men o' war. It was reported that the galleon intended to make landfall at Shannon, there pick up half a dozen more escorts, and continue on to Spain.

I should have questioned the veracity and source of these rumors and reports because I knew of no reason that such a fat prize would come so far north. I surmised that the vessel was probably coming from somewhere in the Caribbean or even the coast of Colombia or Venezuela, for Cartagena was, at that time, reputed to be one of the wealthiest cities in the New World. If, as was rumored, it was flying the flag of Spain, it should not have been near any land controlled by the English, the French, or the Dutch. Common sense would have dictated that such a floating treasure trove would stop at the Azores or the Canary Islands, or at any one of a dozen ports more friendly to Spain.

My instincts told me something was very strange about the whole situation, but I figured there'd be no harm in keeping a lookout for such a ship, if, indeed, it existed at all. I was not in so great a hurry to return home to Clew Bay and I found myself actually enjoying the lovely and ever-changing landscapes as I plowed north. Just west of Ballyheige Bay, the next protected harbor south of the Shannon Estuary, I caught sight of a large galleon flying the Spanish flag. It fit every description I'd been given and it was indeed surrounded by four protective warships. It was two miles out. My *Sea Ghost* and its two brethren were, at that moment, lying at anchor in Ballyheige roads.

The galleon continued north at a lazy pace. Just as that ship reached the peninsula separating Ballyheige Bay from the Shannon Estuary, its escort vessels broke off from their charge and turned southwest toward the Dingle Peninsula, where they could continue to guard the galleon against any attackers which might come from that direction. The Spanish treasure ship, once inside the estuary, would be safe from attack, since this was the Earl of Desmond's demesne and the Earl was honor-bound to afford protection. The captain of the galleon had obviously not reckoned on danger from that very small area between Kilbaba and Carrigaholt – a wide mouth just west of the narrows – where the large vessel would be an easy target for attack and plunder.

Slowly, unobtrusively, my three ships seemed to drift north and west, hugging the coastline so nothing would look suspicious. When we rounded the westernmost point of the peninsula separating the bay and the estuary, the large treasure vessel sat almost motionless in the very middle of the Shannon's mouth. There were no ships anywhere in sight, and our three vessels, the caravel and two galleys, continued hugging the coastline to the south of the estuary. Slowly, ever so slowly, we came closer to the galleon, and still there was no discernible movement on its part and no other ships visible anywhere.

It was almost as though we were lovers gently courting the large treasure galleon. We approached our intended prey so slowly, so cautiously, our eyes so carefully aimed at the large vessel that it was too late before we noticed that the mouth of the Shannon had suddenly closed as ten warrior vessels stood between us and the open sea. As I looked east, toward the narrows. I swore as viciously as ever I'd sworn before. There were eight heavily armed boats blocking the strait. As slowly as we had approached the galleon, so those eighteen warships now approached us in a classic purse-string maneuver, drawing the circle around us ever tighter.

With the odds eighteen-to-three, it would have been suicidal to attempt to fight through the blockade, and I was anything but a suicidal fool. The flagship of the enemy fleet ignored my other two ships and sailed straight toward the *Sea Ghost*, as if knowing exactly who was on board the smallest of our ships.

"Permission to board?" a voice called out from the vessel. As if they needed permission.

"Granted," I called out. Then, to preserve what little negotiating power I thought I might have left, I continued in the same tone, "State your name and your business."

A tall, hefty man, a couple of years older than I, stepped to the forecastle and returned my challenge. "The Earl of Desmond, Granuaile ni-Mháille. You should know me. You've been plundering and pillaging my land for four years last past, and now it is my turn to be, shall we say, your host for the foreseeable future."

"My host? We are, you and I, people of the world, Desmond. Let us not mince words. Why not call a spade a shit shovel? You mean to take me captive."

"Well said, Grace," he said, bowing mockingly in a way which increased my anger, but which, even more so, made me realize how truly helpless I was. To add insult to this macabre scene, he gingerly stepped aboard the *Sea Ghost* with four huge men in tow. He bestowed the "honor" of shackling me himself, my wrists tied behind my back, and the toughs with him lifted me, as if I were a sack of feathers, and carried me to Desmond's flagship.

To put the finishing touches on his masquerade of civility, Desmond turned to the pilot on board the *Sea Ghost* and airily said, "You and the other two ships are free to go hence. You are dismissed and discharged."

The captain looked at me questioningly. "We are ready to fight, M'lady."

I was well aware that the loyalty of my men was such that they would readily die fighting for my honor, and while there was no chance we would emerge victorious and it was far more likely than not that they would certainly die, I had no desire to have these good men's deaths on my conscience.

"No, Captain McNally," I said. "Do as my captor says. You'll tell Richard, of course?"

"Of course he will, Granuaile," Desmond said, "for all the good it will do you. Or, if you've not noticed, this is Munster, not Connaught, and The MacWilliam *tanaiste* has neither power nor place here."

There is little to tell about the next eighteen months. The Earl of Desmond installed me in Limerick Gaol. Is one prison any different from another? Not really. The dungeon is below ground level and always damp. The bars on the cells were clammy and, in the case of Limerick, overgrown with moss. During my life, I had allowed no bounds, neither those of activity nor those of convention, to bind me against my will. My "home" was a square cell, ten by twelve feet. When I needed to relieve myself, I did so in a bucket, which was emptied once a day or, if the gaoler was lazy, as was often the case, every two or three days. The stench throughout the cellar was overwhelming.

Once a day, the inhabitants of the gaol – there were five of us, four men and myself – were herded upstairs and into a small courtyard – where we were free to do what we wanted, albeit in a greatly confined space, sometimes for an hour, sometimes for as long as six hours. The longer times seemed to be maliciously planned to take place during the coldest, most inclement seasons, although I must here say that the winters in flat, inland Limerick were far milder than they had been in Connaught.

So confined, I resolved to survive as best I could. For hours on end, I retreated into my past life. In addition to the almost complete lack of activity – I had walked around and around the courtyard at first, but within a month that became so boring I did little more than stand in the warmest place I could find – the food was the same day in and day out. We had two meals a day, a mushy gruel in the morning, and a "dinner" served in the late afternoon that consisted of half-rotten turnips and carrots swimming in a broth with a skin of fat on top that indicated that maybe – *maybe* – a bit of fatty meat had been dragged through the slop to tease us with the hint of a meaty taste.

Given this diet and want of activity, I soon found that what little was left of my youth had given way to the spreading of my hips and the thickening of my waist that so often serves as a harbinger to middle age. After three months, vanity was the last thing on my mind. I concentrated on sheer survival.

I also learned to abide my own foul body odor, and that of my fellow prisoners, since we were allowed to bathe in cold water only once every fortnight. My sexual needs, which had always been voracious, were now somnolent and nonexistent. I kept track of time in the oldest way known to man. Early in my imprisonment, I found a small stick in the courtyard. I secreted it in my cell, and each day when we came back from the courtyard, I would make a small scratch in the earthen wall of my cell. I'm not certain I marked every single day. I probably didn't. However, I was reasonably certain that it was the late summer of 1578, or close to it, some eighteen months after I'd first been unceremoniously thrown into Limerick Gaol courtesy of the Earl of Desmond, when, one day, a female guard approached me and signaled me to follow her to the upper floor of the gaol.

Once there, I was allowed to thoroughly cleanse myself in hot water, with ample soap and a towel with which to dry myself. I was provided a reasonable set of clothing – trousers and a loose-fitting brown blouse – which were large enough to afford my new, heftier figure a degree of comfort – and a pair of sandals. I was led into a room where I was presented to a man only a little taller than my own height. This fellow, who was in his late fifties, had a moderate pot belly and wore a periwig, breeches, and a daycoat.

"Granuaile ni-Mháille, I adjure you to curtsey to your superior, Lord Justice Drury, the President of Munster." I found Desmond's fawning obsequiousness to be demeaning and disgusting, far different from the courageous man who'd once been my friend in the past.

"Lord Drury," I said neutrally, neither bowing nor deferring to him.

"Ah," Drury said. "So this is the notorious woman that hath impudently passed the part of womanhood and been a great spoiler, chief commander, and director of thieves and murders at sea to spoil this province."

"Ah," I responded in a tone equal to his. "I find your charm to be underwhelming, Mister Drury."

"Silence woman!" he thundered.

"Of course," I said, smirking. "Your forcefulness in the face of a woman certainly betrays your strength of character. Does Mrs. Lord Drury accept this sort of treatment, or are you only allowed to do this when confronting a prisoner who has no power to so much as move."

"I suggest you mind your tongue," he said, obviously fighting back his anger.

"Why? If I don't, will you cut it out? And why not cut off my breasts and my arms while you're at it. Isn't that the English way?"

"Well, Granuaile," he said, smiling – a rather malevolent smile I thought – "we seem to have gotten off on the wrong foot. The Earl of Desmond has performed the admirable service of bringing you to me in order to prove his loyalty to the Crown. Would you agree that turning you over to me would demonstrate his fealty?"

"No, Lord Drury," I said, summoning up my own dignity. "He seems to believe I'm going to die in his prison and he'd just as soon not have my blood on his hands. He knows that sooner or later, regardless of what he might think, my death would be avenged, if not by the O'Malleys, then by the Burkes, the O'Flahertys, or other clans throughout this island who will recognize the infamy of his betrayal."

"Strong words," Desmond broke in. "Easy to say when you're housed in the comfortable accommodations with which I've provided you. I think you'll remember Limerick Gaol with fondness when you settle down in your next abode."

"And where would that be, Desmond?"

Lord Drury answered the question. "Granuaile ni-Mháille, regardless of how we started out, I am not unaware you are famous throughout Ireland for your stoutness of courage and person and for your sundry exploits at sea. You will have ample opportunity to test that courage. At the conclusion of this interview, you will be transferred to Dublin Castle, where you will remain in my care until..."

He didn't finish his sentence, and didn't need to. I shuddered. The dungeons of Dublin Castle seldom released any of their convicted tenants to relate the grim happenings which occurred behind the dark, dank walls.

The ominous words of Lord Drury, "where you will remain in my care until..." could mean only one thing. Until I died or was murdered in Dublin Castle.

I had been less than thirty days in Dublin Castle when I was summoned to the upper storey of that frightful place. As with my interview at Limerick Gaol, I was allowed to bathe and dress in "civilized" clothing. When I entered the large room accompanied by two guards, I was shocked to see not one, but three well-dressed gentlemen waiting for me, all of whom I recognized. There was Lord Drury, of course. But it was the other two men who turned to face me, who saw my astonishment.

"Good day, M'lady. It seems we meet in a different place and under different circumstances. I trust you have maintained your courage and your spirit?"

"Aye, Sir Henry, but not without difficulty. And Sir Phillip, if anything you look more dashing than ever. A shame I have changed in appearance as much as I have, but I've been in rather different circumstances than the two of you."

"I can't say I don't appreciate your setting me free. Indeed, I owe you my life. But why the devil did you wait so long?"

"Politics, Granuaile," Sir Henry replied. "As you are only too well aware, the Crown considers you a thorn in its side. Roaming free, you are the very symbol of rebellion. Don't get me wrong, we don't trust the Earl of Desmond much farther than our ability to see him, but if he wanted to 'prove' his loyalty to the Queen by capturing and holding you, we were in no position to interfere with him."

"So you let me rot in Limerick Gaol for a year-and-a-half..."

"I did, and for that I apologize – privately, of course. But, as I said, it was..."

"Politics," I finished the sentence, not without some bitterness. "And this transfer to Dublin Castle? Its reputation is known far and wide, and if you wanted to frighten me to death, you couldn't have done a better job."

"Perhaps I can explain," Lord Justice Drury interjected politely. "I realize you perceived me as the devil incarnate, and if you could have spat arrows at me when we first met, you would have done so."

"You'll get no argument from me on that."

"I, too, can only apologize. It was part of a charade to cut you loose from Desmond, who'd have continued holding you in Limerick Gaol until you quite probably would have died. Fortunately for you, we represented a superior force, and one which the Earl of Desmond wanted to impress with his fealty. I seem to have forgotten my manners again, Lady Grace. Would you care for some more hot ale?"

"Yes, thank you, Lord Justice." He poured me a fresh mug and passed me a plate of pastries, which I gobbled most impolitely, not having had sweets for more than a year-and-a-half. "I trust you have news of my husband? My children?"

"Aye, Lady Grace." This from Phillip Sidney. "All well, all concerned. My father and I met with Richard-an-Iarrain shortly before we departed for Dublin. He's aware we're setting you free."

"Final question, gentlemen. Why are you doing so, knowing what you do about me?"

"Ahem." Sir Henry Sidney coughed uncomfortably. "There are problems, Lady Grace," he said. "It seems that my annual levy, which was designed to fund a central government militia for Ireland, has caused discontent among the wealthy landowners. My colleagues in the Privy Council tell me that those landowners, Protestants, of course, carried their grievances to the Queen. She has summoned me to return to London next month, where I'm told that I will not be happily received. I fear that notwithstanding my loyal services to the Crown, once I return to England I will be relieved of my duties as Lord Deputy and will not be returning to Ireland."

"I'm sorry," I said, and earnestly, for Sir Henry had truly been a decent man.

"Oh, I'll manage to survive," he said ruefully. "I've no doubt my position on the Privy Council is secure, and, if need be, I've got the wherewithal to simply retire to Ludlow Castle and serve as president of the Welsh Marches. But to answer your earlier question, you have always been honest with me, Lady Grace, and I respect such candor. Who knows what would happen to you were you to remain in Dublin Castle after my departure? You probably *would* perish. As someone whose honor demands that he be a decent human being, notwithstanding our differences, I felt it incumbent upon me to arrange for your freedom as one of my final authorized acts as Lord Deputy of Ireland."

"Thank you, Sir Henry, Sir Phillip, Lord Justice Drury," I said. Tears of thankfulness had come to my eyes, and I didn't try to stop them. I actually curtsied and then, uncharacteristically, burst into a full scale bout of weeping. The men initially watched uncomfortably, but then Sir Phillip, bless him, came over to where I stood, took me in his arms, and simply, gently hugged me at patted me softly on the back until my crying abated.

Alas, Sir Henry, as good a man as I had known since Edmund O'Flaherty, was prescient. Queen Elizabeth received him coldly, censured him for his extravagances, and permanently recalled him from his position as Lord Deputy of Ireland. He was replaced by the elderly Lord Leonard Grey. Much later in my life, I saw a letter from the Queen to Lord Grey directing him "to increase the revenue without suppressing the subject, to reduce the army without impairing its efficiency, to punish the rebels without driving them to desperation, and to reward loyal people without cost to the Crown." All in all, this was, of course, an impossible task. In reflecting on my years of dealings with the English and their Queen, I must say that Elizabeth's primary difficulty throughout her reign was lack of sufficient revenue. As a result, she constantly employed pence-pinching and stop-gap measures in the reconquering of her Irish demesne.

Chapter 24

Sir Henry's mistrust of the Earl of Desmond proved to be justified. When I arrived back in Connaught at the beginning of 1579 there were rumors that, come summer, there would be a major uprising against the English incursion. I was cautious against us playing any part in what I felt to be needless folly. Richard, on the other hand, was eager to engage in battle, although he hadn't yet decided on which side. In order to allay any suspicion that I had resumed my old ways, my husband and I met at Kildawnet Castle, far away from both Rockfleet and the Hen's Castle on Lough Corrib. Although it was known that Kildawnet Castle was owned by O'Malleys, it held unhappy memories for me, so it was not a place I frequented.

When I had returned to Connaught late the previous year, Richard had been diplomatic enough not to mention the substantial weight I had gained or the shift of my figure brought on by age, and I was courteous enough not to mention that he, too, had become rather portly. The physical changes in both of us had in no way lessened our eagerness to cleave to one another. I did notice, however, that my Iron Dick was exhibiting other signs of age. For one thing, he would frequently go into the antechamber during the night to relieve himself. He was gone far longer and more frequently than he had been only a few years ago, and when he returned he complained that he was not able to empty his bladder. Often, he lay awake for several hours each night, tossing and turning in discomfort.

Both of us had learned in our three decades together to be thoughtful and considerate of one another – to be nearsighted when it came to seeing faults in the other, and to be a bit deaf when either said a harsh word. I suppose this comes with all couples who have established a loving friendship that transcends time.

"Well, husband," I said after we'd had a filling, if Irishly boring, dinner that evening, "what think you of the talk of this newest rebellion?"

"There's more than a shred of truth to the rumors," he replied. "There's no question Gregory wants to recapture the countries the Church lost to the Protestants. As far as he's concerned, Elizabeth is the archvillainess of the world."

"How does that concern us, Dick? We've given little but lip service to the Church over the years. The clans have been far more important to us during our lives, but I fear even they are breaking down."

"If the Romans are only interested in our *immortal* souls and they're willing to leave how we run our *earthly* business to us, it seems to me they're the better choice."

"I don't know," I said, pondering my mug of hot ale. "We should think carefully about who's going to win if there is a rebellion. Shane MacOliverus is an old man and he can't last forever. You're the *tanaiste*, so under *Irish* law you're in line to become the next MacWilliam. But under *English* law, the MacWilliamship would go to Shane's next of kin, his brother Richard, unless, of course, the English see you as being closely aligned with them, in which case they'd be more politically astute by conferring the title on you."

"But if the Irish rebellion were successful," he rejoined, "and the Gaels saw me as being in England's pocket, I could be named *tanaiste* a dozen times and never succeed to The MacWilliamship."

"An interesting problem," I mused. "God could have done a better job than to mess in the political alliances of Ireland."

Ugo Buoncompagni, who'd taken the name Gregory XIII when he ascended to the Shoes of the Fisherman, was already an old man of seventy when he'd been elected Pope in 1572. He'd sat on the papal throne for seven years, far more than the average tenure of a Pope at that time. His election had been greeted with great joy by the Roman people, as well as by the rulers of France, Spain, Portugal, Hungary, Poland, Russia, and the various Italian states. During the next few years, he spared no effort to restore the Catholic Faith in the countries that had become Protestant. Gregory was awash in money, something that annoyed the penurious Elizabeth no end. Thus, his efforts to procure religious freedom for the Catholics of England were completely unsuccessful.

Last year, he had sent Thomas Stukeley with a ship and an army of eight hundred men to foment rebellion in Ireland, but Stukeley had joined forces with King Sebastian of Portugal against Emperor Abdulmelek of Morocco, so Stukeley's expedition had never even made it to the Irish shores. It became obvious that Gregory would send another force to Ireland, sooner rather than later.

During the months that followed our talk at Kildawnet, Richard and I assiduously avoided becoming involved in what was happening far to the south, even though we heard the news within a week or two of it happening.

Early in June, 1579, Sir James Fitzmaurice Fitzgerald, together with the English Jesuit, Doctor Nicholas Sanders, departed Corunna, in Galicia, Spain, with a small contingent of Spanish, French, and breakaway English troops. A few days later, Fitzmaurice captured two English vessels in the channel. Less than a month after that, they landed in Smerwick on the Dingle Peninsula, where they garrisoned at Dún an Óir. The following week, they were joined by two galleys with over a hundred fresh troops. Four days later, their ships were captured by the English fleet under the command of Sir William Winter.

Fitzmaurice appealed for help to most of the Gaelic chieftains in the west of Ireland, as well as to the Earl of Desmond, the same Desmond who'd captured and imprisoned me two years before to show his "loyalty" to the English crown. The O'Flahertys and some of my distant O'Malley clansmen set sail with a flotilla of galleys to help Fitzmaurice, but the English quickly forced them back to Clew Bay.

By the beginning of August, confusion reigned. Fitzmaurice left the fort to await the arrival of Stukeley, who, unknown to him, had been killed during his misguided alliance with the King of Portugal. After running out of patience, Fitmaurice went on pilgrimage to the Monastery of the Holy Cross in Tipperary. There, he became caught in a skirmish with his cousin Theobald Burke's forces. During the fight, Fitzmaurice was shot, but he somehow managed to cut his way through to Theobald, whom he killed with his sword. Fitzmaurice won the battle, but as he was leaving the battlefield, he knew he would not survive his injuries. He ordered his friends to cut off his head after his death, so that his enemies might not mutilate his body.

When he died, shortly thereafter, a kinsman decapitated him and wrapped his head in cloth. His friends tried to conceal the rest of his body under an old tree, but a hunter discovered Fitzmaurice's remains and brought them to Kilmallock. For weeks, Fitzmaurice's headless trunk was nailed to the gallows, until it was shattered by musket fire and collapsed. At this point, Sir John of Desmond, the Earl's brother, assumed command of the rebellion. Shortly thereafter, the Earl himself, reneging on his previous vow of loyalty to the Crown, joined Sir John and Doctor Sanders in their growing rebellion against the English.

I was not concerned with which side won or lost the ongoing squabble. I spent the summer months of that year attending to business. Although my fascination with the sea had never abated, I was now forty-nine, somewhat corpulent, and it pained my joints to be constantly at sea. While I enjoyed my yearly trip to Portugal and Spain, where the warmth did wonders for my physical comfort, I was content to let my captains do the hard work, while I supervised their labors.

The war was exceedingly profitable for me, as wars generally are for those who sit on the sidelines and sell necessaries to both sides. Scarcely fifty years ago, the firearm was a rare, expensive, and deadly curiosity. Most wars had still been fought as they had been from time out of mind, by sword and hand-to-hand combat. No longer. He, or in my case, she, who had the larger and more powerful cannon generally prevailed at sea, while land armies were now being outfitted with modern muskets and flintlock rifles, which had replaced the unwieldy blunderbus. When it seemed that this latest Irish rebellion would be long and vicious, everyone from landholders to publicans, and certainly those directly engaged in the battles, required – demanded – arms at any cost.

While the turnip and carrot crops were good that year and sheep and cattle seemed to abound, one never knew what would happen in future. Both sides engaged in a new form of war, a policy where they destroyed the land all around them. Because of this, wheat, barley, salt, sugar, and such, were in demand as much, even more, than guns and ammunition.

With twenty ships under my command, our fleet became a primary purveyor of such goods. Since we flew neither the English flag nor the Rebel flag, we were reasonably welcome and reasonably safe in ports from Munster to Connaught, with the exception, of course, of Galway.

In September, I returned to Rockfleet to find Richard pensive and restless. "What is it, my love?" I asked him. Over the years, we'd developed a directness of communication that came from being attuned to one another's moods.

"This," he said, showing me a letter from my erstwhile captor, Gerald Fitzgerald, the fifteenth Earl of Desmond. "He's made a formal request to The MacWilliam and one to me asking us to join in the uprising."

"You've refused, of course," I said.

"The MacWilliam has refused, but that puts me in a more difficult position than ever. If the English prevail, and Shane MacOliverus has certainly sided with them, then he's in a better position than ever to invoke *English* law to make his brother Richard the MacWilliam upon his death. MacOliverus' refusal now forces me to join Desmond, if for no other reason than to protect my claim to the title under Irish law."

Richard and I climbed the stairs to our great room. I noticed he exhibited a great deal of pain and stiffness as he made it from one flight to the next, and he had to stop every half dozen steps to catch his breath. When we got to the large room on the fourth floor, he moved close to the fireplace, warming his backside.

"Do you believe the rebellion will be successful?" I asked.

"Not a chance, Granuaile."

"Then why would you even think of aligning yourself with Desmond?"

"You hate him that much?"

"Of course not," I replied. "When he captured and imprisoned me, he was doing so to save his own skin and to make sure he was covering his rear as well as his front. I'd have done exactly the same thing in his place. Both you and I have been around long enough to know that an oath of eternal loyalty is good for a day at most."

"Which is exactly why I think I should join forces with Desmond."

There was a companionable silence between us for a few moments. I understood exactly what he was thinking. In fact, I had reflected that very thought earlier. "You're saying, it doesn't matter which side you're on. In the grand scheme of things, the English prefer power to loyalty. Richard MacOliverus, Shane's brother, is untested, and if Shane adheres to the Crown, it will make no real difference because it's The MacWilliam who's backing England and Richard simply stands in his brother's shadow. On the other hand, if you give a good account of yourself in opposing the Crown, you'd ultimately be able to make your own deal with the Lord Deputy."

"Certainly that, Granuaile. But there's another reason, too."

"Which is?"

He sighed and sat heavily down on one of the stone hobs near the fireplace before he answered. When he did speak, I heard an ineffable sadness in his voice. "Granuaile, although I don't say it frequently, I love you more than anyone I've ever known. We've never kept secrets from one another, and I won't keep a secret from you now. I'm getting on in years..."

"Fifty-six is not that old, Iron Dick."

He smiled, but ruefully. "I'll not say I don't appreciate the double meaning of that name, dear Granuaile, but as you may or may not have discovered..."

"That doesn't matter, Richard. There are numerous ways... and you've always kept me happy."

"It's not just that, my Granuaile. I fear there may be something more seriously wrong with me than either of us know or suspect."

"The night voiding?"

"Aye. It's getting worse, and more painful. I've started getting pains in my lower back, even when I lie down. And it's more difficult to lie down because I fear I've contracted the disease that so distressed the late King Henry."

"The gout?"

"Aye."

I didn't know what to say, but inwardly I trembled. From the day I'd first met him, nearly thirty-four years ago, Richard-an-Iarrain had been the strongest, most masterful man I'd ever known, except, perhaps for my late father. Richard had never been hesitant to take whatever life had to offer with great humor and good grace. It pained me desperately to see him starting to fade.

"Granuaile," he continued. "Everyone needs another hill to climb, and beyond that yet another hill. When the hills stop, life ends. Joining the Earl of Desmond is the next hill."

"I thought The MacWilliamship was the next hill, the ultimate hill."

"Aye, but unless I show myself to be Richard-an-Iarrain, the infallible Iron Dick of old, I may not even succeed in becoming The MacWilliam."

"So you're set on doing this?"

"I am."

"God bless you, then, Richard-an-Iarrain. While I may not *publicly* support you, since it's best that both of us keep our opportunities open on either side, I believe I can make a meaningful show of how much I love you."

"How?"

"Come with me, down to my ships."

He did. When he saw what I was about, color returned to his face, and there emerged the great manly smile that had swept me off my feet so many years ago. That day, I presented my husband with five shiploads of goods – six hundred muskets and flintlocks, several thousand rounds of ammunition, enough clothing, heavy boots, and dry goods to keep his Burke army in suitable warmth and comfort for most of the winter, and a hundred new saddles and tack, and fodder for his animals.

"My Esteemed Earl of Desmond," Richard wrote back. "I am pleased to grant your request to join in your revolution against the English Crown. I believe I would best serve the interests of the cause not by coming to Munster, where my forces would only compete for what food and supplies are there, but rather by remaining in my own territory, from whence I might protect the northernmost reaches of your frontiers.

"While I am certainly willing, indeed eager, to see action once again, I enter this fray not to be defeated, but to emerge victorious. In Mayo, I am confident, not only in the remoteness of my demesne, but in my familiarity with this country. Environed as it is with woods, bogs, and mountains, to no man's memory has any English governor ever ruled over this land, nor even set foot here."

In Munster, the war raged on inconclusively, with each side claiming small victories while Ireland bled.

The Earl of Desmond assumed leadership of the rebellion in a spectacular manner. On November 13, 1579, he and his followers sacked the town of Youghal, massacring its English garrison, hanging the English officials there, looting the town, and abusing the civilian population. Desmond's forces then blockaded Cork itself, before withdrawing westwards into the mountains of Kerry. Meanwhile, the Clan MacCarthy joined the rebellion and sacked Kinsale.

Chapter 25

True to his promise, my Richard remained aloof from the engagements in the south. In Connaught, he gave not only a good, but a magnificent account of himself. He first convinced the Clandonnells, the most fearsome of the Gallowglass forces, to join him. The Clandonnells were, to put it simply, the best of the best the mercenary Gallowglasses had to offer. For more than a hundred years, the Gallowglasses had been the best forces money could buy. They'd been employed both by the Irish chieftains and by the Anglo-Irish Lords. My own family had used them from time to time. If the Clandonnells were the mercenaries of the dry land, the O'Malleys were the mercenaries of the sea. No sooner word went out that the Clandonnells had come to the aid of Richard-an-Iarrain Burke, then they were joined by the O'Malleys, the Burkes, and the O'Flahertys.

During the winter of 1579-1580, Richard's forces roamed and plundered Connaught at will, decimating the O'Kelley and Athenry territories, but taking almost no lives in the process and leaving those lands intact.

At the beginning of 1580, when we met on the *Sea Ghost*. I saw that whatever illness had befallen my husband was becoming more pronounced. "Well, husband, have you had your fill of fighting and glory? You look awful, by the way," I said, hugging him gently, as a mother would her child.

"You've always been direct, Granuaile, and for that I thank you."

"You're my man, Dick. If there's anything to be done, I want to help you do it. You've made your showing and demonstrated your strength. Why do you need to prove more?"

"Because it looks like the rebellion may succeed. Isn't this the best time to consolidate my power base?"

"Looks can be deceiving, Richard. I met Nicholas Malby three years ago, when he was Henry Sidney's Deputy. The man's courageous, he's got initiative, and he has survived political upheavals before. The Earl's had his tactical victories and he believes he has the upper hand now, but I cannot see Malby losing to the Earl of Desmond in the long run."

"What do you suggest?"

"This would be the perfect time to 'surrender' and submit to Malby."

Richard was not one to let his temper get in the way of practicality, and he did not do so now. He'd been with me long enough to know that my judgment, while not always sound, was not to be lightly dismissed. "Why do you say that, Granuaile?"

"Even as we speak, my own spies have advised me that Malby is going to try to cut a deal with the Clandonnells. You've done well over the winter and they've been promptly paid, but if it comes down to the ultimate battle of the purse, the Crown can outlast you."

"Shane McHubert's castle at Donamona can hold out," Richard started to reply stubbornly. Then, thinking better of it, he said, "But perhaps not against the Clandonnells. Desmond's got Malby's main forces tied up down in Munster."

"All the more reason for him to divert to the north and show the Queen a victory. What better way can you think of to get into his good graces than by giving him a submission at this low point of Malby's campaign? Besides, you've given enough to the clan and you've shown your mettle several times over, my love. It's time we were tending to your own condition."

"I suppose you're right, Granuaile. How best to accomplish what we want and salvage my position?"

"Let me attend to that, Richard."

During the second week of February, I learned that Sir Nicholas Malby would be spending the night of the 16th at Ballyknock Castle, less than fifteen miles from Rockfleet, in advance of setting up his garrison headquarters at Burrishoole Abbey. This was convenient to me, for I had thought I'd have to hazard a secret journey overland to Galway.

On the afternoon of the sixteenth, I arrived with a retinue of six of my O'Malley kinsmen. By prearrangement, neither Richard nor any of his Burkes accompanied me. Sir Nicholas was the model of courtesy and decorum when he greeted me. Because he was surrounded by his own retainers, his countenance was studiously neutral.

"Lady Grace, there's been much blood under the bridge since you and I last met in Galway," he began. "I fear there will be far more blood spilled before the troubles are over."

"Rather silly, isn't it, Sir Nicholas?" I said.

"That depends on which side you're on. You must be aware I'm here to contest your husband's joinder in this rebellion."

"I am, Sir Nicholas. I'm also aware that the Clandonnells have come over to the English side and that within the last three days you've taken Donamona from Shane McHubert, Richard's chief counselor, and put all its inhabitants to the sword."

His eyebrows lifted. "You seem to know everything that goes on around here, Lady Grace."

"I've made it a point to do so for thirty-five years, Sir Nicholas. That's one of the reasons my head remains firmly atop my neck. With thanks, of course, to Sir Henry and Lord Drury."

"You remember your benefactors well, M'lady." He moved to an oak table and lit up a small pipe of the kind that had come into fashion after Sir Walter Raleigh's return from the New World. "Now, shall we make small talk for the rest of the afternoon, or would you favor me by telling me why you came?"

"Of course, Sir Nicholas. You are Lord Grey's second-in-command, but to all intents and purposes you are the Lord Deputy charged with the administration of Ireland for Queen Elizabeth."

He nodded. "I am here to offer you my submission and that of my husband."

At that, Sir Nicholas Malby breathed in, hardly masking his surprise. "You *and* your husband?"

"Aye."

"May I ask why, Lady Grace?"

"You may. My Richard, as you might have surmised, is a bit headstrong. Not foolish, mind you, but headstrong. I believe that with his usual eagerness for action, he probably flung himself headlong into what he calls the Desmond Revolt without due regard for the obvious consequences. You'll note he has not so much as set foot or sent any troops farther south than Lough Corrib." Malby puffed contentedly on his pipe, wordlessly urging me to continue. "I don't care about this war one way or the other, except to tell you it's been good for me."

"I'm aware of that, Lady Grace. You've been supplying war stores to both sides." This time it was my turn to be surprised at

Malby's knowledge. "So let us agree we both have spies whom we'd rather not disclose. That's perfectly all right with me and, might I add, you need have no fear of prosecution from the Crown. What you've done is neither more nor less than war profiteers have done throughout history. I accept your submission and in the name of the Crown I regrant you everything you had before you submitted, save and except I must demand payment from you of, shall we say, one cow each year."

We both laughed. I was delighted to find Sir Nicholas Malby had his predecessor's grace and sense of humor.

"But really, Grace – may I call you that in private?"

"Of course, Sir Nicholas."

"Why would Richard-an-Iarrain submit? And do you truly have a warrant to bind his submission?"

"That I do," I said, handing him a writing from my husband attesting to my authority to negotiate with the English Crown for his submission. "The reasons are, as Sir Henry told me when he arranged for my release from Dublin Castle, 'political.' Richard is *tanaiste* to The MacWilliamship."

"Under Brehon law that would stand him in good stead. English law is somewhat more complex."

"So I understand, Sir Nicholas. In many instances, but not all, that would mean that Richard MacOliverus Burke, the present MacWilliam's brother, would inherit the title on Shane MacOliverus' death."

"Yes." He eyes betrayed that he had immediately seized upon the reason Richard-an-Iarrain was offering to submit to the Crown. "You must understand, of course, that Shane MacOliverus has shown loyalty to England since his original submission."

"True, Sir Nicholas, but has Richard MacOliverus shown any real leadership ability in Connaught?"

"That's an unfair question, M'lady. When has he ever had the chance?"

"When the Burke clan held elections for the *tanaiste*."

"Madame Burke, need I remind you that your *former* husband, the late Donal-an-Chodaigh O'Flaherty was *tanaiste* to becoming The O'Flaherty."

"If you know that, Sir Nicholas, you must be aware of who was the *de facto tanaiste*."

"Touché," Malby replied, smiling equably. He gazed out one of the slit windows of Ballyknock and changed the subject. "I'm going to Burrishoole Abbey tomorrow."

"So I've heard."

"What's the place like, Grace?"

"It's an ideal choice for your garrison, Sir Nicholas, and it will give you a good opportunity to rest in the middle of the fray. Burrishoole is situated beside the river that drains Lough Furnace, within three miles of the sea. The lough has ample timber, marble, and other supplies. The iron mine near there has functioned for hundreds of years, and the land around the Abbey is arable as well as being good pastureland."

"In addition to all those good things you say, Lady Grace, the English fishing ships that anchor off the coast have paid the O'Malleys great tribute each year for the past twenty years."

"All the Crown's when I submit, Sir Nicholas."

"Aye, that's true. I trust Richard-an-Iarrain's submission is not without conditions, Lady Grace?"

"You trust correctly, Sir Nicholas. My Richard is ready to turn his troops over to the Crown, and there need be no writing necessary before he shows his good faith. I only ask that you remember when the time comes, that Richard-an-Iarrain came to you at a time when he did not need to do so, and at a time when the sun was somewhat low in the sky when it shone on England's Irish empire."

As it turned out, our submission was well-timed, for the following month the Crown repaid the Earl of Desmond's ferocious actions in kind. By the end of March, 1580, the Crown enjoyed an important strategic victory, taking the Desmond's stronghold at Carrigafoyle Castle at the mouth of the Shannon. They had now cut off Fitzgerald's forces from the north and prevented foreign troops from landing at Limerick. A number of other Desmond strongholds fell swiftly: Askeaton was abandoned, with its Spanish defenders blowing up the walls, and the garrisons at NewCastle West, Balliloghan, Rathkeale and Ballyduff surrendered soon afterwards. Many of the lords who had joined the rebellion surrendered as well, judging the English to have the upper hand. By the summer of 1580, it appeared as though the rebellion was beaten.

But then, a new rebellion broke out in the eastern province of Leinster.

For the first time ever, Iron Dick accompanied me on my annual journey to Portugal and Spain. Praise God, my great friend, Doctor António Manso Pinheiro was still alive, albeit a very old man of nearly eighty. His angel of mercy, Maria, was still his closest friend and companion, although when I found them, both had retired to Doctor António's villa near Sintra. Maria's sons had taken over Pinheiro's medical practice. Although their practice was not graced by the same wide-ranging worldview as Doctor António's, they were capable practitioners and had learned the art of diplomacy well from their mother and her great friend.

I sent word in advance of my coming that I was bringing my husband with me. In a very private, sealed letter to Maria,

I described Richard's symptoms and begged that she arrange, if at all possible, for the ancient, retired, but still brilliant, Doctor António to come out of retirement for even a day, so that he might consult with my husband.

I had always been honest with Iron Dick, and this was no time for either of us to hide the truth from the other. Before we had even set out on the journey, I told him I wanted him to see my friend and that he should tell Doctor António all of his symptoms, sparing him no details. I was gratified, but also worried, when Richard not only readily agreed to go, but also told me that of late his symptoms had gotten worse.

I should not have been surprised that Maria, Doctor António, and Maria's sons were there to meet us as the *Sea Ghost* pulled into port on June 15, 1580. Without so much as a "by your leave," they housed Richard and me next to their clinic from the first night we arrived.

The following day, all three doctors poked, prodded, and questioned Richard-an-Iarrain, then cut pieces of skin and tissue from various parts of his body, which consumed another day. The following morning, they asked us to come into their conference room. We arrived to find the three of them and Maria Correia already seated around a large table. Each looked serious and very concerned.

Doctor António Manso Pinheiro rose when we entered and bade us be seated. He commenced speaking in the gentle tone I remembered from eighteen years before. "My friends, I don't have to pretend you don't know that Richard is quite ill."

"How ill?" I asked.

"It's the crab disease," he responded.

I gasped and felt the blood draining from my face. I looked at my husband, my strong, brave, courageous companion since

I'd been sixteen, and saw the color drain from his face as well. "How bad?" he croaked.

"That's difficult to say, Lord Burke," António replied, elevating my husband's rank by several degrees. "We've found places where it *hasn't* spread," he said, not trying to raise false hopes, but not making things worse than they were. "So far as we can tell, the heaviest concentration of diseased tissue is in the area of your stomach and your midsection," Doctor António continued.

"Can you perform any kind of surgery?" Richard asked. His voice wavered and I felt he was near fainting.

"We will cut into you to see what we can find. When we touched the area where the diseased tissue was greatest, we thought we felt a growth of some kind. We could better evaluate your condition if we could enter your body and, if there is such a growth, cut out what we can."

"How soon would you want to perform this surgery?" I asked.

"Tomorrow morning," Doctor António replied.

I looked at Richard and he looked back at me. Richard, who'd just been handed what might well be a death sentence, reached over and patted my hand comfortingly. "We really have no choice, darling," he said. "I've never been one to run from a battle and I'm not about to run from this one. Can you doctors explain what you propose to do?"

"Yes, Lord Burke," one of Maria's two sons said. "Within the next hour, we propose to give you a mild sedative. My mother will remain with your wife throughout the night, since she, too, should have a sedative. Every two hours, one of us will force increasing doses of morpheus poppy down your throat, with water, of course. Within four at most, you will have no recollection of anything that happens after that."

"In the morning," the other son took up, "while you are still and continuously unconscious, we will feel the area where we think the growth is, and we will carefully measure where we think it ends. Then, we will cut three incisions in your midsection, only as deep as we need to go, and, hopefully, without cutting into any part of what we think is the growth. Once we have opened you up, we will be able to see if there is a growth, and, if there is, we will, with God's help, cut it and try to remove it."

"As simple as that?" I said.

"My dear Granuaile, nothing we do in this operation can be called 'simple,' but that is the short, direct version of what we hope to accomplish. Now, my friends, when one is dealing with the crab disease, every day is precious. With your kind and trusting permission, we'd like to start as soon as possible."

Chapter 26

I cannot remember what went on during the next two days, not because I wanted to shut it out of my mind, but because Maria insisted that for my own good it was best that I be sedated until the operation was over. On the morning of the third day, I awakened to full consciousness. Maria was holding my hand in such a way that I feared for the worst. I could not even bear to say anything. I simply looked miserably at her, much the same as I imagine a cow or sheep would look as it was being led to the slaughter.

"He's alive and he's resting," she said, in answer to my unasked question.

"That's all you can tell me?"

"That's all we know for now. My sons found a growth the size of my fist," she said. "They were able to remove it and close Richard up. When they tested the growth, they found it was filled with bad things."

"He's alive," I mumbled, feeling faint and dizzy.

"Yes. You should gather your strength, Granuaile. Richard will be fully conscious by this afternoon and we'll talk then."

"Richard-an-Iaraiin, it seems you are truly a man of iron," Doctor António said. "Although my colleagues gave me leave to speak with you, I claim no credit for what they did." The four of us were seated on wooden chairs at some distance from my husband's bedside. "Are you in pain?" Pinheiro continued.

"Yes."

"Unbearable?"

"Not unbearable, Doctor António."

"That's because you are still somewhat under the influence of the morpheus poppy," he said. "As your body starts to heal, we will administer less and less of that substance, and you may experience greater pain."

"I can live with that, so long as you can assure me that I will live, Doctor."

"That's the attitude we want you to have," Pinheiro said. "I'd like to tell you what we found and what we did."

"Please do," I said.

"As we suspected, we found a lumpy growth. Praise God, it was in such a place that we could cut it and reconnect the tubes around it. As Maria told you earlier, Granuaile, the growth was the source of the crab matter we initially found."

"Did you cut it all out?" I asked.

"We cut the lump out. Unfortunately, we have no way of knowing whether any of the bad humors have spread beyond the lump. The crab disease is tricky, and many times it appears in many places throughout the body. We can only cut out what we can see."

"So you don't know?" Richard interjected.

"We don't," one of Maria's sons replied. "If we can find more, we can keep cutting, but for now we have done the best anyone could possibly do."

"How long do I have to live?"

"There's absolutely no way we can tell you," Doctor António said gently. "We can tell you that had the lump been left inside you, it would have killed you fairly quickly, six months to a year at the most. But the lump is now gone, and we can only pray that you will live until the Lord God calls you home."

"Will there be any change in my ability to void myself?" Richard asked. Now that he felt his *life* had been spared, he was concerned with his *comfort*.

"Unfortunately not," Doctor António said, this time in a much lighter vein. "Unless you'd been born a woman, and of course you'd then have been cursed with your *menstruus* each month, you are doomed to an old man's fate, just as I am doomed to an old man's fate. You will, alas, continue to have difficulty voiding your bladder. Uncomfortable, yes, but in no way fatal."

At the end of September, 1580, we returned home. Richard complained far less of pain and malaise, and although he still experienced the "old man's condition" that he shared with Doctor António and so many others, he was far more energetic than he'd been only a few months before. My angel-medicus had even placed Richard on a very bland diet, which made his gout bearable. The crisis seemed to be over.

On November 24, 1580 Shane MacOliverus, The MacWilliam, died. My husband, Richard-an-Iarrain Burke, as *tanaiste*, was, according to Gaelic custom, next in line to succeed him. However, MacOliverus' brother, Richard, disputed my man's claim. Richard-an-Iarrain, now recharged with his second chance at life, immediately took up arms, engaged Scots mercenaries, and prepared to defend his rights. The Earl of Clanrickard's two sons, Ulick and John, sided with my husband.

Sir Nicholas Malby, no friend of the Scotsmen, sent for my Richard, so that they might negotiate how best to resolve the impasse. Shortly thereafter, I received by messenger a sealed letter from Sir Nicholas.

"My Dear Lady Grace,

"I spoke frankly with your husband, Richard-an-Iarrain, and asked why he wanted to go to war, why he was raising forces, and why he was paying the Scots. Your husband replied that when The MacWilliam had died and the title descended on him as a matter of right, his friends, particularly the Earl's son, had informed him that I intended to set up his enemy, Richard MacOliverus, as The MacWilliam.

"I told him he should have ascertained my intentions before making war, and that I was not his enemy, but that my duty was to uphold every man's rights. He replied that he really had hoped for mercy, particularly in light of his service to Her Majesty. He said he would do anything in his power. I asked him to expel the Scots and told him that if he did so, I would promise him my help."

My husband then aided Malby against the Scots, whereupon some fifteen hundred of those outlanders left the province. True to his promise, Sir Nicholas ordered the two contenders for The MacWilliamship, Richard-an-Iarrain and Richard MacOliverus, to meet with him.

Much to our delight, Malby appointed Richard-an-Iarrain as The MacWilliam and Richard MacOliverus as shire rief. My Richard was obliged to pay Sir Nicholas a fine of one hundred cows and to permanently banish the Scots from county Mayo. My husband had secured a good bargain, obtaining The MacWilliamship title at a low cost, in view of his turbulent and often anti-English record. He also got rid of the Scots whom he had employed, without having to pay them the money he owed them for their services.

With Richard-an-Iarrain installed as The MacWilliam, I attained what was to that time the pinnacle of my power and influence. My Richard conceded not only that I was the best wife imaginable, but that I had been instrumental in securing The MacWilliamship for him. Sir Nicholas wrote me again, stating:

"You have made a favorable impression in your encounters with the English authorities who, although we are aware of your illegal activities, are nevertheless impressed by your ability, your courage, and, ultimately, your proved loyalty to the Crown."

At the same time, my credibility as a Gaelic leader was not adversely affected by my show of cooperation with the English, which my clansmen and their allies recognized would be forthcoming only so long as it suited my own purpose.

In September, 1581, my Richard was knighted, and I was now officially Lady Grace Burke.

Shortly afterward, Richard MacOliverus, still smarting from being denied The MacWilliam title, slew some of my husband's followers who'd been sent into MacOliverus country to collect rents. My Richard retaliated by killing one of MacOliverus' sons. The pretender to The MacWilliamship rose up in arms and sought aid from the O'Neill and O'Donnell clans. Sir Nicholas speedily quelled this rebellion.

On October 28, Richard-an-Iarrain and I were invited to a gala gathering at the governor's residence in Galway. It was an impressive assembly, a gathering of all the principal powers of Connaught.

We arrived to find the residence glittering with what must have been hundreds of candles. The wealthiest and most beautiful people in Ireland must have all been arrayed there that night. Even at my age, given the lands I'd seen and my own sexual adventures in an earlier day, I was shocked at how daring some of the ladies – and I admit they seemed such very *young* women – dressed. To a woman, each of them seemed to wear brighter colors with necklines so low and busts pushed so high that very little was left to the imagination.

The gentlemen, as well, seemed, all of them, tall, straight, and dressed in the tightest of breeches, white, yellow, red, and even bright green waistcoats, and matching jackets with contrasting piping down the arms and around the lapels.

Though he was older than most, my husband cut a dashing figure and I was so proud to be seen with him. Richard and I even danced some of the latest, most popular dances come lately from England – or so I was told they were among the most popular dances. Even at my age, I felt young again, and beautiful. It was that kind of a magic evening. My friend, Sir Nicholas, wrote me afterward,

"My dear friend, My Lady Grace,

"In addition to all your many talents, you were clearly the *Belle Dame* of our gathering. I salute you, who has been a warrior queen all your life, as peacemaker and socialite to absolute perfection. I foresee only good in your life to come."

During the next year-and-a-half, Mayo was quiet as my Richard consolidated his power and reputation for fairness as The MacWilliam. We maintained our close relationship with Sir Nicholas Malby. To the outside world, we were an island of peace in a sea of turmoil. Only I knew, by January, 1583, that my husband was in his final decline.

I was saddened by what I believed would be the imminent passing of my lover, my husband, and ultimately my dearest friend, who, from 1546 to 1583, had been all things to me, and who had respected my independence. We knew his last days were upon us, and we spent them not in the governing role of The MacWilliam for Richard, and not in the role of Pirate Queen of western Ireland for me, but rather in our home at Rockfleet. While there, we spent untold hours in our marriage bed, not wild with passion, but simply holding one another, and talking, crying, touching, and trying to maintain what time we had left together in the best way we knew how.

My Richard-an-Iarrain passed away peacefully on April 30, 1583 in his sixtieth year. His was the final appointment to The MacWilliam title according to the Brehon law of *tanaistry*.

I was devastated by Richard's passing, but since I had known for months that it was only a matter of time before he would not be with me for much longer, and since I had had time to mourn ahead of his death, Richard did me the great final kindness of dying slowly and gently, never complaining or telling me how painful it must have been for him. He had been as brave as a lion in his youth, and he carried his courage with him to the very last.

I wept, not as I had wept for Ballyclinch and not as I had wept for Hugh deLacy, but more quietly and, mayhap, possessed of a greater depth of feeling, for now I was truly at childhood's end.

And what of the rebellion that had erupted in Leinster after the English had all but put down the revolt in June of 1580? The wars continued. It was a war of attrition and the ultimate result, given the unification of the English and the disarray of my countrymen, was a foregone conclusion. The innocent civilian population suffered tremendously as a result of the war, being targeted by both sides and having their crops, livestock and homes destroyed. The result of this was famine and the outbreak of epidemics of diseases caused by malnutrition. In the summer of 1582, Elizabeth removed Lord Grey from the office of Lord Deputy for his excessive brutality. By mid-1582, thirty thousand people had died of famine in Munster alone. Hundreds more were dying in Cork of starvation and disease.

For the Earl of Desmond, there would be no pardon. He was pursued by Crown forces until the end. For the remainder of the war, the Earl and his remaining allies evaded capture on the run in the mountains of Kerry and Tipperary and engaged in guerrilla warfare. In early 1582, John of Desmond was killed in a skirmish north of Cork. The rebellion finally ended in 1583, when the Earl of Ormond assumed command of Crown forces. Ormond took a less ruthless approach to the campaign than the English officers had, preferring diplomacy to scorched earth tactics. He contained the rebels to the west, in Cork and Kerry, and persuaded many of Desmond's closest relatives to surrender.

On 11 November 1583 the end came when the Earl of Desmond was killed in the Slieve Mish mountains by the local O'Moriarty clan. The clan chief, Maurice, received one thousand pounds of silver from the English government for Desmond's head, which was sent to Queen Elizabeth in London. His body was triumphantly displayed on the walls of Cork city.

Chapter 27

On my husband's death, I harbored no illusions that Richard's clan would allow me to keep my fair inheritance. Thus, I immediately gathered my followers and one thousand head each of cattle and horses, and laid claim to Richard's property. It was imperative that I act quickly. According to Gaelic custom, the widow of a deceased chieftain inherited one-third of her husband's property, but Connaught had never yielded any thirds to any woman surviving the chieftain. I had experienced this before, on the death of my first husband, Donal-an-Chodaigh O'Flaherty. This time, however, I established my claim by simply moving myself, my followers, and my herds into Burrishoole, Rockfleet, and the Hen's Castle.

As I look back on those days, I realize now that there was a vast difference between our old Gaelic Ireland and the new Europe. An alliance between, say, France and Spain produced an army of fifty thousand forces, while a similar alliance between the O'Malleys and the Burkes could field a force of one-fiftieth that number. Add to that the fact that the English crown could impose and enforce taxes and tolls, and whereas I could increase my *personal* wealth by plundering any number of ships, including English vessels, my navy consisted of two hundred men. It was only a matter of time before England or France or even Spain could wear me down through sheer numbers.

I saw what was happening in Munster to the south and Ulster to the north: slowly, but irresistibly, the Gaelic gentry were being replaced with English lords. With increasing certainty, the clan chiefs were more and more siding with the English. My Richard had been elected The MacWilliam by Gaels, but he was the last one so elected. Word spread throughout Connaught that the English Deputy would appoint the next MacWilliam, *if that title were even allowed to continue to exist.*

In retrospect, what was happening was inevitable. A group of feuding clans, no matter how large and powerful, was simply no match for a unified country. Swords and brute courage were no match for cold, passionless muskets and flintlocks.

Now, twice widowed and fifty-three, I was still a power to be reckoned with in western Ireland. Connaught, however, was soon to be placed in the charge of a new governor under whose severe rule the fortunes of the province and the people, and of myself, Granuiale-ni-Mhaille O'Flaherty Burke, were to change dramatically.

Chapter 28

Sir Nicholas Malby died in March, 1584, a month before my fifty-fourth birthday. While I had not always been on the right side of Sir Nicholas, I think, when history judges him, he will be treated kindly. Due to his adroit handling of the Desmond rebellion, not to mention his diplomatic finesse in dealing with my late husband, the spirit of revolt against England never spread to Connaught, which quietly paid its taxes, continued with its old ways, and was nominally loyal to the Crown.

After Richard's death, I was too busy concerning myself with my O'Malley naval forces, consolidating my power base as far removed from the English bastions as I could be, and, of course, ensuring that my coffers were full and my troubles few. I had neither the time nor the inclination for any romantic dalliances. I no longer ventured far from Clew Bay. While I still loved the feel of the salt-air wind on my face as much as ever, my joints perennially pained me while I was at sea.

I no longer had the same exuberance and confidence I'd enjoyed in my youth. Where once the thrill of the hunt – whether for a Spanish galleon or a Barbary pirate vessel – stirred my blood and warmed my passions, nowadays I found more and more that piracy was just another means of earning a livelihood, no different from cattle rustling, soldiering, or farming. I suppose it is ever thus. When one has been engaged in an occupation for a long time – in my case nearly forty years – there is a certain sameness in everything you do.

I found myself sympathizing with the few large, old fish I often saw swimming lazily in Clew Bay – survivors – as well as the older clan chiefs, who sat around the fireplaces in their castle-fortresses rather than making war as they had done in their youth.

I was amused by a story Sir Nicholas had told me on a visit he'd made to Carraigahawley shortly after my Richard's death. An old bull and a very young one were standing atop a hillock, surveying a herd of cows. The young bull said, "Let's run down the hill and we can each mount us a cow!" to which the old veteran replied, "No, son, let's *walk* down the hill and we can mount *several* cows."

"What you're saying, Sir Nicholas, is that old age and treachery will defeat youth and vigor every time?"

"Well put, Granuaile," he'd said, chuckling gently.

Now Sir Nicholas was dead and Iron Dick Burke was dead, and I was not of a mood to fight the battles of my youth any longer.

On Malby's death, Sir John Perrott succeeded to the position of Lord Deputy of Ireland. Two months later, on the eighth day of May, 1584, a date I shall remember until I, too, am buried, Sir Richard Bingham was appointed the administrator of Connaught.

Let me here describe Sir Richard as I first saw him from a distance, shortly after he assumed his position. He was a tall man. Everything about him seemed longer than normal. He had a face shaped like an elongated heart, dark hair, which he combed to one side to try to fool people that he was not balding, a very high forehead, which made his face seem longer still, and facial hair that descended from his temples to a full moustache and goatee. His dark brown eyes were as cruel as I later found the man himself to be.

Bingham wore a shirt and waistcoat of shiny material that simulated iron, but was actually composed of thin metallic threads cleverly sewn into cloth material. He wore a high-necked scarf, which seemed to add to his already prodigious height, and a wide brass collar. A "V" shaped overlayer of artificial chain main descended to his waist. The sleeves under his waistcoat were ruffled and emphasized the longest fingers I'd ever seen on anyone, man or woman. Sir Richard fancied the tight trousers and leggings so popular in England at that time, as well as the pointed-toe delicate shoes of a nobleman.

At fifty-six, he was two years my senior, and, though our paths were to cross all-too-frequently and all-too-viciously, Sir Richard was darkly handsome in the way arrogant and powerful men can be.

When Sir Richard assumed the governorship of Connaught, I was firmly established at Rockfleet Castle and had once again resumed my career of maintenance by land and sea. My two sons by my first marriage to Donal-of-the-Battles vigorously opposed the Queen's appointment of Murrough-ne-Doe as The O'Flaherty. Donal Crone, the ousted O'Flaherty, was still alive. Despite the Crown's appointment of Murrough-ne-Doe, most septs of the O'Flaherty clan still supported Crone.

I have previously said that it was the wars between the clans, and wars *among* the clans that made us so susceptible to the Crown. The useless battle over The O'Flahertyship was one such example. Murrough-ne-Doe captured Ballynahinch Castle. It was a small, insignificant fortress, but it occupied a strategic position in Iar-Connaught. Barely two months after that, my two sons, Owen and Murrough, recaptured that bastion. Murrough-ne-Doe's son, Teige, retaliated by plundering my sons' lands. The stupid, needless, petty warfare continued for years, while, of course, the English sat on the sidelines, knowing that when there had been enough killing, they would simply walk in and take control.

At this time, the main bone of contention in Connaught was the practice of *cessing*. For many years, the English authorities had quartered troops and retinues of government officials in peoples' homes, often causing them great hardship, As time went on, neither the English nor the Gaels were enamored of *cessing*, but if it were to be abolished, it would be necessary to raise revenue so that the English could be properly quartered. As 1584 came to its end, the principal chiefs of Connaught met with the Queen's representatives, and they entered into the Composition of Connaught.

Under that agreement, which I never signed and was never invited to sign, all the lands in Connaught were surveyed, and a rent of ten shillings per quarter of tillage or pasture land was fixed. The chieftains were also obliged to surrender *their* rights to collect rents and taxes, in return for which they were "allowed" to keep their land and castles, but here the English sharply departed from the old Gaelic law. Under Brehon law, when a chieftain died, the sept or clan would elect his successor, always a male. Under the new English system, succession was by primogeniture – the firstborn son took everything.

Although my sons refused to sign the Composition, since their enemy, Murrough-ne-Doe O'Flaherty was the principal signatory to that agreement, they were nevertheless named as contracting parties. As time went on, although there were many complaints and even small rebellions stemming from displeasure with the Composition, even I had to admit that the abolition of *cessing* in favor of rents was a tolerable relief.

Of course, there was no way *I* would accept either of these alternatives. I owned Rockfleet Castle and its environs, and I defied anyone, Gael or Englishman, to challenge my hegemony or take one shilling of rent from me.

In January, 1586, Sir Richard Bingham fired the first salvo of what was to become our longstanding war with one another. He insisted that the provisions of the Composition of Connaught would be obeyed *to the letter* throughout Connaught. To show that he meant exactly what he said, with absolutely no room for negotiation, he held a session at Galway in which he ordered seventy people, many from the chief families of the province, to be hanged.

Such vicious and unwarranted action led to widespread unrest, which came to a head in Mayo. Edmund Burke was *tanaiste* to The MacWilliam title under Gaelic law. The English refused to uphold his claim and Sir Richard took the rancorous and unheard-of step of declaring that the Crown would no longer recognize *anyone* who claimed the title of The MacWilliam. Edmund, aided by septs of the Mayo Burkes, rebelled.

In April, 1586, my only daughter, Margaret O'Flaherty, and her husband, yet another Richard Burke, this one known as Deamhan-an-Chorrain – the "Devil's Hook" – came to Rockfleet Castle the day after my birthday.

I truly liked the Devil's Hook, partly because he'd always been solicitous and respectful toward me and mostly because he was a faithful, gentle, and caring husband to my Meg. It was one thing for Margaret to cozy up to me, as a small girl will always do to her mother. Still, I found it unnerving when her handsome, manly husband, who was a mature twenty-eight, referred to me as "Mama." Although I was now a very matronly fifty-six, I could not really be *that* old.

"Don't tell me you're here to wish me a happy birthday," I growled. "You're a day late."

"We didn't come here for that, but happy birthday anyway, dear Granuaile," Devil's Hook said. "You don't look a day over..."

I glared at him. "Don't say it," I warned.

"A day over the way you looked last year at that this time," my son-on-law continued smoothly. "As a matter of fact, I have some news that might interest you, and I've come to solicit your help."

"Say you so," I said. "Speak your piece, Richard."

"Sir Edmund has rebelled against the English. Last month, he fortified Castle Hag in Lough Mask and we joined him."

"You came over from Achill Island to tell me that?" I asked, referring to his demesne.

"Aye."

"You're soliciting my help?"

"Aye, again, Granuaile. You've heard what Bingham did to the seventy who opposed the Composition?"

"I have, and it did not please me."

"There's been no officially recognized MacWilliam for three years."

"Since my own Iron Dick died. But I understand most of the septs want Edmund to be The MacWilliam."

"Then you must know why we're in need of your aid," Devil's Hook said, walking over to the fireplace and tossing a large log on the ever-burning fire, as if it were a small stick of tinder.

"Having The MacWilliam's widow – God, how I hate that word – in your corner gives Edmund Burke credibility."

"You are a perceptive woman, Granuaile."

"Don't flatter me, son-in-law," I said archly. "You're aware I've no desire to pick a fight with the English."

"I don't ask you to make war on the *Crown*," he replied. "Sir John Perrott, the Lord Deputy, is a good and compassionate man. It's Bingham who's set himself up as arch enemy of the Gaelic ways."

"That may well be," I said, walking over to the fireplace, which was now more brightly alight, and turning my backside to the fire. Even in the early springtime, the aches in my joints were now such that the fire's warmth, which might have been intolerable in my youth, was now a welcome respite. "But so far he's left me alone and I've left him alone. I see no reason to change that – and every reason to keep it that way."

"Even if it means sacrificing your independence to Bingham?"

That gave me cause for thought. The prior English overlords had at least gone along with the fiction of letting us pretend we were still in control, allowing us to live by our own laws, while we realized they were slowly, but diplomatically, taking control of the reins from the clans. Now, Sir Richard Bingham, arrogant man that he was, was seeking to show us exactly who was the *ruler* and who were the *ruled*.

"What exactly did you have in mind, Hook?"

"Our spies tell us Richard Bingham's about to attack Castle Hag to teach The MacWilliam and all the Mayo Burkes a lesson."

"And?" I asked, stepping away from the fire and sitting myself down in a clever device Richard had brought to the house during his last years, a rocking chair.

"I'm told Bingham intends to circle the castle. The Burkes have always had powerful land forces, but the Crown claims to control the sea."

"Do they now?" I said, realizing too late I was rising to the Devil's Hook's bait.

"Aye. He's confident if he attacks Castle Hag from the sea, the English will prevail and our army will be useless."

"You're asking me to form a protective blockade?"

"Actually a little more than that."

"More?"

"Aye. The blockade will be a temporary feint. We believe Castle Hag will ultimately fall, sooner rather than later."

"You're sending me on a fool's errand, then?"

"Not at all. While we'll seem to be mounting a suicidal defense of Hag Castle, the Burkes and other clans have united and will be forming a massive force a hundred miles north of the castle. We'll be able to stave off the English for at least two rounds of battle. We'll run desperately low on ammunition, although Bingham's land and naval forces won't realize this. One night, our protectors, the O'Malley ships, will simply disappear, abandoning the Burkes to Bingham."

I began to see where Devil's Hook was leading, and I admired the originality of his plan.

"And when Bingham's troops awaken the next day, they'll renew the battle..."

"Against ghosts."

And so it went. Indeed, things turned out better than we'd have thought possible. Since Bingham's forces would take at least a fortnight to debark from Galway, I had time to reprovision my ships with new, much heavier cannon. We wouldn't be traveling any distance once we were abeam Castle Hag, and we'd have no need to outrun Bingham's pocket navy once we were positioned. We could carry sufficient ammunition to withstand many days' worth of attacks from the English fleet.

As the time for Bingham's attack on the castle grew closer, our information became more detailed. His initial force would consist of ten medium-sized ships, armed with between four and eight cannon each. Our informants advised us that the English cannon had a maximum range of a hundred yards. I decided to keep our smaller, faster ships, including my *Sea Ghost*, at home in Clew Bay. Our seventeen largest ships, galleys, were outfitted with eight heavy cannon each. These weapons had twice the range of the English guns, and the balls they fired were half again as large as the Crown's cannonballs.

I was certain Sir Richard's own spies had told him there would be a sea blockade awaiting his fleet, but with supreme arrogance, obviously believing his ships could blow anything out of the water, he directed his vessels to enter the waters abutting Hag Castle. Indeed, he stood on deck of the first ship to close on the castle, where he might be the most visible.

In those days, the accepted manner of a sea blockade-defense was for the defending ships to group in a semicircle around the protected castle-fortress. Since cannon were generally mounted at the broadsides of the protecting ship, that ship was normally positioned with one side facing the castle and the other facing the incoming attacking forces.

Much to the apparent consternation of Bingham's fleet, I had planned and now executed a totally different kind of blockade-defense. I commanded eighteen ships. Each had three mounted cannon on each side *and* one large cannon in the bow and one on the stern of each galley, so our boats could attack from any position. Since a ship's sides presented the largest target, Bingham's forces had not reckoned with being attacked head-on by our ships. To further confuse and frustrate Sir Richard's fleet, our eighteen vessels were lined up in alternating ranks. The four ships nearest Castle Hag faced straight out to sea, then three were positioned broadside, then another four faced frontwise, three more were turned broadside, and the four ships nearest Bingham's approaching force faced the enemy ships directly. Thus, the established English naval strategy of "break through one defender, break through the entire defense," simply didn't work. The Crown's fleet would have to break through *five* ranks of ships to get to the castle.

When Bingham's flagship drew into Castle Hag's sheltered bay, we hoisted the Hen's colors to the top of our mains, so Sir Richard could know exactly whom he was confronting. Simultaneously, the two outside galleys of our forward rank positioned themselves so they were turned inward, facing the governor's lead vessel.

When Sir Richard's flagship hove to within a hundred yards of our forward line, I put my mouth to the same type of cone-shaped speaking device I had used during the attack on Hen's Castle so many years ago, and called out, from my own lead ship, which was in the center of the front rank, "Sir Richard, you are surrounded. For your safety and those of your troops, begone, Sir!"

"Grace O'Malley, you damned harridan, how *dare* you challenge the might of England! How dare...?"

His words were drowned out as the roar of cannon fire erupted from the bow of my ship, shattering the foremast of his vessel.

"There's more where that came from, Sir Richard! I suggest you show respect for the queen of the Connaught seas!"

"Queen? You? Hah!" he exploded, deliberately spitting toward the front of his ship.

At that moment, a middle-aged man, who, by the decorated braids on his shoulders, must have been the captain of the ship, approached Bingham hurriedly. He spoke too quietly for me to hear, but he gestured frantically toward my two flanking ships, their cannon aimed directly at Bingham's head. Even from the distance separating our ships, I could see Richard Bingham darken with barely controlled rage.

Without another word, he turned smartly around and stomped out of sight, no doubt into the hold of his ship. Two sailors came smartly up to the bow of that vessel, waving white flags. The ship turned and limped away from the confrontation.

During the next two days, the lines of ships, English and O'Malley, sat facing one another, our men and theirs glaring stonily at each other. While we outnumbered them by nearly two to one, I thought it prudent not to dare the might of England by cavalierly blasting away at Bingham's fleet. Likewise, the two ranks of English ships did not venture to run the gantlet of our five lines. So it came to pass that neither naval force played any part in the battle for Hag Castle. Worse yet, the English governor of Connaught, trapped on his vessel, was as useless as teats on a bull. From time to time, he could be seen on the deck of his flagship, fuming and cursing, but it was all in vain. Our forces ensured that not so much as a rowboat debarked from any of the Crown's vessels.

On land, the indomitable Burkes made an admirable show of it, rebuffing the English forces as they mounted wave after wave of unsuccessful assaults. But, as the Devil's Hook had told me, the clan's resources were limited and the two hundred defenders were using their ammunition at a prodigious rate.

On the morning of the third day, Burke signalmen, high on the ramparts of the fortress-castle, ran two green pennants up the flagpole. To the English attackers, this meant nothing. It was the prearranged signal that tonight would be the night.

That day, the Burkes not only defended against the day's attacks, but they counterattacked and actually drove the English army to the low hills, a mile east of the castle. For the first time, it appeared the defenders might actually become the attackers and could drive the Crown's forces out of the area altogether. Worse, the English knew that with our ships ringing the castle, they could expect no assistance from their sea forces.

Midnight. All lights aboard our vessels were out. Earlier that evening, after the sun had gone down, the four galleys nearest to shore had drifted silently landward until they got to within two hundred yards of the land. I was not worried they would run aground, for I had surveilled the bay two weeks earlier and found an area of deep water near the beach that was more than sufficient for our needs.

The ships' longboats were lowered so slowly and carefully that they made scarcely a ripple as they touched the water's surface. Each rowboat could accommodate ten men, and each ship carried two longboats. To ferry the two hundred Burke soldiers out to our boats would take only three forays for each boat

Suddenly, unexpectedly, as the boats were completing their last runs, the English, in a surprise move, started firing from the sea at the brightly-lit castle, carefully making certain that the cannon were aimed high enough to avoid confronting our ships. While this was undoubtedly meant to be a ghastly surprise to our forces, in reality it proved to be the worst blunder the enemy could have made. The noise and sudden nighttime flurry of activity covered any sound made by our ferrymen.

At my command, our own ships started firing back, deliberately aiming high or low or sideways to avoid a direct hit on the English ships. So concerned was the enemy that no one noticed four of our galleys repositioning themselves toward the front rank, but far to the right of the action.

The firefight lasted more than an hour. During that time, the four vessels bearing two hundred land defenders, including the Devil's Hook and Edmund Burke, The MacWilliam himself, quietly slipped out of the bay, headed north toward the reinforcements who at that moment were on their way south. Four additional ships formed a protective blockade and ran interference for the convoy as far as the open sea, then returned to join the "battle" with the enemy.

As the sun rose the next morning, the English were surprised to find that where there had been eighteen ships protecting Hag Castle the night before, there were now only fourteen defenders. Even more to their astonishment, my own flagship ship raised a white flag and the thirty oarsmen rowed directly toward Sir Bingham's vessel.

When we got to within a hundred feet of that warship, my captain called for their leader to come on deck, and when that man did, our senior officer asked permission for me to board and speak with Sir Richard Bingham. Their captain sent a sailor scurrying downstairs. It took an inordinately long time for the man to return, and when he did, he seemed flushed with embarrassment. He whispered something in his captain's ear and that man, too, seemed uncomfortable. When he finally spoke, it was in a low voice, but one that carried well across the water separating the ships.

"Sir Bingham says he has nothing to say to your lady," their captain said to ours. I was near enough that I could hear every word he said.

In an equally quiet voice, I said, "Captain, I can see you are disturbed by your governor's lack of grace and even more so by his lack of good manners." The captain looked down at the deck of his ship and said nothing. "Very well, if Sir Richard refuses to face me man-to-man, or even man-to-woman," here, I stopped and chuckled mirthlessly, "I will give you the message I would have given him. You'll notice that four of our ships have departed. Sir Richard may have Castle Hag, if that is his wish, without firing a shot, and your bloodthirsty governor will find there is not a man-jack left to kill within a hundred miles of the castle. If he wishes to fight with shadows, that is his choice. As between you and me, I suggest we disengage from our useless endeavor and that each of us be discharged to go hence."

The captain looked up. Even from the distance separating us, I could see the shadow of a smile cross his face. Graciously, he tipped his right hand, fingers extended, to his forehead, the universal sign of a respectful salute.

"I heard that!" screamed Sir Richard as he mounted the stairs from belowdecks. "So you think you've made a fool of me in front of my legions? Very well, Grace O'Malley – *Lady* Grace," he said with as much venom and disdain as his voice could muster. "I concede that perhaps this day seems to be yours. But we will be here many years, you and I, and our paths will cross again. Make no mistake, *Lady* Grace. I will crush you as one crushes the carrion worm beneath his boots, and I will live to see you despair of your own life. Fitchet bitch!"

With that, he turned on his heel and went belowdecks once again.

Shortly after Bingham's ignominious "victory" at Castle Hag, the Irish of Connaught demonstrated once again that they knew how to lose everything they had won. Richard Roe Burke, a distant relative who had not been actively involved in Edmund Burke's revolt, "turned coat," and submitted to the governor. Bingham "rewarded" the loyal Richard Roe by promptly trying him and hanging him on the gallows within a fortnight. The governor engaged in such vicious reprisals that the incipient revolution began to wane. It did not escape my notice, however, that neither Bingham nor his armies came anywhere near Rockfleet.

A month later, I heard that all was not well in Bingham's demesne. Friction had arisen between Bingham and Sir John Perrott, the Lord Deputy in Dublin. Rumor held that Perrott was secretly compiling charges against Connaught's governor, accusing him of cruel and unjust practices which had resulted in the revolt in Connaught. Within three weeks, the Lord Deputy ordered that the remaining rebels be protected by the Crown and returned to their homes. I am certain that Sir Richard fumed inside, but there was nothing he could do, since he was Perrott's subordinate. So it was that despite Bingham's threat of retribution, there was peace. For now.

Chapter 29

The peace did not last for long. In June, Lord Deputy Perrott announced that Edmund Burke was to receive a small part of The MacWilliam lands, while William, Shane MacOliverus' nephew, received the greatest portion. Edmund and his followers were incensed at this decision and rose again in revolt. This time, Edmund was joined by the Joyces, the O'Malleys, and various septs of the Mayo Burkes.

Meanwhile, Sir Richard's brother Captain John Bingham, acting as the governor's agent, boldly entered my territory, no doubt with bad intent, since Sir Richard was still smarting from the humiliation I had dumped on his head at Castle Hag.

On July 30, 1586, in the fifty-seventh year of my life, Captain John Bingham finally subdued the Burke rebellion. Showing that he was as cruel as his brother, that same day John Bingham held sessions and tried and hanged Edmund Burke, who was then ninety years of age, and who, under Gaelic law, was the rightful heir to The MacWilliam title. Thus ended the rebellion in Mayo, but in Iar-Connacht, in my eldest son Owen O'Flaherty's territory, Captain Bingham proceeded to loot the land, seizing booty and cattle to pay for the expenses of the Crown incurred in the rebellion.

My son Owen, although married to Katherine Burke and a relative by marriage of the hanged Edmund Burke, had not taken part in the rebellion. Nevertheless, Bingham's brother, bastard that he was, brought me one of the greatest heartbreaks of my life. I heard the story from my son-in-law, the Devil's Hook, one evening in July, when he rode alone to my castle at Carrigahawley. It was one of the few times I'd ever seen this brave man cry.

"M-m-mama Granuaile," he stammered. "I bring you dreadful news. I pray only that you don't hold me to account."

"Of course not, Devil," I said. My heart dropped, and I suspected that whatever he had to say would be beyond my ability to deal. "These are bitter times indeed. Thus far, I've managed to elude Captain John Bingham, but barely."

"I'll not mince words, Granuaile. Your Owen has been murdered." If someone had taken a jackhammer and slammed it into my stomach and then beaten me over the head, I could not have been more battered than by that news.

Oh, God, my Owen, my firstborn. So gentle and giving throughout his life. Owen holding onto my skirts. Owen defending his sister against baby Murrough. Owen, the perfect little gentleman, the perfect son. Never, never, never a harsh word from his lips about anyone. Owen, my Owen, too good for this life, too gentle a man to be anything but an angel. At the moment my son-in-law delivered this news, a large part of me died. More so than when I lost Ballyclinch, more so than when I lost Hugh DeLacy, and, God help me, more so even than when I lost my beloved Richard-an-Iarrain.

I was dead inside, and no matter what anyone would do to me in future, it could not compare with the incredible pain and emptiness I felt at that moment. I wanted to cry out, to scream, to kill those responsible – and there was not a damned thing I could do. There was no way to bring him back. I wanted to vomit and I wanted to leap from the highest castle battlement to join him. Oh God, God, God, you have damned me more than any other woman! As wicked as I had been in my life, why did You not visit this death on me rather than on my angel Owen? If I lived another fifty years, I would never again be without pain, without emptiness, without coldness.

I knew I was in shock, but for the sake of the Devil's Hook, a good man, I must somehow force myself to stay calm, at least until he departed. There would be time to suffer and to grieve, and that would be long and slow. It would be for the rest of my life.

"Is it that bastard John Bingham's doing?" Surprisingly, I was dry-eyed and I managed to control the fury and the unbearable sense of loss I felt inside.

"Indirectly."

"What mean you, 'indirectly'?"

"Captain John was pursuing the Joyces and other rebels. When the English troops failed in their effort to capture the rebels, they were furious, frustrated, and hungry. Unluckily, they happened to come to the mainland abutting Owen O'Flaherty's island that evening."

"But my Owen would not think to tamper with the Crown," I said stonily.

"To the contrary. When Captain Bingham's troops called over for food, Owen ferried all the soldiers over to his island, where he provided them with the best of food and drink."

"That sounds like my son." My shock was giving way to desperate sadness.

The Devil's Hook continued, gathering a semblance of self-control at last. "That very night, Owen was apprehended by his guests. He and eighteen of his followers were bound together with a rope. In the morning, the English soldiers seized four thousand cows, five hundred stud mares and horses, and one thousand sheep, leaving the poor people on Owen's island destitute. The English marched the prisoners and the cattle to Ballynahinch, where they met Captain Bingham."

"Go on," I urged him.

"Bingham hanged the eighteen prisoners, including ninety-one-year-old Theobald O'Toole. He spared Owen and left the area. The next night, a false alarm was raised in the camp at midnight. Owen was bound in Captain Molloy's tent, and in the melee that followed, he was stabbed twelve times and died. No one took credit for the murder, and Captain John Bingham uttered a perfunctory 'apology' the following day.

The next several days went by in a blur. I could not eat, and my days and nights were consumed in endless crying, shouting imprecations to the heavens, and mostly in suffering an agony that could never be erased, I cursed the God who had too early taken my son. Better he'd have been ripped from my body before I'd birthed him, for then I would not have had a chance to know him, to watch as his fat little legs pummeled the air long before he could walk; to hear his squeals of joy as he discovered new vistas everywhere. To hold him to my breast – he had even been gentle when he gave suck, as if he did not want to bother me or hurt me in any way. I could still smell the milk-sweet aroma of the little fellow after he'd eaten his fill of the most natural sustenance I could give him.

Owen, who suffered Donal-an-Chodaigh's rages with equanimity and patience. Owen, who never held a grudge. Owen, whose entire life was a paean to the kindness of the human soul. And now he was gone. Gone forever. Or, at the very least, gone until the time when I would cross over to a better place, and he and I and Richard-an-Iarrain and Ballyclinch and Hugh DeLacy and Maria Correia and António Manso Pinheiro and my father and mother would all be together once again.

As much as I hated, as much as I damned the inequities of the harsh governor and his equally cowardly brother, I felt the ineffable helplessness of knowing – *knowing* – that they commanded a power greater than mine. I could only hope they would get their comeuppance when, as all men eventually do, they faced their Maker. At this point in my life, I came to understand how even the bravest human being can be beaten down until they submit, until they grovel, until they lose their humanity.

But I would not lose my humanity. I would not lose my identity. I was Granuaile ni-Mháille, daughter of the Black Oak, widow of The MacWilliam, Queen of Connaught. The time would come, I swore. Regardless of what happened in the future, part of my soul was dead. But regardless of what happened in future, the rest of me would live.

The Devil's Hook, God bless him, came back the following week, and started spooning warm broth into me, bathing me, even washing the bedclothes, which by that time were rank with the festering pustules, which had formed when I tried to stab myself, to create physical pain that might, perchance, balance the pain I felt inside. By the time he left, it was a fortnight after he'd told me of my son's death. While I had wished myself dead a thousand times, I kept on breathing. Day continued to pass into night and there were times when I even managed to sleep a few hours before the sun rose once again.

His parting words were, "Always remember, you are Granuaile ni-Mháille, Grace O'Malley, and you must now live not only for your departed loves, but for your departed son as well. If you allow Owen's death to kill *you*, then the evil ones would have won, and to what purpose?"

Although I was in no mood to be comforted, I started to feel a small measure of peace within my soul.

A week after that, I finally chose to leave my castle, to smell the salt air of Clew Bay and feel the breeze on my dried and puckered face, which, I daresay, was now truly that of an *old* woman. It was a beautiful sunny day, rare even in summer, and its very warmth and brightness consoled me.

I'd gone about a hundred yards on the path to the sea, when suddenly I felt some sort of netting thrown over my head. As I turned to retrace my steps, I found the net drawing tighter on all sides. I was pulled to the ground. Despite my kicking and screaming, my entire body was soon tied so tightly that I could not move in any direction. I lay there panting and furious, as I am sure a wild animal does when it is brought down and secured by a strength greater than its own.

Bound and helpless as I was, when I looked up, I found myself face to face with the cruel Captain John Bingham, he who was responsible for murdering my son.

"Well, well, well," he said, with malicious glee. "What have we here? Why, I daresay it appears to be the redoubtable Grace O'Malley. I am sure you have many things to say, for my brother tells me you've never been one to spare a caustic word."

I looked up. Without saying a word, I hawked up such spittle as I could muster and spat full in his face, and this in

front of his lieutenants. Stunned, he reacted by slapping me as
hard and viciously as he could, so hard in fact, that tears came
to my eyes and I could hardly see. But even if he killed me
right then and there, I would never give that bitch-spawn the
satisfaction of seeing me cower or hearing me cry. No sooner
he stopped hitting me for a moment to catch his breath, I spat
in his face once again.

He responded by punching me with closed fist until
both my eyes swelled up so black and puffy that I couldn't see.
Then, becoming aware that I was tied up and on the ground,
he started kicking me anywhere he could find a place. The pain
was unimaginable – worse than giving birth, but it was nothing
compared to the pain I'd experienced over Owen's death.

As Captain John Bingham kept up his raging onslaught,
I was carried away to another time, another place. What was
going on was meaningless. Since my throat was so swollen I
could not talk, I went outside myself. It was as if I were floating
above what was going on below, watching a tall, wretched,
infuriated beast pummeling and kicking and bestially mauling
a helpless old woman. And through it all, my mind repeated
over and over and over again, without stop, "I am Granuaile ni-
Mháille, daughter of the Black Oak, widow of The MacWilliam,
Queen of Connaught. The time will come. I am Granuaile ni-
Mháille, daughter of the Black Oak, widow of The MacWilliam,
Queen of Connaught. The time will come. I AM GRANUAILE
NI-MHÁILLE, DAUGHTER OF THE BLACK OAK, WIDOW OF
THE MacWILLIAM, QUEEN OF CONNAUGHT. THE TIME WILL
COME. THE TIME WILL COME..." and I lost consciousness.

I was half-dragged and I half-stumbled along, bound
with heavy chains, for two days. Along the way, ten others
were snared and these ten and I were shackled together and
whipped from time to time if our footsteps faltered. We were

fed once each day, in the evening, and then only a thin, sour, oily gruel that smelled as though soldiers had urinated in it. While I gagged and felt like throwing it back up, it was the only sustenance I had.

A thousand head of cattle – *my* cattle – accompanied us. That low and despicable heap of human garbage had asserted his dominion over what been, and by rights still was, mine.

On the afternoon of the third day, our sad party reached Ballinahinch Castle in the shadow of the Twelve Bens. Captain John went into the castle and emerged with the arch-bastard, his brother Sir Richard Bingham, the English governor.

"Ah, Lady Grace," he beamed, with cynical humor. "We meet once again, this time on land. Last time we met, I told you I would not forget what I owed you, and I have not. Come see what I have prepared for you."

Despite the dryness in my body, I somehow managed to gather enough spittle to broadcast it into *his* face. Unlike his brother, he refused to allow his court to see his rage explode.

"You seem to be enjoying your last wish early, Your Ladyship," he said, grabbing me hard by the arm and propelling me forward. "That's fine. Come around to the other side of the fortress and see your gift."

When we got to the rear of the fortress, there was a tall, newly-built gallows. I had not a doubt that Richard Bingham fully intended to ceremonially hang me as a lesson to any would-be rebel. Such was his reputation, and such had been his actions in the past, so why should I be any different?

But I had died a thousand deaths already with the passing of my darling Owen, and if he thought I would give him the satisfaction of pleading for my life, or weeping, or begging, he was dead wrong. When I saw the gallows, I held my head high and managed to croak, dry throat and all, "As you have prepared what you think will be for me, know you, Richard Bingham, that one day it will be for you as well. I damn you and I damn the mother that fed and weaned you. I damn you ten times ten generations from now and, like Onan of old, I pray your only sexual pleasure comes when you spill your own demon seed on the ground."

"Silence, impudent woman!" he growled.

"What will you do if I am not silent? Hang me higher? Kill me more slowly? Make it more painful than you did for my Owen? I do not fear you and I do not fear the likes of you, Richard Bingham. You are a bully, and a bully is nothing more than a coward, a mouse turd pushed high."

"It seems you *want* me to hurt you, to physically abuse you in front of my retinue. Well, Grace O'Malley, I have no intention of dignifying your empty prattle by battering a mere woman, a weak vessel of no account." He whistled sharply, and two burly men came forward. "Guards! Take this worthless old slut to the dungeon, where she will stay and rot for three days, during which time she will be tried for treason. On the fourth day, she will be led to the gallows, there to be hanged by the neck until she is dead."

At fifty-six, I had already lived longer than most, and if I was to die, it was in the fullness of my years. If Richard Bingham thought I would spend my last days moping and crying, reflecting on my past life, or ruminating like some poor cow about to be led to the slaughter, he was sadly mistaken. I never considered myself a heroine or someone of such bravery as to be emulated, but in this circumstance I did not care if I died by Bingham's hand on the gallows or by drowning in the sea. I determined to die with my head held high and I would not give him the least satisfaction by showing that Granuaile ni-Mháille had died a sniveling coward.

As promised, on the morning of the fourth day I was led out to the gallows. The morning was foggy and dour, a perfect day for death. The assemblage was few, and all of them were English, so far as I could tell.

"Well, my dear Grace," Bingham said mockingly. "Have you any final words of wisdom you wished to impart to us?"

I turned my back to him and did not utter a word.

After a brief period, Bingham nodded and the hangman ascended the scaffold, the black head shroud in his hand. My two guards roughly turned me toward the gallows and prepared to march me to my death, one on each side to ensure I would not bolt and run.

The assembly was startled by a noise coming from the other side of the castle. I stared in wonder as my son-in-law, Richard "the Devil's Hook" Burke rode straight up to Richard Bingham, dismounted from his chestnut gelding, and calmly walked to within two feet of the man.

"Sir Richard, the Lord Deputy commands that you read this letter immediately."

"Who are you?"

"You really don't know?" Devil's Hook asked.

"I believe I have seen you before," Bingham remarked. "Very well, whoever you are, I will deal with this in a few moments. As you can see, I am busy with a hanging this morning, and I will have this finished first."

"I think not, Richard Bingham," Devil's Hook said, deliberately omitting the "Sir" to which the governor was entitled to be called.

"What? How dare you presume to speak to me thus?"

"I speak for the Lord Deputy, Sir John Perrott, Bingham, and if I am not mistaken, he is your direct superior."

"That he may be, whatever you call yourself, Snark or Hoke, or something like that."

"Ah, so you know my name after all, or something like it. Listen, dog turd, I think you'd best read the letter from your superior *before* you carry out something for which you'll be sorry later."

"How dare...?"

"Are you going to read the letter, or shall *I* read it to the witnesses standing around, waiting for you to perform an unlawful as well as unnatural act?"

Sir Richard rudely grabbed the envelope and ripped it open. He extracted a sheet of vellum paper, read it quickly, and threw it on the ground. His face turned a scarlet. "What drivel is this? A forgery, no doubt."

"Read the seal, Bingham," Devil's Hook said. "If you want to risk disobeying this document, that's certainly your prerogative."

By that time, a group of some dozen men gathered around the letter. One of Bingham's courtiers read the contents out loud.

"To Sir Richard Bingham, Governor of Connaught, from Sir John Perrott, Lord Deputy of the Province of Ireland, Greeting. We are advised that you have in your custody one Lady Grace O'Malley, and that you propose to try her for treasonous acts. We find no records or evidence of such acts, and, of course, if Grace O'Malley is to be tried, she is to be afforded due process guaranteed by the law of England.

"Richard Burke, also known as the Devil's Hook, is known to be a loyal supporter of the Crown and a worthy man. He has agreed to stand as bondsman on behalf of said Grace O'Malley. Therefore, under Richard Burke's recognizance, you are hereby ORDERED to set Grace O'Malley free from your custody forthwith, and discharge her to go hence, and you are further ORDERED to appear at the regular assizes in

Dublin thirty days hence, then and there to SHOW CAUSE IF
ANY YOU HAVE, why all charges preferred or contemplated
to be filed by you against said Grace O'Malley should not be
dismissed and vacated altogether, AND IF YOU DO NOT SHOW
SUCH CAUSE, then the bond of said Richard "Devil's Hook"
Burke shall be exonerated, and he shall be quit of such bond..."

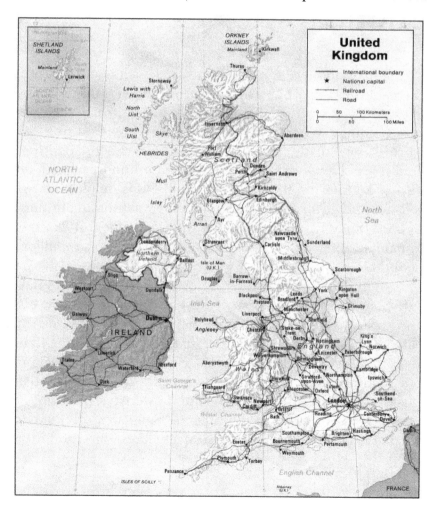

Chapter 30

Sir Richard did not show cause sufficient to press charges against me, but while I had my freedom, the English forces in Connaught had raided and stolen nearly all of my cattle holdings. Where immediately before my capture, I had had three or four thousand head of horses, sheep, and kine, I found my holdings reduced to less than a hundred head, and these of an inferior grade. Worst of all, I was helpless to fight back, for the governor, even though he was nominally under the Lord Deputy's administration, was very much in charge of Connaught. He had the ear of the Queen and a substantial force of militia to do his bidding.

While I still retained my ships. Richard Bingham's naval contingent kept me under such close scrutiny that I had little room to maneuver. My ability to maintain myself by sea was, to all intents and purposes, foreclosed. For the first time in my life, I suffered deprivation of funds. Not content to restrain me from making my living around Clew Bay, the English harried my ships when they tried to journey south to Munster, Leinster, and beyond. As word reached me that the Spanish were readying an Armada of a size never before imagined, to once and for all smash the English, it became near impossible for my ships to navigate the waters between Ireland and the Continent.

To further infuriate Sir Richard Bingham, my son-in-law, the Devil's Hook, never a friend of the governor, rebelled, thus annulling his pledge of my own good conduct. Shortly thereafter, as if nature itself were conspiring against me, half my ships were destroyed in a tempest off Clew Bay. It was time for me to take what little I had left and seek my fortune in a safer area, a place where I'd never previously been.

Ulster was the northernmost province of Ireland. The O'Neills and the O'Donnells ruled the land, one of the few Brehon bastions not yet seized by the claws of the English lion. For many years, the O'Malleys had maintained a close association with those fine clans, based on both friendship and business. When conditions became intolerable in Clew Bay, I left Rockfleet with my ten remaining vessels, commencing on June 11, 1587, and headed toward Ulster and the sanctuary I hoped the O'Neils and the O'Donnells would provide me.

We started out two vessels at a time, so as not to alert the ever-present English ships who, in all but name, were my gaolers. The *Sea Ghost* was the sixth vessel to depart, and it was fortunate that I chose to go on the third night, for I later learned that the following morning the English forces became suspicious that six out of the ten ships had gone missing, and immediately impounded my remaining four galleys. This was a severe blow to me, because my own armada had now been reduced from twenty ships to six.

From Kildawnet, my sad little fleet scurried up the channel into Blacksod Bay. On the fifth day out of Rockfleet, we regrouped at Donegal Town, where we were met by young Hugh Roe O'Donnell, son of The O'Donnell himself. Hugh was a handsome, strapping man. I assumed he was close to the same age as my son-in-law, the Devil's Hook. He'd been educated in England and had already been given the title Earl of Tyrone.

Yet, although O'Donnell had been a beneficiary of Queen Elizabeth's largesse, he was no admirer of Connaught's governor and my nemesis, Richard Bingham. He bade me follow him to a two-storey high, wood-beamed inn, in Donegal Town itself, where we sat companionably, quaffing ale and nibbling at hard scones.

"The only good news I can give you, Lady Grace," he said, "is that Bingham has been ordered by Her Majesty to serve in Flanders. He leaves next month. I suggest you consider staying in a remote area of Donegal for the next few months."

"Where would you recommend, Hugh O'Donnell?"

"*Oileán Thoraigh*, Tory Island. Even though we're still nominally in control of Ulster Province, I think it's best for your safety that you remain as invisible as you can."

"Where is Tory Island?"

"Eight miles off the northwest coast of County Donegal." He unrolled a chart he'd brought with him, and pointed how we'd get there. "From Donegal, you travel west to the open ocean. Then you head northeast, navigating Glen Bay, which is fairly small, then the larger Gweebarra Bay and Rossen Bay. Northeast of that, you'll cross the Tory Sound, and here," his index finger tapped the map, "is Tory Island."

"Doesn't look like a big place."

"It's not. It's three miles long and about a mile wide. But it'll be sufficient for your needs. Large enough to house you and feed you and hide your ships. There's a protected hidden cove on the northwest edge of the island. The O'Donnells and the O'Neils will make sure you're well-provisioned and well-guarded."

"It was good of you to welcome me, Hugh Roe O'Donnell, better yet that you've made arrangements for my stay. How's your father?"

"He's well, thank you."

"I'm told he passed The O'Donnell title to you last month."

"Aye, he did." Hugh smiled broadly and proudly.

"And the O'Neil?"

"Tirlough Luineach's growing old and feeble. Mayhap when he dies I'll acquire the O'Neil title as well," he said, not mean-spiritedly, but in a quite natural tone. "If we're to survive the English onslaught, the clans will inevitably have to unite."

"My thoughts exactly, Hugh O'Donnell."

"Might I suggest that six of the O'Neil masters sail your ships to Falcarragh, the jumping-off point for Tory Island, and that you ride with me by land to see what the countryside is like?"

"I'd like that very much, Hugh O'Donnell," I said, and sincerely.

During the ride through County Donegal, from Donegal Town in the south to Falcarragh in the far north, I had ample time to consider my now straitened circumstances. Where a year ago I had commanded a thousand men and twenty ships that raided other vessels at will and traded as far east as Spain, I now had less than a third of that number in ships and less than half the men. I was twice widowed and my eldest son had been killed by the English forces. Yet, I had much to be thankful for. My head was still sitting on my shoulders and, except for the continual aches in my joints and the occasional difficulty hauling my large body about, I was in good health.

Donegal is the northernmost county on the Irish mainland. As we rode through the land, I noticed it consisted chiefly of low mountains – about the height of the Twelve Bens – with a deeply indented coastline forming natural loughs. There were two mountain ranges, the Bluestack Mountains in the south and the Derryveagh Mountains, which hove into view as we moved farther north.

Donegal was cool and damp, even in the height of the summer. At Falcarragh, a small and remote settlement of fifty souls, my six ships sat serenely at anchor. Hugh O'Donnell insisted his captains pilot our vessels over to the island and that he accompany me on one of the O'Donnell ships, which would then return the six masters and himself to the mainland. I soon found out why. The turbulent Tory Sound could shut off the island from the mainland for several days at a time. We were fortunate to cross the strait during clement weather.

Tory Island was windswept, and the wild winds that battered the island made it almost devoid of trees. A small settlement of five families lived in the southeast corner of the island. We'd be left to our own devices on the opposite end of the island. Four hundred-fifty men would be a lot to feed, but the O'Donnells had thoughtfully provided for us. We found grain and fodder, sheep and cattle, and even a few buildings which would house those of our crews who were waiting for us when we pulled into the protected cove Hugh Roe O'Donnell had promised would await us.

I felt freedom from worry during my first week on Tory Island. But I knew I'd have to return to my practice of maintenance by sea if I were to keep the loyalty of my troops. In the past, it had been easier to find vessels on which to prey, for Galway was an important international port. In Ulster, the ships plying the sea were almost invariably from Scotland, and the Scots, dour and warlike, did not ferry treasure to County Donegal. Rather, they carried soldiers. Thus, the opportunities for predation were limited indeed.

On the other hand, the fishing off Tory Island was magnificent. Hake, mackerel, and cod were plentiful, no doubt because Tory was situated in the warm gulfstream current. Farther north, we caught more herring and ling than we could load on board at any one time. Thus, my return to the original O'Malley means of maintenance, fishing, staved off poverty and privation allowed me to continue feeding and succoring my crew and even enabled me to recover part of the purse I had lost.

I could well have stayed on Tory in peace for the rest of my days, but having once seen a new and different land, my curiosity was piqued, as it had not been since I was a young girl. For the first time in many years, I longed to travel farther afield, to places I'd never been, and I felt strangely drawn to move north.

During my third week on Tory Island, I called my captains, my masters, and my men together. "My worthies," I asked, "are you pleased with what we've been able to do thus far?"

"Aye," said the most senior master. "But many of the men are homesick and want to return to their wives and sweethearts back home."

"I understand," I said, "and we will as soon as it is reasonably safe to do so. Seamus," I continued, addressing the master, "while we are constrained to stay in Ulster, I believe that fishing will make us wealthier than we've been all year. I suggest we stay in the area for the next two months, building our reserves. I would like, however, to explore places where it is always daytime during the summer months. I would like to call out as many men as would like to accompany me. The rest may stay here until I return."

The greatest number elected to stay close to home. Fifty men volunteered to travel north with me – more by ten than I could comfortably accommodate in the *Sea Ghost*. I proposed we draw lots to determine who would go north and who would stay on Tory.

After some discussion, six of my good men withdrew their names from consideration for the journey north, leaving forty-four, plus myself, and that number we could accommodate. Thus, the necessity of drawing lots and disappointing some of my men was avoided.

Since this was to be a voyage of discovery in unknown seas, traversing unknown lands, we planned neither to pirate anyone nor to fight with anyone. Nevertheless, we would need to eat. We offloaded all but one cannon, brought sufficient lemons and limes, hardtack, and salted fish to last us for three weeks, installed fishing gear, warm woolen coats and trousers, rain slickers and rain hats in the storage area, and prepared to cast off.

Although I actually took the helm for part of the journey for the first time in more than five years, for the most part I was content to allow a younger master to take charge of the *Sea Ghost*. It took the better part of a day tacking northeast from Tory Island to round dramatic Horn Head and the Rosguill Peninsula before we reached Malin Head, the northernmost point in Ireland. We dropped anchor for the night in the lee of the Head. Although the landscape may not have seemed different to untrained eyes than most of western Ireland from the Cliffs of Moher north, so excited was I to be on a voyage of discovery that I marked every stone and hill and headland in my mind's eye, as if I might never see it again.

The following morning, we left Ireland, the land that had come under the cruel yoke of Richard Bingham and his ilk, behind, and continued north and east toward fiercely independent Scotland, which had bravely refused to bow under the English yoke.

"Where to, now, M'lady?" the master asked.

I'd been thinking about an answer to that question since we'd awakened that morning. The O'Donnell had left me charts that covered Scotland, all the way to the Orkney and Shetland Islands, the latter so far north it was within that area sailors called "the land of the midnight Sun." Then and there, I decided this would be my destination. If only once in my life, I would see the land where it never got completely dark during the summer months.

"The Hebrides," I responded. That area was quite well charted. Our first step would be Islay, some twenty-five miles from Malin Head, on the same parallel as Glasgow, but much farther west, then to Mull, half a day to the north.

As the morning was sunny and calm, we decided to land at Port Ellen to reprovision. When we made landfall, I found that the natives spoke a language which was at once both foreign-sounding and familiar. It was Gaelic, but not the Gaelic we spoke in Connaught.

"Scottish Gaelic," the master told me.

We had taken several skeins of Irish wool and numerous Irish handcrafted sweaters, just in case we might trade with the locals. This proved to be propitious, for we sold all of what we had, very quickly and at a very good price. Since I was in no hurry to leave Islay, not knowing if I would ever return, the master and I walked to the outskirts of Port Ellen. Outskirts was rather an overstatement, since the entire town, the largest on Islay, had but six hundred inhabitants. When we reached the end of town, it seemed every available space along the loughs were laden with birds of all kinds, barnacle geese, choughs, hen harriers, oystercatchers, cormorants and other wading birds I'd not seen in Ireland. We were still in the gulfstream, so the weather was warm and balmy that day.

So pleasant was the area that we decided to lay over that night, and for the first time in months I experienced the camaraderie of a public house, this one filled with singing and fiddlers and the extremely strong, smoky-tasting Scots whisky.

Mull Island, the next of the Inner Hebrides, lay about the same distance from Islay as Islay was from Malin Head. At a steady six knots each hour, it took the *Sea Ghost* four hours to reach the southwestern tip of the island. There were no settlements of any size or interest there, but I'd been warned by Hugh Roe O'Donnell to steer well clear of the *coire breckan,* the "cauldron of the plaid," that comes up west of Mull between the sparsely inhabited islands of Scarba and Jura. Hugh told me that although he'd never experienced the cauldron, it was reputed that the Atlantic tide comes and goes so quickly that the narrow gap between the islands creates waves that slap up twenty feet tall.

I was familiar with the old Norse legends about the *coire breckan*. This tub of violence is where the great winter hag Cailleach – the ancient and malevolent goddess of the sea – was said to wash her cloak. When storms came on, especially in the autumn, people told each other, "The Cailleach will tramp her blankets tonight."

I'd heard tales of the Cailleach since I was a little girl. She was said to be lean and vicious, with a blue face, rust-colored hair, a single tooth, and one eye. It was said that she created the mountains and the islands of western Ireland and the Scottish highlands by dropping stones from the creel she carried on her back.

Depending on where in Ireland you were, the tales, and even the name of the Cailleach changed. South of Clew Bay, the Cailleach was called the *Muileartach*. She was said to have come from the west, over the waves. She lived in the ocean with her lover and enjoyed having her body massaged by sea merchants. Like the Cailleach, the Muileartach often took the shape of an old woman. It was said she visited houses on shore to ask for lodging, pretending to be a cold and weary traveler. If the door was slammed in her face, she would retaliate by kicking it open furiously and creating gusts of wind and water that would destroy the entire building in an instant.

Whether they were one and the same goddess or not, I was not about to challenge either the Cailleach or the Muileartach head-on, so we kept far to the east of the cauldron and sailed very close to the northwestern mainland of Scotland for the rest of the day. We put in at a bay or inlet so small it didn't have a name, but it was calm and protected, and I slept well that night.

When the afternoon sun was halfway between the zenith and the horizon the next day, we made landfall at the southwestern edge of the Isle of Skye. I was immediately struck by the dramatic beauty of this largest of the Inner Hebrides. At one point, it was less than a mile from the Scottish mainland, but it also jutted out into the sea, halfway to Lewis with Harris, the largest of those islands known as the Outer Hebrides.

Even back at Rockfleet, Richard-an-Iarrain and I had read Gaelic poetry about *Eilean a' Cheò,* the Misty Isle to the north. I spent two entire days on the island, wandering on foot through the Cuillin Hills, the Red Hills, and Blaven. The coastline was deeply indented, and I was never far from the sea. On my walks, I made certain to tread quietly, so as not to disturb the tiny goldcrest, the magnificent golden eagle, the pygmy shrew, and the red deer. On my second day, my guide, a young woman taller than me and half my age, suddenly pointed toward the sea. My eyes were sharp enough to catch a pair of otters frolicking on the shore. Even though it was full summer, there were plenty of colorful wildflowers still in bloom. Where we came to settlements, we heard snatches of Scottish Gaelic. I was truly charmed by the place, and vowed to return.

As the sun came up on the third day, the master inquired whether we'd make the twenty-mile journey to Lewis in the Outer Hebrides or follow the Scottish mainland to Thurso, at the northern tip of that country. By that time, I was eager to reach the land of the midnight Sun, so I pushed for the shorter mainland route.

Between John O'Groats, land's end at the northern tip of the Scottish mainland, and the southernmost point of the Orkney Islands, there is a channel known as the Pentland Firth. It is said to be one of the most dangerous stretches of water in the world, not because of the relatively short passage through it – only seventeen miles from the North Sea to the Atlantic Ocean, and, at its narrowest point, less than seven miles wide. It is dangerous because of the tides that sweep through it twice a day, from the Atlantic to the North Sea. These tides can make the passage rough even on the most pleasant of days, but very often it is not a pleasant day in the area of the Firth, which is why sailors preferred to stay well out to sea and approach the Orkneys from the north, or to make the equally long voyage from the English channel to the southeast. This could easily add an entire day, and sometimes more, to the time it took to get to the Orkneys, but one simply could not rely on the benign sea goddess, the *Mither o' the Sea* to overcome the power of the Cailleach.

Although the master of the *Sea Ghost* was a young man, he was, by nature, cautious and conservative, so instead of turning east toward Thurso and John O'Groats, we kept sailing due north until we saw Orkney's largest island, *Mainland* in the distance.

The Orkneys and Shetland Islands were now owned by Scotland, but that had only occurred a little more than a hundred years ago. In 1468, Orkney and Shetland were pledged by King Christian I of Denmark and Norway as security against the payment of the dowry of his daughter Margaret, who was betrothed to James III of Scotland. The cash dowry was never paid, so the islands were forfeited to the Crown of Scotland. In 1471.

Just as the sun was setting, the *Sea Ghost* pulled into port at Stromness, a lovely little village in a protected harbor in the southwest of *Mainland*. We'd evaded the treacherous Pentland Firth, and I was eager to see how close we were to where there'd be light every hour of the day or night. As it turned out, it was dark for only about three hours that night, and even then it was more twilight than full dark.

I found Stromness delightful. It was surrounded everywhere by water – the harbor, small bays, and three loughs – and the settlement was remarkably clean. The buildings were painted in bright colors and the people of the place seemed uniformly friendly and happy. But as much as I enjoyed it, an irresistible force kept pulling me northward, and by sunset of the second night, the master could tell I was anxious to embark on the next leg of our voyage.

It was as if my destiny called, and I hastened to meet it.

Chapter 31

It was ten in the evening when the *Sea Ghost* departed Stromness for the Shetland Islands. The sun still hung in the sky, though the settlement, protected by a rounded arm of hills against the Atlantic winds, was in shadow. A line of gold fire ran along the top of the ridge above the town. Standing on the top deck of my beloved caravel, I was high above the dock and at eye level with the upper houses and trees of Stromness. I stood in daylight, while the village below turned to thoughts of sleep.

At a signal from the master, we moved off calmly, the fifteen pairs of oarsmen rowing us gently out of the harbor. There was rain in the air, more a fine mist through which the sun sparkled. The harbor waters were gold, overlaid with a scalloped pattern of frost and dark green.

When we rounded Point Ness, I found myself staring at the largest rainbow I'd ever seen, whose perfect arch created a gate. The arch had one foot on Mainland and the other on another nearby island. Although all the colors were present, it wasn't the brightest rainbow I'd observed. It was almost more white than multicolored, with glinting filaments the colors of emeralds, rubies, and sapphires.

A little later, we came into Hoy Sound, and the island of Hoy rose majestically to our left. The sun was dropping fast over the western horizon and a strong, cold wind met the prow of the ship head on. The oarsmen started rowing once again, and soon we were able to tack into a favorable wind. It was long after eleven when I finally went below deck to my cabin. The world was still in twilight, and as I lay down I felt the sea beneath the boat rolling gently.

When I awoke, it was dim in my cabin. Outside, through the porthole, spattered with rain, I saw misty cliffs and raw, rocky shores. These must be the Shetland Islands, I thought, and I felt a momentary stab of inexplicable fear. How dark everything looked out there, how gray and wet and inhospitable. I'd heard stories that in olden times the Shetlanders would not rescue a drowning person, even when it was safe and easy to do so, for they believed the sea demanded a sacrifice. If you took away the sea's victim, someone else, perhaps you yourself, would be taken instead.

I curled myself back into sleep, rocked by the waves. Despite the surliness outside the ship, I felt enveloped and safe and warm in my berth, in my cabin. When I next woke up, the *Sea Ghost* was docking in Lerwick. The thick, gray mist was lifting and as I stepped onto the deck, the sun shown through the clouds and onto the green, green land below.

Lerwick had a distinctly different feel than anywhere I'd been in the north. For one thing, the town was substantial – by my reckoning at least a thousand souls lived here – and there was an air of busyness about it. There were a number of ships in port, and by their markings and the dress exhibited by fat burghers attending the ships, I surmised this was a polyglot town housing as many Dutchmen and Norwegians as Scots.

Indeed, the Norwegian coast was only three hundred miles to the northeast, and since the tip of Scotland was well to the south, it was open water between the Shetland Islands and the Flemish coast.

Strangely, I felt myself being drawn more than ever to another place, and the force was such that I knew it was not far from here. I was equally certain that I must go there by myself, or, at the very least, with someone other than my crew. I told our ship's master he should search out trade opportunities in Lerwick and that I needed to be alone.

"I've had a difficult year," I said, almost sorrowfully. "I need three or four days just to myself, to think on my life and to determine where I go from here."

The master was understanding, more so than I'd hoped he'd be. He told me he would make my excuses to the crew and that, in any event, they'd be thrilled to be out from under the thumb of authority, particularly in a port town such as Lerwick, where sailor's delights awaited.

I found lodgings just south of the center of town, and settled in waiting... waiting.

The knock came very early the next morning. I didn't know what I'd expected, but I was surprised nonetheless to see a young lad of ten. "My da said to fetch you," he said. The boy did not even ask my name or give any other greeting, yet I, Granuaile ni-Mháille, the Pirate Queen of Connaught, reputedly one of the strongest and most willful women in Europe, followed the fellow as obediently as a lamb following its mother.

We must have walked for a great distance, because soon Lerwick was well behind us and we were in the countryside abutting a narrow bay or a small lough, I could not tell which. The boy led me to a well-kept stone house, where a man stood waiting. He was fair-haired and light-complexioned, but his large, reddened hands showed he was not a stranger to hard work, either on land or at sea.

"We're going to Unia," he said.

"You're a man of few words," I replied shakily.

"Don't need many. Come along, then." He led me south. The waterway widened a bit, and a small single-sail boat waited at the end of a wooden jetty. He signaled me to join him on board, and I did. There was no one on the skiff except the two of us.

The boat left its slip easily, and I noticed that the man was expert in the way he handled the vessel. The bay widened into an outlet and then into a channel, and I saw the high rocks of an island some five miles distant. Low clouds scudded between the channel and the island, and while the water was choppy, it was not the precursor of a storm.

"The only decent harbor is far around on the western side of the island. I'll take you along the high eastern shore because I know of a little half-moon cove here, where the water is deep enough for a mooring. It's also the habitation of an aged and demented Norsewoman whom you are destined to meet. You may want to have a word with her. Who knows? She may prove to be your own many-times-great-grandmother."

I shivered involuntarily, and it was not because of the cold.

The man brought the skiff in to a scooped-out cavity in the cliff wall, where the rock columns loomed above a tiny shelf of shingle, and there he anchored. We sat in silence for more than an hour. I looked at the man who'd borne me here, but he said nothing. Oddly, he looked much older than he'd been when I'd met him at his cottage only a few hours ago. Perhaps it was the slant of the light, but it did not much concern me, and I let my mind wander on to other things.

My thoughts were interrupted by a thin but urgent outcry from somewhere. I looked over to the man in the boat. He shrugged his shoulders, but otherwise said nothing. Looking around, I found that the shouting was coming from the shore. Over there, a small and nondescript figure was doing a sort of dance on the shingle ledge, gesticulating and calling incoherently.

"What is that?" I asked my host

"Nothing to be worried about. It's only old Nehalennia. She gets wildly excited when any vessel puts in here because every master brings her a gift of provisions. Since Unia is uninhabited but for her, I think it is all she gets to live on. I do not know how she manages between feedings. He reached into a small storage bin that was sitting in the stern of the skiff and handed me a large slab of smoked meat and a skin of whisky. "You may as well make friends with her," he said, lifting a tiny coracle from amidships. "There's only room for two in this small boat," he continued, "and since you'll be carrying her a gift, I trust you know how to pilot this little craft yourself."

In a few moments I easily negotiated the fifty feet between the deep water and the tiny shelf of welcoming land. When I stepped ashore, the woman danced up to me, dressed in gray rags and ribbons of some kind of very limp and flimsy leather. Without ceasing to dance – her lank white hair flopping, her sharp old knees and elbows madly jerking – she babbled and plucked at my sleeve as I hauled the tiny boat up onto the shingle. I could tell that she was speaking a dialect of some very old language, but little more than that. Here and there I caught a word or two of very primitive Gaelic, but for the most part I was unable to decipher what she said because she went on so rapidly.

After some time, I understood she was thanking me for whatever I had brought her. Still jigging and jogging in her old-bones dance, she moved jerkily over to the coracle where she extracted the meat and the skin of whisky. She clasped them to her scrawny chest, blithered some more, then turned and scuttled away toward her cliffside hut, beckoning for me to follow.

The pull that had lured me to this place was now stronger than ever. I followed the old woman and had to get down on my hands and knees to squeeze into the hut behind her. There was nothing inside except a smoky fire of faggots laid in a ring of stones, and a pallet made of dried seaweed and filthy rags. The single room was scarcely big enough to contain the two of us, but there was unused space beyond. I could see now that the hut had been built by leaning pieces of driftwood about the dark opening of a shoulder-high cave in the cliff wall.

However, if there was anything to show me, the crone had other things to do first. Without even heating her smoked slab of meat – I could not tell whether it was beef or mutton or pork – she was already tearing at it with her few snaggle teeth, and swigging from the whisky skin. Nehalennia was incredibly old, so wrinkled and gnarled and leather-brown and ugly that she could have been one of the legendary three Furies, *Clotho* the Spinner, *Lachesis* the Measurer, or *Atropos* the Cutter – Creator, Preserver, Destroyer – of Greek mythology. She possessed only one eye, with a vacant hole where the other had been, and her nose and chin nearly touched when she munched.

Her chewing did not stop her babbling, but it slowed the articulation to where I could comprehend it. I heard her say, quite clearly, even quite sanely, "That fellow in the skiff will have told you I am mad. All say that I am mad. That is because I remember things from long ago, things other folk never knew, so they do not believe in those things. Does that prove me mad?"

I asked gently, "What sort of things do you remember, good Nehalennia?"

Chewing hard, she waved a greasy old hand, as if to indicate that the things were too numerous for her to list. Then she swallowed and said, "Achh, among others... the great sea beasts that used to exist... the monster Kraken, the creature Grindl, the dragon Fafnir..."

"Mythical monsters," I said. "Seaman's superstitions," I added softly, so as not to antagonize Nehalennia.

"Myths? *Ni allis*," snapped old Nehalennia. "I can tell you, Sigurd hooked and netted and beached many of them in his time." With the haughty pride of a grand lady, she fingered the sleazy rags she wore. "Sigurd slew those beasts so he could dress me in fine raiment." Seeing her leather rags up close, I could recognize them as eelskin.

I said, "Good Nehalennia, you are a Norse woman?"

"Aye."

"Would you remember any of the others who once inhabited these islands?"

Spraying chewed matter, she exclaimed, "Weaklings! Fainthearts! Softlings! Nothing like Sigurd they were! These islands were too harsh for them, so they fled. Some returned to the Viking strongholds from whence they'd come when Harald Hårfagre took control over these islands. Ach, I was respected and a woman of valor and renown until that bastard Ragnvald Christianized the Hjatland."

My mind reeled. I was not unfamiliar with the names Harald Hårfagre and Ragnvald. They had lived and ruled these islands more than seven hundred years ago, so if old brown Nehalennia was claiming to remember them, she was either mad indeed or old indeed. Humoring her fancy, I asked, "Why did you not return to the Continent with them?"

"*Vái!*" Her one bleary eye looked at me with astonishment. "I could not leave my Sigurd!"

"Are you saying that your Sigurd and Harald Hårfagre and Ragnvald lived at the same time?"

She bridled, as if insulted, saying loudly, "Sigurd *still* lives!"

I did not care to dispute her. The master of the skiff had said she was demented but not dangerous. Still, one could never tell. I asked, "Good Nehalennia, do you perhaps remember any other names of those times? Besides Harald Hårfagre and Ragnvald?"

"*Ja!*" Her one eye now gave me a measuring look, and she chewed for awhile before continuing. I had not yet said anything to her about history, but surprisingly she said, "If you would know the very beginning of things, you must cast back... beyond history... beyond Sigurd and Harald Hårfagre and Ragnvald... back to where you touch the night of time. There you would find no Norsemen, no Gaels, no Goths, no people, no human beings at all, but only the *Aesir* – the family of the Old Gods – Wotan and Thor and Tiw and all the rest..."

When she paused to tear off another bite of meat, I said encouragingly, "I have heard such names."

She nodded and swallowed. "Back there in the night of time, the *Aesir* appointed one of their minor kinfolk to become the father of the first human beings. His name was Gaut, and he dutifully sired many peoples. Over the ages they took various names, the Svear, the Rugii, the Seaxe, the Danisk..."

When she paused for a swig of the whisky, I said, "I see. All the Germanic peoples. In the south they took the names Alamanni, Franks, Burgunds, Vandals, Celts –"

"Notice!" she interrupted, pointing the skin's spout at me. "Of all those peoples, only the Goths kept the name"

That was the single most antique piece of historical information I had been given yet. I may be thought slightly mad myself to have taken that as worth remembering, coming as it did from a madwoman. But Nehalennia sounded sane enough on this subject, and she certainly *looked* old enough to have been present in person at what she called "the beginning of things."

Now, rending the meat again, she said through a mouthful of it, "Good... tastes good," and that obviously reminded her of something. She swallowed quickly so she could tell me, "It was also from our original father's name of Gaut that all the many peoples derived the word 'good.'"

Then she laid aside the meat and the whisky skin, saying, "Come, young woman. I will take you to Sigurd." She picked up a brand from the fire, blew it to flame and, carrying it for a torch, shuffled into the cave mouth behind me.

I had to stoop to get inside the cave. It was not very deep, and at the farther end of it the aged woman was holding her torch with one hand, using the other to scrabble at a heap of damp seaweed until she uncovered a long, pale object lying on the rough stone floor.

"Sigurd," she said, pointing a withered finger.

I went closer and saw that the object was a solid block of ice, as big as a sarcophagus. I motioned for old Nehalennia to hold the torch closer, but she croaked an objection. "I must not risk melting the ice. That is why I keep it here the year around, and keep it covered with weed, so it melts not even by a fraction."

As my eyes adjusted to the dim, flickering torchlight, I could see that the ice block truly *was* a sarcophagus, and the crone truly did possess a "Sigurd" – or at least a preserved male human being. Although the ice block's irregular surface blurred my view of him, I could make out that he was clad in rude leather garments, and that in life he had been tall and muscular. Squinting more closely, I saw he had clear young skin, an abundance of yellow hair, and that his still open, surprised-looking eyes were a bright blue. His features were those of a peasant youth, somewhat slack and stupid, But, all in all, he had been a handsome young fellow, and still was. Meanwhile, old Nehalennia went on talking, and now that she was not chewing, her speech was getting again indistinct, so that I could catch only disconnected words and phrases.

"Many, many years ago... a bitter winter day... Sigurd went out... in fishing boat. Sigurd overboard... Companions dredged him out... encased in ice... brought him ashore thus... thus he has been ever since..."

"How tragic," I murmured, and sincerely. "Was he perhaps your son? Your great grandson?"

Her reply was slurred, but it was unmistakably indignant. "Sigurd... my *husband!*"

I gasped. "I'm so sorry. I honestly console you in your grief, Widow Nehalennia. And I admire your devoted caretaking of Sigurd. You must have loved him very much."

I would have expected the hag to sniffle or simper or give some other such widowly response, but old Nehalennia seemed much more emotionally moved. She flailed her torch about and fluffed her eelskin rags, and screeched so that the cave echoed, and I shrank back against the wall in fright. But I was able, just barely, to comprehend the wretched old crone's words of angry lament.

"Grief?... Love?... With all my heart I *hate* the spiteful Sigurd! Just look, young woman! Look at my husband, then look at me. I ask you, is that fair? *IS IT FAIR?*"

Chapter 32

When the old woman had quieted down, she beckoned me follow her back to her small and filthy hut. She gestured that I should sit on the greasy rags that served as her bed. I did, and she pushed the skin of whisky toward me. As repulsed as I felt, I could not refuse her, but, realizing that one could never know when she'd have another visitor, or be afforded replenishment of those supplies, I took the smallest swig, and sloshed it around in my mouth before swallowing it, so she'd surmise I welcomed her gesture.

She, herself, sat contentedly on the floor near me. I noticed that despite the filth and squalor in which she lived, and her own wildly unkempt appearance, she did not give off an offensive odor, neither from her body nor from her mouth. She sat awhile, still munching bits of meat companionably, then reached over and took the whisky skin back from me. After a draught far more substantial than mine, her single eye fixed me with a benevolent stare, and to my utter shock, she said, in perfect, clear Irish Gaelic, "So, Granuaile ni-Mháille, you are fifty-seven years old – a mere babe so recently torn from your mother's breast – and twice widowed, and now you are here."

So astonished was I that I must have turned white. I could not even find words to answer her, so stunned was I.

"I... I did not come of my own accord," I stammered, for want of something – anything – to say.

"They never do," Nehalennia responded equably. "From Harald Hårfagre to Ragnvald, from Alexander of Scotland to King Håkon..." she murmured. "You know, it was far better before Christianity came. I was revered then, worshiped even..." she mumbled, almost to herself.

"You are *the* Nehalennia?" I gasped. Once, long ago, I had heard of a sea deity, a *benign* sea deity, who had borne many names through history – Isis, Artemis, Saint Gertrud, and, yes, Nehalennia. Sanctuaries to Nehalennia had been found in many lands abounding the North Sea. I felt a strong grasping in my innards as even that one small taste of whisky took hold. I had not had anything to eat that day.

The old woman did not answer directly, but started rocking back and forth. "You were the Queen of the Irish Seas a moment ago," she said. "You had it all, The MacWilliam to husband, the gentlest son of all... You are angry because the ill-gotten seed survived and the good one is gone..."

"Aye," I choked, and angry tears started to come.

"The power of the Norman yoke has come upon your land, and you are powerless to resist it," she continued. At that, I started moaning uncontrollably. "And you fear your death is near." She continued rocking slowly, quietly, the very antithesis of the dancing madwoman I had seen on the ledge an hour before.

"Is... is that why I am here?" I asked in a tiny girl's voice. I recalled saying the same thing in the same tone of voice more than half a century ago, when I was three or four years old and frightened, and when my mother had comforted me.

Nehalennia waited a goodly while before she responded. "You are not yet ready to leave this earth, Granuaile ni-Mháille. Donal an-Chodaigh, yes, and Ballyclinch and Hugh DeLacy and Richard an-Iarrain and Owen Dubhdarra O'Flaherty, but not you, girl."

"And Richard Bingham?"

"*Ach*, that man will harry and harass and distress you almost interminably, but in the end you will survive him, too."

"And Ireland?"

"Alas, Granuaile ni-Mháille, that poor and hurting and troubled and tragically beautiful land will fall under the English yoke, and while it will never wrench itself free during your lifetime, or for a long, long time thereafter – which is but a moment in time if we hearken back to the night of time of which I spoke. But there will come a time... and you will be remembered, Granuaile ni-Mháille. Oh, yes, you will be remembered..."

It was a day of amazement, a day on which I felt I had touched eternity, a day of epiphany. Nehalennia and I spoke – or rather *she* spoke as a goddess-mother and I listened raptly – for some time, I don't know how long. When I returned to the skiff, it was late in the afternoon. In the morning, I had come to this place in the company of a vigorous, youngish man, who might have been a many-centuries later reincarnation of Nehalennia's Sigurd of that long-ago time. When I returned to the skiff, I was greeted by a gnarled and grizzled old seaman who looked thirty years older than I. But for the fact that he was about the same height as the man who'd brought me here this morning, and that he wore precisely the same clothing as that other had worn, I would have sworn he was a completely different fellow.

"I told you old Nehalennia was mad but harmless," he said. "Now it is time for you to return home."

Chapter 33

Having learned why I had been summoned to these climes so far from Connaught, I felt at greater peace than at any time since my Richard-an-Iarrain had passed. I returned swiftly and directly to Tory Island to find my men impatient to return to Clew Bay, but well-provisioned and enriched by fishing in Donegal's fertile waters.

Sir Thomas Le Strange had been appointed to replace Richard Bingham and Richard's younger brother George, certainly a more benign sort than the former governor of Connaught, assumed the rule of deputy governor. I took up residence once more in Rockfleet Castle. With Richard Bingham, my arch enemy, out of the way, it was time for me to make up for lost time. The remains of my depleted fleet once more put to sea in search of sustenance and to recoup my losses. Since Richard Bingham had confiscated my sheep, my horses, and my cattle, maintenance by sea was now my only option for survival.

The *Sea Ghost* was still my pride and joy. It had been a very special gift to me from my father, and it came at a time when I was recovering from a low ebb. But that was a quarter century ago, and although I had scrupulously kept the caravel in the best repair of which my shipwrights were capable, I could not escape the fact that just as I was showing my age, so was the *Sea Ghost*.

In September, 1587, I ordered my flagship placed in dry dock, where she was to be completely torn town and refurbished to her original condition. Any piece of wood that showed even the first sign of rot was to be replaced by strong new beams, flooring, coverings, decks, everything. With Richard Bingham gone, I had refilled my coffers, and it was essential that I remanufacture my fleet so long as I could afford to do so. Richard Bingham had preyed on me before, and who knew when that evil man, or someone equally his like, would return to a position of power in Connaught and try to break me once again?

The *Sea Ghost* was in dry dock for six months, and during that time my fleet was reduced from six to five – one-fourth of what it had been during my wealthiest days. But they would have to do for now.

Meanwhile, my youngest son, Tibbott-na-Long, Toby of the Ships, remained in John Bingham's custody. Although John was almost as much a nemesis to me as his brother, I could not overly complain of Toby's upbringing. As I have earlier said, it was only a matter of time before the English encroachment was complete. Toby had been brought up speaking English and he had adopted English manners as well. Thus, even though he had participated in the Burke Rebellion, he had been only peripherally involved and the English did not regard him as a criminal.

Early in 1588, I received dreadful news. Hugh Roe O'Donnell, who had arrogated to himself the cognomen "Eagle of the North," and who had been my great benefactor while I was in Donegal, was lured to his capture and imprisonment in

Dublin Castle by, of all people, the good Sir John Perrott, the same Perrott who had been my own beacon of salvation when Richard Bingham had ordered me hanged.

Now the English were once more in strong control of Connaught and the Gaelic resistance was, for the moment, in tatters. Such were the politics of the day that I thought it prudent to travel to Dublin and meet with Perrott. Although I had been to Dublin before, it was when I had been a "guest" in Dublin *Castle*, that great and much-feared gaol in Ireland's largest city. That dreaded place now held my friend Hugh Roe O'Donnell.

I have earlier told that the collapse of Ireland as I knew it was in large part due to the divide-and-conquer strategy of the unified English presence. As I look back, I cannot but feel great guilt, for by my own acts in trying to save my own skin, I contributed as much as any to the breakdown of our independence. In my day, I have been called courageous, but I feel that had this truly been so, I would have stood firmly, even if I had been but one among the many. And while I could take the easy road and say I was neither better nor worse than my neighbors, who saw what the Bible called "the handwriting on the wall," in truth a single man or woman, if they have any integrity, must take responsibility for his or her own acts, and for no one else's.

Hugh Roe O'Donnell had succored me and mine, and had given me comfort and protection while I was in his demesne. Now, I proposed to repay that kindness in a most callous and shameful way. I went to Dublin not to throw myself on Sir John Perrott's mercy on behalf of the Eagle of the North, but rather to ask pardon for *myself*, for my sons Tibbott and Murrough, and for my daughter Margaret and my son-in-law, Richard "Devil's Hook" Burke. Blood is thicker than water. Sometimes it is almost impossible to expunge the blood from one's hands by dipping them in water.

In April, I arrived at the Lord Deputy's door in Dublin. The doorman was polite and cordial, but told me, "Alas, Sir John has been called to London for consultation."

My face dropped, betraying my great disappointment, "But I thought..." I started lamely.

At that moment a tall, exceedingly handsome man of my own age, darker complected than most, but not a Moor, walked dignifiedly into the entry hall. "Grace O'Malley, or may I say Granuaile ni-Mháille? I am so sorry Sir John is not here to meet with you. He specially requested I remain here in Dublin to address your concerns." The man's voice was beautifully modulated, soothing, and by his pronunciation and easily natural use of Gaelic, I might easily have mistaken him for an Irishman native born. "But I forget my manners, Lady Granuaile. I'm Thomas Butler – 'Black Tom' my friends call me, and I would feel honored if you would call me that."

I was caught completely off my guard, so charmed was I. "Black Tom?" I asked. "But you're not...?"

"No, I am not," he said, laughing easily. "I don't know how I got the nickname myself. It might be for the black clothes I favor, the black gelding I used to ride many years ago, or my reputation among certain Catholic circles. You've been traveling a while and you're no doubt disappointed not to find the Lord Deputy here. Would my inviting you to walk about Dublin with me ease your disappointment?"

I shrugged. "I can think of worse things than to be seen in the company of a gentleman of your obvious stature – unless, of course, you're some kind of impostor claiming to be a friend of Sir John Perrott."

As we exited the Lord Deputy's residence, we walked north toward the River Liffey. "Dublin – he pronounced it

'Doob-linh' – actually means 'Black Pool.' It was named after a dark pool of water, which formed where the Liffey meets the much smaller Poddle River. It was an obvious place for the English to site their capital."

"You said *the* English, Tom. As if you weren't one of them."

"I'm not, Granuaile," he said. "I'm as much a Gael as you, other than the fact that I'm a 'damned Protestant.'"

"That doesn't make much difference to me," I said. "I never felt one way or the other about any religion. As long as we all believe in God and act according to our beliefs, one dogma's as good as the next."

"Ah," he said, wagging a finger playfully as we crossed an ancient bridge over the Liffey. "Talk of morality coming from the Pirate Queen of Connaught?"

"Should I act surprised that you know about me, or proud that you know of me?"

"A little of both," he said. "Your reputation preceded you. You knew the Earl of Desmond?" I grimaced. "I'd make that same face were I you. He was responsible for your imprisonment for eighteen months."

"Politics," I replied.

"Aye, but you were the pawn in that game, and to what end? He turned coat."

"You sound like he's no friend of yours."

"You're perceptive, but anyone who's been to Munster would have known that. We've been hereditary enemies for generations, the Desmonds and the Butlers. Ah, here's one of my favorite pastry shops in the city. Perhaps we should sit where it's more comfortable and talk?"

"I'd like that very much, Black Tom," I said, feeling quite comfortable with this distinguished man. "Connaught is

a land of corned beef and lamb stew. Pastry is one of the great
English gifts."

"I trust you don't believe Richard Bingham is another."
At that, my eyelids arched and my eyes narrowed. "Ah,
Bingham's your Desmond, then?"

"You could say that. I've experienced enough of the
English to know they're not all like him, thank God. There were
the Sidneys, Sir Nicholas..."

"Malby was a very good man," Thomas mused. "I miss
him." He stopped a serving girl and smoothly ordered pastries
and coffee, the latter a new import into Ireland. "Sir Nicholas
was a good man and a good ally, one of the best."

"And Sir Richard?"

"Not the type to make a good impression abroad for
our gracious Queen, but whereas Sidney and Malby and even
Perrott are the silken glove, he's the mailed fist. I suppose you
need both kinds, the carrot and the stick, when you're trying to
subjugate a country as wildly independent as Ireland."

The server brought small cups of steaming black coffee.
I'd drunk coffee before, and I preferred it with milk and sugar.
Tom, however, drank his black.

"Don't you find that bitter, Tom?"

"Yes, but a nice kind of bitter," he replied. "It seems
to give me unparalleled energy. Ah, thank you, young lady,"
he addressed the serving woman. "Have some of these lemon
cakes, Granuaile. You're in for a treat."

Conversation flagged as I tried the small cakes. They
were moist and tart and very light. My mouth puckered slightly,
but then there was a wonderful sweetness and smooth texture.
"These are delicious, Tom."

"Yes, but they're not really English. The French across the
Channel perfected these particular types of lemon-butter cake."

I looked around the room. There were numerous wooden booths and candelabra hung from the ceiling, their candles lit even during the day. There were ten other people in the room.

"Tell me, Tom, you referred to 'Our gracious Queen.' Have you actually met Elizabeth?"

"Yes, Granuaile, I have. Many times, as a matter of fact. She's about our age."

"*Our* age? I daresay, you flatter an old lady, Sir. You must be ten years my junior."

"Try *one* year your junior, Grace. And two years older than the Queen."

I had ceased to be surprised at Thomas Butler's wide-ranging knowledge. Still, it was unnerving to wonder how much he really knew about me. To deflect the conversation, I asked, "What is she like, the Good Queen?"

He paused, steepled his fingers, thumbs hooked under his chin, and thought for a moment. "She's not that different from you or me. She has her father's mercurial temper, and you try not to get too close to her for long periods, lest you end up on the trash heap of her past favorites."

"Lovers," I interjected.

"Some. She is not the Virgin Queen she purports to be."

"You sound as though you know."

"Rather forward, Granuaile, aren't you?" he said, blushing slightly.

"No, Tom. You seem a man of the world. If you've slept with her, I suppose I should congratulate you. Not that you've bedded the Queen, but that you've kept your head on your shoulders in spite of it. What is she like, the Queen of England?"

"Would it surprise you if I told you she's as direct as you? And, I might add, although she functions in dramatically different circles, I think you'd find her determined and courageous."

"The kind of person I could talk to directly?"

"If she granted you an audience, yes."

"And say exactly what I think?"

"Provided you were reasonably diplomatic when you did so."

"Thank you for that information, Tom. Since you seem to know everything about me and I know less than nothing about you, I trust you are aware of why I wanted to see Sir John Perrott?"

"Yes. Shall we continue our walk along the Liffey?" he asked, getting out of his booth seat. He walked over to the serving girl, put a couple of coins in her hand, and stood by me courteously while I got up from my bench.

As we continued our walk, he said, "The most recent rebellion in Connaught has come upon hard times. I understand you were involved in ferrying the rebel soldiers from place to place."

"Aye, that's true."

"And all three of your surviving children, Murrough, Margaret, and Tibbott were involved in the Mayo County troubles."

"Also true."

"Then why should our gracious Queen pardon you and your whole family?"

"The enemy of my enemy is my friend. I am not without connections and who knows? I might be of some future use to her. I hear tell the Spanish are raising a great Armada"

"A wonderfully political answer, Granuaile. Without committing anything to you, might you consider doing a small favor for me?"

"I wasn't even thinking of asking *you* for anything, Tom Butler, but yes, if it is within my power to do so, I would be happy to avail you.

He frowned and looked down at the ground. "I have a... special friend... in Blackpool. She's... married, as am I, and we meet by chance in different venues. I need someone who is circumspect..."

"Who doesn't give a damn about your private life, but who could act as a courier," I finished the sentence for him.

"You are as wise as you are brave."

"As we've both said, 'political,' Tom. And, I believe we understand each other's needs. Give me the details on what you want me to do and where you want me to do it. I'm in Dublin for some little while, with nothing much better to do..."

Three weeks later, I had just returned from one of Thomas Butler's "errands," when I was summoned to the Lord Deputy's residence. This time, Sir John Perrott himself was there to greet me. He was as friendly as the late Richard Malby had been. He drew me into conversation immediately concerning Sir Richard Bingham. The Lord Deputy was aware of my negative feelings toward the Connaught governor and seemed quite sympathetic. Never one to hold my opinions in check, I let him know exactly what I felt. "Further, Sir John, I must respectfully state that although he demonstrates military victories, he is not winning the hearts and minds of the Gaels for England."

"Mmmm, yes, I understand that, Lady Grace."

"There's no doubt that thus far he's won battle after battle, but do you ever wonder why, no matter how victorious he may be at any time, the rebellions keep on springing up in different areas?"

"I've heard many reasons. What say you?"

"There were far fewer rebellions when the Sidneys, father and son, and Richard Malby were in charge. Bingham will have to kill every Gael in every clan if he expects to expunge us, and no man has enough years to do that."

"I understand, Lady Grace. Tea?"

"Please."

"Black Tom fancies coffee. Dreadful stuff, that." He rang a silver bell and shortly thereafter a serving man arrived bearing bone china mugs.

"Black Tom seems to have the ear of your... our Queen."

"Oh, yes, My Dear Grace," he chuckled. "That he most certainly does, does our Earl of Ormond."

"The *Earl of Ormond*?"

"Yes. Actually, the line goes back a way. He's the tenth Earl of Ormond. Don't look so shocked. He is rather plain-spoken for nobility, and he does manage to cross between Ireland and England with ease."

"I figured he was high-born and he alluded to some, umm..."

"Yes. Oh, and by the way, he asked me to give this to you," the Lord Deputy said, extracting a heavy cream envelope. I opened the envelope and below the letterhead "E.R,"

I read, "Pardon to Grany ni-Maly, Tibbott Burke son of Richard an-Iarrain and Grany, Margaret O'Flahertie, daughter of Grany, and Murrough O'Flaherty, son of Donal an-Choggie and Grany. The pardon not to include murder nor intrusion into the crown lands, or debts to the crown."

Chapter 34

In the spring of 1588, Sir Richard Bingham returned and resumed his duties as governor of Connaught. The rumors of a Spanish invasion became a reality when, in July of that year, the Invincible Armada set sail for England. Despite its mighty strength, after a series of naval battles against the English fleet under the command of Howard and Sir Francis Drake, the Armada lost its crescent-shaped formation and the slow-moving, ponderous galleons became scattered and easy prey for the lighter, faster English warships. The elements then took sides and prevented the Spaniards from either regrouping or retreating.

The unwieldy galleons were driven helplessly along the coast of Scotland, across to Ulster, and down the west coast of Connaught, where the terrible winds and rocky headlands took their toll of men and ships.

I had mixed feelings about interfering in what was happening. Some months earlier, the English government had made it a crime punishable by death to aid or protect any Spanish invasion forces. On the other hand, there were strong rumors that the Armada vessels contained incalculable treasures, and, in my straitened – but never defeated – state, I could have used some of that treasure far more than our English overlords.

As usual, and tragically so, our clans could not – and did not – prove united in their reception of the Spanish. The O'Neill in Ulster sent provisions to aid the survivors who had been shipwrecked in his territory. The O'Donnell, on the other hand, aided the English in rounding up the Spaniards. I'm sure that Hugh Roe O'Donnell's imprisonment in Dublin Castle had something to do with the O'Donnells' actions.

There was even dissension within the O'Malley ranks. Don Pedro de Mendoza's mighty ship foundered on Clare Island with three hundred men on board. Don Pedro refused to surrender and Dowdarra Roe O'Malley, chieftain of the island at the time, killed every survivor. It was a terrible slaughter, resulting from greed for the spoils of the shipwreck on the one hand, and out of ignorance and misunderstanding of the reasons for the invasion on the other. The O'Malleys of Clare Island were not alone in their treatment of the Spanish.

Farther up the coast, the second in command of the entire Armada expedition, Alonso de Leyva's ship the *Rata*, with four hundred nineteen men, was driven by strong winds into Blacksod Bay, where the Devil's Hook's son – my grandson – robbed and imprisoned some of the survivors.

My own feelings continued to be mixed. The lure of treasure and plunder was a way of life to me, and I dearly needed treasure. On the other hand, my family's connections with Spain were long-established and my understanding of the Armada's aims led me to believe that if Spain succeeded, this would ensure Irish independence.

Unfortunately, there was very little I could do to hide or protect the survivors. My arch-nemesis, Sir Richard Bingham, was now giving his undivided attention to the coastline of Connaught in general, and to me in particular. Worse, the new Lord Deputy, Sir William FitzWilliam, decided that even Bingham's horrendous methods were too lenient. He commissioned his deputy marshal to seek out, dislodge, and kill any of the unfortunate survivors who had managed to obtain refuge from the Gaelic chiefs.

When it was over, seven thousand Spaniards had perished in Connaught. The remains of the Armada, the pride of Spain, had found itself no match for the still more powerful Atlantic. A few – very few – of the high-masted galleons eventually reached Cádiz and Coruña. The days of the Spanish sea dominance in Europe had ended.

A year earlier, I had told Sir John Perrott, now back in England, that force would only beget more force, and that the way to secure the loyalty of western Ireland was by honey, not by steel. While Perrott was more than willing to listen, his successor FitzWilliam and his cat's paw Richard Bingham were most certainly not.

And just as I had predicted, the severe treatment meted out by FitzWilliam and Bingham gave rise to deep-rooted discontent. With the English forces in Connaught spread very thin, the chieftains' outrage erupted into rebellion. Bingham ordered the county *shire rief*, John Brown, to bring the rebels, including my son Tibbott na-Long, my son-in-law, Richard "Devil's Hook" Burke, some of the O'Flahertys, and the Clan O'Donnell, to heel.

Two-hundred-fifty troops reached my fortress at Rockfleet on February 7, 1589. My ever-loyal Devil's Hook met the *shire rief* and objected to him trespassing on my territory. *Shire rief* Brown then turned and marched his men directly into the heart of the Devil's Hook's territory. This proved to be horrendously bad strategy, for Brown was attacked and killed. It was a significant success for the Burkes, and they were immediately joined by other septs of the clan, and by Sir Murrough ne-Doe O'Flaherty, who had previously been the Queen's foremost loyalist in Connaught. Then William Burke, nicknamed the "Blind Abbott" joined the fray. The Blind Abbott had a special reason for joining the rebellion: he was, under Gaelic custom, *tanaiste*, successor to The MacWilliamship, the title and status that Richard Bingham had dissolved.

For the first time in years, the coast was clear for me to repay that bastard, Sir Richard Bingham. My galleys – I had in the interim acquired four more, raising my fleet to ten – provided an efficient means of transporting fighting men from Erris to Iar-Connacht. There was no question that the Gaels were finally getting the best of the fight. Indeed, soon after Bingham's return to Connaught, the Lord Deputy ordered Sir Richard to cease the hostilities and sue for peace. During the peace talks that followed, my clansmen went to Galway to parley. I received a note back from Robert O'Malley, a kinsman of my own age, stating thus:

"Dear Granuaile:

"Things are at an impasse. We demanded that The MacWilliam title be restored, that no officials should reside in The MacWilliam's territory, and that Sir Richard Bingham be removed from the position of governor of Connaught. In return, our men promised to abide by the law and pay their Composition dues.

The Lord Deputy's reply was, 'They shall have sheriffs and they shall not have a MacWilliam.'"

The Burkes' strength increased. Bingham, still under suspicion by the Lord Deputy, was forbidden to take the field against them. By this time, all Mayo had sided with the Burkes and the revolt reached a strength never achieved before. In June, the Burkes compiled a Book of Complaints against Sir Richard Bingham, signed by all the principal chieftains of the country.

In September, seven of my galleys arrived from Ulster with Scots mercenaries. By that time, the Burkes didn't need them. The faithless Scots helped themselves to seven hundred Burke cattle and left for the north.

The following month, the Burkes once again reiterated their demands for the restoration of The MacWilliam title. On October 15, in open defiance of the government, they elected and installed William Burke, the Blind Abbot, as the new MacWilliam. The Burkes were now the masters of Mayo and even parts of Galway, and the rebellion was going from strength to strength.

From time to time, I still "ran errands" for my friend, Black Tom Butler, and in December of 1589, we met in Dublin.

"Granuaile, I think now would be a good time for you to distance yourself from the rebellion and go back to 'maintenance at sea' instead of transporting Burke troops."

"Why, Tom?"

"Our gracious Queen advised me she is royally upset – she used a much stronger term in private – because she feels her Lord Deputy has mishandled the rebellion. She told me that restoring The MacWilliam title has given the Burkes a central figure around which the rebellion could revolve."

"That's true, but, if anything, it makes the revolt that much more likely to be successful. So why are you telling me to lay low now?"

"Because when you combine that with the fact that your favorite, Richard Bingham, will probably be acquitted of the charges of cruelty leveled against him by the Book of Complaints, I'll wager Bingham will try to teach the Burkes a lesson they'll not soon forget."

Indeed, Tom's prediction proved to be all too accurate. When that evil man, Bingham, was exonerated of all charges at the beginning of January, 1590, he moved swiftly and ruthlessly, indiscriminately killing men, women, and children, and plundering everything before him as he attacked the Burke strongholds at Castlebar, Barnagee, and Erris. Bingham's tactics, cruel as they might be, were effective. Three weeks later Edmund Burke sued for peace. As a result, the Burkes ended up paying nearly five thousand pounds.

While there was no way Richard Bingham could implicate me in direct involvement in the rebellion, he was certainly aware that I had participated actively in writing the Book of Complaints against him. Thus, I knew it was only a matter of time before he would turn his attention to dealing with me once again.

Early that summer, when Bingham was raging through Connaught, I accepted an invitation from Black Tom Butler to spend time at Ormond Castle in Carrick-on-Suir. In order to get there, I sailed the *Sea Ghost* down the west coast of Munster, clear to Mizen Head, where the Atlantic meets the Celtic Sea. So clement was the weather and so calm the usually boisterous Atlantic, that I myself piloted the vessel the entire way, until we dropped anchor at Tramore Bay, far from Richard Bingham's jurisdiction.

I felt an almost trembling excitement as I hired a private
carriage and rode inland from Waterford, the largest town in the
county, to Carrick. It was not as if I had any romantic notions
of a liaison between Tom and myself. If anything, Black Tom,
with his constantly smiling face, reminded me of my brother
Donal na-Piopa, who, thank goodness, was still alive. No, what
made me feel young again was that I had been on this particular
high road, coming south rather than going north, on the way
to my honeymoon with Donal an-Chogaidh O'Flaherty at the
beginning of my adult life, forty-four years ago. My God! How
could time have gone so quickly? An entire lifetime in the blink
of an eye.

It was bitterly hard to imagine that I was, by the count of
years, an old woman. Aside from the pains in my joints, which
I had gotten so used to that I would have missed them had they
not been there, I felt as young and strong as ever I had. True, it
had been more than seven years since I'd lain with a man, my
beloved Richard an-Iarrain, who had been my very first. But I
was still very much the Pirate Queen of Connaught, and I could
still fight next to any man and command any Irishman willing
to come under my Hen's Flag. As I was busy living in the past,
being – or at least feeling – youthful again, the carriage breasted
a small rise.

I gasped with undisguised amazement at what I beheld.
Tom had never told me about his residence, nor had I deigned
to imagine what it was like. I'd become aware that Tom was
highly placed nobility, but I considered myself a noble as well.
Ormond Castle was, quite simply, the most beautiful manor
house I had ever seen, and this included the Lord Deputy's
sumptuous abode in Dublin.

As Tom and his wife, Elizabeth Sheffield Butler, a regal-looking lady of thirty-five, came out to the crescent, graveled carriageway to greet me, I must have seemed like a country bumpkin staring in frank awe at the huge residence.

"Lady Granuaile," Elizabeth greeted me courteously, "Tom has told me much about you. I've admired your feats from afar before my husband ever met you. I'm frankly amazed at how you've succeeded in a man's world."

"Thank you, Lady Elizabeth," I replied. "You yourself are no stranger to me, since the Earl has spoken often of you as well." That wasn't entirely untrue. I had made it a point to study about Lady Elizabeth in the Book of Peers before I sailed for Tramore. She was as finely bred as an English racehorse. She'd been a double baroness in her own right, even before her marriage to Earl Thomas Butler. Her father, John Sheffield, Second Baron of Sheffield, had married the daughter of the first Baron Howard of Effingham, and Elizabeth was a product of that marriage. "He's told me about your son as well."

"Ah, young James," she said, brightening. I had often noticed in the past that the way to engage a woman's interest immediately was to mention her children, particularly her boy children. "He's around here somewhere, like all six-year-olds, he's sometimes more trouble than he's worth," she said affectionately. "Do you have children, Grace?"

"I had four, three boys and a girl. The first was killed by Bingham's men," I said, not without rancor.

"I'm so sorry," Lady Elizabeth said sincerely. "Your others are well?"

"One would hope, although Murrough and I have never been close. Last I heard, he was working with Bingham."

HUGO N. GERSTL

"I'm glad you said 'Bingham,' not 'the English,'" Tom joined in.

"I've not hesitated to align myself with the English in the past, provided it's to my advantage to do so. But Bingham's another story. I'm sorry to trouble you with my personal feelings, Lady Elizabeth, particularly since you're the epitome of an Englishwoman."

"No offense taken, Grace," the Earl's wife replied. "He can be rather brutal."

"If you don't mind my changing the subject, M'Lord, M'lady, your manor is the most beautiful I've ever seen."

"Thank you, Granuaile," Tom said. He was outfitted in a casual, but elegant frock coat of pale yellow silk and shiny black satin breeches. With his full black beard and merrily twinkling eyes, he looked both rested and very handsome. "My family originally built it in 1350, shortly after the Crown gave the Butler family their title. We've installed a new façade in the past five years. But once again I forget my manners." He snapped his fingers and two large men appeared as if they'd been waiting for this very signal. "Gentlemen, the Lady Grace's portmanteau is in the carriage, please fetch it up to her room."

If I'd found the outside of the manor impressive, the inside was stunning. We entered the front hall, then walked through a long, festooned gallery. Its stuccoed ceiling was studded with heraldic crests of the Butler family. The commodious room boasted large, square windows, totally unlike the small slit windows of Rockfleet, and two ornately carved fireplaces. There were oil-on-canvas paintings of people I assumed were Black Tom's ancestors. Two huge paintings hung on a long wall. One I recognized as my host. The other was of a woman I'd estimate to be in her early thirties, who looked vaguely familiar.

"The Queen," Tom said. "Of course, she was much younger then."

Farther down the hall there was a particularly riveting painting of an extraordinarily beautiful young woman, one of the most alluring I'd ever seen. "Who is that woman, Tom?"

Tom smiled indulgently. "Anne Boleyn, Henry VIII's second wife and the present Queen's mum. Alas, she lost her head, and Henry went on to others."

"Is there any reason why you keep a portrait of her in your home?"

"Yes, Grace, legend has it she was born in this very castle."

"Really?"

"Actually, there are many castles that claim that distinction today, so who knows if it's true or not? But on the assumption it is, you're in for a treat. Your quarters are in the very room where she's said to have been born." He chuckled. "If she had been born here, she'd be related to the Butlers, and if she was related to the Butlers, then Queen Bess of England might well be a distant cousin."

"So there you have it, Granuaile. Richard Bingham detests you as much as you hate him. He's got a long memory and he doesn't forget slights and insults."

"I really don't care what he thinks, Tom," I replied. "My worry is what he's doing to me. He's confiscated my landholdings and my cattle. The only way in which I now survive is by sea, and he's made it pretty obvious that he intends to close off that avenue too."

"I can't deny anything you say," the Earl responded. We were walking through a finely sculpted rose garden separated by boxwood. It was a rare cloudless day in the southern province, and there was only a slight, balmy breeze. "Neither Perrot nor even FitzWilliam particularly likes him, but that's more for his methods, rather than his intentions. He views himself as a servant of the Crown, and he'll do anything it takes to serve his master, er, his mistress, well."

"But it doesn't serve the Queen if he offends the clan chiefs so badly he incites them to rebellion every few years."

"It's hard to tell if he's successful or not. Every time he's gone, the clans seem to get the upper hand. Whenever he returns, it's only a matter of weeks before he manages to quell the uprisings. You'll have to admit, as cruel as he is, he's damned effective."

"Yes, but..."

"You're not accepting anything I say?"

"About England eventually dominating Ireland, yes. About Richard Bingham, I'll die rather than submit to him."

"You've submitted to the English in the past."

"When it benefited me to do so."

"Enough." More quietly, he said, "How did Maude react to the last message?"

"I think she agreed it was time to end it as loving friends, rather than prolonging things until they became bitter."

"I'm relieved," he said. "Imagine what a mess it would have been had she gotten with child."

"Only if the two of you had made an issue of it," I replied. "How long were you together?"

"Two years."

"And neither her husband nor the Lady Elizabeth were suspicious?"

"I never asked. We were quite careful." He grinned, a bit ruefully I thought. "You know, that time she and I were on the *Sea Ghost* together...?"

"No, Your Earlship," I said, winking. "I do not know – and I do not *want* to know."

"You really are a true friend, Granuaile. One day, perhaps, I might be able to repay your many favors."

"What do you mean 'repay', Tom? As I recall, it was you who got me the royal pardon."

Chapter 35

In May, 1591, I decided it was time to teach my faithless son Murrough a lesson not to mess with his old mother. He'd actually sided with Bingham against the Burkes and me that spring. What galled me was not so much that he helped the English – I'd done so myself on more than one occasion – but that he would align himself with that son-of-a-fitchet-bitch Bingham against his own mother.

On the thirteenth day of that month, I sailed into Bunowen with eight of my galleys and plundered and spoiled a good segment of Murrough's lands. In the skirmish that followed, my men killed four of my son's forces. We then loaded our galleys with the spoils of our attack and sailed unmolested back to Clew Bay.

By June, whether by purchase or outright capture, my fleet of ships was up to fifteen. When some Scots mercenaries who'd come down from Ulster in search of booty killed the Blind Abbott's two sons, I pursued them with my entire fleet. Surprisingly, Richard Bingham did not interfere with my actions. As a result of this foray, I added three more vessels to my small navy.

My friend, Black Tom Butler, was so amused by the dispatch Bingham sent to the Lord Deputy that he hand-copied the document, which FitzWilliam had shown to him, and sent it to me.

"It may please Your Honour that I have lately received credible advisements that in the conflict between the Scots and the Burkes, two of the Blind Abbott's sons were slain, and many of the bad and notorious Burke knaves were killed. Likewise, two of the principal leaders of the Scots and many others on their side were slain as well. What a happy circumstance this is. As a result of the cutting of those bad members, there is now general quiet and tranquility in this province. The Scots departed from hence towards their own country, and Grany O'Malley is preparing herself with some fifteen boats in her company to repair after them in revenge of her countrymen, and for the spoil they committed, which I am contented to tolerate, *hoping that all or most of them on both sides will take their journey towards heaven, and the province will then be rid of many bad and ill disposed persons.*"

Of course, Sir Richard's ironic humor gave me scant comfort. Time as well as Bingham had caught up with me. I was now sixty-one years old, and although I managed to conceal it from all but a very few close associates, my strength was waning. The possibility of continuing my previously active and, I must say, remarkably successful, sea life was rapidly fading. Bingham had robbed me of my livelihood on land. The prospect of a life restricted to my remote and dour fortress of Rockfleet was grim indeed. I knew that as I was aging and my only means of support was to extract it from the tempestuous Atlantic, it was only a matter of time before I'd be reduced to near starvation.

By the autumn of 1591, most of the older Burke leaders had died. The Blind Abbott was no longer in contention for any position of power. Happily, my youngest son, Tibbott na-Long – Toby of the Ships – who, more than any of my other children had acquired my instincts for survival in the ever-changing political field – emerged as the principal leader of the Mayo Burkes.

But even in that emergence, I could see the old ways were breaking down. Toby's rise was contrary to the old Gaelic system. Many members of the clan, especially the Ulick sept, were his seniors. Under the old system, Ulick would have been elected leader. But because of the power vacuum created by Bingham among the Burkes, Toby – just as I would have done – seized his opportunities as they arose and acted accordingly.

Despite the political intrigue and activity which would normally have attracted my attention, by the time my sixty-second birthday rolled around, the few O'Malleys who attended a small party in my honor at Rockfleet were diplomatic enough not to call it a *happy* birthday. I was now struggling for survival, not in the political sense, but for my very existence. Six months later, Bingham wrote to the Lord Deputy, and, as usual, my friend the Earl of Ormond surreptitiously sent a copy of the dispatch to me:

"I find the Devil's Hook's son, Edward MacRichard-an-Iarrain, and Tibbott MacRichard-an-Iarrain, Grany O'Malley's son, to be men of no possessions, or to have any goods, not even so much as half a dozen cows apiece."

Although this insulting note was exaggerated, Bingham's observations demonstrated the depths to which my son and grandson had fallen. It became imperative that Edward and Toby align themselves with a power – Gaelic or English, it mattered not which – so that they could restore their lost wealth and position.

Worse was yet to come. Despite all the problems I had encountered with the English authorities over the years, I had always managed to retain control of my fleet and my immediate coastline. This freedom of movement had enabled me to remain a leader of free Irish in Connaught longer than any other leader. Then, in April, 1593, Bingham tightened the screws. He sent an immense force of forty warships to Clew Bay and blockaded my ingress and egress from Rockfleet. Sir Richard Bingham had finally cinched the noose in the hangman's rope. What he did was neither more nor less than impound my fleet.

I had been cut off from making a living off the land for some years, Now I found myself barred from making a living from the sea. This was the greatest single financial setback I'd suffered in my life. By June of 1593, I was reduced to eating gruel and porridge and the occasional rockfish that came close to my shores. There was no wood to light the fireplaces in Rockfleet Castle and the aching in my joints had never been so fierce.

Richard Bingham had exacted his own revenge on me at last. There was one – and only one – way I stood any chance of restoring my rights and those of my family. I had to appeal to the one force higher than either Bingham or FitzWilliam. The only person to whom I could appeal was Queen Elizabeth herself. And there was only one person I knew who could get my desperate message to the Queen.

"In most humble wise showeth unto your most Excellent Majesty: Your most loyal and faithful subject, Granuaile ni-Mháille of Connaught in Your Highness' realm of Ireland, that where by means of the continual discord and dissension which heretofore long time remained among the Irish, especially in West Connaught by the sea-side, every chieftain for his safeguard and maintenance and for the defense of his people, followers and country – took arms by strong hand to make head against his neighbours, who in like manner forced Your Highness' fond subject to take arms to maintain herself and her people by sea and land the space of forty years past...

"Despite my great age and what little time I have left to live, I most earnestly and humbly beseech Your Most Excellent Majesty to grant unto your said subject under Your most gracious Hand of Signet, free liberty during what days remain to her, to invade with sword and fire all Your Highness' enemies, wheresoever they are or shall be, without any interruption by any persons whatsoever..."

In early July, 1593, Black Tom Butler, the Earl of Ormond, personally sailed into Clew Bay and landed at my much humbled Rockfleet Castle. Whether from sheer charity or genuine pity for an old friend, now in the direst straits, Tom's lieutenants offloaded and brought into the castle three sides of salted pork, two sides of salted beef, several bushels of wheat and rice, and two cords of wood.

I was so thankful all I could do was weep, and with my last shred of dignity, I begged the Earl to remember me as I had been, rather than as I now was.

"Is this the Granuaile I knew only a few years ago?" he intoned, his voice strong and invigorating. "You who are frightened of nothing and no one?"

"Do I need say anything to you about what's happened, Tom?"

"No, Grace, you need not."

"I don't know why you've come, but I can only tell you how much I appreciate even seeing your face, let alone thank you for the incredible bounty with which you've blessed me."

"Bounty, Granuaile? Three years ago, you'd have disdained what I brought as not worthy of even one of your ships."

"Times change, and people do, too."

"Oh, balderdash!" he exclaimed. "Are you telling me the heart of the pirate queen of Connaught no longer beats in your chest?"

"Is that statement intended to mock what I've become?"

"No, Granuaile. It is not intended to mock anything. Do you remember the petition you sent to the Queen last month?"

"Aye. One of thousands, I am sure. That great lady has many more pressing concerns than an old, lame pirate."

"So say you. For your information, I was asked to deliver this from the Queen's Private Secretary, Sir William Cecil, Baron Burghley."

He handed me am ornately embellished scroll with very clear handwriting and the purple seal of Elizabeth Regina.

"EIGHTEEN ARTICLES OF INTERROGATORY TO BE ANSWERED BY GRANY NI-MHÁILLE:

Who was her father and mother?

Who was her first husband?

What sons had she by him? What be their names and where do they live?

What countries they have to maintain them withal?

To whom they be married?

What kin was O'Flaherty, her first husband, to Sir Murrough-ne-Doe O'Flaherty that is here now at the court?

Answer the like question for her second husband and for his sons and their livings.

If she were to be allowed her dower, or thirds of her husbands' living, of what value the same might be.

Where in the Composition of Connaught there are any provisions for wives.

Whether it be not against the Customs of Ireland for the wives to have more after the deaths of their husbands than they brought with them?

How she has maintained herself and made a living since her last husband's death.

Of what kindred are Walter Burke FitzTheobald and Shane Burke MacMoyler to her son?

What captains and countries lie next to her first husband's possessions?

Who possesses the Castle of Murrisk upon the seaside in Owle O'Malley?

What lands doth MacGibbon possess in that country?

Who doth possess the country named Carramore and Mayn Connell?

Who doth possess the island of Achill and Killdawnet Castle?

What kin was her last husband to Walter and Ulick Burke?"

My eyes widened in confusion and surprise. "What does all this mean, Tom?"

"It means you have generated the Queen's interest."

As promptly and completely as I could, with the blessed help of the Earl of Ormond, I responded in writing to the Queen's Interrogatories. Without here overlengthening this remembrance, I pretty much told the Queen what I have said here, although in much more abbreviated and formal style, and I posted the same with Thomas Butler, the Earl of Ormond, when he departed Rockfleet after three days.

Shortly after I dispatched my responses in the care of my great friend, an incident occurred which added new urgency to my petition. Bingham arrested and imprisoned my son, Tibbott na-Long, on charges that he had communicated with Brian O'Rourke of Breffni and had offered to raise Mayo in support of yet another rebellion. Two days later, I received word that Bingham had imprisoned my brother Donal na-Piopa O'Malley for allegedly killing some English soldiers three years earlier. Bingham brooked no trial in this matter. He summarily confiscated all of their lands and cattle, reducing them to nothing – nothing at all.

Regardless of the low station to which I had sunk, I was still the matriarch of the Burke and O'Malley clans. I recalled a day long past, when I stood erect, ready to face the gallows erected by Bingham: I am Granuaile ni-Mháille, daughter of the Black Oak, widow of The MacWilliam, Queen of Connaught. The time will come. I AM GRANUAILE NI-MHÁILLE, DAUGHTER OF THE BLACK OAK, WIDOW OF THE MacWILLIAM, QUEEN OF CONNAUGHT. THE TIME WILL COME. THE TIME WILL COME...

The time for written petitions was past. There was now only one way to deal with this situation. I would sail to England myself and confront Elizabeth. Queen to Queen.

Chapter 36

The problem: how to escape the blockade Richard Bingham had set? Granted, there were no longer forty ships guarding the bay, but even the twelve that were strung from the south to the north entrance to Clew Bay were sufficient. The English had taken Kildawnet Castle, the gateway to Achill Sound, and they had then used the same device the Byzantines had used, albeit unsuccessfully, against the invading Ottomans – they strung two large chains from Achill to the mainland, thus effectively blocking off any access to Achill Sound.

I had seven ships in Blacksod Bay, which were under the watchful eye of four additional English Men O'War. They could not run the blockade *into* Clew Bay, nor could my eight ships *in* Clew Bay, including my beloved *Sea Ghost*, escape to the Atlantic.

The idea of how to run the gauntlet came to me in a dream one night. I dreamt I had been reduced to one small boat, a decrepit old hulk that could barely limp *around* Clew Bay, let alone venture out into the Atlantic. I shuddered as I thought of how low I'd sunk. But when I awakened and looked about me, I was still in Rockfleet and, as had been my custom for years and years, the *Sea Ghost* was securely hawsered to my bedpost.

Over the next two days, I fleshed out my plan. It was dependent on three elements: first, I had always been a gambler and I was about to take the greatest gamble of my life, literally risking everything on gamble. Second, I knew more about the waters between Clew Bay and Dingle Bay than just about anyone else in the area. I had sailed these seas for more than half a century. I knew every inlet, every bay, and every rock. More important, I had an innate sense of the tides in each of these areas. Third, all my life I'd been an aggressor, not content merely to defend a position, and I was, so to speak, on my home turf, something the English were not.

I was sixty-three, a great age, and I wasn't about to question whether or not I could make my plan work. There was simply no question; if it did not work, I would be dead, but I would rather die defining who I was and what I was fighting for, than die a starved-out old woman.

I approached Shane O'Malley, who had been my friend for nigh onto forty years and had been my da's friend before that. Shane could not have been a day younger than eighty, with gnarled hands and a face that was so wrinkled and leathery he looked like the oldest man who'd ever lived, but for his bright, blue eyes, which sparkled with a life not yet over. There was no better shipwright in all of Ireland. I knew that because not only had he maintained all of my ships, from my very first one, but he'd been the man responsible for singlehandedly refurbishing, nay, *rebuilding* the *Sea Ghost* only a few years before.

When I outlined my plan to him, Shane's face turned into one huge smile. "You're really going to do it, Lassie?"

"Aye, Shane O'Malley, that I am."

"Your da would be so proud of you, darling girl. Even better, I kept many of the boards from the *Sea Ghost* so it shouldn't be hard to do what you ask."

"How long will it take, Shane?"

"Less than a fortnight, particularly since it's going to be a complete sham."

"The English are ten miles away."

"They could be ten *feet* away and they wouldn't be able to tell the difference."

"And the other?"

"That's the easiest part of all. It'll take less than a day to make it so old and pitiful looking the English would feel bad even if they knew you were aboard."

"One other thing, Shane..."

"I'll not even discuss taking a penny from you, Granuaile O'Malley. The sheer fun of twisting the English lion's tail hard will be more than enough payment for me. And from ten miles out, they wouldn't see the change, even if I did it in broad daylight."

One week before the execution of my plan, I called forty of my most trusted senior lieutenants, as well as old Shane O'Malley, to my castle for a late evening meeting. When they got there, we all assembled in the great room. As a last bit of extravagance, I had a large fire going, since even July nights on Clew Bay were chilly.

"Gentlemen," I began. "I'll not lie to you and I'll not tell you we're better off than we've ever been." The room echoed with bitter laughter. These men, as trapped as I was, had been reduced to eating turnips and carrots, for beef and sheep were no more. "I plan to confront the Queen of England face to face and see if she truly is the 'Good Queen Bess' her subjects call her."

"What do you intend to do?" a man ten years my junior asked.

"I intend to petition her to her face and request that our rights be restored."

"A fine idea, Lady Granouile," he said. "But how do you get the hell out of Clew Bay?"

"That is why I asked each of you here. But before I tell you my plan, I have something I must say to each of you. You've all been loyal to me through good times and bad. There's no question these are the worst times of all. I'm gambling for my life, but each of you will be part of that gamble as well. My benefactor, the Earl of Ormond, secretly brought in six months worth of supplies of all kind, salt beef, salt pork, dried beans, wheat, even logs for the fire. I will leave this castle at the beginning of next week. I don't know when I'll return, or even *if* I'll return, or, for that matter, whether I'll even make it out of Clew Bay. But I intend to make it, or, by God, I will die trying."

I felt a surge of excitement in the room. My next words were to seal the loyalty of these good men. "My friends, the night before I leave, I want each of you to bring in carts. I intend to give you every flitch of meat I have, every bean in every sack, every last stick of wood, and every supply in this castle. You've been with me long enough – and you've been with one another long enough – that I have no doubt you'll divide this bounty honestly among yourselves."

There were cries of, "No, no!" but I silenced them with a single look – a look they'd all learned over the years meant *Grace O'Malley has spoken thus, and you are not to question it.*

"Gentlemen, now that that's settled, it's time for us to discuss the plan. We'll need every one of you to be sharper, shrewder, and tougher than you've ever been. If I am successful – *when* I am successful..."

I had been aware for many years of Sean O'Malley's expertise, nay, his *artistry*, but even I was not prepared for what I beheld as sunset yielded to twilight on the evening before I was to embark. The newly fabricated sham *was* the *Sea Ghost*, and I could not tell from even ten feet away that it *wasn't* the *Sea Ghost*. And the derelict old hulk that sat alongside it was so forlorn and pathetic looking that no seaman worth his salt would ever dream of boarding it for a trip around a quiet *loch*, let alone a trip around Clew Bay, and anyone who thought this scabrous hulk intended to sail into the Atlantic Ocean would have been condemned as insane.

Only Shane and I – and the crew of eight who'd be venturing out with me on the morrow – knew that the old, unutterably sad, and decrepit thin sheets of junk wood were the mask, the outer false clothing, of the *Sea Ghost*, and that once safely out into the Atlantic, she'd shed this temporary skin, which would become food for the whales and the monsters of the deep.

And what of the "real" *Sea Ghost* anchored beside the junk heap? Well, it, too, was an outer skin, and since it employed many of the old boards that had been stripped from the original *Sea Ghost,* to the sight of anyone who'd not gone aboard, it *was* the *Sea Ghost*. But once on board, a body would have to be extremely cautious, for the deck was only the thinnest veneer of plywood, and there wasn't even a bottom to the boat! It had been sunk into the muddy shallows by means of stout poles, and it would be a miracle if it lasted more than a couple of days, given the wind that was endemic to Clew Bay.

Hopefully, it would accomplish our goal. The English knew that the only way Grace O'Malley would travel anywhere by sea would be on her flagship – and indeed, as a final touch to the charade, come morning, the *"Sea Ghost"* copy would fly the largest Hen flag I could find. Yet the *"Sea Ghost"* would remain where she'd been for the past few months, and even using their most powerful eyepieces, the English would see nothing amiss with my *Sea Ghost*. They would, however, notice *something* was amiss.

"Remember," I told the pilots of my eight galleys that night. "You are to come out of the harbor and head directly for the English fleet. You are to open fire on their ships well before you are within their range and well before they are within your range. The English may be blockading us, but Richard Bingham, not the English, is our enemy. They will think it is only gunnery practice, and they may try to return fire. That's why it is imperative you stay beyond their range. While all the firing is going on, the *New Hope* – that is what I had rechristened the 'derelict' – will limp slowly around the south edge of the bay, stopping briefly at Murrisk Castle and at Carrowmore, before continuing west. In the event any of the English vessels turn toward the *New Hope*, whichever galleys are nearest me when they do, I expect you'll also abandon the 'battle' and come to my aid."

Over the years, I have learned that things do not always go according to plan, and this was to be one of those days when they did not.

The first mishap occurred when our galleys came to within half a mile of the English. Our ships started firing early and harmlessly, as they were supposed to have done. However, the northernmost of the English Men O'War was piloted by a very young and apparently impatient captain. His aggressiveness was most likely the result of inexperience in battle, and although I saw the largest of the English ships, the one sitting in the very middle of the line, signal the young man to desist, he would have none of it. He chased down my galley before our pilot was able to turn tail and run, leveled a broadside attack on the O'Malley vessel, and sank it quickly.

While this was a tragedy, both in terms of economic loss to me and perhaps with loss of life – although I later found out that only two men had been injured, and not badly at that – it did have the salutary result of the two English ships immediately next to the aggressor diverting to give aid to the helpless galley.

My remaining vessels continued their harmless exchange of fire with their English counterparts. I had just about reached the southern entrance to Clew Bay, between Carrowmore Castle and Clare Castle, where I'd been born, when not one but two Men O'War broke off from the mock battle and turned toward the *"New Hope."* I was not surprised. Clew Bay was off-limits to *any* ship that had not first cleared its passage with the English. Although I'd hoped the "derelict" could quietly slip out of Clew Bay during the confusion, I had not counted on it.

As if on signal, two of our ships turned and interposed themselves between the English and the *"New Hope."* Although our ships had a shorter distance to sail to the intercept point, the Men O'War were faster and more heavily armed. The four vessels traded warning fire, but now my worry was that they were getting much closer to one another, and if so much as one stray ball from our cannon were to strike an English vessel, it would not look good when I presented my petition to the Queen.

As the *"New Hope"* rounded South Clew Head, I faced my first dilemma. Should I hug the western coast of Connaught or make a run for Inishbofin Island, which would place me on the direct sea route to Munster and England?

Although the Men O'War were faster than my galleys, they were slower than my caravel. It would all depend on the tides and the wind, of course, but I might just be able to outrun them all – my galleys and the Men O'War. I gauged my distance at a little more than half a mile ahead of my closest English pursuer.

Suddenly, as I turned to look behind me, I saw the second English pursuer turn sixty degrees starboard and head directly toward one of my galleys. Surely the English warship would not be so inhumane – or stupid – as to try to ram the galley. But, as it drew closer and closer to the galley, I foresaw that's exactly what it intended to do. It closed to less than a hundred feet from the O'Malley vessel when a huge rogue northwesterly wave shot under the Man O'War and lifted my galley up so it was higher than the English ship.

What happened next seemed as though the two ships were dancing a strange mating dance in slow motion. With a gnashing crunch that I could hear more than a mile away, my galley came down, literally on top of the Man O'War. The weight of the galley was enough to force the larger ship deeper into the water. Neither ship could disengage from the other. Ultimately, the galley might get away, but for now it looked as though both vessels would go to the bottom of the sea.

I cannot blame my second galley for what happened next. It was falling behind the larger English ship, and there'd be no way it could hope to catch that vessel. It did the merciful thing, and I must say I would have done the same in similar circumstances. It turned back to help its sister ship and, for all I know, the Englishmen as well.

So now it was down to a race between the Man O'War and the much smaller, lighter caravel. In that moment, I made my decision. The English navy patrolled the entire coastline from Killery Harbour to Galway Bay. The chance of my negotiating that section of coast without running into the Crown's main force was nil. To add to the risk, the English had patrolled that area of coast long enough that the Limeys were probably as familiar with the waters and the rocks that abounded as I was. What I had viewed as a choice of two options was not a choice at all.

Then another thought struck me. If I could outrun the Englishman and get as far as Inishbofin – the Island of the White Cow – I would find not only a safe harbor but protection, since my fellow pirate and long-term confederate, the Spaniard Don Bosco, had his headquarters there.

Having made up my mind, I gazed ahead. To the southwest – directly where I was headed – heavy storm clouds were gathering, presaging a strong gale. With not much time to lose, it became incumbent upon us to shed the *"New Hope's"* skin, and that we did in less than an hour, tossing the flotsam in the path of the oncoming English vessel. In a matter of minutes, we raised all of the lateen sails on the *Sea Ghost*, and that proud vessel sprinted ahead of our pursuer. As I lifted a telescope to my eyes and looked back, I measured the difference between the ships at half a mile – the excess weight of the deadwood had slowed us down – but now it became apparent that the Englishman was no longer closing on us.

I felt the thrill of the wild wind against my face, something that might have frightened anyone unfamiliar with this area, but I knew the gale would not last a long time. However, I was equally aware that at this time of the year the tides and eddies and high waves were extraordinarily unforeseeable and tricky in the vicinity of Inishturk, north of my destination. I had been so busy mentally calculating where I would need to be to make safe harbor at Inishbofin that I was unaware until almost too late that the Man O'War had picked up a favorable tide and had now closed to a scant quarter of a mile behind the *Sea Ghost*. It was only a matter of a couple hundred yards before the English warship would come within firing range.

As I glanced back in horror, I saw that was exactly what the Englishman was preparing to do. The Man O'War had ten cannon on each side and was starting to position itself to fire. Crewmen were tamping balls into the heavy cannon. Unless we could catch a faster current immediately the *Sea Ghost* was doomed!

"Shall we prepare to fire on them, Captain?" my second-in-command shouted above the freshening wind.

"No, that would be useless!" I shouted back. "I unloaded everything but four light guns. We'd be blown to kingdom come before we got off a shot."

"What then, Captain?"

"Pray with all your might. Pray for the biggest damned wave the sea gods are capable of hurling!"

"For us or them?"

"Doesn't matter, as long as it gets us away from each other!"

We ran directly into the squall line. The *Sea Ghost* bucked and its wood beams screamed in protest. But I'd ridden these squalls out before, and I commanded the pilot to turn northwest and *away* from Inishturk, which was looming on the horizon. Fortunately, my mate knew exactly what I had in mind, and in seconds the caravel was turned oblique to the gale.

Not so the Man O'War. Its captain, showing the same cocky arrogance I'd seen in many a seaman, turned south, directly toward the coastline. Almost instantly, the English ship was awash in ten foot waves and a tide that spun the large ship in an even more southerly heading, directly toward the high, sharp, and deadly rocks of Inishturk's northern coast. The Englishman did not stand a chance in stars. Just before the squall between us and our pursuer closed off any vision between the two ships, we saw the Man O'War founder and slam into the rocks with a great, grinding crash and the splintering of the once mighty ship into a hundred or more fragments. We could hear the wail of the hapless, hopeless souls, but there was nothing we could do to save them, even had we wanted to do so.

Chapter 37

"So you outran one, and crushed another. Not a bad day's work, I'd say. Of course, when Bingham hears of it he'll go crazy."

"Worse things have happened, Bosco. We lost two. At least I can say honestly we didn't fire a shot that did any damage."

Don Bosco was a little taller than me, very, very round, with pockmarked skin and a still-reddish beard salted with gray. He'd shared the Atlantic with me for a goodly while, and although we plied the same profession there had arisen a genuine warmth between us. He and I had both run afoul of the English from time to time, he because he was Spanish, me because I was independent and Irish, and both of us because we'd been despoiling their trading ships. He was as politically astute as I, however, and there had been times when we'd both served the English cause as well. The only difference in our present fortunes came because I was a quite visible thorn in Governor Bingham's side, whereas Don Bosco had stayed out of independence movements and because his demesne had so little to offer – a population of fifty people that was simply not worth the time or the effort it would take to bring Inishbofin to its knees.

"So you're down to thirteen ships?"

"And no way to use them."

"It seems to me that once you've run the blockade you could open up the sea routes again."

"If – and that's a very big 'if' – Her Majesty will let me. She'd have to directly countermand Bingham, who's probably at this very moment plotting how to stop me from getting to England at all."

"There's no reason we couldn't sail together to the Celtic Sea and thence to St. George's Channel."

"You'd do that for me, Bosco?"

"Might be fun, Granuaile. Hell, we're both of an age and we've never sailed together. It might not be a bad idea to disguise the *Sea Ghost* a little bit, and maybe even fly some pennant other than your cocky Hen Flag. Besides, the pickings might be good this time of year,"

"That's your department this trip, my friend. But I thank you both for the provisions and for the safety your companionship would offer."

Two days after that, we left for Munster. We gave wide berth to Galway Bay and the Arans, for we knew that Sir Richard Bingham would be looking all up and down the coast for the *Sea Ghost*. Once we passed the Mouth of the Shannon and Dingle Bay, we were clear of the main English force. We came upon balmy seas and easy sailing once we'd rounded Mizen Head. At that point, my friend Don Bosco and I bid a fond farewell to one another.

Once across the Channel, my caravel eased past Wales and within a week I arrived at the mouth of the Thames, that large and famous and sometimes filthy and mucky river which led to the greatest city in the world, London.

In all my years, I had never been to that huge and noisy and busy metropolis, and, although I am not a timid person by nature, I was overwhelmed by what I saw. For one thing, the *Sea Ghost* seemed so small and insignificant as it sailed by much larger and brawnier ships. I had attacked ships as large as these in the past, but that was when I had a pack of galleys at my command. Even then, the galleys were smaller and we had mastered the larger ships only by attacking them singly, and only when my forces operated in tandem.

I'd gotten word to Tom to be on the lookout for me, that with God's help and blessing I should be in London sometime between the beginning of August and the end of September. It was mid-September when the *Sea Ghost* pulled into New Quay, which was not new at all, but run down and shabby, and certainly in a less than fashionable part of London.

I must here correct myself, for I said "London." The actual city of London is only one mile on each side, but its environs, all of which were different cities, were still collectively called "London." The *Sea Ghost* berthed on the southern bank of the Thames, where it was able to slip in simply because it was smaller than most vessels.

Black Tom, bless him, came round the morning after I'd arrived. Although I was no longer a vain woman, age having cured me of that, I took pains to look as presentable as I could, for I was now expected to comport myself with some degree of dignity and the trappings of that dignity demanded I dress for the occasion.

"Quite nice," Black Tom said, as he boarded my ship. "But it may take some time to get you an audience with Her Majesty, not that I haven't been working on it. Today, I'm going to squire you around part of London so you can gain your own impression of the city, Granuaile. We might even buy you an... alternate outfit... not to insult you, but simply to give you the opportunity to have more than one change of clothing should your meeting with the Queen consume more than one session."

Tom pointed out that London was truly the hub of the universe. Indeed, the city was daunting in its sheer size and magnitude. When I was small, Lisboa had been, to me, the largest and most exciting city on earth. It had remained beloved to me, mostly because Doctor António Manso Pinheiro had been there, and Maria Correia had been there, and because I'd eaten my first truly 'different' foods there, and because I'd been there with the two men who had mattered most in my life, Owen Dubdharra O'Malley and Richard an-Iarrain Burke.

But surely London dwarfed Lisboa, just as it dwarfed any other place I'd ever seen, Cádiz and Dublin, Bordeaux and... and... Suddenly the magnitude of the great English capital overwhelmed me so that I couldn't even think of other cities I'd seen. London was so... so *busy*. It was filled with narrow cobblestoned streets and alleys. Magnificent public buildings stood next to hovels, and while one building smelled of rich meats and sauces, the one immediately adjacent to it smelled of urine and cheap wine.

I was baffled by the extremes of this city of cities, poverty nestled next to extraordinary wealth, color and pageantry everywhere, milling crowds that made me feel so closed in. It was as far removed from the wilds and lonely hills and loughs and bogs of Ireland as Unia Island, where I'd met the sea-witch Nehalennia, was from Ormond Castle. The city was so *alive* that I could feel its inner heart pounding and pulsating night and day. It truly was the epicenter of the world.

On my second day there, Tom insisted I accompany him to a sartor and a sutor of some repute, so he said, where he purchased two dresses of a quality and style I'd never experienced in my life, as well as some accoutrements which pushed my breasts higher while the neckline of the blouse he purchased for me plunged quite scandalously low.

From there, he took my to see two young women he introduced as ladies-in-waiting to the queen's court. They cut and coiffed my hair in a way that seemed most unnatural. I refused to even consider a wig, since God had given me a full head of hair, even in my advanced age, and I found no need to augment it.

For lunch, the Earl of Ormond took me to one of his favorite restaurants. You must understand that in my day I had eaten quite well, although for the past year I'd been reduced to hard tack and oatcakes, carrots and turnips, with the occasional slice or two of lamb or bully beef. But this restaurant – and my repast there – was surely beyond any meal I'd ever eaten.

There were long tables where you helped yourself to anything you wanted – and as much as you wanted, and you could come back as often as you felt the need. There were vegetables the likes of which I'd never seen or eaten. Tom pointed them out and explained each to me.

"Those things that look something like turnips? They're not. They're called potatoes. They're brought in from the Americas – the New World – and there's talk that one day they'll import them to Ireland. Here is asparagus. It has a very strong and distinct flavor, and it's said to be very healthy, although I must warn you when you piss after you've eaten it, it will smell very funny. And this, my dear, is the most precious vegetable of all. It's called an eggplant – aubergine in French – and it has no relation whatever to an egg. It can be cooked a dozen ways, each better than the last, and here they mix it with onion and tomato and salt and cook it 'til it's as soft as butter."

Moving on, there was another table filled with sea creatures, most of which I had seen and eaten in my day, but never in such variety and profusion and amount. At the end of a third table, a large, muscular man stood beside a huge roast of beef, slicing it for patrons as they carried their already bulging plates to his station.

"I can't help but feel guilty, Tom. In Ireland, we are reduced to eating the same poor fare nearly every day. Even in London, I've seen such heartbreaking poverty. Yet here we are, gorging ourselves on what would be ten or even twenty meals for most people."

"I won't deny that, Granuaile," he said, "but regrettably that's the way it has been and always will be in every society. There are those who rule and those who are ruled, those that gorge and those that starve. It is unfair, but that is simply the way of the world. If you think you've seen opulence here, wait 'til you see the court."

"I've never seen so many people in one place in all my life. How many live in London?"

"Close to a million."

"A *million*?" I gasped, stunned. "There are not half that many people in the whole of Ireland!"

"London has a greater population than many countries," he said.

"How do they all manage? I mean, men and women need food, water, shelter, clothing..."

"Some say they don't manage very well, which is why you see so much poverty in the midst of all this wealth."

"Why do they come to London, then?"

"Because everyone truly believes there is more opportunity here than anywhere else. That if you work hard enough and smart enough, you'll be able to join the ranks of the wealthy. Or, if it's not you, it may one day be your sons or their sons."

There seemed to be validity in what Tom said, for even among the poor, I saw goods being exchanged or bartered or sold in such amounts which would have seemed profligate in Ireland, where even those of middling wealth would scoff at having more than two or three changes of clothing at any given time, and underclothes were an unheard-of luxury.

"Have you any word on when I might see the Queen?" I asked, as we were walking back to my ship at day's end.

"I am still trying to inveigle the earliest moment. Lord Burghley has become a good friend, so I believe we should be hearing from him within the next few days.

The "next few days" became a week, and while I had been cautioned to exercise patience, I was becoming more and more frustrated. Did not this woman realize my very life and the lives of my children were at stake?

Finally, just as my patience was coming to an end and I was about to present myself at the castle with or without an invitation, the summons came the evening before I was to arrive at court. That gave me time to select my outfit. I decided I would not dress to impress anyone, but rather to reflect who I was. Accordingly, on the morning I was to be presented to the Queen, I selected a long linen saffron smock – a *léine* – reaching to my ankles, with long, wide sleeves, under a long dress with the sleeves slit and tapered to allow the long sleeves of the *léine* to show through, with a low-cut bodice laced in front. Over that, I wore a large, woolen sleeveless cloak, with a fringe of wool all around, which reached to the ground. At the neck, there was a deeper fringe to give the appearance of a fur-like collar. This was to be a serious meeting, and I dressed for the occasion.

Promptly at two hours before midday, a carriage arrived at Chelsea House, where I'd spent the night, to take me to Greenwich Castle, where the Queen lived during the summer months. I was comforted to find that Black Tom Butler would ride with me. As the carriage bounced over cobblestone streets near the Thames, Tom said, "She's as nervous about this meeting and as anxious to meet you as you are to meet her. I think both of you are a bit curious about the other."

"That I certainly am, my friend," I said. "I'm eager to meet the woman whose orders and plans have so drastically and completely affected my life."

"Elizabeth is eager to meet you, too," the Earl replied. "She's amazed at how you, a woman, without the supporting facilities of state she enjoys, has successfully led and governed so effectively, and how you've managed to do this for forty years. Not all the reports about you are bad, Granuaile. Even the Queen's Irish deputies and governors – Richard Bingham excepted – have given you credit for an awful lot. Ah, we're approaching Greenwich Castle."

I gasped as I gazed at the long irregular building standing close to the river bank. It was punctuated by towers, the largest of which projected forward so that its foundations were washed by the river at high tide. The whole structure was crowned with battlements, but as someone who had both attacked and defended fortresses for so many years, I could tell these were for show, since there were high, wide, transomed windows looking outward all along the river's curve. Then I looked frankly at my friend. "It's impressive, Tom, but it doesn't have the pleasing lines of Ormond castle."

"It is rather a hodge-podge," he laughed. "Elizabeth wanted it to be big, bold, and overwhelming, but she wanted it built on the cheap. One way she did that was by kicking out the Observant Friars from their building next door, and moving her own retainers into the structure. It's pretty special inside. While I appreciate your loyalty to my Irish manor, you might withhold judgment 'til you see it."

When we entered the Palace, I saw how right he was. The stone castles in the west of Ireland, including my own, were not built for comfort, but for security. The walls of Rockfleet were, for the most part, bare, and they were constantly exposed to the wild Atlantic Ocean. The luxury of Greenwich Castle was overpowering.

As Tom escorted me to the grand hall, everywhere I looked I saw tapestry-covered walls, carved oak wainscots and furniture, and ornate ceilings with fancy curlicued plaster-work – scrolls, cherubs, monsters, and such. As I walked down the long corridors which led to the royal apartments, they literally hummed with the subdued and modulated tones of courtiers, emissaries, petitioners, and many outrageously attractive court ladies. These "court decorations" wore exquisite dresses and shining jewels. They were powdered and coiffed, and they reminded me of birds, flitting hither and thither, trading the latest court gossip.

In that way, our lives might not have been that different, for I had found over the years that no matter what the gathering of people – and particularly females – and no matter where such meetings took place, there was always gossip. I suppose the need to know something that someone else does not know, or pretends not to know, preferably something scandalous or titillating about someone *else,* has oiled the wheels of society for as long as there have been people on earth.

As I passed one of several oversized mirrors in the palace, I observed myself critically. I had been a leader of men, a seawoman without equal, a pirate, a trader, a self-appointed ruler contrary to law and tradition, but too powerful to be dethroned. Looking back at me was an elderly woman whose lined and weather-beaten face proclaimed the harsh conditions of her – my – profession.

"We're about to enter the great hall," Tom whispered. "I will simply be a fly on the wall watching as the two titans meet…"

Chapter 38

As I entered the great room, I had my first glimpse of the sovereign who, with only a few words, could save or destroy my life. She was seated at the far end of the room on what looked like not so much a throne as a comfortable stuffed chair. Rich, complex, and colorful tapestries seemed to hang on every wall. Elegant crystal chandeliers gave off light that sparkled off every piece of jewelry worn in the room.

I came closer and noticed that the Queen of England herself was a *tiny* woman, at least two inches shorter than I. The sober dress I was wearing contrasted with the elaborate, overly done raiment of the Queen. Although her gown must have cost as much as one of my galleys, I was not overwhelmed by her refinement of taste. Rather, it was a magnificent display that might have done well in a costume parade or a masked ball, but it was clearly worn to *impress* rather than to *express*.

The Queen's gown was a rich vermillion color, embroidered and encrusted with jewels and ornaments. On at least six of her fingers, she wore gold rings from which sprang forth stones of every color: blue, red, green, clear quartz, and even one multicolored stone.

As I drew to within three feet of Her Majesty, ruler of England and Wales, and nominally, if not entirely, of Scotland and Ireland, I examined her face up close. It was an old, well-used face, yet Elizabeth's skin was a combination of chalk-white, from the makeup she wore, and bright, splotchy red from the rouge on her cheeks. Her eyebrows were tweezed into a squared arc. I had difficulty ascertaining whether the huge fringe of tightly-curled, thin red hair on her head was natural or an artificial wig. If it was her own, it certainly must have been colored, for it was bright reddish-orange, with not a single strand of gray and I knew the woman was more than sixty years old.

Queen Elizabeth held her hand high to greet me. I nodded in what might have seemed a deferential manner, but I neither bowed nor curtsied, for as far as I was concerned, I was her equal.

"Your Majesty," I said respectfully.

"Grace O'Malley," she replied, her tone neutral, but not cold.

I suppose I should have been frightened, anxious, even nervous unto trembling, but all I could think of was here was a somewhat frumpy little old woman trying to act like some gussied-up girl, sitting in a large chair, and attended hand and foot by richly dressed, self-importantly sycophantic men and women. It made me cough to keep from laughing out loud, and at that moment one of the ladies-in-waiting perceived I needed a handkerchief. She handed me a minuscule one of cambric and lace. After using it to stifle my cough, I threw it into the nearby fire.

The Queen raised her eyebrows, and the effect was quite comical. "Perhaps you may not be aware of it Lady Grace," she said politely, if a little stiffly, "but the handkerchief was meant to be put into your pocket after use."

"Say you so,?" I responded. "In Ireland it would be an insult to pocket an article that has been soiled."

I could not help but notice the good humor that suddenly overcame the Queen. She didn't even try to mask the gleeful glint in her eyes. Now she was the one who coughed to avoid laughing out loud. This time, I signaled one of the ladies in waiting to hand me another handkerchief, which I promptly gave to the Queen. When she had ceased coughing, she held the handkerchief away from her.

"Well, Your Majesty," I said. "What will it be – courtliness or cleanliness?"

There was a shocked collective gasp in the room, whether at my impertinence, my arrogance, or my unwillingness to humble myself before Elizabeth.

In response, the English queen stared fixedly at the handkerchief for a moment, then, with a flip of her royal hand, tossed it into the fire, just as I had done.

The room froze for just an instant. Then Black Tom Butler, the Earl of Ormond, started to applaud the Queen. The others in the room watched carefully to gauge the Queen's reaction. Then, as one, they broke out into hearty applause as well.

"My dear Grace," the sovereign said, "it seems you have started a new tradition at the palace, one which, I'm sure will make the purveyors of handkerchiefs most happy."

"Thank you, Your Majesty," I said, curtseying, "but I believe it was you, not I, who started the tradition."

"You know, Grace O'Malley," the Queen said, "we think we like you. Indeed, we think we would very much enjoy your company in private meeting. Would you care to join the Crown in the small anteroom yonder, where we might talk?"

"I would be delighted, Your Majesty," I said.

Her Majesty Queen Elizabeth, sovereign of an area much larger than the whole of Ireland, stood to her full height – she really was shorter than me – and reached out her arm to me. I took it in mine, and we strolled companionably to the anteroom. Two menservants were waiting at the doors to the room. Each held one side open and after we'd entered, they closed the doors quietly behind us.

The room was not large, twenty by twenty feet at most, and it was far more intimate, elegant, and comfortable than the great hall.

"Shall we sit, Grace O'Malley?"

"If it is your desire, Elizabeth Tudor."

"You dare call me by my given name, without the title?"

"I do, Elizabeth. After all, we are both queens, are we not? Granted, your demesne is far greater, more established, and more secure than mine."

Her eyebrows raised and her eyes widened. I did not know whether she was offended, angry, or amused, such was the wonderful self-control the woman exercised. She walked over to the large window, which looked onto the Thames, then returned and sat down in a chair opposite mine.

"I note you were respectful enough to afford me the deference due my station when we were in public."

"Of course, Your Majesty. You are the Queen and I am a guest in your residence. Make no mistake, Elizabeth, I respect everything you have done, even if I have sometimes opposed your governors, and I am impressed beyond anything I could ever tell you about how you, a woman, have succeeded so mightily."

"It was 'Your Majesty' a moment ago. Now it's back to Elizabeth?"

"Or 'Bess' if you prefer."

Her face crinkled in a genuine smile, and I am sure it wasn't for my benefit. "As I said in the other room, Grace, I think I like you very much indeed. At another time, in another place, we could be the greatest of friends, even though what I've heard of *you* from certain others might not be so flattering. Very well, my dear, as long as it is only the two of us and *no one else – ever -...*"

"Agreed," I said. Suddenly I took her hand in mine, reached over and brought it to my lips, and kissed it. "You are indeed more gracious than I ever believed you could be. You'd have made a helluva pirate!"

"How dare you say that?" she snapped. Then, "You really think so?"

"The best," I responded. "Indeed, I'd love to take you out on the *Sea Ghost* so you could see what it feels like to be free, to have the wind blowing in your face, through your hair..."

At that she laughed heartily. "Did I say something wrong, Bess?"

"No, not at all, my dear Grace," she said. "I'm just recalling that long, long ago, when you and I were still young, one of my governors, Henry Sidney I believe, told me you'd offered to squire him around Galway Bay in one of your ships – and you *charged* him for the privilege."

"I promise I'd take you for free," I replied. "You know, you talk about being young again. We can't roll the clock back, but I'll wager we two old hens would have a bang-up time on the sea. I think you'd actually get a thrill out of raiding a treasure ship – not an English one, of course."

"Would you like some tea, Grace?"

"Please, Your Majesty, and some butter cream cookies if you would be so kind."

"Are we being a bit greedy?"

"No, Bess, just a bit hungry. I've not eaten today. I was nervous thinking about our meeting, but you've been so incredibly gracious I feel I'm in the company not only of a sovereign but of a true friend – a sister queen, as it were."

The Queen pulled a cord situated between the chairs. Within a few minutes, a serving maid appeared with two delicate china cups, a silver tea service, and a plateful of various cookies and sweetmeats. While we were nibbling at the treats and sipping the delicious tea, we made small talk about people we knew, or had known, the Sidneys, departed administrators, Black Tom Butler. At one point, Elizabeth displayed a bawdy side of her wonderful sense of humor.

"Grace," she said, "I'd like to ask you something in confidence. You don't have to answer if it offends you." This time it was my turn to raise my eyebrows, not knowing what was coming. "They say your second husband was nicknamed 'Iron Dick.' Is there, you know, some truth to the double meaning?"

We looked directly at one another, then burst out laughing like two schoolgirls sharing a naughty secret. "If I answer you, Bess, can I trust you to keep the confidence?"

"Of course."

"He was my second *husband*. But he was actually my *first man*. I was sixteen at the time, and he'd rescued me from highwaymen. It took place in the barn of an inn where we stayed that night. He was twenty-three, seven years older than me. I was engaged at the time, and..." I said dreamily, thinking back. "To answer your question... yes, yes, yes..."

"How incredibly romantic," Elizabeth said. "Did your first husband ever know?"

"Didn't know and frankly, wouldn't have cared. He was either engaged in some silly little battle somewhere or off with one of his many 'friends.'"

"Were there... others?"

I began to feel as though I were truly talking with a sister under the skin. "When I got lonely. Did you know I took a fire arrow just below my eye when I was thirty?"

The Queen gasped. "I didn't know. I'm so sorry. But how can you say that? I see no sign of such a dreadful injury."

"That's because of an incredibly kind physician. Alas, he died some years ago. His assistant may still be alive. If so, I hope she's enjoying the life she so richly deserves."

Even though I was spilling my soul to a woman I'd just met, I knew enough not to invade *her* privacy. After all, even though I felt very much Elizabeth's equal, I was still here as a supplicant.

After several minutes, Elizabeth said more seriously, "Grace, I need to show you something and ask you about it. My secretary, Baron Burghley, brought it to me yesterday." She extracted a letter bearing the seal of Sir Richard Bingham, my hated nemesis and governor of Connaught. I read it slowly, digesting it.

"Your august and worthy Majesty. Greeting from your unworthy servant, Sir Richard Bingham:

"There be two notable traitors gone over to London, Sir Murrough Ne-doe and Grany O'Maly, both rebels from their childhood and continually in action. I believe they will complain against Your Majesty's duly appointed officer and they will ask some reward or dispensation from Your Majesty. If such complaints be sustained or such requests be granted, they will only feel empowered to make yet more rebellions. Their reward *should* be Brydewell Prison, for notwithstanding they have been pardoned many times, there is matter enough of late found out against them to hang them justly. Grany O'Maly is mother-in-law to that notable traitor, the Devil's Hook. Howbeit Your August and Merciful Majesty, let them directly accuse me of anything, and if I discharge not myself honestly, let me be punished for it. But if they be allowed to make general accusations against me, I do not doubt but Your Majesty will most honourably and indifferently consider what they say, for if they lie about me, I care not, whatever they might say against me."

What amazed me most when I read this prattle was that I felt neither anger nor bitterness, nor even a rise in feeling. For the first time, I realized that my enemy was desperate. Sir Richard Binghan, who had hounded, harassed, and harried me for years, who had thought to bring me to my knees, to humble me, and to destroy me was *worried*. He was worried about his position, he was worried about how his sovereign the Queen would react to me, and I believe he was most worried of all that all of the calumnies he had spread about me might explode in his face. For all his bluff and bluster, at heart he was, as most bullies are, a coward who did not even have the courage to come to England and make his accusations against me face to face in front of the Queen.

"Well?" the Queen asked, daintily sipping her tea.

"If you're asking me if I slept with him, the answer is no."

There was a brief moment during which the clock in the room ticked three times. Then, Queen Elizabeth, most august ruler of the burgeoning England laughed so hard and heartily that she most unregally lost control and spat out the few drops of tea she'd been in process of swallowing. The tension broke so soundly that she started laughing and she kept laughing and there was simply no way she could – or wanted to – stop laughing. Another person might not find the event or the statement funny, but somehow it struck the most responsive chord in the Queen's body. Finally, she breathed in and out, gulping air, and managed to bring herself back into check.

"Oh, Grace, that is *so* rich, so..." She broke into gales of laughter again. Even I had to smile at her efforts to stop, but I patiently waited for her to do so. Finally, she said, "Not that it matters, but do you care to 'tell me lies' about Richard Bingham?"

"Not really. I truly feel sorry for the man if he had to resort to such desperate tactics. But I cannot say I appreciate that he's taken all my land and my ships and my way of making a living away, any more than I can say I am pleased that my sons and my son-in-law are in gaol and their properties have been taken."

"That's a pretty strong charge, My Dear."

"Would you care to take a trip back to Ireland on my ship and see for yourself?"

"No, that won't be necessary," she said more seriously. "Would you mind if I changed the subject?" she asked, refilling both our teacups.

"You're the Queen," I said.

"And you claim to be the queen of Connaught."

"I won't deny it."

"Tell me then, friend to friend, if *I* may be so bold, why is there so much difficulty in Ireland?"

"It'll take some time."

"Perhaps, since it's such a nice day, we might repair to the garden."

We did, and since it was late summer and balmy, there were lovely roses all about. "This is gorgeous, Your Majesty. Other than the Earl's garden in Munster, I've never seen anything so colorful and well-tended."

"Thank you. I feel that way about it myself."

We strolled a little while, toward the far end of the garden. Then I started to speak. "You asked about difficulties in controlling Ireland. You may as well ask about Scotland as well."

"Ah, yes. There was that trouble with Mary before I ascended the throne."

"It seems to me we're all angry animals roaming the same neighborhood. The Gallowglass Scots mercenaries will kill indiscriminately for whoever hires them. Then they'll come back the following week and kill for the other side. No loyalty there. But the Scots will fight directly, whereas the Irish Gaels will go to ground and strike from any one of a dozen places. It's sort of like a game I saw at a carnival in Portugal. There was a box with a dozen holes in it. There was a leather imitation head sticking out of the box. The customer paid a few pence and he was given a mallet. The proprietor promised the customer that it was a very easy game. All he had to do was hit the head into the hole so nothing would stick out of a hole in the board, and he would win ten times his investment. The only problem was, as soon as the customer hit one of the heads into the hole, another leather head would immediately pop out of another hole. Then, when the frustrated dupe hit *that* head down, *another* one popped up out of yet *another* hole, and so it went until the unlucky fellow had spent far more money than he intended to.

"It's like that with Ireland, Bess. The English governor or the English army or the English navy will beat down one head, but then another will pop up in a different area of Ireland."

"Like the Hydra-headed monster in Greek mythology," Elizabeth mused.

"Never heard of that story."

"Every time you cut off one of the Hydra's many heads, the monster grew two in its place. That certainly is an apt explanation of *what* happens, but it really doesn't answer my question of *why* Ireland is so hard to govern. There are so many benefits to Ireland uniting with England."

"Perhaps England sees it that way, but how well do you know the Irish, Bess?"

"My Lord Deputies give me news about it. And, of course, I have friends like Black Tom, who *are* Irish."

"Are they, now?" I asked.

"You look cynical."

"I am cynical, Bess. Tom's a truly good man, but he's Protestant. Your Lord Deputies and your governors are not Irish, and perhaps that's at the heart of the problem."

"Why do you say that?"

"Because England makes the same mistake that other occupying powers have made throughout history. The English come upon the land by force, and they impose their laws, their religion, and their administrators on a people used to being free. Indeed, one of the reasons Ireland will never prevail *militarily* over the English is that the clan is the dominant social focus of the Irish Gaels, and no amount of promising or threatening or cajoling will ever get them to unite. An Irish chieftain considers himself a king, even if his 'kingdom' consists of one small hill and his 'subjects' number thirty. He considers himself the equivalent of Brian Boru."

"The great king of Ireland who ruled several hundred years ago," she murmured.

"They say, 'One's greatest strength is one's greatest weakness, and vice versa.' I've found that to be true. It is that very spirit of total independence that means Ireland will never be *entirely* conquered, and that same independence spells disaster for any resistance movement."

"Sounds like a wise observation to me."

"Not so much wise as speaking from my own experience. I've been an O'Flaherty and a Burke, but I've always kept my name O'Malley to let the world know where my true loyalties lie. While the O'Flahertys, the O'Malleys, and the Burkes have always been aligned with one another, they have, from time to time, been on opposite sides of one another, even, from time to time, on opposite sides of the same clan. Case in point, the Burkes who support the English and the Burkes who will go down to their final graves fighting the English every step of the way."

"So you're saying it's useless?" Queen Elizabeth said, a bit sadly I thought.

"Not necessarily. There was a civilization once that got it right."

"Dare I ask who?"

"The ancient Romans. They conquered most of what was then the known world and they managed to hold it together for almost half of their eleven hundred year history."

"How?"

"I don't know. I wasn't there, so I couldn't tell you." Elizabeth punctured my talk with genuinely warm laughter.

"I don't disagree, Bess, but it must be done slowly and naturally, and the subject people must be charmed into *wanting* those laws over the long term. Let's put it in the easiest terms for us to understand. Despite what many people call you, I doubt you're any more of a 'virgin' queen than I am."

The sovereign blushed, but not maidenly coquettish. "True."

"All right, woman to woman, I'm sure we've each had lovers. Some felt their manhood was somehow less if they didn't plunge right in. Others understood the needs of a woman. They caressed, they fondled, they took their time and they were infinitely patient. And in the end, which ones did you enjoy most?"

"The latter, of course," Elizabeth said with no hesitation.

"Yet you expect the Irish to enjoy being little more than raped – 'fucked' to use the common word, whereas if England *courted* Ireland slowly, 'made love' instead of 'fucked' her, Ireland would become England's lover instead of trying to fight the Crown every step of the way."

By that time, we'd walked around the entire perimeter of the garden. During our subsequent circuit, Elizabeth said not a word, but seemed very deep in thought. Finally, as we re-entered the palace, she said, once again, "I thought I'd like you very much, Grace O'Malley, and I was right. I do."

"And I enjoy your companionship as well, Elizabeth Tudor. We seem to see eye to eye on many things. Now that we're returning to the palace. I suppose I should reclaim my tongue and refer to you only as Your Majesty."

"Quite. Grace O'Malley, before we go inside, might I ask you in private to do me the honor of allowing me to proclaim you a Countess?"

I smiled. "Elizabeth Tudor, I'm sure you know my answer to that, speaking not only in private but as sister-to-sister. As much as I respect you and honor you, if I allowed you to confer on me the title of 'Countess,' that would be downgrading me. You and I are both queens of equal rank. But you can bestow on me the greatest honor any human being can grant to one another. You have the power to command that I be given my lands, my cattle, and my ships back. You have the power to free my brother, my sons, and my son-in-law and restore them to their previous wealth and position. Unquestionably we are of equal rank, but equally unquestionably, you are by far in a stronger position than me. Thus, you have the power to show your *grace* as well as your power, Your Majesty."

Elizabeth smiled enigmatically. "You have given me much to think about, Grace O'Malley. Have you any further requests?"

"Yes, Your Majesty, I do," I said. When I told her what that request was, the enigmatic smile widened and became beatific.

"Grace O'Malley, I might only give you my answer by referring to this letter from your friend, Sir Richard Bingham. 'I do not doubt but that Your Honour will most Honourably and indifferently consider of it.' You shall have my answer in appropriate form, coming from Sir William Cecil, First Baron Burghley, my Private Secretary, upon your return to Connaught. Now, shall we go back into the great room where my entourage has no doubt been impatiently waiting?"

Queen Elizabeth did not answer my petition that day, nor did I push her for a response. Once we had re-entered the great hall, I knew my place. I was in *her* court, in *her* demesne, and was a guest. The remainder of our formal visit was quite brief, since the Queen had other affairs of state to attend to and other petitioners to see that day. Respectful of her time and schedule, I bowed, then, on the spur of the moment, knelt and kissed one of the rings on her fingers, my eyes downcast, my head bent toward the ground.

Playing her role as well, Elizabeth the Sovereign of England waited the requisite period before she said, "You may rise, Lady Grace." No "countess" or any other title, but simply "Lady Grace," the neutral appellation by which she had greeted me when first I arrived at the Hall. I bowed and backed out of the room, giving her the honor and deference of not turning my back on her until I had departed from her presence.

As Black Tom Butler, the Earl of Ormond, escorted me back to the carriage and then back to my ship, he smiled knowingly and asked, "Well?"

In reply, I simply smiled enigmatically, and that was answer enough for him.

Chapter 39

My return to Clew Bay was uneventful, save and except I was trailed the entire way by an English ship of a new type I had not seen before – a *frigate*, which was, to my eye, a modified and much faster version of the Mediterranean *galleas*. I didn't know if the ship meant to provide safe escort to me or to make certain I behaved peaceably, but as long as it didn't interfere with my passage, I made no attempt to impede its passage.

Needless to say, I was consumed with concern about what the Crown's decision would be. My very life and my living were at stake. Although Elizabeth had been much more than cordial and polite to me – indeed, I had never heard of her giving any petitioner, particularly one from a subject province, a private audience that had lasted more than two hours – I was aware that she was by no means an absolute ruler. She must answer not only to her ministers and to Parliament, but she must also be seen to support her appointed administrators. I was but one supplicant combating a governor of several years' standing, reputation, and, to a greater or lesser degree, success. On the other hand, I knew the Lord Deputy, Sir John Perrott, was by no means an admirer of Richard Bingham.

The first augury I had of what might be was when I rounded the head and entered Clew Bay. There were a number of ships in the bay, but, without exception, they were *my* ships. There was not an English vessel to be seen, except my frigate companion, which turned south and left me once I had passed Clare Island.

As I neared Rockfleet Castle, I heard loud cheering from my loyal forces, who had somehow been informed I was returning, and these were not the sounds of dismay, bur rather shouts of genuine happiness and appreciation.

When I disembarked from the *Sea Ghost* and came at last to the entrance of my home, my fortress, there were three men waiting for me. "My lady," the tallest, a distinguished-looking redbeard of early middle age said, "I bring you greetings from Her Most Excellent Majesty, Elizabeth of England. The office of the Lord Deputy requested that I dispatch her decision to you. Another courier is handing the decision to the governor at this moment as well."

"I thank you," I replied. "Have you been journeying far? I'm afraid I have not much in my home to offer, but you are more than welcome to come inside, warm yourself by what fire I have, and share whatever is available."

"That is most kind of you, My Lady," the redbeard said, "but my orders were to await your coming and to depart immediately I delivered the writing to you."

I waited until I had entered the castle and was alone before I opened the envelope containing the document which would seal my fate. My hands trembled as I took it from the envelope. I read the four pages slowly and thoughtfully.

Elizabeth Regina
September 6, 1593
To: Lord Deputy Sir John Perrott, Governor Sir Richard Bingham, and Grace O'Malley, known in Gaelic as Granuaile ni-Mháille

GREETING.

The Crown has taken under submission and consideration the petition of Grace O'Malley and now finds as follows:

Whereas our Treasurer of England, by his letters of July last, did inform you of the being here of Grace O'Malley of our province of Connaught, requiring to understand your opinion concerning her suit, and

Whereas we perceive by your late letters of answer what your opinion is of them, and their causes of complaint or of suit, whereof you have given them no just cause.

But where said Grace O'Malley hath made humble suit to us for our favour toward her sons Murrough O'Flaherty and Tibbott Burke, to her son-in-law, Richard Burke, known as the Devil's Hook, and to her brother, Donal na-Piopa that they might be at liberty, we perceive by your letters that her eldest son, Murrough O'Flaherty, is no trouble but is a principal man of his country, and as a dutiful subject hath served us when his mother, being then accompanied with a number of disorderly persons, did with her galleys lay spoil to his property and possessions, and therefore by you favoured, and so we wish you to continue.

I must have turned pale when I read those words, for they seemed to favor the governor and my restive son Murrough, with whom I had never enjoyed good relations. Did this mean that my petition would be denied in its entirety? Perhaps there might be some small consolation, 'throwing a bone,' as it were, to me. I read on.

But the second son, Tibbott Burke, one that hath been brought up civilly with your brother and can speak English, is by you justly detained because he hath been accused to have written a letter to Bryan O'Rourke, the late traitor's son, though it cannot be fully proved but is by him entirely denied; and for her brother Donal, he hath been imprisoned seven months past, being charged to have been in company of certain disorderly persons who killed some soldiers in a ward. But for those two, you think they may both be dismissed upon bonds for their good behaviour, wherewith we are content; and likewise, her son-in-law, Richard Burke, known as the Devil's Hook, hath in past stood bond for said Grace O'Malley. And so we GRANT said Grace O'Malley's request and ORDER that you free all of said persons, and each of them, forthwith, and restore them to their previous state, viz. their properties, their cattle, their holdings, and all that was to them bequeathed, devised, and given before.

And as to the petition of Grace O'Malley, known in the Gaelic tongue as Granuaile ni-Mháille,

WHEREAS we are content that she may understand we yield thereto in regard of her humble suit: So she is hereof informed and that she may depart with great thankfulness and with many more promises that she will, as long as she lives, continue to be a dutiful subject of the Crown, yea, and will employ all her power to offend and prosecute any offender against us. And further, for the pity to be had of this aged woman, having not by the custom of the Irish any title to any livelihood or position or portion of her two husbands' lands, now being a widow, and yet her sons enjoying their fathers' lands, and

GOOD CAUSE APPEARING THEREFORE, IT IS HEREBY ORDERED AND DECREED:

That Grace O'Malley is hereby restored to all of her lands, cattle, possessions, and property, whether real, personal, or mixed, of whatever character and wheresoever situate.

That Grace O'Malley is hereby afforded the right and privilege, with no interference from the Crown, its agents, employees, officers, or representatives, to maintain herself by land and by sea, henceforth and for the rest of her life.

That the Crown, and its agents, employees, officers, and representatives of every kind and nature shall favour said Grace O'Malley in all her good causes and shall protect her so that she might live in peace and enjoy her livelihood.

That the Crown, through its disbursary, shall pay to Grace O'Malley as and for a pension, and to ensure her maintenance for her living the rest of her old years, the sum of £240 per year in equal monthly installments, commencing forthwith; and

That said Grace O'Malley is herewith afforded a licence and official sanction of the Crown to act as privateer in our quarrel with all the world.

And this we do write in her favour as she showeth herself dutiful, although she hath, in former times, lived out of order. She hath confessed the same with assured promises by oath to continue most dutiful, with offer, after her aforesaid manner, that she will fight on behalf of the Crown and will justly and with her life defend and protect all who offend England.

Entered this day and by my hand. s/ Elizabeth Regina

Chapter 40

Nor was that the end of the Queen's great beneficence. The following month, three large and beautiful galleys sailed into Clew Bay, accompanied by my friend and benefactor Black Tom Butler, the Tenth Earl of Ormond.

"What now, Tom?" I asked, when he was ensconced in my great room, which, when compared to that of the Queen or to Tom's manor, was not very great at all.

"Her Majesty was saddened when she heard that you had lost two ships in your flight to visit her." He smiled the beautiful smile that lit up his entire face. "She has asked that you honor her and England by accepting the 'long term loan' of these three galleys, she has renamed the *Queen of Connaught*, *The Virgin Queen*, and..." Here he burst into laughter, knowing how much we would both appreciate the irony. "The *Governor Bingham*."

After we'd both managed to stop our hilarious giggling, I asked, "What does Her Majesty mean by 'long term loan?'"

"For the rest of your life, provided you use these ships in the service of the Crown. Oh, and one more thing. The three galleys are loaded with every comestible and provision you and your household and your loyal forces may need to tide you through the winter, and then some, until you are once again able to 'maintain yourself by sea and land'."

The actual results of my mission took longer to emerge. Bingham proved reluctant to implement the Queen's commands regarding my welfare and the welfare of my kinsmen, but I was not prepared after my hazardous endeavor to allow the provisions of Her Majesty's decision to be disregarded or negated by deliberate inaction. It took a little more than two months of my threatening Bingham that I would return to the Queen for further instructions, but he finally, if not happily, acquiesced.

In the next year, rejuvenated by the Queen's incredible generosity and noblesse of spirit, I took to the sea once again, even captaining the *Sea Ghost* on many of its forays, and I repaid my Sovereign several times over. By November of 1594, such was the success of my privateering venture against ships flying the flag of every known European country except England, and many Mediterranean nations, and even vessels flying the banner of the Czars of far-off Russia, that I remitted to the Crown the sum of £6,000 – *twenty-five times the annual pension settled on me by the Queen.*

But Sir Richard Bingham was not finished with me yet.

In an attempt to thwart my ambitions and the complete recapture of the wealth I'd once had, Bingham, in direct contradiction of the *English* law of the Composition of Connaught, cessed or quartered soldiers on my land and the lands of my followers. The cost of housing and feeding these hundreds of essentially useless troops was eating away at my wealth faster than I was amassing it. When Bingham ordered a company of soldiers to accompany me and my forces on all of our sea voyages, this direct interference – under the guise of 'surveillance to enforce Her Majesty's edict' – was too much to bear.

By April, 1595, I had had all I could take of the arrogant and offensive Sir Richard, who had tried every trick in his arsenal to thwart the Crown's munificence to me. I sailed to Tramore, then went by carriage to Ormond Castle and to my old friend, Black Tom.

After much talking and considering and "this-ing and that-ing," the Earl and I drafted a second petition to the Queen, which Tom agreed to deliver to Burghley and the Queen herself. The Earl of Ormond delivered my petition for further relief to the Royal Court at the end of June of 1595. For some reason known only to the heavens, the timing could not have been better or more propitious.

Sligo Castle, regarded as the key to the defense of Connaught against invasions by the O'Donnells from the north, was held by George Bingham, Sir Richard's brother, who, up to that time, had been aided by Ulick Burke. In that month, Burke and his followers mutinied, killed George Bingham, and turned the castle over to the O'Donnells. As The O'Donnell marched into Mayo, Tibbott and I flocked to his side, as he had been so kind to me in the past. Richard Bingham, who was now in Dublin, hurried west to quell this latest uprising, but The O'Donnell, not willing to give battle yet, slipped back to Sligo Castle. Bingham did not have men and supplies sufficient to lay siege to the castle. Meanwhile, The O'Neill, anxious for time to regroup and prepare for *his* all-out offensive, made overtures of peace to the Queen.

I'll never know whether Queen Elizabeth heeded the advice I had given her two years before, or whether she was propelled by forces beyond my knowing, but she declared herself eager to end the long, costly, and indecisive war. She ordered her generals to desist from offensive operations against the O'Neill and O'Donnell clans, and truce was declared.

This was the moment that the *English* administrators of the region, led by Mister Justice Theobald Dillon, Anthony Barbazon, and several other commissioners brought formal allegations against Sir Richard Bingham for gross abuse of his powers. Sir John Perrott had returned to England, and a new Lord Deputy, Sir William Russell, was installed in Dublin.

Russell immediately ordered that Bingham stand trial in Athlone and give account of his services and practices during his governorship. Fearing that the trial against him was fixed, Sir Richard fled to England, where he was promptly imprisoned. Sir Conyers Clifford was appointed governor of Connaught in his place.

Mayo was unified in its support of The O'Donnell, and with Bingham's departure, that support grew daily. In December, 1595, The O'Donnell began negotiations for peace with the new governor. To this day, I do not know whether my suggestion to the Queen had anything to do with it, but that very month Governor Clifford and The O'Donnell agreed to re-establish The MacWilliam title, which had been abolished by Bingham.

The longstanding conflict between Sir Richard Bingham and me ended at last, not with a bang, but with a whimper. In less than three years, disgraced, thrown upon the slag pile of obloquy, and suffering from declining health, my nemesis would be dead.

Once it was decided that a new MacWilliam was to be installed, the contenders for the title were the senior Burkes, William of Shrule, Edmund of Cong, John of Termon, Richard, my grandson, and Tibbott-na-Long, my youngest son.

All of the chiefs of Mayo, The O'Malley, The MacJordan, The MacCostello, The MacMaurice, The O'Dowd, and the chiefs of the various septs of the Mayo Burkes were present at the gathering to elect the new MacWilliam, and I was present, too. Since The O'Donnell, my old friend, would serve as the inaugurator and guiding force behind the election, I had high hopes that my Toby would assume the title previously held by my late husband, Richard-an-Iarrain, Iron Dick Burke.

But, alas, this was not to be.

The O'Donnell conferred the title on Theobald MacWalter Burke, who had been active in O'Donnell's cause. The appointment was a grotesquely unwise act for someone I had thought was balanced and far-seeing, for it gave offense to every family of the Burkes, whose rights and feelings had been openly disregarded. It was a devastating personal setback for me. With the departure of Richard Bingham and the decline of English power in the province, and with County Mayo in The O'Donnell's hands, my hopes for improving my own and my son's political status had been rekindled. In return for my friendship and my previous cooperation with Hugh Roe O'Donnell, I had had reason to expect his support for my son's political aspirations. But The O'Donnell had decided otherwise, and in so doing he had alienated Tibbott-na-Long from his cause.

It was a mistake The O'Donnell was to deeply regret.

Chapter 41

Elizabeth's war with The O'Neill and The O'Donnell continued, despite the truce. The O'Donnell maintained and extended his hold over Connaught. His appointee to The MacWilliamship, Theobald, did not have the loyalty of the other septs of Clan Burke. Thus, he was able to continue as The MacWilliam only so long as The O'Donnell was willing and able to support him. With the exception of the disgruntled Burke septs, the chiefs and clans of Mayo continued to rally to Hugh Roe O'Donnell's cause. In the north, The O'Neill continued his show of loyalty to the Queen, who had no option but to believe him.

When Sir Conyers Clifford formally assumed his duties as governor, he found a ravaged land. The O'Donnell's many incursions into Connaught had resulted in the devastation of the countryside, and Governor Clifford found such famine in the province that he had great difficulty feeding his own troops. He recovered Sligo Castle and The O'Donnell returned to his home base in Ulster.

In Mayo, The MacWilliam, unable to muster any strength now that his protector was gone, was driven out. In April, 1597,

Tibbott-na-Long, Richard, the son of the Devil's Hook, and other Mayo chieftains submitted to the Queen and agreed to fight against The O'Donnell.

Now that Bingham had departed, my galleys were freely able to put to sea in search of maintenance. But while my personal fortunes soared, my heart bled for my Ireland, which was once again in total disarray. The land was bare of cattle and produce. Clan after clan were divided in their loyalties, some fighting for the Queen, others for The O'Donnell and The O'Neill.

The fortunes of the combatants waxed and waned, while the fortunes of the land itself and those inhabitants who sought nothing more than to live their lives in quiet obscurity, declined steadily and irrevocably. By the turn of the century, in the year 1600, the power and prestige of The O'Neill and The O'Donnell were at their highest. Within two years, at the Battle of Kinsale, the rebellion, which had become a revolution, was utterly crushed, the final and conclusive milestone in Elizabeth's campaign to reconquer her Irish kingdom.

The old Gaelic order had maintained a resistance, ineffective as it often was, for decades. But resistance, if it were to prove effective, depended on unified opposition and well-planned foreign aid, and neither of these came about. The old Gaelic order provided for separate states and territories ruled by chieftains and lords, independent of each other, yet depending on the strength of alliances. The survival of the fittest was manifest in Ireland's laws, and, as I had told Elizabeth, therein lay its greatest weakness. For Ireland had become detached from the mainstream of Europe. It was still a medieval state.

I had been born when Gaelic power was at its height, Yet the very seeds of its destruction were being sown by Elizabeth's father, Henry VIII. I experienced the effects of English policies on my way of life. At first, I had actively resisted the incursion of the English lion, but it did not take long before I realized the futility of unorganized resistance against the concentrated and effective methods of a unified and determined conquering force. And at the end of the day, I realized where my future must lie.

I am old and I am tired and I am at peace. I look down at my sweet granddaughter, my Maeve, who is to marry in a couple of months, and who has listened so patiently to this tale. How innocent, how like a childlike little girl she looks. I wonder if I ever looked like that. She is now sleeping, which is just as well, since I believe it is time for me to rest for a while. I will finish my tale tomorrow...

Afterword

Grace O'Malley died peacefully at her beloved Rockfleet Castle in April, 1603. She survived Queen Elizabeth of England, her benefactress and ultimately her friend, by one month. Grace's son, Tibbott-na-Long, Toby-of-the-ships, was knighted First Viscount of Mayo by Charles I in 1627. This line became extinct in 1767. In 1669, Grace's great-great granddaughter, Maud Burke, married John Browne of Westport. The present owner of Westport House, Lord Altamont, is a direct descendant of the couple. On the O'Flaherty side, Grace's son Murrough and her grandson, also named Murrough, continued to live at Bunowen Castle, but later, as English settlers and planters moved farther westward, the O'Flahertys were dispossessed of their large holdings. Some of Grace's descendants emigrated and fought in foreign armies, while others remained and clung grimly to the remnants of their heritage to die mainly in poverty.

And yet today, she is remembered... she is remembered...

"Oh, no, 'twas not for sordid spoil
Of barque or seaboard borough
She ploughed, with unfatiguing toil,

The fluent, rolling furrow;
Delighting on the broad-back'd deep,
To feel the quivering galley
Strain up the opposing hill, and sweep
Down the withdrawing valley.

"Or, sped before a driving blast,
By following seas uplifted,
Catch, from the huge heaps heaving past
And from the spray they drifted,
And from the winds that tossed the crest
Of each wide-shouldering giant,
The smack of freedom and the zest
Of rapturous life defiant

"Sweet when crimson sunsets glowed
As earth and sky grew grander,
A'down the grass'd unechoing road,
Atlanticward to wander,
Some kinsman's humbler heart to seek
Some sick bedside, it may be
Or, onward reach with footsteps meek,
The low, grey lonely abbey."

The End

CPSIA information can be obtained
at www.ICGtesting.com
Printed in the USA
LVHW051950290623
751160LV00001B/2